PRAISE FOR KEVIN J. ANDERSON

"Arguably the most prolific,
most successful author working
in [science fiction] today."
—Algis Budrys

"Anderson is the heir apparent to
Arthur C. Clarke."
—Daniel Keys Moran,
author of *The Last Dancer*

"A rare combination of talent and practicality."
—*Starlog*

"Anderson is the hottest writer on
(or off) the planet."
—*Fort Worth Star-Telegram*

Kevin J. Anderson

FANTASTIC VOYAGE

— MICROCOSM —

AN ONYX BOOK

ONYX
Published by New American Library, a division of
Penguin Putnam Inc., 375 Hudson Street,
New York, New York 10014, U.S.A.
Penguin Books Ltd, 27 Wrights Lane,
London W8 5TZ, England
Penguin Books Australia Ltd, Ringwood,
Victoria, Australia
Penguin Books Canada Ltd, 10 Alcorn Avenue,
Toronto, Ontario, Canada M4V 3B2
Penguin Books (N.Z.) Ltd, 182–190 Wairau Road,
Auckland 10, New Zealand

Penguin Books Ltd, Registered Offices:
Harmondsworth, Middlesex, England

First published by Onyx, an imprint of New American Library,
a division of Penguin Putnam Inc.

First Printing, May 2001
10 9 8 7 6 5 4 3 2 1

 REGISTERED TRADEMARK—MARCA REGISTRADA

Printed in the United States of America

PUBLISHER'S NOTE
This is a work of fiction. Names, characters, places, and incidents either
are the product of the author's imagination or are used fictitiously,
and any resemblance to actual persons, living or dead, business
establishments, events, or locales is entirely coincidental.

BOOKS ARE AVAILABLE AT QUANTITY DISCOUNTS WHEN USED TO PROMOTE
PRODUCTS OR SERVICES. FOR INFORMATION PLEASE WRITE TO PREMIUM
MARKETING DIVISION, PENGUIN PUTNAM INC., 375 HUDSON STREET, NEW YORK,
NEW YORK 10014.

To Louis & Louise Moesta
for their years of support, love,
and pride in my work.

Prologue

After a suicide mission wiped out the Russian peace-keeping encampment, Vasili Garamov knew there could be no quick diplomatic solution to the Baku crisis. He gazed off into the distance, paying no heed to the ominous thunderstorm building off the Caspian Sea. Despite the smoldering cigarette clenched between his lips, the Deputy Foreign Minister could smell smoke from burning aircraft fuel and charred flesh.

I should have gotten here sooner, he thought, then cursed the usual bureaucratic mix-ups that had delayed his arrival.

On the other hand, if the misrouted diplomatic airplane hadn't diverted him to Armenia instead of bringing him directly here to Azerbaijan, Garamov himself might have been a casualty of the rebel attack. Then Moscow would have buried their Deputy Foreign Minister with full honors (probably misspelling his name on the tombstone), before sending out the next supposed peacemaker on their list. . . .

It was a wonder anything ever got accomplished when dealing with the Russian bureaucratic behemoth.

Five days earlier, Azeri militants had taken over Baku, one of Russia's most vital oil fields and refineries, and begun a systematic slaughter of all non-Muslims within the city. Russian troops had responded, grinding to a halt beyond the city, just out of range of the hastily emplaced rebel artillery. Refusing to negotiate, the militants had then threatened to obliterate the Baku oil refineries if the Russian army made a move. It was not a bluff.

Through no merits of his own, Vasili Garamov had been called in to end the crisis. Despite his ambassadorial credentials and suitably high political rank, his presence here was a complete mistake. Garamov's expertise was in dealing with American research and industry—*technical* problems, not religious or ethnic ones. Though familiar with cooperative research programs and technology transfers, he had little experience with historical hatreds and cultural clashes. He had no special skills, nor any particular knowledge of obscure ethnic difficulties around the Caspian Sea. He didn't even speak the local language.

But because someone had misfiled his papers, *he* had been selected for this assignment. *Typical.*

Another clerical error had gotten him on the wrong plane, so that he arrived eleven hours behind schedule, well after the situation had fallen irrevocably apart. Though the bureaucratic mistake had inadvertently saved Garamov's life, no doubt some official would be reprimanded for it. . . .

Following the inferno of the suicide attack, the surviving Russian troops howled for revenge. Equipped with the best military hardware in the region, they wanted to level the besieged city, never mind about the 1.7 million innocent civilians or the vital petroleum industry there.

A squadron of SU-35 Typhoons loaded with air-to-air missiles had already been summoned from the nearest Russian air base in the Caucasus Mountains. Mobile land artillery was in position and ready to move in a full-scale assault. The order had already been given, storm or no storm.

Garamov just hoped the fighter jets wouldn't hit the wrong target.

He stood outside the prefab command shelter, knowing in his bones that the impending operation would be a bloodbath. He tossed his cigarette to the ground and crushed it under the sole of his shoe. Even as Deputy Foreign Minister, Garamov wasn't really in charge here, though he'd probably be blamed at the end of the day.

He would rather be back in Moscow reading his technical reports.

He turned his lean, sharp face toward the stiff breeze. His chalky-pale skin emphasized the darkness of his lips as he lit another cigarette, counted how many remained in his pack—three—and wondered if he could make them last the afternoon.

Field Commander Kamenev marched up, holding his cap against the wind. His thick red mustache made him look perpetually displeased. "Artillery is ready to move forward, Deputy Foreign Minister."

"And you are sure they were sent in the correct direction?" he said under his breath, not really expecting a response. The air was electric with the wet-metal scent of ozone; lightning crackled like unexpected anti-aircraft fire in the thick soup of clouds.

Kamenev was deaf to sarcasm and ignored the comment. "If you will come inside the command tent, we can observe the fighter-jet squadron on our satellite screens. I would like to have you at my side."

For political cover? he wondered. "I prefer to watch from out here, with my own eyes." Garamov slicked back his dark hair, but the wind ruffled it again. "When do the Typhoons arrive?" *When can I go home?*

"Due in half an hour, Mr. Deputy Minister. The pilots are confident the storm will not be a hindrance."

"Of course they are confident." Garamov took a long drag of the acrid smoke and exhaled it in a visible sigh.

"It is time to send in the armored vehicles and artillery. I have authorized them to crush the road-blocks and retake the city." Kamenev saluted, his face a waxy mask of controlled righteous anger. "We will have our revenge on the murderous rebels, sir."

"Of that, I have no doubt." *And anyone else who gets in the way.*

During his bungled journey, while Garamov had struggled to rearrange his diplomatic flights through incompetent Armenian officials, a rebel-hijacked C-130 aircraft fuel tanker had taken off on a suicide mission from besieged Baku, headed toward the largest concentration of Russian troops on the out-skirts of the city. A sluggish old prop plane bought long ago from the United States, the C-130 was nei-ther an attack craft nor a fighter jet. It had no weaponry.

But the tanker itself was a weapon. A flying bomb.

By the time Russian troops realized that the rebel pilot intended to crash into their encampment, they could not shoot it down fast enough. The fireball crisped eyebrows a kilometer away and incinerated anyone standing closer. It would be another day be-fore recovery teams could venture into the smolder-ing graveyard to excavate the countless charred corpses.

Though he was a respected politician, Vasili Gara-mov was no field commander. Kamenev had already made up his mind to launch an immediate, if ill-advised, retaliatory strike. It seemed to the Deputy Foreign Minister that a sensible leader would have waited for the weather to clear, but the time for com-mon sense had passed. A bureaucratic error, a mis-take in the chain of command. The Russian army would retake Baku using overwhelming force; the rebels would lose—would, in fact, be exterminated.

A communications officer rushed out of the tent, his face cheesy-pale, blue eyes wide with excitement. "Sir! The rebels have launched their own attack jets. We are seeing activity on the Baku airfields."

"Secondhand Iraqi aircraft," the field commander said. "No match for our SU-35 Typhoons." He brushed down his reddish mustache, unperturbed.

"Yes, Field Commander, but our Typhoons are not yet here," Garamov pointed out. "Very well. Now I will see these satellite pictures."

They ducked into the tent to watch the surveillance images. One tracking screen displayed the Russian jets, which had already crossed the Azerbaijani border and were rapidly closing the gap . . . flying straight into the fist of the brewing storm.

Hotspots on the terrain displays showed long-range artillery bombardment of the Baku airfield. Garamov considered it likely that the Russian counterstrike would cause more damage to the refinery infrastructure than the militants ever would.

"Typhoons are closing," the communications officer said, his Russian thick with a Georgian accent.

As Garamov watched blips on the screen, another dot appeared from out of range and at a high altitude. "What is that? I did not see it before."

"Not one of ours," said the comm officer, tracking the Typhoon squadron. "Just one aircraft, unfamiliar configuration. It does not seem to be maneuvering."

Shouts of surprise rang out as the rebel jets veered from their original trajectory, *away* from the approaching squadron.

Garamov understood immediately. "They do not intend to face our Typhoons, Commander. They will strike *here*, perhaps even make further suicide runs."

The field commander watched the approaching

rebel MiGs, his face grave, his voice decisive. "Mr. Deputy Minister, we have a helicopter ready to take you to safety."

Garamov tried to pull away. "I should stay here."

"You should stay *alive*, sir. You are a diplomat. You do not belong on a battlefield." Garamov had no argument for that.

Less than three minutes later, he found himself strapped into the back of a jostling helicopter. Gray rain began to slash down, and the pilot fought against the wind. Booming explosions in the clouds sounded distinctly different from thunder.

As the helicopter took him to safety in the wrinkled, mountainous folds of the Caucasus, Garamov maintained his command-and-control link and received regular battlefield reports. He felt detached from the action, helpless.

The Typhoons shot three MiGs out of the sky. A single rebel aircraft slipped through and dropped haphazard bombs on the army encampment. Showing no restraint, Russian ground troops broke through the Baku roadblocks, and the Azeri militants were in full retreat into the city. Casualties would be high on both sides.

Then the storm struck with full force. The Typhoon squadron continued its hunt in the clouds, tracking and destroying rebel MiGs, but two Russian jets were already down. Everything was slipping out of control.

Garamov had accomplished nothing here. He'd been unable to. He might as well write his own political obituary.

"We have lost contact with base," an artillery subcommander shouted in Garamov's earphones. "We confirm five major ground explosions, and one rebel jet crashed in the vicinity of the command tents." He paused. "There are no orders from Field Commander Kamenev. We presume he is dead."

What else could possibly go wrong?

The Typhoon squadron leader patched through. "Mr. Deputy Minister, the unidentified radar trace is approaching. Request permission to engage and destroy."

Were there no other high-ranking officers? Garamov groaned. He wasn't a military commander and had no business giving battlefield orders. Because of his status, some bureaucrat had probably designated him second-in-command. He stalled, knowing that failure to make a decision was preferable to making a bad one. "What kind of craft is it? Are there any scheduled commercial flights in this air zone?"

"None, sir! This is no known type of aircraft, unrecognizable to our systems, and it transmits no IFF signal." All military aircraft sent out a coded "Identify Friend/Foe" beacon to keep from being targeted by friendly fire.

"It is heading straight for us, sir, no evasive maneuvers whatsoever. Just like the suicidal C-130 tanker."

Because of the recent massacre, the fighter pilots were out for blood. Even before the rebel fighter jets came within visual range, the Russian pilots had launched air-to-air missiles at them—far more than were necessary, but everyone wanted a piece of this kill. It looked like a disaster waiting to happen.

"Sir! Please respond! Weapons ready."

Garamov saw the blips on the screen, watched the strange craft blundering into the attack zone. He remembered the Korean Air Lines passenger jet that had been shot down over Sakhalin Island—another flaw in the chain of command—and the subsequent political fallout. *Please don't let it be another mistake.*

Rain pelted the helicopter's windows, leaving streaks that blurred the landscape.

"Permission granted," he said over the shuddering drone of the engine.

On the screen, he watched traces as the Typhoons converged on the sluggish craft. The unidentified target did not attempt to escape. Missiles struck the slow-moving target and detonated. A bright blip flashed on the screen.

"Identification?" Garamov leaned sideways in his seat, gripping the side wall as errant gusts shook the helicopter. "Did any pilot actually see the target before it was destroyed?"

"No, sir. Nothing left but smoke and falling wreckage."

Watching the fireball and debris cloud dissipate on the screen, Garamov saw a secondary trace dropping in a parabolic arc. "Looks like the pilot ejected from the unidentified craft, sir!" the squadron leader called. "Maybe there is a survivor."

"Track it. Mark where it falls." Garamov motioned to the helicopter pilot. "We are on our way."

The thunderstorm ripped across the Baku battle zone. Russian ground artillery continued to pound three surprisingly well-defended Azeri strongholds outside the city. All but one of the rebel MiGs had been shot down, and four Typhoons were in a frantic chase after the last one. It wouldn't take long.

Garamov pressed his earphones close as the squadron leader described the rugged terrain around where the ejected pilot had crashed. As the helicopter zeroed in on the area, the Deputy Foreign Minister still hoped he could salvage the situation, rescue a downed rebel pilot . . . do *something*.

He hoped the helicopter wouldn't fly into a mountainside. That would be the perfect end to his career.

The pilot circled over the forested hillsides, looking

for a place to land. Broken, burning trees smoldered in the thick rain, marking the spot where an oblong, coffin-sized object had plowed into a steep slope.

Not a man dangling in a harness and parachute. Not a pilot at all.

Something else entirely.

The helicopter pilot finally landed, his craft tilted at an angle, skids slipping in the mud. Before the rotors had stopped spinning, Garamov climbed out and stood without an umbrella, cold rain streaming down his dark hair and pale skin. The air held a roasted smell with a metallic undertone mixed with the richness of churned earth.

He couldn't believe what he was seeing.

When it struck, the ejected container had gouged a long furrow in the dirt and splintered dozens of dark pines. Yet the armored pod remained intact and sealed, even after such a rough impact.

Leaving the pilot behind, Garamov approached the object. Strange designs and lacings of circuitry trailed all around the exterior, giving it a cocoon-like appearance. Immediately, the design and the technology intrigued him. The markings were in no language he had ever seen.

Through clumps of mud trickling off the misty window ports, Garamov could discern that there might be a survivor inside. Or at least a body. Smooth and gray-skinned, with grossly large eyes squeezed shut in unconsciousness or death. Not an Azeri rebel, not a human at all. An *alien* body.

He knew this was a mistake to far overshadow all the bureaucratic bungling he had ever experienced.

Letting out a long, heavy breath, as if someone had punched him in the stomach, Vasili Garamov realized that his already-impossible assignment had gotten even more complex.

Chapter 1

The unmarked convoy was on its way up the steep, switchbacked slope. Felix Hunter, Director of Project Proteus, could hear the distant engines toiling out there in the darkness.

Delivering an alien body was the sort of thing best done in the dead of night.

High in the isolated Sierra Nevadas, on a rarely traveled road, Director Hunter stepped away from the blazing spotlights in the compound. Motioning to the facility guards, he passed through the sallyport one chain-link barrier at a time and took a few steps down the gravel road to where he could see the stars . . . and think.

At this high altitude, the atmosphere was startlingly clear, like a lens through which billions of pinprick stars shone. Given hours of solitude, he could have walked deeper into the forest, away from human settlements, and let his eyes adjust.

Out of all those twinkling lights, which one did the alien specimen call home?

When his daughter Kelli had been a young girl, Hunter had taught her the constellations. He had enjoyed those times. He was glad he could think of his daughter without feeling the ache of grief. Now only the bittersweet memories remained.

The guards left the fence gate open but remained alert, weapons ready. The main defense of the Proteus Facility was simply to be unobtrusive. Few people accidentally stumbled upon this isolated location, and what anyone saw on first glance looked like an innocuous cellular phone substation and power plant, complete with NO TRESPASSING and DANGER: HIGH VOLTAGE signs. The real security began beyond the first set of fences and gates leading into the mountain tunnels—and no unauthorized person had ever gotten that far.

The chill air made Hunter's ears tingle, but he waited, listening to the rumble of trucks until he spotted the headlights of the approaching vehicles. He would be there to meet the convoy.

In his early sixties and very healthy, Felix Hunter was not a big man, but he carried himself with great confidence and self-possession. Kelli's husband, Major Marc Devlin, had once joked, "Felix, you could walk whistling through a minefield with your eyes closed and never miss a single note." He had an olive complexion, a trim mustache, and dark hair with a fringe of salt-and-pepper around the ears. He wore a suit even inside the lab and felt as much at home in the rock-walled tunnels as at a black-tie function in Washington, D.C.

He took a last glance at the peaceful stars above and trudged back toward the fences and security lights. When the trucks and their extraterrestrial cargo arrived, he and his team would have to get back to work. That was where his real passion lay.

The alien specimen from the Azerbaijan battlefield remained sealed inside its armored pod, undamaged even after being shot down by Russian fighter jets. Deputy Foreign Minister Vasili Garamov, one of the silent international partners in Project Proteus, had been true to his word.

This mission would be a perfect showcase for their capabilities.

Miniaturization technology had been around (and highly classified) for decades. During the 1960s, the U.S. project had been run with an iron hand by General Walter Carson, a gruff and far-too-confident commander who demanded Black Program funding to keep America one step ahead of the Soviets.

Carson's scheme had been to shrink airplanes and armies to microscopic size; he could deliver a fly-speck invasion force invisible to enemy counter-measures, then restore them to normal size for an overwhelming surprise attack. Though the idea sounded preposterous, the general had enough clout—maybe even blackmail material?—to push the program through the attendant red tape.

Back during the Cold War, the original Project's objectives had been strictly military. There had been no discussion about the possible commercial applications of miniaturization technology—transportation, precision manufacturing, integrated circuit design, surgery, much less pure science. All of those things could come much later, after Carson had his own way.

The death knell for the project had involved the lead researcher, Chris Matheson, an old friend and former classmate of Hunter's at Yale. While Hunter had worked his way up the ladder of large interna-tional corporations, dabbling in politics and diplo-macy, Matheson had developed the classified miniaturization project for General Carson. After sev-eral amazing tests with the prototype apparatus, Matheson had boldly insisted on shrinking himself. Even in college, the man had liked to test the limits. Following orders, his technicians had reduced him smaller and smaller . . . until he broke a quantum boundary. Despite their best efforts, the technicians had been unable to reverse the process.

Hunter hadn't been there himself, but he had repeatedly watched the 16-mm film of the test. Chris Matheson had shrunk smaller than a cell, smaller than a nucleus . . . until he vanished into nothingness. Matheson had never come back.

In the furor afterward, General Carson had been removed from his position, and the vastly expensive project was dismantled, its components locked away. With the fall of the Soviet Union in 1990, the urgency for Cold War competition faded. The program records were boxed up and stored in a Top Secret warehouse, where the magnificent technology had languished for decades.

Until Hunter had resurrected it.

Now at last, through a fluke, Project Proteus would have the opportunity to prove its worth—if the Director could get his team together in time and run them through their paces.

The lights of the convoy's first scout car bounced up the road, twin high beams glowing like the eyes of a dragon. It was a black, unmarked sport utility vehicle with run-flat tires and bullet-proof glass. The two armed men inside it had orders to shoot to kill in the event of any perceived threat.

The scout car pulled up to the gate outside the mountain facility. Proteus guards came forward, their high-powered rifles unshouldered. Hunter thought the paranoia might be a bit too intense, but given the cargo, they all had a right to be suspicious and nervous.

The armored convoy—a Safe Secure Transport, or SST—was normally reserved for moving nuclear warheads, but the alien pod could be even more valuable and dangerous, than any atomic bomb. After all, Hunter thought, there were plenty of warheads, but (as far as he knew) only one extraterrestial cadaver.

And that was assuming the thing was actually dead. . . .

He came forward in the headlights' glare and identified himself, showing badges, providing passwords, signing papers. Behind them the armored cargo truck climbed the steep mountain road, shifting gears, its headlights blazing like a ghost hunter's high-powered flashlight in a haunted house. The heavy vehicle showed no intention of hurrying, despite the extraordinary time constraints under which Hunter had to operate.

All too aware of how easily the situation could fall apart through mistakes, apathy, and bureaucratic incompetence, Vasili Garamov had gambled everything and bypassed appropriate channels. Now Team Proteus needed to get to work before Moscow politics got involved.

Hunter expected that his Russian friend would pay dearly for his audacity, especially after the Baku massacre. But if Project Proteus could pull off a miracle, to Garamov's credit, the Deputy Foreign Minister just might survive. At the same time, Hunter would boost his own top-secret project by proving its worth to the narrow-minded skeptics who challenged his funding year after year.

The vehicles rumbled through the sallyport and entered the guarded compound. They were followed by the chase car, the convoy's final line of defense in case the SST were attacked.

When the fence gate rattled shut again, locks clamped down, and the guards—wearing "rent-a-cop" uniforms—took up their positions once more. Motion sensors placed at strategic positions for hundreds of acres around the mountain facility automatically reset themselves. Hunter watched as the red taillights of the truck disappeared into the big semi-circular opening inside the granite cliff. At last he breathed a sigh of relief.

Finally, they could get to work.

After seeing pictures of the alien lifepod, Hunter had shared them with his team members so they could plan a micro-exploration strategy under the tightest possible time constraints. Once word leaked out even through secret political channels, he would be able to fend off diplomats and other scientists for only a day, at most; the Russian government would demand the return of the sealed pod. The Proteus researchers had no choice but to complete their work before Hunter lost control of the specimen. But he was confident his miniaturized crew would be able to gather the necessary data and come back out—armed with enough discoveries to keep the world of science busy for decades to come.

Now that the alien container was inside the Proteus Facility, the clock had really begun ticking.

Chapter 2

As he approached the rundown townhouse in bright morning light, Major Marc Devlin gave a skeptical frown, then shrugged. Not the sort of place he would have expected to find a famous "alien expert."

The UFO business must have fallen on hard times.

Granted, homes on the outskirts of San Francisco were at a premium, their prices driven up by high-salaried programmers or investment execs. Still, Devlin had anticipated something a little more . . . *maintained* for the home of a celebrity.

Battered RVs hunkered in driveways across the street; dogs barked in backyards where old lawn furniture was visibly deteriorating. As a pilot, Devlin had learned how to gather details about his surroundings in a flash, using peripheral vision as well as his main field of view. But aside from the unexpected rundown neighborhood, he saw nothing interesting here. Nothing at all.

The self-proclaimed alien expert was probably spying on him through a window.

Although Project Proteus had reactivated his Air Force rank, Devlin wore civilian clothes today. In spite of his long-standing fascination with aerospace and big planes, he'd taken early retirement five years ago at the age of thirty after losing his wife to cancer.

He'd spent a few lackluster years as an inventor and aircraft designer, until Director Hunter—Kelli's father—had contacted him with an offer to join the unbelievable new miniaturization program. He'd jumped at the chance.

The uneven fringe of Devlin's mussed brown hair looked as if his mother still cut it. He had a prominent dimple on his chin, large bright eyes, and a face just a bit too boyish to look rugged. Kelli had always done a good job picking his clothes, straightening his collar, helping him maintain proper appearances. During those last weeks in the hospital, he had tried to look his best for her.

Alone now, he found that being a snappy dresser was no longer high on his list of priorities. Working on complex engineering problems for Project Proteus was far more interesting than keeping up with the vagaries of fashion.

Leaving his dark government sedan parked at the curb, Devlin walked up the sidewalk. He noted brown grass in the postage-stamp yard, patched stucco on the townhouse walls, flowering weeds in the so-called lawn, weed-infested flowers in a dirt patch under one window.

By reputation and by his own assertion, Arnold Freeth was the foremost specialist in the country in the field of extraterrestrial sightings. The man's biggest claim to fame was that he had hosted a controversial and much-ballyhooed *Alien Dissection*, available on home video.

So why did the guy live in such a dump? (Not that his own quarters would ever appear in *House and Garden*.) Devlin tried to give him the benefit of the doubt. Maybe Freeth was so constantly in demand, always speaking at conferences or giving interviews to tabloids or paranormal magazines, that he didn't have time for yard work.

Devlin, who spent his days tinkering with the *Mote*, the beautiful micro-exploration vessel he had designed, had no time to read grocery-store newspapers or watch TV scandal shows. As a practical engineer, he had never really believed the tales of visitors from other worlds, but he had seen the sealed alien lifepod in the Proteus lab this morning before dawn, so he was not about to sneer at even Freeth's most outrageous claims. Not today.

Dr. Cynthia Tyler, one of the world-class medical experts working for Project Proteus, had downloaded clips from Freeth's *Alien Dissection* videotape to show Director Hunter. The similarities with the lifepod alien were uncanny. "We need this man, Felix. Where else are we going to get a specialist for our mission?"

Hunter had been wary of Arnold Freeth's alleged credentials, but he had no time to run detailed background checks. The alien specimen would probably be theirs for less than a day before the already-brewing political furor wrenched it back to Russia.

Devlin's orders were to enlist the UFO expert's help without delay.

Trying to look professional, he stood prominently in front of the door and pushed the button for the bell, but heard no sound. Probably broken. After a second try, he pounded on the door. He peered into the peephole, hoping to see some movement or change of light. He looked at his watch.

Back at the Proteus Facility, the designated miniaturization team had been thrown into a rigorous, eleventh-hour training routine. Seventeen times already, Devlin had been reduced to the size of a dust mote in order to test his micro-exploration craft. Other potential miniaturization team members had all undergone equally extensive preparation—pathologists, anatomists, microbiologists, structural analysts, organic chemists, materials scientists, even a security specialist.

Yet now, for their first real mission, Team Proteus was forced to bring in outside expertise. It was embarrassing, but who could have planned ahead for an alien expert?

Since hotshot Captain Garrett Wilcox would pilot the prototype *Mote* on its microscopic voyage, Director Hunter had insisted that Devlin was the best man to fetch Mr. Freeth. Perhaps Devlin's love for science fiction would give the two something to talk about during the long drive . . . or maybe Felix just wanted his son-in-law to get his head out of the lab and see other people for a change.

Across the street, a woman yelled at her rat-brown yap-yap dog as it chased children on tricycles. An old man sprayed water from a garden hose onto a hedge of pink oleanders, while glancing at Devlin out of the corner of his eye. Everyone had seen him pull up in the dark car; all of the neighbors wondered what he wanted.

"Mr. Freeth, if I could have just a moment of your time?" he shouted at the door. He would have been far more comfortable in a mechanic's coveralls, a clean-room suit, or a white lab coat complete with pocket protector full of pens to maintain his image. "I promise I'm not selling anything."

Finally he heard someone stirring inside. With an effort, Devlin rehearsed again what he was going to say. He was no politician, no fast-talker. He suspected that his conservative black suit, polished shoes, and dark sunglasses practically shouted that he worked for a secret government agency. Which of course he did. Otherwise he wouldn't be here.

He certainly had something of interest to show a UFO enthusiast.

Devlin heard a gasp behind the peephole, and the

door opened. A pale man with freckles peered out. Arnold Freeth, who according to his file was thirty-seven and unmarried, wore a clean white shirt, blue slacks, no shoes. Beneath neatly trimmed dishwater-brown hair, his muddy brown eyes darted from side to side as if afraid he might miss something. When Devlin stuck out his hand, Freeth looked at it suspiciously. "Can I see some ID, please?"

Devlin reached into his pocket to withdraw a government identification wallet and passed it to Freeth. "Roger that. I had this printed up especially for you. I hope you like it."

He'd always had a cocky sense of humor. No one could laugh harder at a pie-in-the-face jape or Wile E. Coyote falling off a cliff. Devlin and his Air Force buddies had specialized in harmless pranks that had gotten even more outrageous when he'd first met Kelli Hunter, a civilian medical technician at a local hospital. She had rolled her blue eyes in lighthearted disapproval at his antics. Now, she always wore that expression in Devlin's memories.

He flashed what he hoped was a disarming smile. "My project would like to hire your consulting services, Mr. Freeth. As soon as possible."

Freeth studied the government ID as if it were a Polaroid photograph of a flying saucer. He didn't even ask what *Proteus Access* meant.

He handed the ID wallet back and ran a hand through his hair, messing up its neat appearance. "I knew someone would come to shut me up and shut me down. The government can't stand me exposing their conspiracies, can they? I know too many things."

Devlin fumbled the ID into the inner lining of his jacket. Lab smocks had more reasonable-sized pockets. "If it makes a difference, we do plan to reimburse you for your work."

Freeth perked up. "Reimburse me, that's good."
Beyond the door, Devlin got a glimpse of a dark and
cluttered apartment, the walls crammed with book-
shelves, every horizontal surface filled with magazines, papers, photographs, and notes.

The man rattled off words and terms like gunfire.
"I get paid five hundred dollars per day for consulting on paranormal matters, plus expenses. I expect your people to pick up travel costs and provide
my meals and reasonable lodging." He crossed his
arms over his pressed white shirt. "That's not
negotiable."

Devlin looked at his watch again. "Roger that. I
am authorized to make such payment." He hoped
Felix wouldn't balk at the expense, but supposed he
could talk him into it. "Given your track record, I
have no doubt you'll be worth every penny."

Freeth looked at him with an intrigued expression,
a wide-eyed nerd trying not to let his interest show.
"What am I going to be doing for you, and the government? I . . ." He swallowed hard. "I have my
principles, you know."

"Well, I could tell you, but then I'd have to shoot
you," Devlin said with a mischievous twinkle in his
eyes. "Just kidding, Mr. Freeth." He regarded the
UFO expert with a straight face. "If I were telling
anyone else what I'm about to tell you, I would feel
like a complete fool. But I assure you, this is no joke."

Freeth crossed his arms over his chest and
waited expectantly.

"We, uh . . . we have an alien body in our
possession."

The other man drew in a gasp, happily believing
what most people would have laughed off. "A . . .
real alien?" Then he grew skeptical again, as if he'd
been the butt of numerous practical jokes before.
"Where did you get it?"

"The specimen arrived late last night at our facility. It bears a remarkable similarity to the one on your *Alien Dissection* video. Due to . . . political pressures, we have less than a day to complete our analysis." He spread his hands. "That's why we don't have time to learn everything *you* might already know."

Freeth struggled to control his reaction. He seemed on the verge of hyperventilating.

"We need your help, Arnold." Devlin tried to sound comradely. "Are you willing to join our team?"

"Absolutely!" The UFO expert looked as if he might grab Devlin in an overjoyed hug. "But please call me Mr. Freeth. I like to be treated as a professional."

"Roger that, Mr. Freeth. You'll need to get ready to leave at once, and I've got some confidentiality papers for you to sign in the car." Devlin's voice grew stern. "We're a little pressed for time."

Chapter 3

The densely packed integrated circuit was only a few millimeters wide, but it looked as large as Nebraska to Tomiko Braddock and her miniaturized team.

The metal wall stood before her like a sheer cliff ten times her height. The circuit path's face had been sheared off using state-of-the-art processing efforts to smooth its edges, which still left microscopic imperfections, lumps, and curves.

Insurmountable.

No problem.

Garrett Wilcox, the designated pilot and commander of the upcoming mission, would probably try to leap it in a single bound just to show off in front of her. The twenty-eight-year-old captain kept himself in shape, drank orange juice by the gallon, and never complained about Proteus mess-hall food; he often even asked for seconds.

Now, standing on the intricate pathways of the computer chip, Tomiko assessed the straight walls of gold, copper, and germanium dodging right and left at sharp angles, racetracks through a convoluted maze. It was a new-design ULSI chip, or Ultra-Large-Scale Integrated circuit. The light seemed grainy at her minuscule size, shimmering as if in anticipation of a thunderstorm.

For a last-minute proficiency exercise, Director Hunter had sent them into this unknown scenario, just to see how the candidates responded. Tomiko and Wilcox were accompanied by the medical specialist assigned to the upcoming mission.

Dr. Sergei Pirov had participated in the initial Soviet miniaturization research at the height of the Cold War decades before. Although he now had trouble keeping up with the younger members of the team, his skills were vital to the mission. Pirov's techniques for studying cellular damage and pathogens would be crucial to understanding the alien body on a micro-level.

Unfortunately, his expertise wasn't terribly useful here on substrates and nonhomogeneously deposited layers of metal films.

In fact, Tomiko was the only one of the three who knew her way around an electronic map. When she'd been younger, her indulgent parents, busy celebrities, had smiled upon everything she wanted to do. One of her hobbies at age thirteen had been building circuit boards in a little garage workshop in Sausalito.

Improvise, she thought. *Now.*

Tossing her shoulder-length black hair away from her face, she rapped her knuckles on the gold wall, felt the solid metal, then looked down the twisted circuit lines. Somewhere, in all that mess, one tiny pathway was broken. *Shouldn't be hard to find it—if we have a million years or so.*

"I'll go first." Wilcox gave her a cocky grin. "Just like in one of your dad's movies. Remember *Terrorist Tower?*"

Her parents were martial-arts film star Nolan Braddock and Japanese Olympic ice skater Kira Satsuya, but Tomiko had never wanted anything to do with living in the public eye. "Garrett, you're so full of yourself, you should've brought an extra backpack to carry your leftover ego."

"That's what you like about me, Tomiko—my self-confidence and my total assurance." He raised his eyebrows.

"What I *like* about you is you're the only person available," she said. "Not like I have much choice around here."

"You bet. That's the drawback of working inside a secret mountain complex." Wilcox sprang high and released a squirt from his compressed-gas jetpack. Within moments, he cleared the top of the barrier and landed on the upper surface. "King of the mountain!"

Over the suit radio, Dr. Pirov said, "Amusing, Captain Wilcox, but it does not help us complete our mission. The clock is running. Our miniaturization field is set to dissipate in fifty-three minutes." His voice sounded paper-dry.

Tomiko removed several pieces of equipment from her belt. "Okay, let's move it. Taking a test reading." She placed sonic inducers against the rippled gold wall and tucked a receiver pickup into her left ear. Concentrating, Tomiko sent a pulse into the metal. When it rang out like a gong, she studied the scrambled oscilloscope screen in front of her, noting acoustical wave patterns that showed the homogeneity of the circuit path. "No voids or impurities."

"Then this is not the trouble spot," Pirov said with an exhausted sigh. "We will have to check someplace else. Do you have suggestions, Ms. Braddock?"

Wilcox leaned over the abrupt edge and waved. "Hey, come on up!"

Tomiko stared up at the sheer gold wall like a mountain climber ready for a challenge. "Let's get a gnat's-eye view, Doctor P. Like Captain Wilcox suggests."

She coiled her muscular legs and jumped. At this size, with virtually no body weight, gravity had only the tiniest hold. Using her jetpack, she skimmed along the endless cliff face until she reached the golden plateau.

Exhilarated, Tomiko swiveled around and added another spurt of gas to counteract her motion. Wilcox reached out to catch her, but she didn't need his help. She landed on all fours on the sprawling surface.

Wilcox scanned the electronic blueprint. "I'm making sure we're in the right place. The technicians set us down within a very small error tolerance . . . but I don't like that word 'error.' "

On the hand-held screen, he displayed the complex ULSI circuit map. A blip showed their location. Unfortunately, the dot itself was larger than several blocks of circuit paths. Not much help there. He tried to align the blueprint with parallel lines and intersecting overpasses, connected metal pathways doped with impurities to create semiconductor switches and electron gates.

"This place looks like the L.A. freeway system, only designed by someone on hallucinogenic drugs.'

"Figure it out, Garrett. Just think of it as a video game."

Tomiko knew the basic principles of large-scale integrated circuits. A thin metal film was deposited on a slice of semiconductor, usually germanium or silicon. Shining through a mask, short-wavelength x-ray lithography exposed the circuit pattern, which was then etched away, leaving only a dense lace of microscopic wires, finer than split hairs. The whole circuit, smaller than a thumbnail, contained millions of transistors and linking wires in a complete super-processing and memory unit.

The team was supposed to discover why the pattern didn't work, but it was just a practice exercise.

Their real mission into the alien capsule would begin that afternoon. They had to prove themselves *here* first, one last time.

Wilcox finally pinpointed their position. He frowned. "Two paths from where we're supposed to be. We need to cross over to the right circuit line."

"Okay, let's move it." She gestured over the edge to the old medical specialist standing like an ant below. "Come on up, Doctor P, and drop down your guy wire. I might need to catch you." She knew how tough it could be to maneuver against air currents and random molecular motion at their tiny size.

Far below, the elderly Russian man leaped into the air with a burst of compressed gas. As she'd feared, the doctor shot past the plateau edge, tumbling without slowing. "Come on, Garrett—grab him." Tomiko reached out with acrobatic grace to snag the dangling rope and gave it a short, hard yank. The Newtonian counter-motion lifted her off the surface, but Wilcox caught her just as Pirov landed hard.

All three studied the maze looping across the silicon plain. Holding up his illuminated circuit map, Wilcox pointed out the lines and corners they'd need to follow. "There, and then there. Turn right and take that forty-five-degree cross-connector and we'll find ourselves in the right spot."

"All right, Garrett, you've convinced me you're qualified to be a navigator."

"*And* a pilot, among my many skills. Just wait until we get inside that alien body, and I'll dazzle you."

Pirov squinted along the line Wilcox indicated. "I believe I see a dark discontinuity along the path." From his belt, he removed a small pair of Soviet-made high-powered binoculars. "That flaw may be what we were sent to find."

"Let's go have a look. We'll go faster using the jetpacks, and we need to learn how to maneuver with them anyway." Wilcox looked over at Tomiko. "Want to race?"

Pirov looked at his watch, concerned. "Forty-four minutes remaining."

"Plenty of time." Tomiko fired her jets and sailed along, the barest fraction of a millimeter above the intricate surface. "Follow the yellow-brick road."

Cruising along like remoras, the three of them approached the blemish Pirov had spotted. It looked like two twisted hairs as big as telephone poles embedded within the gold wall, pitch black and with an outer structure of layered scales, like fossilized trees.

"Whoa, what is that?" Wilcox asked.

At the age of eight, Tomiko had spent a week in Petrified Forest National Park, while her father filmed his classic *Desert Ninjas*. Between takes, Tomiko had climbed fossil tree trunks that were thousands of years old. These blackened stumps before her were less than a billionth the size of those ancient trees. . . .

"Carbon fibers," Tomiko said. "A dust speck contaminant left in the deposition process. Let's do a little excavating, see if that improves the conductivity."

Tomiko uncoiled her ropes, kneeling at the edge of the soft metal cliff. With a few smacks from her geological specimen hammer, she pounded grappling hooks into the gold surface, one line for her, one for Wilcox.

Securing a laser cutter to his hip, the captain commandeered a rope and lowered himself over the edge, as light as a bit of fluff on the wind. "I'll take the big one." Grinning, he swayed out over the chasm and let himself drop.

Wilcox had gotten himself a high-level security clearance on a whim. Tomiko suspected the young captain fantasized about covert operations and Black

Program secrets. Being isolated inside a mountain lab was perhaps not the commando work Wilcox had been imagining, but being one of the world's first micro-explorers was certainly exciting enough.

Moving with meticulous slowness, Dr. Pirov busied himself with his own equipment, setting up leads and contacts. "I will check it from up here."

Tomiko rappelled down the circuit cliff, holding her weight with just a finger touch on the guy wire. She swung across, widening her arc, until she could grab the second Sequoia-sized carbon fiber with her feet.

Ready to get to work, she unslung her laser and pulled a dust mask over her nose and small chin. Narrowing her almond eyes, she pointed the cutter beam and melted gold around the embedded carbon fiber. Yellow metal flowed like butter, loosening its hold around the containment. Then, feeling like a lumberjack, she sliced into the crystalline charcoal.

When Pirov was ready to test, he sent another sonic boost rippling through the circuit path. Dislodged ebony flakes floated in the air. As the echoes and tremors died down, Wilcox's big chunk of carbon impurity broke free. He nearly lost his balance, but caught on to a rugged hunk of dust, then swung on his guy rope. Crumbling black diamonds fell away like black snow, leaving a scar in the gold. The tiny fiber tumbled ever so slowly toward the substrate far below.

"First one's clear." He sounded as if he had been racing her. Tomiko kept working on the second protrusion.

Pirov's voice came over the suit radio. "My sonic trace picked up those inclusions, but they are too small to hinder current flow."

"Great," Tomiko said. "Now that we've already done the work."

"Think of it as practice, Tomiko," Wilcox said.

"Secure yourself and keep grounded, both of you," Pirov warned. "Stay away from the metal. I am sending an electron pulse to map surrounding terrain."

Wilcox swung out on his rope and straddled the blackened carbon trunk of the second impurity next to Tomiko. The carbon smeared his pant legs with soot, but the microscopic particles could not penetrate the miniaturization field and would vanish as soon as he regrew to proper size.

"Hey, Tomiko, I've seen you making eyes at Major Devlin whenever he isn't looking." Wilcox leaned close with what he thought was his irresistible smile. *Give the guy an inch* . . . "Trying to make me jealous, I think."

"Not a chance."

He misunderstood her answer. "What's wrong with Devlin? He's Air Force, and so was his dad— he's okay."

Tomiko marveled at how simple and straightforward the man's life must be. "*Retired* Air Force, and I wouldn't make a move on him. Not until he's ready."

"Ready? How many years is he going to wait? His wife died . . . what, five years ago? I don't see him moping around and grieving for her all the time."

Tomiko rolled her dark eyes. "You don't see much of *anything*, Garrett. Obviously, you've never had a genuine emotional attachment."

"Thank you."

"That's why I'm only passing time with you."

"Clear, please!" Pirov yelled from above, his voice raspy.

Tomiko held on to the carbon pillar. An electrical burst surged along the circuit line, glowing like heat lightning. After the shimmers flooded past, she crawled to the end of the impurity and went back to work extracting the black stump, though it wasn't the primary problem. She just hated to leave a job unfinished.

"I have additional readings now," Pirov said over the suit radio. "There is some kind of discontinuity up ahead. A major defect. We must fix that in order to accomplish our objective."

Tomiko used the laser's intense, microfine light on the carbon trunk until the second bundle broke away. The black cylinder rolled against the wall, bounced on random air currents, then slid to the substrate. "For aesthetic reasons," she said to Wilcox.

The two scrambled up rappelling ropes to the top. The Russian doctor checked his mission chronometer. "Twenty-three minutes remaining."

"Then let's not wait around." Wilcox jetted off, and Tomiko shot after him. The three team members traveled toward a shimmering change of color and light reflectance in the distance.

When they crossed a boundary between different metal tracks laid down in opposing film layers, Tomiko saw the reason the prototype ULSI chip had failed.

She stared. "Now that's what I'd call a big problem."

Chapter 4

During the three-hour drive across California's flat Central Valley, Devlin kept his mysterious silence even in the face of Arnold Freeth's obsessive enthusiasm. Curiosity was eating the UFO expert alive.

"Where did this alien come from, Major Devlin? What condition is it in? What . . . exactly is my role in this?"

Devlin didn't want to let details slip about the Project. Not yet. "It's a sealed package, Mr. Freeth, straight from a crashed flying saucer. We don't even know if the alien's alive."

Freeth looked alarmed. "You don't want me to perform an autopsy, do you? I—uh, just hosted that video, you know. How are we going to study the specimen?"

Devlin flashed a secretive smile. "No autopsies. We have a much more innovative technique for investigation." He refused to say more.

Before leaving, while Devlin stood waiting on the sunny sidewalk, the UFO expert had bustled around in his "suite," packing a smart-looking briefcase and a snappy garment bag. He had dressed in a stylish tweed sport jacket with suede patches on the elbows, cinched on a tie, added socks and soft black loafers.

"No need to dress up, Mr. Freeth. The project will

provide you with an appropriate uniform." Devlin thought of how much more comfortable it would be to get back into a Proteus jumpsuit again. This tie was strangling him.

"It's a question of image, Major Devlin." Freeth slung his briefcase and garment bag into the back seat. "In my line of work, I always run the risk of being branded a kook, and I have faced the worst that hecklers can dish out. Thus, I make a concerted effort to look as respectable as possible."

Across the street, the old man continued to water his oleanders. The housewife ushered her yapping dog into the garage. Everyone watched as Devlin and Freeth drove off.

Bursting with enthusiasm, Freeth was content to hold up both ends of a conversation as they left San Francisco behind. He launched into his beloved topic, as if intent on earning his consulting fee from the moment he stepped into the car.

"I assume you know about the exploded spacecraft over Siberia in 1908? Some people call it the Tunguska meteor, but evidence clearly shows it was an alien ship that suffered some sort of accident. Trees were flattened in a distinctive radial pattern for miles around, and no debris was ever found."

Devlin watched the farmland flash by as he accelerated, driving with one hand on the steering wheel. "We don't have any debris either. Just some sort of protective pod." He'd flown enough experimental aircraft that a simple highway jaunt like this generated no excitement. He drove ten miles over the speed limit, slipping past large trucks, some piled high with hay bales, others holding cattle or horses. "And our flying saucer came down near the Caspian Sea, not out in Siberia."

"The Russians have all the luck," Freeth said, then brightened. "Well, we have our opportunities on this side of the world, too. Everybody knows about the abduction of Barney and Betty Hill, and the mass sightings of UFOs over Mexico City and Salida, Colorado."

"Oh, sure." Devlin had never heard of either one. "Common cocktail party conversations across the country." He pulled out to pass a slow red Ford pickup, but drifted back into his own lane when he couldn't see more than fifty feet in front of him.

Freeth continued, as if Devlin had encouraged him. "On July 19, 1952, Washington, D.C., radar picked up eight unidentified targets in restricted airspace over the White House. Significant, eh? Air traffic controllers at National Airport contacted Andrews Air Force Base, and airmen there watched an orange fireball circle in the sky, then zip away at impossible speed. But when questioned, the Combat Officer from Andrews said he had referred the matter to a 'higher authority' and was not concerned about it."

As the road wound into the Sierra foothills, the traffic remained annoying. Devlin couldn't remember if this was a Friday or a holiday weekend; it had been too long since he'd paid attention to a calendar.

Freeth reveled in having a captive audience. "Nobody even bothered to report the White House incident to Captain Edward Ruppelt, the man assigned to run Project Blue Book, the official investigation into flying saucers. Ruppelt had to read about it in the newspapers, and by then it was too late. It's like the Air Force was trying to cover up something important."

Devlin accelerated in a short passing lane up a steep incline clogged with trucks. He didn't have time for a leisurely drive. "I'm an Air Force man myself, Mr. Freeth."

"I knew you had to be military, even in a suit and tie. I could tell by your haircut."

Without losing his calm, Devlin scooted around a dairy truck, dipped back to his own side of the road as the lane vanished again, then slipped over to the left to pass a gasoline tanker. He emerged ahead of the clog just as a sharp curve—and an oncoming Chevy pickup—blocked his view.

Kelli had always closed her eyes when he drove like this.

Freeth squawked as they came up fast on a dented guard rail.

Devlin accelerated around the corner, keeping two tires on the pavement and spitting only a little gravel from the shoulder. He avoided the drop-off by at least half a foot.

White-knuckled, Freeth gripped the armrest as if he were trying to strangle it. He squeezed his eyes shut and recited information, distracting himself. "The Air Force investigation was a joke. It started in 1947 with Project Sign, which concluded in a Top Secret memo that said, 'The phenomenon reported is something real and not visionary or fictitious.' That's a direct quote, thanks to the Freedom of Information Act."

"You memorize that stuff?"

"Just the important parts. It's the only way to maintain credibility when you're up against a tough talk-show host." Freeth opened his eyes again, relieved to see a straight stretch of road.

"Air Force Chief of Staff General Vandenberg rejected the Project Sign findings, ordered the whole report destroyed, then reformed the organization as Project Grudge—the name tells it all—with instructions that all reports were to be evaluated 'on the premise that UFOs couldn't exist.' " Freeth shook his head. "Good old military objectivity."

Devlin grunted, keeping his smile to himself. "Roger that. And they concluded that the sightings were meteors, temperature inversions, weather balloons, sundogs, lenticular clouds." He had seen all of those phenomena himself in his flying days. "Up to and including the planet Venus, right?"

"So they *said*. But even the brass wasn't convinced by Project Grudge, so they kick-started the investigation again in 1952, this time as Project Blue Book. They issued Regulation 200-2, which gave official instructions for reporting and investigating UFO sightings. Paragraph 9 states in no uncertain terms that information will be given to the public *only* for cases that have been positively explained and identified. Any sightings that couldn't be brushed aside remained classified." He looked at Devlin with an indignant expression, as if he expected him to argue. "Who knows what's still lurking in their secret files?"

Devlin knew better than to argue, especially after the alien lifepod he'd seen with his own eyes.

"Project Blue Book fizzled due to lack of funding, lack of support . . . and lack of authority. The low-ranking officers in charge couldn't get the cooperation they needed, and so the group was officially disbanded in 1969." Freeth leaned over until he was whispering in Devlin's ear. "But reports kept coming in, and the dusty old files contained so much evidence that only the most unimaginative and stubborn people refused to believe in extraterrestrials."

Devlin kept a straight face. "Don't over-estimate open minds, Mr. Freeth. People still insisted the Earth was flat for quite a few centuries after they should have known better."

The Sierras crouched before them in a line of rugged hills, brown-grass chaparral darkened with live oak and mesquite. Devlin took a left off the main highway while other drivers headed in a caravan toward Yosemite, or south to Kings Canyon and Sequoia National Parks.

Freeth glanced over at the back of Devlin's head, as if looking for a small screw at the base of his neck. "I recently conducted a survey, Major Devlin. Ninety percent of Americans believe that extraterrestrial spacecraft are being kept at Area 51 in Nevada. The same percentage believes that a saucer crashed at Roswell, probably the most inept cover-up in U.S. history."

Devlin whipped around another curve, making Freeth swallow convulsively.

"I've sold over a million copies of my video. That's domestic and international. People *do* want to believe. The government can't keep everything hidden from us, you know. No matter how hard you try."

Devlin gave him a tolerant smile. "I'm not trying to hide anything, Mr. Freeth. I'm taking you there, remember?"

The expert clenched his hand over one knee; his freckled face yielded a suspicious frown. "Why exactly are you being friendly with me, Major Devlin?"

"Just a friendly sort of guy, I guess."

Devlin turned onto a poorly marked county road and left the last remnants of rural traffic behind. Normally, he might have been concerned about giving away the route to the hidden Proteus Facility, but Arnold Freeth was paying no attention to the trip.

Devlin had to reassess his opinion of the UFO expert. He was not just a gullible nerd who'd found his niche in life. He was a credulous firebrand—quick to believe assertions, and just as quick to defend his beliefs—but he wasn't unintelligent, and his passion was real. Devlin couldn't fault the guy for that.

According to Freeth's dossier, he held a bachelor's degree in astronomy and another in sociology from the University of California at Berkeley. Freeth had published numerous articles and essays, some of them quite compelling to the open-minded; he'd been noticed in mainstream magazines as well as stacks of UFO tabloids.

Freeth was an articulate speaker who delivered an intriguing lecture. His passion was enough to keep him circulating on an endless quest through Rotary Clubs and public libraries to deliver his message to anyone who would listen. And he had the energy for it.

Devlin finally slowed as he found a gravel road that switchbacked up a granite mountainside. Ponderosa pines clutched any pocket of fertile soil. Where chaparral grasses grew tall, white butterflies flitted about, seeking weeds and thistles that hadn't yet died in the summer dryness. The sedan bounced up and down on the rutted road, tossing Freeth against his seat belt. Devlin had driven this route enough times to know how fast he could go without jarring the rearview mirror loose.

"We were very careful with that dissection video," the UFO expert said, his teeth chattering together in the rough ride. "We knew people would look for any flaw, and so we took the greatest care to analyze the footage. We made sure there was a clock on the wall at all times. The camera ran continuously, the doctors moved about but never blocked any key view. Special effects experts from Hollywood were convinced it couldn't possibly have been faked." He looked smug. "Computer analysis studied the film grain, searching for discrepancies. There were none."

"As a person would expect," Devlin said, "if it was real. You convinced Dr. Cynthia Tyler in our project. That's why you're here."

Freeth responded as if Devlin had inserted a quarter into a machine. "Still, some people will always be skeptical. They want to lose their sense of wonder. They don't believe in the marvels of the universe."

Freeth was accustomed to getting laughed at, to

being the butt of jokes. His voice took on a different tone now, as if hoping he'd found an ally in Devlin. "Has our society become so cynical that it's a *joke* to believe in something? Should a person be ashamed because he trusts in the inexplicable? Say, how is that different from the religious faith that churches have been spouting for two thousand years? Should we accept only what the government tells us to?"

Freeth took out a comb and reflexively stroked his dishwater-brown hair back into place. "I pity people who can't *see* wonder in the world, people who've become so cynical that their lives are all dull and clear-cut."

Devlin came around the last blind curve between tall pines to a sheer granite face and a fenced-in compound. "Ah, here we are. Welcome to Project Proteus."

Chain-link fences and high shrubbery surrounded the unmarked facility, tall transmitting towers, and satellite dishes. Guards stood at the entrance. Devlin brought the sedan to a halt in front of the gate and looked at the intense man in the passenger seat.

"Mr. Freeth, you are in for a treat."

Chapter 5

It was the opportunity of a lifetime, and no one was going to take it from her.

Dr. Cynthia Tyler stood in the sealed containment room, surrounded by every piece of nondestructive scanning equipment available to Proteus scientists. She leaned over the weirdly beautiful alien lifepod, feeling like the child who had the largest present under the Christmas tree.

The extraterrestrial specimen took her breath away.

Proteus technicians, wearing full anti-contamination gear like herself, used delicate instruments to clean and analyze the pod. Every step of the process was photographed and videotaped, so that the detailed records could be studied later. And in case anything went wrong.

Though the sealed container had been hosed off before it was crated and shipped to the United States, globs of Caucasus mud remained caked within the convoluted hieroglyphics. Metallic lines laced the shell like a complex circuit diagram, or blood vessels.

She still hadn't been able to determine if the specimen inside was even alive.

Behind her helmet faceplate, Dr. Tyler had high cheekbones and a narrow chin. Her shoulder-length blond hair was kinked and frizzed, because a perm required minimal maintenance. Her deep brown eyes and dark eyebrows led some to infer that she bleached her hair—a false impression, since Cynthia Tyler had no time for such things, and certainly no vanity toward her appearance. She was proud of other things about herself, had never wanted to do the Michelangelo routine on her face and hair. She'd seen some women whose makeup tables looked like a chemical weapons armory, their suite of hair-care products better stocked than Tyler's analytical chemistry laboratories.

Instead, she preferred to keep her *brain* conditioned and tangle-free.

Tyler used moistened cloths with gentle solvents to clean grime from the pod's window panels. "There's not a scratch." She rubbed her gloved finger along the smooth, slightly fogged porthole. She already had enough material for at least one journal article, probably more. She tried to prioritize the most prestigious publications in her head. "This thing's ship exploded, and the pod dropped two thousand feet without a parachute and slammed into a mountain." She shook her head, looking at the technicians. "Not a nick, not a mark."

"That means it's going to be tough to get the pod open," said one man.

Tyler studied the incomprehensible patterns that formed a protective web around the tough material. "Too many integrated systems, and we don't understand the controls. Unless we're careful, we could cause irreparable damage." *If the pod hadn't been sent here, Russian scientists would probably have bludgeoned it open already.* "We don't want to waste an opportunity like this."

Director Hunter's voice boomed over the containment-chamber intercom. "Our agreement with Deputy Foreign Minister Garamov is to complete all investigations *in situ*, Cynthia. We have no idea what sort of infectious microorganisms might be carried by a being from another planet. We must maintain absolute sterilization precautions. We will not open the container under any circumstances."

Tyler spread her gloved hands. "Director, we're sealed inside a secret mountain facility, within an armored chamber rated for Hot Zone investigations, certified against the most infectious diseases on Earth." The technicians wore padded spacesuits and breathed through respirator pumps that made them all sound like Darth Vader with a head cold. "What more do you want?" *You're cramping my style, Felix.*

Hunter stood by his control deck in the VIP observation deck above, like a medical professor watching a delicate operation from a surgical gallery. "I'm paid to be cautious. Who's to say that our most infectious terrestrial microorganisms aren't featherweights compared to what this creature carries as benign germs?"

Tyler's brow furrowed behind her transparent face shield. "Have you been watching that silly *Andromeda Strain* movie again, Felix? Look, something that doesn't use our biochemistry *can't* be infectious, any more than I can catch the flu from an iguana. Earth's ecosystem would poison any alien bacteria, or they would just starve to death."

"Not good enough, Cynthia." Hunter remained calm.

Before its arrival in the dead of night, eight hours previously, she had considered the possibility that the "specimen" might be an elaborate hoax, though she couldn't fathom why the Russian government would promulgate such a fake. To make American scientists look foolish and gullible? That made no sense.

Hunter had reassured her. "I know Vasili Garamov, and he's a very careful man. Extremely careful.

I can't believe he'd be taken in by a carnival side-show." The Deputy Foreign Minister himself would arrive that afternoon, straight from Russia. She convinced herself that Garamov would never show his face here if he had any doubt in his mind.

No matter how preposterous it might seem, Hunter had convinced Tyler that the alien must be genuine, and she had begun to calculate how much scientific clout she could earn from this. While waiting for the convoy to arrive, Tyler had studied the images sent on a secure telephone unit facsimile from the crash site in the Caucasus. The STU fax had been short on details, but the alien looked strikingly similar to what she had already seen on a popularized video of a purported "alien dissection." Tyler had found footage from the dissection video (along with immediate ordering information) on the Internet.

She had rushed to Hunter with the news. "This tape might be real, too, Felix. Look at the similar bone structure, its face, its limbs. If it's indeed the same kind of extraterrestrial creature, we ought to bring aboard the man who performed this dissection." She knew how useful Arnold Freeth's expertise could be, even if it meant sharing authorship credit on some of the articles.

Hunter had frowned, his dark eyes sincere but skeptical. His voice as deep and commanding, with a sonorous bass timbre. He stroked his mustache as he pondered. "Dr. Tyler, those videos are widely believed to be ambitious fakes. The men responsible always disappear upon closer investigation, along with any trace of the actual specimens. It would be folly to bring a charlatan into our sophisticated research project."

Tyler had pointed to the specimen inside the pod, tapping her gloved finger on the misty glass. "But there *are* aliens. This man may be the only specialist we can find, and you don't want to include him? Can we afford to take the chance?"

"Cynthia, I remind you that we've barely got a day of turnaround before we have to return the specimen to the Russian government."

She had smiled, intense dark eyes making her face seem tighter, sharper. "The man lives in the Bay Area, Felix, only a few hours from here. How could he turn down our invitation?"

Though she didn't admit as much, she was a bit skeptical about the video herself. As a doctor, Tyler would have performed certain procedures differently if *she'd* had an extraterrestrial cadaver spread out on an operating table. But still . . .

In the end, Director Hunter had capitulated.

Now, while Major Devlin went to retrieve Arnold Freeth, Tyler performed her preliminary analysis without opening the armored lifepod. She'd been at work since daybreak, not even noticing how hot and sweaty her anti-contamination suit had become.

She looked up to the VIP observation deck again. "Director, the alien corpus resists all normal attempts at nondestructive probing." She punched a button on her display screen. Every image was smeared, filled with static, showing only the blurriest outlines. "Nuclear magnetic resonance, CT scans, thermal maps, x-rays—everything is blocked. We can't see deeper than the skin surface."

Hunter flicked on the microphone from the VIP deck. "Is the capsule itself the problem? A defense mechanism of some kind?"

She shook her head, but the voluminous flexible helmet masked her gesture. "We've got plenty of readings on the electronics and design of this pod— Major Devlin will be thrilled to study them. They're an engineer's dream come true." She tapped the curved surface again. "No, the alien body itself seems to scramble signals. It blurs all our readings into static."

"That doesn't make any sense, Cynthia," Hunter said.

"You're telling me. Just let me think about it a little longer. I'm sure I can figure this out."

Tyler had been divorced twice by the age of forty-two. During the breakup with her first husband, to avoid the pain, she had dived deeper into her research. Later, she'd married a colleague who shared her interests, but she'd managed to drive him away, too. "You are a very passionate woman, Cynthia," he'd told her, "but it's not the kind of passion a husband wants."

Though she had accomplished much in her life and convinced many people of her skills, Tyler kept trying to prove herself, and in the process she had a tendency to run over innocent bystanders. She had excelled in school, in research; she'd won awards, published controversial papers. But she kept raising the bar to make it harder for herself.

And now she had the most remarkable specimen in history right in front of her. Just out of reach.

Tyler looked at the unsatisfactory scan images, feeling frustrated and stifled. "We aren't going to get much more with the equipment in this chamber. There's only one way to find the information we need. You know it, Felix, and so do I."

Hunter agreed. "That's why the specimen was brought here, Cynthia. We'll need to send a team inside."

Chapter 6

On the complex ULSI circuit, the discontinuity in metallic paths left a yawning gulf. "It's the Grand Canyon of microchips." Garrett Wilcox surveyed the open gap, as if assessing whether he could jump across it with a motorcycle.

Beside him, Tomiko saw where the deposited line of gold should have intersected a copper tracing, but the two had not merged. One edge had slumped and flowed sideways like lava detouring onto the silicon substrate.

Dr. Pirov looked at the gap in dismay. "We have no equipment to rebuild that. And we obviously do not have the time." He looked at his mission chronometer again. "Twenty minutes before field integrity begins to degrade."

Tomiko tossed her sleek hair behind her shoulders. "Still have to fix the breach and get out of here."

"You bet. With the three of us we must have brought enough chewing gum and duct tape," Wilcox said.

Tomiko put her hands on her slender hips and studied the microscopic strata. The opal gray of silicon was layered with metal films and silicon dioxide, like sedimentary rock made of insulators and semiconductors, gates and electron paths. The ULSI circuit was designed to process instructions millions of times faster than previous generations of chips. *If it functioned properly.*

Wilcox turned to Tomiko and lowered his voice. "Any ideas?"

"Not ready to give up yet." She heaved a sigh. "Electricity doesn't care how pretty the road is, just as long as there's a throughway. Since we don't have time to do reconstructive surgery, let's hope a simple bandage works."

"Piece of cake, then." Wilcox unshouldered his laser cutter. "Come on, Tomiko, let's generate a little heat."

Staying close together, she and Wilcox worked their way down the rubble-strewn slope where the deposited gold had failed to connect with the river of copper. Tomiko and Wilcox took large, bounding strides, while the old Russian doctor picked his way cautiously behind them.

At the bottom of the junction, Tomiko fired up her laser cutter. "Okay, let's move it." She and the young captain shone their beams at full-power, wide-dispersal onto the leading edge of the gold glacier. Heat dissipated through the petrified metal waterfall. The beams pounded the gold, softening it until the barrier slumped.

"I like this," Wilcox said.

Pirov kept a careful watch on the time. "We must begin our exit a full five minutes before we lose miniaturization field integrity. It is now thirteen minutes before we must return to the pickup point."

Wilcox made a pooh-poohing sound. "There's a big safety factor before we *start* to grow back. Five or ten minutes at least."

"Once the metal starts flowing, we'll finish up here fast enough." Tomiko continued to play the beam until the gold moved like chocolate toward the copper junction. "I've done work like this before, though on a larger scale."

While her father had gone off to shoot movies and her mother skated in glamorous traveling ice shows, Tomiko had stayed at home, making circuit boards to drive crude erector-set machines. She read *Popular Electronics*, wrote away for kits in the classified ads, and assembled them herself.

She had followed printed circuit patterns, using a masonite baseboard coated with copper foil, spraying it with light-sensitive resist film. She drew her own stencil patterns as the mask, then developed the boards like an amateur photographer, leaving copper lines behind. With tweezers she hand-stuffed wires into the appropriate circuit holes and soldered transistors into place.

Tomiko's parents wanted to help her become a star, just like them. Her father had even gotten her cast as a hard-fighting streetwise waif in *Little Orphan Assassin*, in which Tomiko played the ten-year-old daughter of a gunned-down hit man. Nolan Braddock had been the kindly FBI agent keeping her safe while rival mobsters tried to rub out the rest of her family.

Tomiko had stolen many hearts in that film, but though her parents loved to perform for crowds, she preferred to perform for herself and meet her own challenges. Such as being miniaturized and attempting a quickie repair job on a complicated computer chip. . . .

Realistically, Tomiko couldn't believe it would ever be cost-effective for tiny crews to slap together repairs on an ultra-complex integrated circuit. Such chips were designed to be mass produced, and not even the most sophisticated ULSI circuit would ever warrant such tender loving care.

But this was only a test mission, practice before

the team went inside an alien body. They all had to be at the peak of their capabilities.

Next, Wilcox swung his beam over to the copper wall, playing heat over the rough surface until it shimmered orange. The two rivers of metal streamed toward each other until the circuit paths collapsed together and fused into a dam. Now the electrons could flow through, and the circuit would function as designed. Almost finished.

"We have seven minutes," Pirov said. "Please hurry."

Tomiko raised the heat to complete her work. "Ready to get out of here?"

Wilcox relentlessly concentrated his beam on the already-molten copper. Unexpectedly, the metals began to boil.

"Hey, enough, Garrett." Tomiko yanked her laser away and switched off the beam.

Hot globules boiled off, wavering spheres bound by liquid-metal surface tension. They sprayed upward, then drifted down in an avalanche of hardening, molten metal.

Tomiko jumped into the air, levitating with her jetpack and dodging the hot spheres that drifted around them. For a moment, it looked like a cascade of sparkling balls from the sky, as if someone were throwing metal flowers to celebrate the team's victory. Then a hot globule passed in front of her face like a comet, and Tomiko felt its blistering warmth, saw the shimmering crystallization of its cooling skin. She bent backward like a reed, out of its way.

Wilcox dove under the rain of molten metal. "Before I call a retreat, we've got to verify that the circuit works." One of the trembling spheres crashed into the floor next to him, but the team captain dodged to the left. When it struck, the globule burst its hardened outer skin and spilled hot metal in a puddle.

With spare movements and careful precision, Wilcox dropped to his knees and removed electrical leads from his test pack. "Sending another pulse through." He slapped down one and then another onto the gold surface. Wilcox glanced over his shoulder, raising his eyebrows at Tomiko.

With the hot spheres still raining down, Pirov crouched, trying to make himself even smaller. "We should get out of here," he said in a tiny voice.

"Watch out, Doctor P!" Tomiko swung the laser cutter and vaporized a globule that tumbled toward the old man. The Russian ducked in surprise. The metal blob ruptured into smaller cooling spheres, which spread out like gumballs floating backward in the air, crackling as they cooled.

"Everybody clear!" Lifting his feet off the surface, Wilcox sent a test pulse into the connector. The metal walls thrummed as a surge of electrons smashed into the newly fused gold and copper microwires—and flowed through. "You bet!" He did a little victory dance. "Full connection."

Then a shimmering ball of molten copper crashed into his right leg, splattering hot metal. He screamed.

Tomiko was already in the air, knocking him away from a second falling sphere. Wilcox writhed, grabbing at his leg and burning his fingertips on the coating of liquid metal. The fabric of his jumpsuit snapped and smoked; the flesh underneath sizzled as his skin and muscles cooked.

Tomiko held him down, shouting for Pirov. "Come on, Doctor P! Need your help here." The splattered metal had hardened into a crust, but continued to burn. Tomiko made a snap decision and grabbed the hot crystalline edges with her fingers, blistering her hands as she pried the copper off, exposing the angry wound.

Wilcox's jumpsuit had charred entirely away, and

the burn dug deep into the cocky young captain's thigh muscle. The smell of cooked meat overpowered the sharp tang of hot metal. He moaned, biting back another scream.

"Come on, be a tough guy, Garrett," Tomiko said close to his face. "*Now's* the time to show off for me." Wilcox grabbed her arm and squeezed it in a death grip.

Dr. Pirov turned his head from side to side, as if searching for miraculous outside help. He looked as if he wanted to back away. "That wound is too deep, too severe. We should wait until we return to normal size, then we can take him to the Proteus infirmary." He nodded quickly. "They will know what to do."

"Forget that. He needs help right away," Tomiko said, ready to slap him across the face. "Do something for him now. Come on, you're a *doctor.*"

Shaken, Pirov snatched packets from his first-aid kit. "But we have less than five minutes." He jabbed Wilcox with a morphine syringe. "I never had much of a bedside manner, you see. My instructors told me I could establish more rapport with a dissection cadaver than with living patients." He spoke quickly, as if to calm himself rather than Wilcox. "That is why I went into anatomy rather than medical practice."

Though dazed, Pirov wrapped the gaping burn with all the gauze he carried. Bodily fluids began to soak through the wrappings.

"See, Garrett. You just needed a little bandage." Tomiko touched the blond hair at his temple, the streaming sweat on his grayish skin. Imminent shock. The morphine began to take effect.

"Got to head for the exit point. Doctor P, help me carry him." She snatched up the captain's discarded laser cutter and tucked it under her arm. If she left the piece of equipment behind, it would grow back to normal size and crush the delicate chip. "No time for caution. Just get to the edge."

She and Pirov grabbed Wilcox under each arm, then raised him with their jetpacks. The wounded captain hung like a dead weight between them. They streaked along low to the surface, trying to get enough thrust from the compressed gas to maintain stability as random air currents jolted them. They climbed higher until the convoluted circuit looked like a tiny city seen from an airplane.

But the paths beneath her began to look smaller, the lines finer. "Growing already. Keep moving."

Tomiko could not sense the weakening miniaturization field, but she increased the outflow of gas from her jetpack nozzle. As the team members enlarged, their mass increased proportionately, and the small gas jets could not provide enough lift and propulsion. The tiny packs had been designed only for use at sizes where air resistance meant a lot and gravity counted for little.

Now, as they grew heavier, the jets couldn't keep up, and Tomiko began to fall. She and Pirov could barely keep Wilcox's boots from dragging along the surface of the ULSI circuit.

Ahead, beyond the edge of the chip, Tomiko could see the bright, pulsing glow of the miniaturization room, although everything seemed light years away. She could discern no details of the technicians or equipment. Not yet.

She hoped Director Hunter had a medical team standing by. They had no time to stop and set up a transmission.

Wilcox finally ceased his writhing and dangled unconscious. "Only a few more minutes, Garrett," she said, though he couldn't hear.

At last, jetpacks sputtering, the team members crossed the edge of the circuitry paths. To the Proteus crew outside, they were already visible, the size of small insects.

Director Hunter said into his voice pickup, unaware of the accident, "Good work, team. We've tested the circuit, and the error in the chip has been corrected." His voice sounded deep and pervasive inside their suit radios.

"Felix, get an emergency medical tech in here, now!" she shouted into the open link. "Garrett's hurt."

Still growing, Tomiko and Pirov dropped to the lab floor and landed heavily as the now-useless jet-packs gave out. She tried to shield Wilcox from the impact, letting him tumble on top of her.

The Russian doctor straightened beside Tomiko, looking perplexed and embarrassed by his own helpless reaction.

While the team approached normal size, two emergency medical technicians hurried toward them like lumbering giants. "Better get a stretcher, take him to the infirmary," Tomiko called, her voice small and piping as she grew. "Let's move it here!"

Hunter rushed forward. "What happened?"

The medical techs hustled Wilcox out of the room, carrying him through the double doors. They took readings, keeping up a running chatter about the best treatment.

"Big problem, Felix." Even shaken, Tomiko forced a no-nonsense tone into her voice. She tossed Wilcox's retrieved laser cutter to the floor. "You've got to launch a mission in a few hours—and now you don't have a pilot for the ship."

Chapter 7

Awed by the successively camouflaged fences inside the Proteus Facility, Arnold Freeth climbed out of the government sedan. Amazement blossomed on his freckled face, and his eyes grew progressively wider. "You've really got an alien body in there, don't you? My God, you want me to—"

A Marine MP in a private-security-guard uniform swung the first sallyport gate shut and padlocked it. He glanced at Devlin's badge and ID, then saluted. "We've been expecting you, sir. Director Hunter needs to see you immediately."

"On my way." He knew that Felix, frazzled with all the last-minute urgent preparations for the mission, probably wanted to double-check something about the *Mote*. Devlin gestured for Freeth to follow him into the perimeter, shoes crunching on the packed gravel.

The UFO expert stretched his neck, risking whiplash as he tried to stare everywhere at once. The high granite bluffs were streaked with black from algae and rain runoff; Ponderosa pines whispered in the breezes, releasing a sun-warmed, resiny scent.

"Not much of a secret installation, right out in the open. Not at all like Area 51." He sounded as if he spoke from personal knowledge. "I expected soldiers with machine guns, razor-wire, motion detectors, land mines. . . ."

Devlin clapped him on a bony shoulder. "If you weren't authorized here, Mr. Freeth, you'd be all too aware of those things." They headed toward the cavelike entrance.

"That tunnel is big enough to drive trucks through."

"The hard part is driving them up the winding road. Thirty-eight switchbacks. A real headache, especially in the winter. The SST from San Francisco took five hours to get here late last night with the alien body."

"When—when can I see it?"

"Paperwork first, Mr. Freeth. This is the government, after all."

Inside the tunnel, a guard sat in a transparent Lexan enclosure surrounded by TV monitors. "Major Devlin! Director Hunter has asked to see you immediately upon your return. There's been an unexpected change in this afternoon's mission."

"Roger that, Sergeant." Devlin took a clipboard the man slid through an opening in his windowed enclosure, then gave Freeth a conspiratorial wink. "There's always an unexpected change, one way or another, and I always manage to fix it." He turned back to the guard. "I'll go see him as soon as we get Mr. Freeth processed through."

The UFO expert stiffened with suspicion when he learned they would have to take fingerprints, retinal scans, and a badge photograph, but Devlin cut off the other man's protests about violated civil rights and privacy. "I can't show you the alien until you go through the red tape. You know bureaucrats."

With a discouraged nod, Freeth submitted to the tedious procedures. When the processing guard finally handed him a laminated badge on a thin chain,

Freeth slipped it over his head and looked unexpectedly pleased with himself.

Devlin led the way along the painted floor, following bright pools from caged fluorescent lights set into the rugged ceiling. The air in the entryway had the damp, chalky smell of caves. Deeper inside, the passages were lined with painted concrete and color-keyed power conduits and pipes. Three-wheeled white Cushman electric carts hummed along, carrying packages, supplies, or technicians.

Freeth seemed to be floating with excitement as they passed laboratories and high bays. Airlocks sealed experimental rooms with a hiss of compressed air. Though intimidated by the size of the complex, he looked as if he'd seen the culmination of his life's work. "Believe me, I knew places like this existed. I *knew* it. This is like the secret hangars at Edwards Air Force Base in the Mojave Desert."

"Actually, the Mojave is where we grow our giant tarantulas and our mutant radioactive ants," Devlin said with mock seriousness. "Here, we work on something . . . *smaller*."

Big Science had always enthralled Devlin. Even during his Academy days, when he was just dating Kelli Hunter, he'd loved to tinker beyond the prescripted class experiments, often at the expense of old equipment.

Once, Devlin had modified a CO_2 laser and accidentally bumped a spinning mirror, which bounced a reflection around the room, scribing black streaks on the cinderblock walls. The sour-tempered professor—a civilian who was counting the years until he could move to the Bahamas and sip piña coladas all day—had banned Devlin from the optics laboratory. After waiting until the professor went off to a physics conference, Devlin had filled hundreds of plastic cups with water late one night and built an immense pyramid in front of the man's office door. He added a note, "Can I buy you a drink, Professor?"

When the professor returned from his conference, it took him and his secretary hours to dismantle the barricade, drenching themselves in the process. Lucky for young Marc Devlin, the professor had made so many enemies among the underclassmen that he'd never been able to identify the real prankster. . . .

Now, as Devlin led Freeth past security checkpoints, the man's expression changed to barely covered anger. "It's amazing what the government keeps hidden from the taxpayers. Do they think we can't handle knowing about this?"

"Project Proteus is a collaborative effort with American and Russian scientists, a few Europeans, a few Japanese. It's too big"—he smiled at the irony—"and too important for one country to handle alone."

Freeth continued to speculate about international conspiracies and military industrial conglomerates. "I've heard there's an engine that runs by burning distilled water, and another one that gets a hundred miles per gallon of gas. But, believe me, the oil companies don't want us to have them. Every one of those inventors was killed in a mysterious accident."

His muddy eyes showed an edge of panic, as if he was afraid a similarly mysterious accident would befall him. "And you know that pharmaceutical companies found a simple cure for cancer a long time ago, but they'll never release it because they make too much money on all those expensive treatments."

"Negative, Mr. Freeth." Devlin's voice grew suddenly cold. He had watched the heroic efforts the oncologists had performed on Kelli, and certainly not because they wanted to keep any miracle pills hidden for their own private use. "You have been misinformed."

Though his wife had worked as a medical technician, she was the last to suspect that something was wrong. She would have chided patients for ignoring such symptoms, but she hadn't seen a doctor until the ovarian cancer had progressed too far. From that point, she and Devlin had had very little time left together. Far too little . . .

A miracle cure, indeed.

Quiet now, Devlin led the UFO expert to a lift cage. He tried to focus his thoughts, get back to business. "You'll see everything with your own eyes soon enough, Mr. Freeth."

Freeth gripped the metal bars as the caged elevator dropped into the deepest levels. Devlin ushered him into well-lit tunnels that smelled of paint, lubricants, and recycled air. "Are you ready?"

Freeth nodded vigorously, still out of his depth, but refusing to admit it.

The last set of smooth-bore tunnels looked like an underground hospital corridor. Ahead was a Class IV isolation chamber large enough to be an operating theater, complete with an observation deck at the ceiling level. Thick bullet-proof glass windows and armor-reinforced access doors surrounded the chamber. Armed Marines nodded to Devlin as he approached.

"There you go, Mr. Freeth. I hope your expertise serves us well. The team is going *inside* this afternoon."

Freeth stepped gingerly forward, cautious but curious. He placed his palms against the large windows, like a child staring into a closed toy store.

In the middle of the isolation chamber, surrounded by sophisticated analytical and medical apparatus, sat a sealed cylindrical case like a coffin, or a life-support capsule. Its angles and curves seemed entirely wrong, and the side walls were marked with stylized hieroglyphics. It did not belong among the chrome and polished surfaces prevalent inside the Proteus Facility.

Visible through the capsule's transparent side and top walls lay a motionless humanoid form, fragile-looking and gray-skinned. It had an enlarged head, similar to those of the alien visitors that had become so popular in the tabloids. The enormous eyes were gently closed in sleep, or death.

"Holy shit! Is this for real?"

"It's very real, Mr. Freeth." Devlin saw that the UFO expert was gibbering with excitement and pale with shock. "I—uh, hope you brought along a clean pair of undershorts."

"I can't believe it. Holy *shit!*"

"And we need you to help us figure it out. You'll be part of the team."

Devlin looked up as redheaded Dr. Trish Wylde, the Proteus chief pathologist, came running down the hall. Trish was also trained in miniaturized missions, though she hadn't been chosen for the upcoming exploration. Her narrow face bore a look of alarm. "Major Devlin, you've got to go see Director Hunter. There's been an emergency."

He was instantly alert, ready to respond. Perhaps Felix wasn't just being frazzled after all. "What kind of emergency?"

"It's Captain Wilcox. The doctors don't think he'll lose his leg, but he's definitely not flying the mission this afternoon."

Devlin's heart turned to lead. "Roger that. I'm on my way. Trish, please see to Mr. Freeth. He needs a jumpsuit in his size. Try to run him through a simulation or two before it's time." He stopped and spun halfway around. "Whoa, I didn't even tell him about the miniaturization yet. He needs a briefing before we go inside the alien." Devlin raced off to where he could find the Director.

"Miniaturization?" Freeth said. "Going inside the alien? What is he talking about?"

Trish Wylde smiled at the UFO expert, taking him by the arm. "You're going to be reduced to the size of a cell so you can join a microscopic exploration team that's going to be inserted directly into the alien's bloodstream. The rest of us envy you the opportunity."

Freeth's mouth opened, closed, and opened again. "But that's . . . ridiculous. Shrinking a person down to a dust speck—"

"Smaller, actually."

"But that's preposterous! It can't be done."

Trish Wylde arched her thin eyebrows. "Says the man who believes in alien abductions?" Freeth reddened, but couldn't counter her argument. She nudged him down the corridor. "Aren't you glad you agreed to come along?"

Chapter 8

The main miniaturization lab was the crown jewel of Project Proteus, capable of safely reducing a test subject to an infinitesimal fraction of its original size. At least, so long as everything went according to plan.

Director Hunter stood inside the chamber, hands locked behind his back. Enough had already gone awry for one day. Captain Wilcox had come out of surgery and remained in recovery. Marc Devlin still hadn't checked in, and Deputy Foreign Minister Garamov should be landing in San Francisco any moment now.

"Are we ready for our test?" Impatient, Hunter turned to Dr. Rajid Sujatha, who had suited up in full clean-room garb. "We'll only have time for this last check."

They didn't have the luxury to make this a model mission, but Hunter and his crew would pull off a miracle anyway. He couldn't pass up a chance like this.

The Bengali doctor nodded vigorously from across the room. "As soon as we bring in Fluffy Alice, Mr. Director, sir."

In Hunter's considered opinion, the miniaturizing apparatus itself appeared to have been inspired by an alien spacecraft. Indeed, after he had pulled strings to resurrect this mothballed program, he'd never asked where the equipment had originated. The technology seemed beyond anything the most ingenious minds—American or Soviet—had ever created. Back in the 1960s, how could mere human scientists have developed an apparatus so much more complex than even the Manhattan Project's atomic bomb or NASA's Apollo moon landing?

Some things Hunter didn't want to know.

Waiting behind the barricade, he brushed a hand over his mustache. His neat hair was a shade too dark to be called iron-gray, but it gave his lean face an extremely distinguished appearance.

Technicians in gloves and clean-room suits moved around the chamber, fine-tuning the prismatic grid, double-checking the outputs of myriad devices behind the interlocked focusing plates.

"Ten minutes to activation!" a jumpsuited woman called.

"Check. Everybody finish up your procedures. Bring in the rabbit."

Dr. Sujatha wheeled a cart into the center of the projection area, his sparkling black eyes framed by his dust-filter mask and bushy dark brows. Inside a cage sat a contented-looking white rabbit, all twitching ears and blinking pink eyes.

Sujatha positioned the test animal at the focal point of the miniaturization beams, then stepped behind the barricade, out of the clean zone. He had a wife and three daughters at home, but they had no inkling of what he did for Project Proteus. Eleven times now, he had gone out of his way to show Hunter snapshots of his lovely girls.

Sujatha yanked down his mask and removed his latex gloves. "Fluffy Alice is ready for another test run, Director, sir."

Only a few more hours . . . The mission must proceed, despite the problems, despite the speed bumps.

Hunter's stomach wouldn't start to unknot, though, until Marc Devlin got back. What was taking him so long to bring the alleged UFO expert? He hoped his son-in-law had had a nice, quiet drive, because all hell was breaking loose around here.

"Five minutes," a technician called.

Unexpected sparks crackled from one of the control panels, accompanied by a thin curl of smoke and the smell of burning plastic insulation. Shouting, two technicians shut down the preliminary run and yanked the cover plate off their main panel.

"Do we need to cancel the test?" Hunter growled. "We can't afford another setback."

One tech yanked out a circuit board and pried at a blackened component. "We can get this replaced in a minute, sir. Put the countdown on hold for sixty seconds. That's all we need."

Inside the miniaturization grid, the rabbit sniffed around her cage, as if looking for something to nibble.

"We expect no surprises, Director, sir." Sujatha tried to sound reassuring.

"If we *expected* them, they wouldn't exactly be surprises. After what happened to Captain Wilcox, I insist on total safety for my team members."

Hunter remembered why the miniaturization research had been shut down in the first place. No matter what the cost, Hunter vowed that no microexplorers would be lost on his watch—not even a rabbit. He hoped.

The technician slid the board back into place, closed the cover plate, then powered up the system again. He studied the yellow lights until each one turned green. He ran another quick circuit check, then nodded. "All ready to go, sir. Picking up the countdown."

The rabbit poked about for a way to escape from

the cage. She hopped from one side to the other, trapped. The green lights flickered off again, then came back on, weaker than before.

The double door swung open into the main chamber, and Major Devlin hurried in, his face flushed. He saw them behind the observation barricade. "Felix! I got your message. What's wrong?"

The sight of his son-in-law flooded Hunter with relief, followed by a heaviness about what he'd have to ask. "Marc, I'm glad you're here. Did you fetch Mr. Freeth as expected?"

"Affirmative. Dr. Wylde is running him through the hoops. The *Reader's Digest* condensed version."

Hunter brushed a tanned hand across his forehead. "At least something went as planned today."

Devlin's hazel gaze remained intense. "Don't dance around the problem, Felix. What happened to Captain Wilcox? Where does that leave us for the mission, sir?"

Hunter drew a deep breath. "Garrett had a run-in with some molten metal during this morning's training exercise. Tomiko brought him out, and Doctor Pirov kept him alive. The medics here did what they could, but he'll be a long time healing and will probably need a walking stick for the rest of his life."

Devlin's voice was hoarse. "I'll try to find him a stylish one."

"Ready for miniaturization!" the first technician announced. "Powering up the system, Director Hunter. All apparatus has stabilized."

Hunter leaned forward to the viewing window in the shielded wall. "Are you certain the systems are optimal?"

"Absolutely, sir." He tapped the panel again. "Everything checks out."

"Be damned sure," Hunter said. "Another glitch

at this stage will cancel our primary mission. We'll never have a second chance at that alien."

And Project Proteus would be back to square one.

Thanks to a slip of the tongue from a drunken ambassador, Hunter had learned of the mothballed miniaturization program years ago. He'd done some digging, using connections he had accumulated for decades. Regardless of its problems, the shrinking process *worked* and should not have been forgotten.

Hunter had spent years gathering the people and resources necessary to work the bugs out. The original prototype apparatus had disappeared somewhere along the line, but the blueprints and specs remained. He had scouted funding from various countries to keep Project Proteus alive, and also to muddy (and, he hoped, defuse) the politics of one government having sole access to such breakthrough technology.

In the chaos of the crumbling Eastern Bloc, Hunter had negotiated with Vasili Garamov himself to purchase the classified Soviet miniaturization equipment. He'd brought over the Russian program's top researchers, including Sergei Pirov, people who were only too willing to be given a new life in the U.S. For years, Hunter's hand-picked scientists and engineers had refined the shrinking technology, taking the best parts from the old American program as well as the Soviet equipment they had purchased.

After his daughter's unexpected diagnosis of cancer, her death had been so sudden that the Project had rolled on its own momentum for a time, while Hunter and Marc Devlin stayed by Kelli's side. He had done his best to watch over his son-in-law ever since.

"Felix, how can you go without Captain Wilcox?" Devlin asked. "He's been trained and tested on the *Mote*. You didn't have time to assign a backup pilot, and there isn't anyone—'' He stopped in mid-sentence.

Hunter had known Devlin would figure it out for himself. "It's got to be you, Marc. You designed the *Mote*. You've flown her on a number of tests." His heart sank. "I'm very sorry. I never wanted to send you into danger, because I don't trust my objectivity where you're concerned. But right now I don't have a choice."

Devlin squeezed Hunter's shoulder in a strong grip. "Felix, you're a captain of industry, and I've seen you wrestle politicians to the ground. You've never been one to let emotions get in the way of an important decision."

"I won't let anything happen to you, Marc. I promise."

"I know." His hazel eyes glittered with growing excitement. "I'm honored to go, I really am. Nobody can take better care of the ship than me. The *Mote* and I have a special bond."

Buzzers sounded in the chamber, warning that the miniaturization process was about to commence. Automatic fail-safes locked the doors, and air-exchange systems roared inside the sealed chamber.

"Activating miniaturization beams."

The prismatic lights in the floor and ceiling began to pulse out of phase, an alternating sequence that glowed from outside the visible spectrum. Behind the filtered observation window, Hunter's eyes adjusted to take in more of the fringe illumination. He saw a flicker of static discharge around the rabbit cage.

"Good-bye, Fluffy Alice," Sujatha said. "Come back to us in one piece."

A throbbing sound grew, like the bass of a rock group playing miles away. Slowly at first, the table, cage, and rabbit shrank down in perfect symmetry, until Fluffy Alice was the size of a hamster, then a mouse, then a fly.

The technicians worked at their panels, scrambling with touch-screens and keypads, whispering furiously at each other. Hunter did not like the concerned expressions on their faces. One of the green lights burned out. He considered calling off the test, but held his tongue. He did not have time to be obsessively cautious.

"The technology has been proven safe many times, Mr. Director, sir," Sujatha said, picking up on Hunter's uneasiness.

In an adjacent room, walled off behind thick shielding, the primary miniaturization apparatus hummed, its huge engines sucking power through high tension lines from the nearest hydroelectric plant. Behind the walls, where only physicists dared to go, the true shrinking process took place.

Safe in her cage, Fluffy Alice didn't seem perturbed as the entire table and cage diminished to a pinpoint and became an exhibit for bacteria and dust motes.

The glowing lights stopped, the pulsing fell silent. The interlocked prisms dimmed, and the technicians heaved a sigh of relief. One mopped his forehead, noticed Hunter looking at him, and quickly focused back on his work.

The loudspeaker proclaimed, "Phase One successful. Miniaturization accomplished, factor of ten to the minus fifth."

"Never ceases to amaze me," Hunter muttered.

"That'll be me in a few hours." Devlin sounded as if he still couldn't believe he would be going along after all.

Sujatha looked over at Hunter. "Would you like to be miniaturized yourself, sir? As Project Director, I am certain you have the authority to assign yourself to an exploration team."

Devlin laughed at the suggestion. "While Director Hunter has complete confidence in the technology, Dr. Sujatha, I don't think he's cut out to be a daring adventurer. Maybe someday . . . when he's younger."

The rabbit still had not returned. Video monitors projected magnified images of the central miniaturization zone, but Fluffy Alice had been reduced far beyond conventional, nondestructive observation techniques. "Thirty seconds. Condition stable, as far as we can tell."

"How long are we going to wait before restoration?" Hunter asked. Every second that ticked by raised his concerns.

"Relax, Felix," Devlin whispered. "You're going to keep *us* reduced a lot longer than this."

"It is only a routine short-term shrinkage and restoration, sir. The weak field will degrade rapidly," Sujatha said. "However, I am certain we will be able to keep our exploration team intact for the maximum five-hour time allotment."

All movement inside the sealed miniaturization chamber had ceased. No ventilation stirred, no machinery hummed. Hunter waited, unable to dispel his ever-present tension.

"We're at the one-minute point," the disembodied voice reported. "Prepare for re-enlargement."

The prismatic grid hummed again. Hunter instinctively shielded his eyes, but studied the focal point in the center of the beams until a black dot appeared and expanded rapidly into a discernible shape, a rectangular cage on a table. Everything looked normal.

Hunter held his breath. The rabbit twitched. Fluffy Alice sniffed about, her pink nose wiggling, ears erect.

"We've already had our quota of mishaps for one mission," Devlin said, reassuringly. "Have faith in us, Felix. The rest will be smooth sailing."

When the interlocked plates ceased glowing and the enormous machines fell silent, an all-clear signal sounded from the loudspeakers. With a loud *thunk*, the electronic security seals on the doors unlocked.

"Nothing to worry about." Disheveled from his long round-trip drive and eager to get ready, Devlin turned to go. "I'm going to see Captain Wilcox in the infirmary, if he's awake by now. Trish Wylde will still be putting our UFO expert through the paces before our final briefing. Still in an hour, sir?"

"Yes, and Team Proteus is scheduled for miniaturization at sixteen-hundred hours this afternoon."

Putting his mask and gloves back in place, Sujatha ran to check Fluffy Alice. He removed the plump rabbit from her cage, holding her up for a cursory checkup. He gave a thumbs-up sign and petted the animal before putting her back inside. "I am pleased, sir, that you do not require us to dissect our specimen after each journey."

"I'm sure Fluffy Alice appreciates that too," Hunter said. "It's the only way we can study the effects of repeated miniaturization. Your rabbit has been shrunk down more times than any other living creature."

"Fluffy Alice is happy to serve." Carrying the wire cage, Sujatha strode toward the exit. Hunter knew the Bengali doctor would reward his precious test rabbit with snippets of carrots and parsley.

"Bring the *Mote* through the hangar doors and position it in the field," he instructed the other workers. "No time to waste."

Hunter headed out of the miniaturization chamber, back toward his office. He had to pick up the dossiers and prepare for the briefing. He hoped the specialists he'd selected for this first, all-important mission would return in one piece, just like Fluffy Alice.

Chapter 9

When Garrett Wilcox returned to consciousness, the last thing he wanted to see was the man who would replace him on the mission.

Devlin stood by the recovery bed in the infirmary, arms crossed over his chest. "Can't leave you alone for a second, can I, Garrett? I go away for a simple pickup, and look what happens." He regarded the blond-haired patient with a frown. "What is it they say about young fighter pilots—balls the size of grapefruits, brains the size of peas?"

Struggling to raise his head off the pillow, Wilcox managed a smile that looked a little like an attack of gas pain.

While the Proteus infirmary did not have the equipment of a large medical center, Wilcox received the full attention of the project medical staff. If they had taken the time to airlift him to the nearest hospital after the accident, the young captain's burned limb might have needed amputation. Here, at least, the surgeons had salvaged his leg.

Still fighting off the painkillers and the anesthetic, Wilcox tried to focus his eyes. "Sorry . . . guess I'm just an attention grabber."

Devlin feigned a disappointed frown. "Roger that,

and now I'm stuck taking your place on the *Mote*. Man, I wanted to watch my soaps this afternoon."

Wilcox had trouble orienting himself, finding his voice. "You mean you don't really want to go?"

Devlin gave a reassuring laugh. "Of course I do. It's my dream come true. Unfortunately, this is probably the only way Felix would ever let me fly the ship. He tends to be a bit overprotective of me, you know."

Wilcox managed a disbelieving snort. "Lucky you. The Director runs the rest of us ragged." He leaned back, obviously groggy and in pain. "So, did you get that UFO guy? Is he for real?"

"Who can say? At least he's *earnest*. And he certainly doesn't know less about the alien specimen than we do."

Devlin wondered how Arnold Freeth was handling his introduction to Project Proteus. Trish Wylde would no doubt select the most rigorous, most comprehensive training routine she could fit into the available time. Afterward, Freeth would probably consider the strangest Abductee's convention to be a walk in the park.

One of the medical technicians came in, wearing a look of disapproval. Devlin glanced at his watch. "Hey, I'm on my way. Just wanted to check up on you. There's a briefing in half an hour, and I've got to get up to speed on everything *you* were supposed to do. Slacker."

"Hey, watch out for Tomiko, okay?"

Wilcox had seen all of Nolan Braddock's action films and could discuss them in more detail than even Tomiko could. Devlin suspected that must embarrass her greatly.

He smiled at the very idea of needing to rescue the beautiful Asian powerhouse. "I suspect you'd have to ask Tomiko's kindergarten teacher for the last time anybody needed to watch out for *her*. Our collective butts are in her hands."

Wilcox grinned at the image. "You wish." He let out a bittersweet sigh of disappointment and lay back in the bed, ready for the comforting embrace of more sedatives and painkillers.

Devlin stopped at the infirmary door. "You'll go on the next mission, Garrett."

"Don't think so . . . probably be hobbling around for the rest of my life." His voice was slow and slurred. "And I got a security clearance for *this*?"

"Look on the bright side. You can always spend hours and hours listening to CIA wiretaps."

"Gee, thanks," Wilcox said.

Plucking at his rubberized environmental suit, Arnold Freeth looked over at the chief pathologist. She kept glancing at her watch, urging him to begin the simulation. "Time, Mr. Freeth. We don't have all day."

"But why would I ever need to use this?" He rubbed at the polymer sleeve, then adjusted his waist belt. The outfit looked like a scuba-diving getup.

Trish Wylde draped a comfortable Proteus uniform on one of the plastic chairs lined up against the wall. "You can wear this when you're finished. You'll find it much more pleasant than that environmental suit." Her voice sharpened. "But this test exercise is rather rigorous. Since you're going on a real mission in a few hours, we'd better hit you with the hard stuff now."

She led him toward a deep tank filled with slow-moving amber liquid. Freeth looked into the container with an uneasy frown. In panic, he glanced back at the elfin face of the redheaded pathologist. "But I don't know what you're doing, what you expect me to—"

"Your full mission briefing is in less than an hour. You'll learn everything you need to. But if the *Mote* gets trapped in bodily fluids and starts sinking, don't you want to know how to swim to safety?"

"Trapped . . . in bodily fluids?"

"Don't worry." Somehow, her smile did not comfort him in the least. "For the most part, you'll be sitting in your seat the whole time. But you need to be aware of the *differences*, if nothing else. On the microscopic scale, you can't just move the same way as you might swim in a pool. When your body is only about a millionth the size it is now, you have to worry about factors such as air or fluid resistance, not to mention Brownian motion."

"What's that?" Freeth asked, as if it were some sort of deadly hazard. He turned away from the thick fluid in the tank, hoping to stall her.

"Random disturbances caused by the movement of molecules in a liquid or gas. Have you ever seen an image waver around in a microscope? That's Brownian motion. When you're miniaturized, tiny ripples can seem like a thunderstorm."

"But how am I going to be shrunk down to microscopic size?" Freeth raised his voice. "And for what purpose?"

"Why, the better to see the alien, of course." She gestured impatiently toward the tank. "Now get in."

"I'm not sure I like this," Freeth said.

"You signed the papers, didn't you? Anyway, I thought aliens were your business. I can't imagine what would happen to your reputation if word got out that you refused a chance to explore a genuine extraterrestrial."

Freeth squared his shoulders. "You're right. I survived the *Jerry Springer Show* . . . so how bad can this be?"

"Good attitude. Now that you're suited up, I'm

going to have you practice moving through thick oil. It has a significantly different viscosity than water or air . . . and we didn't have time to prep the gelatin tank."

"A *gelatin* tank?" The UFO expert took a step backward, picturing himself drowning in lime Jell-O.

She ignored the comment. "When you swim through oil, the difference will make you think in alternative ways, make you use different tactics for simple movement. You'll need to question your instincts and react according to your surroundings."

Freeth looked at the tank of sluggish, translucent liquid. "Is it vegetable oil or motor oil?"

She sealed the breathing mask over his mouth and nose and pulled the transparent visor down over his eyes. "Consider it a surprise."

Then, none too gently, she nudged him into the tank.

Chapter 10

Even buried within a secret maze of guarded tunnels that would have confused the most cheese-hungry experimental rat—the Proteus briefing room looked just like any other conference room in any other office building.

The first to arrive for the meeting, Devlin lounged back in a chair. He breathed deeply to relax his muscles and bring his reflexes to peak performance. He had to shift his mindset, pinch himself to believe that he was actually going on the mission, rather than standing by as a troubleshooter and mechanic.

A projection screen filled one wall in front of a long table marred with water rings from drinking glasses and coffee cups. A box of doughnuts sat on a table in the far corner, brought in from Fresno two hours away. A coffeemaker exuded sour smells on a black-metal credenza.

Wearing a crisp, official Proteus jumpsuit, Arnold Freeth entered the room after a guard led him to the door. His freckled face looked pink, freshly scrubbed; his hair was damp and mussed. "Major Devlin! Are you coming along on this crazy mission, too?"

"Roger that. There was an accident, and I'm the only other qualified pilot. So I got promoted."

"An accident?" Freeth paled. "Are we going to be

in any danger ourselves? Do you even know how to fly the ship?"

"Affirmative, to both questions." He gestured toward the box of doughnuts. "You'd better eat something, Mr. Freeth. There's no restaurant on board the *Mote*."

The UFO expert chose a frosted jelly doughnut and used an institutional brown paper towel for a napkin. He fingered the laminated badge on the chain around his neck, as if to prove he'd been brought here for a legitimate purpose. "How many other people are on the team?" He blotted sugar from his lips with the rough paper.

Tomiko Braddock sauntered in as if she were stalking someone. "Depends on how many show up for the meeting. Around here, if you don't attend briefings, you don't get miniaturized." She placed her hands on her hips. "Okay, let's move it. The Director should know better than to be late for his own show."

Freeth stuck out his hand, after carefully wiping raspberry jelly from his fingertips. "I'm Arnold Freeth, UFO Specialist."

Tomiko looked at him as if analyzing a specimen and returned his handshake firmly enough to show that she could have ripped his arm out of its socket, if she'd felt like it. "Good to meet you, Arnold." Her glance slid to Devlin. "Sorry you had to come to the party at the last minute, Marc. I should've taken better care of Garrett."

"Well, I'd hoped we could avoid disasters at least until the mission *started*," he joked, "but I'm grateful for the unexpected opportunity."

Devlin had always gotten along well with Tomiko. If he ever decided to start dating again, he would probably ask her out. He was fairly certain her current relationship with Garrett Wilcox was less a matter of emotional attachment than one of convenience for the two of them. Aside from being relatively compatible people working at close quarters, both available, both attractive, the two had little in common.

The next person to enter was Sergei Pirov, with short-trimmed, gray-brown hair, leathery skin, and reddened eyes. The old Russian doctor looked drained and uncertain, as if he'd been through too much already for one day. He sagged into his chair and meticulously began studying a blank laboratory notebook he had brought with him.

Finally, Project Director Hunter strode in, talking with Dr. Rajid Sujatha and a slender, intense woman with permed blond hair. Seeing the UFO expert, she smiled in satisfaction. "Ah, Dr. Freeth! Welcome, I'm Dr. Cynthia Tyler. I've seen your *Alien Dissection* video. Very impressive. I brought it to the attention of Director Hunter, which led to your being invited to join this mission."

Freeth didn't know what to say. "Thank you . . . I think. And, by the way, it's *Mister* Freeth."

Devlin chimed in, "They don't give doctorates in his area of expertise."

Freeth blushed.

Felix Hunter offered his hand. "Despite my initial skepticism, Cynthia here convinced me your expertise could be useful. She can be quite persuasive when she puts her mind to something. We'll be glad to have your . . . unusual perspective aboard."

"Perhaps someday you'll host *this* video, Mr. Freeth," Tyler said, tossing her curly blond hair. "Call it *Alien Dissection II* . . . if they ever declassify the footage." She sat next to him.

Hunter placed his long fingers on the water-stained table and waited until the chatter died down. Finally, he activated the projection screen to display an image of the alien's sealed lifepod.

"As you can imagine, it was difficult to bring the extraterrestrial here intact without letting a thousand scientists tinker with the capsule first." His dark mustache curved downward in a frown. "But Russia's Deputy Foreign Minister is a friend of Project Proteus."

Dr. Pirov, still shaken and uneasy from the Wilcox emergency only a few hours earlier, perked up. "Yes, Mr. Garamov has proved quite helpful to me in the past."

"And he's fully aware of what we can do here," Hunter said. "Through what may prove to be a stroke of luck for us, Garamov was assigned to Azerbaijan in the recent Baku crisis, and he was on the scene when Russian Typhoons shot down the extraterrestrial spacecraft."

Freeth bit back a squawk. "Fighter jets downed a flying saucer? What if it was carrying an alien ambassador? That could start an intergalactic war!"

Tyler agreed fully. "An absolutely valid point."

"I hope Mr. Garamov hasn't inadvertently started a war here on Earth, either," Hunter continued. "He's one of only a few witnesses who actually saw the lifepod. On the official record, it was listed as a pilot who ejected from a downed rebel MiG. Even the Russian higher-ups will take a while to figure that out."

Devlin leaned forward. "So, what really happened to the flying saucer? Still no sign of any wreckage?"

The Director shook his head. "When the air-to-air missiles struck, the UFO seems to have vaporized. Possibly some sort of automatic self-destruct system to prevent their technology falling into other hands."

"Especially into the hands of primitive folks like us," Tomiko said.

Dr. Pirov took half-hearted notes in his lab book, looking as if he wanted very badly to be somewhere else. His hands were shaking.

Hunter tapped his laser pointer on the table, waiting for quiet again. "Mr. Garamov is a very cautious man. When he understood what he had, he realized that extraordinary precautions would have to be taken—both for secrecy and for safety. An overzealous technician might crack open the case and kill the specimen. Worse, the alien might contain extraterrestrial bacteria, viruses, or even bodily toxins that are perfectly normal to *its* biochemistry, but could be deadly to humans."

Tyler made a rude noise. "We've been over this already. Our Class IV chamber has full defenses, including an automatic sterilization/incineration protocol in the event of a worst-case scenario. How many triple fail-safes do you want?" She looked over at the UFO expert, as if for approval.

Arnold Freeth sat forward, surprising everyone. "Sorry, Dr. Tyler, but the law requires you to follow the quarantine guidelines in the Code of Federal Regulations. Title 14, Part 1211, regarding 'Extraterrestrial Exposure.' "

Hunter gave him a blank look. "Is that really in the CFR?" Devlin had never seen the Director taken so completely off guard. He tried to cover his smile, watching his father-in-law handle the situation.

Freeth spoke smoothly, in his element at last. "A fairly arcane law, adopted in July 1969, states that anyone 'extra-terrestrially exposed' can be quarantined under armed guard for an indefinite period. A person can also be jailed for up to a year and fined as much as five-thousand dollars for *letting* himself become exposed. The text goes on at great length." He blushed as he realized everyone around the conference table was staring at him. "Uh, you can look it up yourself."

"I have never heard of that law." Hunter looked at Devlin, who shrugged.

Cynthia Tyler pursed her lips, impressed even though the UFO expert had disagreed with her. "See why I suggested we bring him on board, Director?"

Hunter cleared his throat. "No one knows how to work the capsule's mechanics or life-support systems—unless you have some inside knowledge to share, Mr. Freeth?" The expert quickly shook his head. "Therefore, there's only one way to perform a thorough investigation and retain the integrity of the capsule and the extraterrestrial specimen."

Devlin loked around the table. "If we're smaller than the size of a cell, we can explore without leaving a mark. Assuming we can get inside the pod in the first place."

Hunter looked very proud of himself. "Exactly what Garamov realized. In order to transport the specimen here without disturbing it, he bypassed so much red tape that heads are likely to roll—including his own."

"Unless we pull off a miracle," Devlin said.

"So we'll have to do just that," Tomiko said. "No problem."

"It seems a . . . sensible approach," Pirov said, but his voice sounded uneasy.

"My arrangement with Garamov is that we must return the alien lifepod, intact, within twenty-four hours. He can impose diplomatic delays for no longer than that. There's a chance we can curtail an international incident before it begins. That doesn't give us much time to prepare."

Hunter flicked the screen to a diagram of the lifepod capsule beneath a bulleted list of the mission sequence. "I had already chosen team members late last night, but recent events have forced me to reassess my choices. Since Captain Wilcox is now unable to fly the exploration ship, Major Devlin has agreed to take his place as pilot. Tomiko Braddock will still act as security."

The Director looked at Cynthia Tyler and Rajid Sujatha. "I want you two to stand by to assist inside the Class IV room in full anti-contamination suits."

Tyler, in particular, did not look happy with this turn of events. "But Felix, I—"

He cut her off. "Mr. Freeth will go along to provide his insights into alien anatomy. I would have preferred to give him more thorough training, but time does not permit it."

Freeth wrung his hands, his skin as pale as milk, looking as if he wanted to crawl off to the nearest UFO convention. "Remember when you asked if I brought along a clean pair of undershorts, Major Devlin?" he whispered. "I think maybe I . . . need them right about now."

Hunter continued, anxious to finish the briefing. "Because of his long association with Project Proteus, I have selected Dr. Pirov to serve as the on-board medical expert. He will direct the biological exploration, though Major Devlin can veto his suggestions if there are any safety concerns. I don't want to lose crew members over this."

Instead of being excited, the Russian doctor looked deeply disturbed. "Director Hunter, I believe I must ask you to make another choice. My responses during this morning's emergency were not . . . acceptable. I am perhaps too old to undergo such rigors. My reflexes are not as good as they should be." He looked down at the doodles in his lab notebook, as if they might offer some arcane answer. "I would be better qualified to assist . . . in some other capacity."

Cynthia Tyler practically jumped to her feet. "Director, you know I'm the best qualified person to go. I've studied that alien body from the outside, I've run all the possible scans, I've trained for these mis-

sions—and I'm the one who found our UFO expert."
She gestured toward Arnold Freeth. "You owe it to
me."

Surprised, Hunter looked at the Russian doctor.
Pirov leaned across the table, resting his elbows on
two circular water stains. "I would be glad to take
Dr. Tyler's place in the isolation room. I am qualified
to assist in an external capacity, and I honestly think
my younger colleague could do a better job aboard
the *Mote*."

"And I would be happy to have your assistance in
the isolation room, Dr. Pirov, sir." Sujatha smiled at
the older man.

"I don't have any objection to the switch, Felix,"
Devlin added.

Every face around the table looked at the Director,
waiting. Hunter saw the fearful and uncertain expression on Pirov's face and realized that the Russian
might indeed be a liability. Pirov had been a political
choice, but Cynthia Tyler was much more intense
and determined . . . perhaps too much so.

"Don't get the idea that this is a democracy," he
said, his voice deep enough to be a growl, "but I can
accommodate the change if it increases our chances
of success." He waited only a moment for his people
to object, and no one did.

"Be prepared for miniaturization and launch in
two hours."

Chapter 11

Time to mission: 2:00 hours

Before launch, while the other team members completed their final mission preparations, Devlin devoted every moment to the vessel that would carry them through the alien's body.

Though qualified inspection crews had given the *Mote* a clean bill of mechanical health, Devlin didn't trust anyone else's assessment. Extensive pre-flight checks were not just a matter of pride, they were also a matter of survival. He wanted to touch the ship's hull, polish the control board, test the systems himself, check the engines to make sure everything was up to *his* specifications.

Wearing clean-room overalls, rubber gloves, and elastic-trimmed booties, Devlin adjusted the mesh over his unruly dark hair and passed through a line of air blowers and scrubbers. Next he crossed a pad of gray stickum that grabbed loose debris from his feet on his way into the echoing, white-tiled room.

Brightly lit in the center, surrounded by the prismatic reflectors of the miniaturization apparatus, sat the *Mote*, a vision of engineering style and grace. She was raised off the floor on landing struts, ready to go.

Engrossed in the challenge of the impending mission, Devlin felt more alive than he had for a long time. He was glad he'd accepted Felix's invitation to join Project Proteus three years earlier.

After Kelli's death, Devlin's dad, a retired Air Force colonel, had been unable to help him through the period of mourning. The gruff older man simply didn't have the emotional tools to face such distress. His best commiseration had amounted to "Keep your chin up. You'll get over it."

But Devlin didn't want to "get over" his wife, had no wish to brush aside his years with her. He wasn't looking for another love of his life. Still, five years after losing Kelli, Marc Devlin had fallen in love again. With a ship.

The wedge-shaped *Mote* had a creamy white hull, aerodynamic lines, sensual curves. To him, few things were sexier than a ramjet configuration or thruster assembly, and the unusual impeller engines (his own design) made him giddy. The ship was a work of art, a cross between a jet fighter and a submarine, with inspiration drawn from his favorite science fiction shows—everything from *Star Trek*'s shuttlecraft to the Flying Sub from *Voyage to the Bottom of the Sea*.

When he'd first been invited to join Project Proteus, Devlin had been afraid that working for his father-in-law would provide too many reminders, bring raw emotions to the surface, cause too much strain between them. But when he realized how lackluster his consulting career had been after his retirement from the Air Force, dabbling with silly inventions and marking time, Devlin had accepted the offer.

Over coffee one day, Felix Hunter had explained the Project's overall parameters, then given the young man carte blanche. By hand, Devlin had drawn the vessel's original schematics, incorporating innovative ideas that other engineers might have considered too impractical or unorthodox.

Curved windows made of reinforced plasglass gave
an unobstructed view from the ship's front and sides.
Directly behind the cockpit, the main cabin held laboratory tables, a full suite of analytical equipment, and
movable work chairs where Arnold Freeth and Cynthia Tyler would sit. High-powered, fast-processing
laptop computers had access to the *Mote*'s main computer and its extensive library of CD-ROMs packed
with reference material.

While useless at full size and mass, the impeller
engines and exhaust cones could push a *miniaturized*
vessel at great speed. Though Captain Wilcox had
been slated as the first mission pilot, Devlin had designed the *Mote*'s cockpit controls to fit his own grip;
buttons and dials were arranged to match his personal preferences. It was *his* ship, and he had designed everything to the most exacting specifications.

Kelli would have been proud . . . and probably a
bit jealous.

Devlin's dust-protective booties made no sound on
the polished floor as he walked across the grid of
prismatic projectors. He ran his hands over ivory hull
plates that would have made a space shuttle proud.
He closed his eyes and "saw" through his fingertips,
as if he were a psychic healer searching for an imbal-
ance in a person's aura.

"We'll be on our way in two hours. Ready to show
everybody what you can do?" Alone, he wasn't embarrassed to talk to the ship; after all, some people
talked to their *plants*.

Because Felix Hunter had to deal with so many
hands controlling the purse strings, Devlin's original
designs had been adapted and "improved"—then
built by the lowest bidder. As a result, the finished
vessel had been created by committee, with all the
quality and reliability that implied.

On miniaturized test flights, Devlin had taken his

vessel through rigorous enviroments, testing her limits. At the conclusion of each run, he'd spent hours tinkering with the controls, modifying them to be more responsive. He had disconnected and reconnected the subsystems until he had an intuitive grasp of every wire, every circuit, and every control board. No one understood the *Mote* better than he did—which was just the way he liked it.

Devlin ducked around the landing struts and hunkered down to climb through the bottom hatch. Inside the craft, he inhaled the new-car smell of fabric, paint, and metal. He scanned the cockpit, making sure not a single paperclip was out of place.

His black-leather pilot seat was fronted by the curved control board, a Christmas tree of lights and dials, some cryptically marked, some with grease-penciled annotations. Following tradition, he reached into his pocket and removed a snapshot of Kelli and himself (laughing and drenched after a water-balloon fight). He taped it just at the edge of the cockpit window, where he could easily see it. Beside the photo, he'd handwritten his new motto on an index card: THINK SMALL.

From the copilot's seat, Tomiko Braddock would control all the weaponry and defense mechanisms. During the ship's final modification phase, she had insisted on adding high-powered laser projectors ("cannons," she called them) to use against obstacles in the uncharted microscopic terrain. "At our size, even a dust mite will look like Godzilla romping through Tokyo. Give me some firepower."

When miniaturized, the streamlined vessel would be surrounded by a containment field, a barely visible force that maintained their reduced size and dispersed quantum forces. Once they entered the hostile micro-universe, the team would be entirely on their own. Self-sufficient—or vulnerable, depending on how one looked at it—without the possibility of outside intervention.

A vertical airlock cylinder ran through the center of the vessel like an apple core, with its hatch on the underbelly of the craft. When miniaturized, the crew would be able to explore outside in environmental suits. Devlin walked past the airlock to the back bulkhead and opened a hatch into the cramped engine compartment. Shining a handlight inside, he inspected the impeller cowlings, the turbines. *Perfect.*

"You're beautiful," he said to the ship. Compliments never hurt.

He carried his "little black bag," in which he kept every conceivable low-tech gadget to repair those engines, even rebuild them from scratch, if the sophisticated modular systems failed. Torque wrenches, needle-nosed pliers, screwdrivers . . . cotton swabs, toothpicks, chewing gum, Band-Aids, and the ubiquitous duct tape. All the essentials.

While Devlin understood his tools and every system aboard the *Mote,* it bothered him no end that he could not fathom the scientific details of the miniaturization process itself. The two senior project physicists, Quentin and Cutter, were so absorbed in their esoteric work that it seemed they could barely dress themselves or eat their meals without assistance. Brilliant to the edge of being idiot savants, they never took furloughs, even to Fresno, unless the Director ordered them to. And then they had to be escorted.

National treasures, Felix called them. Who was Devlin to argue?

The physicists loved to explain their pet theories to anyone who had a security clearance and the possibility of comprehending what they were talking about. Someone like Devlin. Quentin and Cutter spoke of quantum effects, overlapping waveforms, the arbitrary space between the electron cloud and an atomic nucleus. It all made sense to them.

In his post-grad engineering training at MIT, Devlin and his fellow classmates had engaged in a friendly rivalry with the head-in-the-clouds physicists. Trusty engineers knew how to make things *work*. They solved problems and made useful items based on pie-in-the-sky theories that physicists cooked up. But these two geniuses went farther beyond the mental fringe than anyone Devlin had ever met in his professional career.

Cutter, whose wild hair looked as if it had been combed with a ceiling fan, cited holographic theory, explaining how a three-dimensional pattern could be stored in a hologram, which, when illuminated by intersecting laser beams, would project the original image at any size. Counter-intuitively, the complete information was stored in every part of that hologram; a sliver cut from the overall piece could project the entire image.

"And what does that have to do with miniaturization technology?" Devlin had asked.

Cutter had scratched his unruly hair. "It seemed an interesting analogy."

Quentin, tall and lantern-jawed, had furrowed his brow when Devlin asked, "But what happens to the *mass* when we miniaturize? If we shrink a ship down to the size of a cell, why don't we still have several tons worth of matter? Where does it go? Is there some sort of *mass sink*?"

The lantern-jawed physicist cleared his throat. "An imaginary-space quantum reservoir where all the mass goes? Intriguing idea." Quentin looked toward the armored walls at the far end of the chamber. "Recent theoretical extrapolations suggest that mass is a tensor property, not a scalar. Therefore, a simple four-by-four space-time transformation *can* yield a zero or infinitesimally small mass."

"Fine theory. And how do you perform a four-by-four space-time transformation on a real object?"

"Why with our apparatus, of course."

Devlin wondered if he should duck while the physicist vigorously waved his hands. "Roger that. So what you're saying is it all functions by magic?"

Quentin scratched his heavy jaw and quoted Clarke's Law. "Any sufficiently advanced technology is indistinguishable from magic."

After that, Devlin had stopped asking questions.

With a glance at his watch, he closed the engine cowlings and backed out to the main compartment. Soon the team would regroup for miniaturization and insertion into the alien capsule. His heart fluttered with excitement rather than anxiety.

Devlin patted the cockpit controls again. "Let's get ready to dance, baby. You and me. We'll make them all proud."

Chapter 12

Politics.

Felix Hunter enjoyed challenges as much as the Project scientists, but *his* battles were fought in a political arena, not a technical one. Engrossed in their own pieces of the puzzle, the Proteus crew never saw all the troubleshooting Hunter did from the battleground of his office.

He spent hours on secure phones, facing teleconferences, sending faxes and documents over scrambled lines. He had to smooth the feathers of ambassadors, industrial leaders, and world-class scientists—all of whom had agendas of their own.

No wonder his wife preferred to stay by herself at their house in Carmel, dabbling with watercolors and interior design. Their marriage was like a pair of old slippers, a bit ragged but too comfortable to discard. Helen had never much cared for the overblown elegance of upper-crust diplomatic functions. After losing their only daughter, Hunter and his wife had both withdrawn into private interests. Instead of retiring to the California coast with her, Hunter had chosen to helm a major classified project.

Hunter sat back at his desk, a clunky old army-issue monstrosity painted seafoam green. He could have arranged for extravagant mahogany furniture, an ambassadorial relic to flaunt his status. Years ago, in his Washington, D.C., offices, he'd bowed to such ostentation. His priorities and preferences had changed since then. Here, deep in the mountain, the metal desk reminded him of the scientific glory days of the 1950s and '60s, when people had believed technology would solve the world's problems. Hunter wanted to recapture that sense of infinite possibilities. . . .

Few things, however, were as dull or as tedious as sifting through treaties, agreements, regulations. Taking a heavy breath, Hunter opened the immense volume he'd taken from the document room, the *Code of Federal Regulations*. There, exactly as Arnold Freeth had claimed, under Title 14, *Aeronautics and Space*, he found the lengthy and convoluted guidelines that theoretically applied in this situation. Trust the government to write a regulation for everything.

" 'Quarantine' means the detention, examination and decontamination of any person, property, animal or other form of life or matter whatever that is extraterrestrially exposed, and includes the apprehension or seizure of such person, property, animal or any other form of life or matter whatever. For example, if person or thing 'A' touches the surface of the Moon, and on 'A's return to Earth, 'B' touches 'A' and, subsequently 'C' touches 'B,' all of these—'A' through 'C' inclusive—would be extra-terrestrially exposed ('A' and 'B' directly; 'C' indirectly)."

Hunter's eyes glazed from the bureaucratic definitions. And the *Code* applied only to U.S. law; finding a common ground with international law would be more difficult yet.

In only two days, the alien lifepod had become a political hot potato behind the scenes. Vasili Garamov had so far managed to stall with red tape, but the clock was ticking.

Once word got out, a flood of so-called "experts" would insist on seeing the specimen. Some would want to pry open the containment vessel and begin dissection; others would demand that the alien be summarily destroyed to avoid any risk to humans and prevent a "world-wide panic."

Shooting down the UFO had been an unprovoked act of aggression. If the aliens had other ships in the vicinity, they could launch a full-scale assault upon the entire Earth. Before it was too late, the human race had to learn everything possible about this species—preferably without causing more damage to the sole "survivor."

Deputy Foreign Minister Garamov was scheduled to arrive before the launch of Team Proteus, as an official observer. Upon completion of the miniaturized mission, he would oversee the return of the alien body to Russia.

Unfortunately, Hunter had just learned that Congressman Edwin Durston had intercepted Garamov upon his arrival at the San Francisco International Airport. The Congressman, a long-time opponent of Project Proteus and its level of secret funding, intended to escort the Russian to the mountain facility so they could watch the mission together. Although Durston would accomplish little here, he insisted on being present.

And Hunter would have to play the host, all smiles. It was an opportunity, really. At last, he could demonstrate the value of Project Proteus, even to a perennially tough customer like Congressman Durston. This was the Director's chance, and he was sure his lost friend Chris Matheson would have been proud.

Hunter slid shut the clunky drawers and straightened papers on his desk, rearranged the pencils, checked to make sure the stapler and the tape dispenser were full. He looked at his watch again. The four team members would be getting prepared.

Since she was to be the medical expert on board, Dr. Cynthia Tyler had taken the time to double-check all the analytical and recording equipment that could be crammed into the laboratory space. A nervous Arnold Freeth had finished another rushed simulation. Devlin had completed a full systems check on the *Mote*.

Hunter knew he shouldn't be uneasy about sending his son-in-law on the mission. Marc Devlin was perfectly qualified, probably more so than Captain Wilcox. But it was hard to risk losing one of the few remaining connections to his daughter. . . .

The intercom crackled on. "Director Hunter, the group is suiting up in the prep room. We are ready to proceed to the *Mote* for the final countdown. Everything's on schedule, sir."

Though he was tired, his eyes scratchy from too much time without enough sleep, Hunter smiled. This was the moment he'd been waiting for. "Excellent. I'll be right down."

Before he could go, he turned to find senior pathologist Trish Wylde standing at his door. She looked flushed, as if she had worked herself up to a confrontation. Her gentle, narrow face was lovely, though she didn't seem to realize it.

"Felix, I know it's too late." Trish managed to cover her hurt feelings with a veneer of pride. "Cynthia's fully qualified in the technical area, but she's a loose cannon. She can't hold a candle to my skills. When Dr. Pirov asked to be pulled from the team, I should have been your next choice. I'm the best person for this job."

He could see that Trish had rehearsed her words over and over. "Did I do something to make you lose faith in me?"

He had to fight to keep his shoulders from slumping. Trish Wylde, a talented pathologist who had worked in many exotic situations, had an extraordinary talent for determining what had gone wrong inside a living body. She could find clues, chemical traces, and damage marks with an ease and speed that put most analytical teams to shame.

"It was an on-the-spot decision, Trish. Dr. Tyler is a perfectly credible pathologist, and she also has expertise in microbiology, which you don't have."

"Come on! Familiarity with Earth-based microorganisms won't mean squat once they get inside the alien. None of it is going to apply." Trish crossed her arms over her chest, daring him to deny it. "And you *know* I'm a better choice than putting Dr. Pirov in the isolation chamber. Or was it in the agreement with the Russians to have him as part of the hands-on team?"

Hunter frowned. "Hundreds of factors enter into every decision I make, Trish. After this mission is successful, we'll have other opportunities for miniaturization missions. You're next on the list. I trust your expertise. Now you have to trust mine."

"But it's just *politics*, Felix." She said the word as if it were an insult.

"Yes, and we need to keep politics in mind—just as much as we do the laws of physics." He held up a finger. "If we don't play this first one exactly right, our whole program could be dismantled and shut down. Congressman Durston and Deputy Foreign Minister Garamov will be arriving at any moment. I want you to get the two VIPs cleared and usher them to the observation deck. You are my chosen representative, and I expect you to make a good impression."

Trish looked somewhat mollified, but not convinced. "As long as you promise I'll be on the second mission."

"I guarantee it," Hunter said.

Marc Devlin arrived, flushed with excitement, saving him from further discussion. "Ready to go, Felix?"

Trish thrust out her hand, grasped Devlin's, and vigorously pumped it. "Good luck, Major Devlin. I'll see you next time." She shot Hunter a satisfied glance, then departed.

Devlin grinned. "Ah, so you've already decided that I'm piloting the *Mote* next time, too? Glad to hear it."

Hunter's heart warmed to see his son-in-law's rekindled enthusiasm. Though the two men had always gotten along, Devlin had at first been in awe of the busy diplomat who flitted around the world, working with industrial barons and government officials, taking part in ambassadorial functions.

As soon as Hunter realized how much his daughter loved this man, he'd accepted Devlin wholeheartedly. He'd been intrigued by the young engineer's innovative aerospace designs, but anyone with the money to develop and test those strange craft was generally too conservative to take such risks.

Hunter and his son-in-law had drawn closer while Kelli had faded in the hospital. The two had occasionally had awkward dinners together, but Felix hadn't been able to talk about his classified Proteus work, and Devlin hadn't had the energy to keep up his end of the conversation. Now, though, he seemed exuberant again.

"Are you sure you're okay with this, Marc?" He met the younger man's hazel eyes and saw a depth there that few other people noticed.

"Absolutely, Felix." Devlin had repaid the man's confidence by producing his best work. Both men, for different reasons, were completely engrossed in Project Proteus. Underneath, their relationship was deeply personal, but that was overlaid with a veneer of professionalism. "The *Mote* is anxious to show off what she can do. Don't worry about me."

Hunter forced a smile. "I'm sending you into the unknown. It's my job to worry."

"And you're very good at your job, Felix. Let's get on our way." Devlin clapped the older man on the back, uncomfortable with the emotions that threatened to spill over. "We've got places to go, corpuscles to see."

Hunter hesitated a moment longer. "I promise you'll get out, Marc, safe and sound." With a queasy knot in his stomach, he realized he had held his daughter's sweat-slick hand in the hospital and promised her a similar thing. Perhaps he made his promises too easily.

Devlin gave him a sincere smile, the kind he never showed to co-workers. "Affirmative, Felix—but if you go all mushy on me, I won't be able to concentrate on piloting the ship."

The discussion over, connections still strung between them, Hunter straightened his jacket and followed Devlin down the hall toward the prep room.

It was time for Team Proteus to launch.

Chapter 13

Wearing full Proteus jumpsuits, the four micro-explorers walked together toward the miniaturization chamber with serious, ponderous steps. Tomiko shook her head. "This looks like a scene from one of those 'brave astronaut' movies."

Devlin raised an eyebrow. "Like Nolan Braddock's *Reentry Burn*?"

She regarded him with just the hint of a smile. "For example."

Throughout her college years, Tomiko had downplayed her parents' fame. She'd once declined going with friends to a Braddock film festival, afraid they might recognize her from *Little Orphan Assassin*—or worse, that they might make rude jokes about her father's cornball, high-powered action scenes.

Although Tomiko had always liked athletics, she actively avoided the public eye, so participating in professional or even Olympic sports was out of the question. She had many diverse interests, but no deep ones. She flitted from fascination to fascination, believing in the philosophy of diminishing returns: Beyond a certain point, if a subject didn't keep giving worthwhile information, she moved on.

Years ago, she had befriended one of Nolan Braddock's young female costars, and as they had walked away from a coffee shop late at night, they'd been accosted by two switchblade-wielding youths. After Tomiko had finished with them, the young men could barely limp out of sight, leaving bloodstains and a couple of teeth behind. Awed, the starlet had hired Tomiko as her personal bodyguard. "It's perfect! Look at you. You're tiny and pretty. Nobody expects you to be a landmine like that."

Tomiko had guarded her friend for four months until it became apparent that the starlet's star had burned out and she needed no further protection. Tomiko then told her parents she wanted to become a military policeman or security guard. Though he'd played MPs, Marines, and Army veterans in many roles, Nolan Braddock had been concerned. "You deserve something better than that, Tomiko."

"I don't want people fawning all over me, Daddy. I know you and Mom love it, but I'd rather keep a low profile."

Braddock had smiled at her. "Sweetheart, with what I've got in mind, you won't have to worry about *anybody* noticing you."

Nolan Braddock had met Felix Hunter at a celebrity fund-raiser for international relief. Though he didn't know exactly what work the mysterious "Proteus" comprised, he knew Hunter was putting together some sort of top secret project . . . and he wanted his daughter to have a chance at working in high-end security.

Tomiko had bested some of the top-notch Marines who also vied for her position. She possessed the right combination of fast reactions, cleverness, and sheer body strength, and Director Hunter had hired her immediately. Her father didn't know exactly what Tomiko did, and he drew satisfaction and excitement from the realization that she couldn't tell him.

Oh, how he would love to see his daughter now. . . .

Tomiko gave Arnold Freeth an encouraging nudge as they approached the door of the miniaturization room. The UFO expert had removed his ID badge from its chain and clipped it to the right pocket of his jumpsuit, just above the Proteus logo; now he looked like a genuine member of the team.

Just before they entered the bright chamber, Director Hunter made a point of shaking every team member's hand. With the same formality he had used when speaking before important Congressional committees, at the United Nations, or behind the closed doors of government residences, he said, "The four of you represent the best we have. You're all qualified, all fully trained in your fields—"

Arnold Freeth raised his hand as if to argue the point, given his few hours of crash-course instruction, but Hunter did not acknowledge him.

"You are about to embark on a great adventure, into a landscape no one on Earth has ever seen. Your success will prove the worth of Project Proteus."

Devlin leaned close to Tomiko and muttered, "If he mentions 'where no man has gone before,' I won't be able to keep a straight face." She smiled and endured the speech as part of their mission.

"We'll be following you, and praying for you. Once Major Devlin pilots you into the sealed lifepod, you will be on your own, with only your resources and your imaginations. You will have a maximum of five hours to learn what you can and return with as much knowledge as possible for humanity."

"Roger that. Back in time for dinner, Felix," Devlin said.

Inside the chamber, the prismatic focusers glowed on stand-by around the waiting *Mote*. Technicians checked and double-checked readouts on control panels behind the safety barricades.

Devlin led his three crewmates through double doors into the clean-room area. A noticeable breeze blew in their faces from a positive-pressure current that kept foreign particles out of the room.

"Is that it?" Freeth asked, visibly shaking but also enthralled and eager. "Is this where it happens? Is that our ship?"

"Affirmative, Mr. Freeth." Devlin smiled with pride, looking at the *Mote*. "Beautiful, and she's got brains, too." He gestured for Cynthia Tyler to climb aboard, using the lower hatch. "You first, Doc."

Arnold Freeth was gray and sweaty, and Tomiko teased him. "Don't worry, Arnold. We haven't had an accident in . . . oh, quite a while."

Devlin looked over at her. "Not since this morning."

Freeth struggled to maintain his composure. "If it's so safe, why do we need a microscopic-sized security specialist?"

Tomiko tossed her black hair. "Hey, if you find yourself face to face with a mean macrophage, *I'm* the one you want at your side."

Rattled, the UFO expert climbed aboard. "Believe me, this isn't exactly the way I'd imagined my first real extraterrestrial experience." He began looking for where he was supposed to sit.

Dr. Tyler pointed him toward the seats in the main compartment. "But you already did work on an extraterrestrial like this for your alien dissection video. We're counting on you to help focus our efforts." She checked her analytical equipment, running a quick diagnostic of the systems before she strapped herself in.

Her eyes regarded him intently, and Freeth seemed to squirm under the scrutiny. "Um, er—no. The alien cadaver I studied seems to have been a . . . different species.''

Tomiko swiveled in the copilot's chair, intent on her banks of weapons controls. As he strapped into the pilot seat, Devlin looked across the miniaturization room to where Felix Hunter stood behind the shield barrier. He looked deeply concerned. Devlin gave him the high sign through the cockpit window.

Moving to her seat beside the UFO expert, Tyler said congenially, "This technology's been perfected by both the Soviet Union and the United States." She adjusted her seat belt, checked his, then looked out the side window, anxious to go. "We've all been miniaturized plenty of times with no ill effects. Nothing to worry about."

From her seat in the cockpit, Tomiko turned with an impish grin. "Unless, of course, someone steps on us."

Freeth didn't say another word until the miniaturization began.

Chapter 14

When the shrinking beams came on with a pulsing hum, Devlin drew a deep breath to steady himself. No matter how many test missions he had completed, the activity never became routine for him. He leaned back in the pilot's seat, hands stroking the controls. "This one's for real."

Though it went against common sense, Devlin felt no physical change when the miniaturization process began. Seen through the cockpit windows, the outside chamber suffered an odd, disorienting perspective shift. The walls rushed way from them.

His body, his cells, even his DNA, were being made more compact. His mass was somehow shunted to an "imaginary quantum reservoir," or a "diagonal matrix transformation," or whatever the project physicists had built into this technology.

Think small.

The humming resounded until the *Mote* itself vibrated. Ambient light sparkled and fizzed behind his eyes. Devlin looked down at his arms, expecting to see his skin rippling and puckering, but he felt only a giddy sensation of falling that was more his imagination than an actual effect of the process.

"Is it really happening?" Freeth said from his back seat. "Right now?"

"Just look out the window," Tyler said, her own eyes narrowed with fascination. She smiled at him, then turned back to watch outside.

"Team Proteus." The comm speaker crackled to life. Hunter's rich voice boomed so loudly that Devlin adjusted the volume with a flurry of fingertips. "This is Project Director Hunter, checking on your progress."

Tomiko leaned over and said brusquely into the voice pickup, "We know who you are, Felix. Who else would be calling—a telemarketer asking about our long-distance phone service?"

"Has he got a deal for you," Devlin said with a smile.

Hunter's voice was dry, barely tongue-in-cheek. "Thankfully, Ms. Braddock, others have a bit more patience."

The pulsing lights from the prismatic projectors flickered and stopped.

"Stage one complete. The *Mote* is now two centimeters in length," Hunter continued. "We are bringing in the glass capsule. Major Devlin, if you could engage your engines, we'll need you to move your vessel."

With thunderous footsteps, two technicians entered the chamber dressed in sky-blue clean-room outfits. They wheeled a cart that held a thick-walled glass cylinder a meter long. Viewed from inside the reduced *Mote*, the cylinder looked as big as a fallen skyscraper. The cart wheels rumbled forward, and each step sounded like the approach of a tank platoon.

"Roger that." Devlin fired up the impeller turbines and raised the *Mote* on a cushion of air. The engines strained, designed to work best when the micro-exploration ship was even smaller. "On our way." He raised the ship above the prismatic grid as the cart came to a halt. Cruising in a circuitous route, Devlin tested the *Mote*, checking out its handling, then flew up toward the glass cylinder. The technicians looked like titanic redwood trees.

"The *Mote* actually functions better under her own power." Devlin looked over his shoulder. "It's easier to trust me than to hire suitably delicate workers. And finding a delicate worker with a security clearance is a thousand times harder still."

The UFO expert looked from side to side so quickly he was bound to hurt his neck. Dr. Tyler said, "Earlier missions used precision apparatus to move the miniaturized vessel. But every motion caused a lot of shock and jostling. Very cumbersome. Our chief pathologist, Trish Wylde, even sprained her wrist in one accident."

"Believe me, I'm familiar with Dr. Wylde," Freeth said with a groan, "I'm just glad to have missed out on her 'gelatin tank.'"

"Still got five more orders of magnitude to go in Stage two," Devlin said. "Everybody, prepare yourselves to move a few more decimal points."

When the vessel was safely inside the glass cylinder, the technicians screwed a cap on each end, one of which had an opening large enough for the miniaturized *Mote* to fly through.

Once the ship flew free inside the big glass cylinder, like a fly trapped in a soda bottle, the technicians withdrew beyond the prismatic floor grid. Soon they vanished into the distance. The horizon of the room was too far away.

Though he was in charge of the whole project, Director Hunter felt like a mere observer. He stood behind the protective barricades, from which he had watched the experimental rabbit reduced to microscopic size and enlarged again.

Unlike Fluffy Alice, though, he could converse with Team Proteus. "Prepared for Stage two, Major Devlin?"

He could hear Tomiko drumming her fingers on the weaponry panels. "We don't want to stay *this* useless size for very long. Let's move it, Felix."

Hunter wished Deputy Foreign Minister Garamov had gotten here in time, but he could not scrap the detailed schedule because Congressman Durston wanted to stop for a hamburger, or whatever had delayed them.

Hunter signaled the technician at the miniaturization controls. She adjusted a flux parameter, and the pulsing beams came on again. The brightness emanating from the interlocked prismatic focusers hurt his eyes, but he refused to blink as the cylinder shrank. Marc Devlin was inside there, in command, ready to launch into the unknown.

When the beams faded, the *Mote* was no longer visible inside the syringe-sized cylinder. "Stage two complete, sir." The technician stepped away from her controls and wiped a strand of sandy hair from her forehead.

"Team Proteus, you are now at optimal size." At the control panels, Hunter set the mission chronometer running. "Establishing zero point for miniaturization field integrity, Major Devlin. Five hours."

"Affirmative. Time remaining, five hours."

Two handlers cautiously came forward, approaching the small glass tube like dog catchers facing a rabid St. Bernard.

"I hope you did your math right, Felix," Devlin said into the voice pickup. "If we're miniaturized to the wrong faction, we won't be able to get through the hole in the base of this glass cylinder."

Hunter replied in his calm voice, "Marc, if our people can handle the quantum miniaturization technology, I'm confident we can manage simple percentage calculations."

Devlin still sounded doubtful. "*I've* got a degree in engineering, and I still have trouble balancing my checkbook." Indeed, Kelli had always handled the couple's financial matters.

One of the men grasped the slick cylinder with a gloved hand. Devlin broadcast, "Whoa, remember to handle with care. Every tiny movement gets amplified by many orders of magnitude."

While one man carried the cylinder with precise, ponderous steps, the other handler went to the chamber wall where a sterilization cabinet led into the Class IV containment room. *Where the alien was.*

Following strict procedures, the tech opened the autoclave door. Inside the Class IV room, Sergei Pirov and Rajid Sujatha had already suited up to receive Team Proteus.

Hunter transmitted an update to the miniaturized crew. "The technician is now opening the sterilization portal."

"Just tell him not to drop us, Felix."

Operating his impellers, Devlin balanced the ship against stray air motions. The *Mote* swayed back and forth, but the thrusters and stabilizers kept them on an even keel. "Smooth ride so far."

All details of the room were so huge and far away that the ship was surrounded by a blur. Even the cylinder's glass walls had faded into a distant curved barricade. Devlin's eyes couldn't comprehend what they were seeing.

Outside vibrations and distant rumblings must have been noises or conversation in the containment room, but on their tiny scale nothing was comprehensible.

With a loud thump, the miniaturized glass tube

was set down inside the autoclave, originally designed to sterilize items passing in or out of the containment room. Then a sound like a reverberating gong clapped through the hull—the outer door of the transfer chamber being sealed.

The chronometer on the panel clicked down the time remaining before the miniaturization field began to lose its integrity. Four hours, fifty-five minutes to complete their mission.

With a rumble like a series of far-off explosions, disinfectant mist sprayed down upon the outer capsule wall in raindrops the size of asteroids. But the *Mote* remained high and dry. Her external hull and everything aboard had already been sterilized before the initial miniaturized process.

"We're wasting so much time before we even start," Cynthia Tyler said, looking to Freeth as a kindred spirit. "We won't have enough time to explore the alien's biosystems as it is. You and I are going to have to work overtime."

The inner hatch of the autoclave opened, and Devlin could see the shadowy shape of a gargantuan gloved hand reaching toward them like King Kong grabbing Fay Wray.

"Dr. Pirov is extracting you manually," Hunter said.

"All conditions optimal, Felix," Devlin said. "Team Proteus is ready to proceed."

The Director paused, as if pushing aside all second thoughts. "Prepare for insertion into the alien's lifepod."

Chapter 15

Fully suited inside the isolation chamber, Dr. Sergei Pirov breathed hard inside his flexible helmet. Moving slowly, he worked the autoclave latch, broke the seal, and opened the heavy interior door.

Within the supply portal a transparent cylinder as long as his gloved finger rested on a little stand that had once been a full-sized metal cart. Inside the glass tube, beyond the limits of his vision, hovered the miniaturized vessel and the team of specialists ready to explore the alien's biosystems. Though he couldn't actually see the smaller-than-a-dustspeck exploration team, he tried to scrutinize them through his curved faceplate.

Pirov frowned, not at all envying his colleague Cynthia Tyler for the chance to see what no living human had ever witnessed.

He fumbled for the cylinder, but the tiny droplets of disinfectant mist made the glass tube slippery. Inside the cumbersome suit, he felt even less self-assured than usual. He almost dropped the tube, but somehow held on.

Despite the assurances of Dr. Sujatha, Pirov knew he didn't belong here, either. Other members of Project Proteus—Trish Wylde, in particular—were better qualified, but the old Russian doctor had been working on miniaturization techniques for four decades. Director Hunter felt obligated to give him important tasks, especially with Vasili Garamov coming to observe the mission.

That was not the way decisions should be made.

He focused his concentration and carried the reduced cylinder across the equipment-crowded floor toward where Sujatha peered boyishly into the alien's lifepod. The Bengali doctor's eyebrows were thick and bushy, a forest above eager brown eyes and a comfortable, well-worn face.

They both looked like spacemen in their blue anti-contamination suits—bulky arms, legs, and boots. Every seam was coated and sealed with polymer tape. Tubes from a breathing apparatus fed compressed air into the flexible hood attached at the collar. The air echoed in Pirov's ears, hissing from tanks on his back, permeated with a dry, metallic smell.

He moved with careful steps past trays of sterilized surgical equipment, battery-powered laser scalpels, sample tubes, and portable chemical analysis decks. His sleeves were so padded he could barely bend his elbows. He wouldn't be nimble enough to complete an appropriate dissection of the specimen, and he was glad it wasn't supposed to come to that.

He misjudged a corner, brushed a rotary bone saw from its tray, and knocked it onto the floor. The sound startled him and he froze, careful not to drop the glass tube. The shock of impact would kill every member of Team Proteus. What was he doing? Sweat broke out on his forehead.

"Gentle, Sergei. We must be kind to the people in there. They have a hard task ahead of them." Sujatha gently slid the miniaturized cylinder out of his hands and carried it over to the lifepod. "Here, I will insert it into the cradle."

Behind the observation windows above, Director

Hunter sat in front of his bank of controls, watching. Pirov liked the Director very much—the man had been helpful and supportive when he, Pirov, had been brought over to the United States—but now Hunter's scrutiny intimidated him. He could feel the Director's intent gaze and made sure he followed appropriate procedures. Cameras were mounted all around the room, recording every movement he made, for the sake of documentation and history. No mistakes.

"I apologize for giving them a rough ride." Trying to catch his breath, Pirov moved to one side of the alien lifepod and prepared for the next step.

The micro-explorers grasped the arms of their chairs as violent motion rocked the vessel from side to side. Devlin wrestled with the impeller controls, trying to dance with the attitude jets.

"Proteus, we're encountering turbulence here," Devlin broadcast to the outside. At their size, the momentum from the departing signal made the *Mote* lurch backward.

Tomiko said, "Hey, Felix, this cylinder isn't a snowglobe."

"Dr. Pirov got a little too jittery moving you across the room," Hunter's voice came through the panel. "He offers his apologies."

Their high-frequency transceiver allowed them to send burst messages to the outside world and constantly scan for incoming messages, but at an extreme energy cost. Once they entered the extraterrestrial body, Devlin was concerned that the strange scan-blocking interference would hinder direct communication. They would find out soon enough.

He leaned back in his seat, mentally gearing up to make his way across an unexplored biological wilderness. No doubt Dr. Tyler had already outlined half-a-dozen research papers she intended to write. In uncovering totally new microscopic territory, he wondered fleetingly if he could plant some flags or name any alien landmarks after himself. "Devlin's Duct," for instance. What the heck, maybe Cynthia would throw him a bone.

"Dr. Sujatha is preparing the laser drill now," Hunter said. "Insertion into the lifepod should occur in less than ten minutes."

Pirov glanced up again at the VIP observation deck, but he still saw no sign of the Russian Deputy Foreign Minister. Once miniaturized, Team Proteus had a limited amount of time, and they could not wait for their diplomatic audience.

Worried and intent, Hunter swiveled in his chair. With the intercom muted, he picked up the phone, argued into it, but remained firm. He hung up and continued to stare at Pirov, his expression interested. "Please continue, doctors. We will have to bring our visitors up to speed whenever they arrive."

Absorbed in his own activities, Rajid Sujatha stood by the multiple-jointed arm of the precision laser drill. Using slow, step-by-step manipulations, he maneuvered the angular elbows and the precise point into position. "Now preparing to test, Director, sir." With deep brown eyes he studied the displays and calibrated the gauges, then glanced through the broad windows to the standby laser drill outside in the corridor.

Rated for only a single use without replacement, the tiny lasing component would burn out once it was used at full power to drill an appropriate hole through the lifepod glass. If needed, a second component could be sent through the autoclave, but that would waste an hour. The big spare machine in the outer corridor provided little more than reassurance, since it would take an inordinate amount of time to bring the second laser drill through the anti-contamination barriers.

Sujatha would have only this one opportunity.

Uttering a barely audible prayer, he fired a low-wattage laser pulse through the misty lifepod window. Reflections and interferometry measured the glass thickness with absolute precision. He rattled off numbers from the readout, "Calibration complete."

Pirov stepped back and let him work, relieved that his colleague knew what he was doing.

"Locking down gyros and bearings." Through gloved fingers, the Bengali doctor adjusted the controls, fixing the big laser drill in place. "Setting burst intensity at—"

"Please," Pirov interrupted, feeling too much anxiety, "we must not waste time."

Sujatha made a wry expression through his face-plate. "Tension and impatience pave the way for mistakes." He went about his preparations just as slowly as before. "I have three young daughters, you know. Children teach a person more patience than meditation or schooling."

"Unfortunately, I never had children," Pirov said. He had been divorced for years. His state-sponsored marriage to a Soviet official journalist had given him no sons, no love, and no regrets when it was over. Now Pirov devoted himself to Project Proteus, grateful to be doing something he cared about. Anxious to be useful, he locked the end of the glass cylinder into a cradle with a hair-fine hollow needle already attached at the end.

Like a proud father, Sujatha studied his laser apparatus. "Firing now. This one is for real, Director, sir." He pushed the power button.

A burst of intense red light struck the curved surface of the lifepod, burning a precise needle-width hole. Before Pirov's eyes could adjust, the beam switched off, its drilling work completed after tunneling a hole precisely 99.99% of the way through the cloudy window material.

A curl of smoke spiraled up from the shaft, difficult to see without close inspection. Sujatha stepped back the power in the laser and then shone the calibration beam into the hole again. "Within tolerances. One micron of material remains on the inner edge." He turned to the old Russian doctor. "Time to insert Team Proteus, Dr. Pirov."

Sujatha flicked controls on the laser drill, then stepped back with a sigh. "Laser component no longer functional, as we feared, sir." He powered down the big machine. "No opportunity for us to drill a second hole. Team Proteus will have to make do with what they have."

"It'll be fine, Doctor," Hunter said over the intercom.

Pirov moved the cradle containing the syringe and the miniaturized *Mote*. The microscopic vessel was so small, he couldn't even see a fleck inside the cylinder. He shuddered as he thought that *he* might have been inside there. Some people wanted glory; some opted for safety.

He used his gloved fingers to guide the hair-fine shaft into place. He tried to get a better grip without fumbling and accidentally pricked the fabric at the end of one gloved finger. Just a scratch.

Pirov cursed his clumsiness and hoped the Director hadn't seen. Thankfully, Garamov wasn't there yet. He felt embarrassed, but it was a minor thing, and he didn't bother to report it. No one even noticed his brief pause. Instead, Pirov finished threading the needle into the laser-drilled hole and raised the cylinder into position.

"It is in," he said with a heavy sigh. "Tell Major Devlin that it is up to him now."

Once the *Mote* had successfully traversed the needle shaft and entered the drill hole, Sujatha would cover the opening with quick-drying epoxy before Team Proteus breached the inner containment.

With a crackle from the short-wavelength transmitter, Devlin sent an update. "Impellers at half thrust. Proceeding forward, down the hole."

Motionless and rubbery, the oval, peaceful face of the alien seemed to stare at Pirov through the lifepod window, as if wondering what these humans were up to.

Team Proteus was on its way.

Chapter 16

The miniaturized *Mote* shot along the hair-fine hollow needle like a bullet through the barrel of a gun. The ship's forward lights splashed their beams along the pitted metal shaft.

"On our way, with plenty of room to maneuver." Devlin corkscrewed the ship, testing impeller and rudder controls, delighted with the freedom. Everyone else hung on. Arnold Freeth searched in vain for a barf bag.

"Now you're showing off like Garrett always did," Tomiko said.

Devlin's grin dissolved into mock dismay. "You mean Captain Wilcox flew my ship in a reckless manner?"

Leaving the tip of the needle behind, they plunged into the wider drill hole in the armored glass-like substance. The translucent material reflected ambient light like a glacier with shimmering walls of blue and gray.

"Withdraw the needle," Devlin transmitted to the outside. The communication burst jostled and slammed the tiny ship, but he managed to keep from scraping against the glass walls. He picked up speed, heading through the thick glass barrier.

With a loud scraping noise, the needle cylinder retreated like a locomotive pulled backward through a tunnel. Behind them, seen through the thickness of the misty lifepod window, a shadow covered the entrance hole with a smear of epoxy to maintain the pod's atmospheric integrity until the ship came back out. Outside in the containment chamber, Dr. Sujatha applied a "pinger" to the drill hole, a small location transponder so that the *Mote* could find their return passage. *Less than five hours from now.*

They had a lot to accomplish in the meantime.

The precision laser drill had left a micron-thick wall on the inner surface of the pod window—the only thing that stood between them and direct contact with the alien environment. It came up fast, a giant roadblock in front of them.

"Whoa!" Devlin slammed the impeller engines into reverse as the tunnel came to an abrupt dead end. With the backwash of furiously turning turbines, the vessel rocked from side to side. Behind him in the main compartment, the hastily added medical CD-ROMs clattered out of their storage rack, and three long sampling poles crashed to the deck. "Sorry," he said quietly, leaving the others to wonder if he was talking to the crew or to the ship itself.

Tomiko gripped the weapons controls with a wry smile. "Let me take care of this little speed bump." Using the ship's forward lasers, she scribed a circumferential opening large enough to accommodate the *Mote*. Then, setting the laser cannons to full power, Tomiko let out a *whoop* as she fired. Vaporized material sprayed thick droplets into the air.

As the lifepod's atmospheric pressure equalized with the hairfine shaft, the *Mote*'s stabilizer fins scraped against microscopic irregularities in the walls. Debris spanged off the windshield and side hull. Devlin winced as he imagined all the superficial scratches and dents. "So much for my low insurance rates."

Steady again, the vessel hovered at the threshold, impellers humming. The giant open emptiness lay ahead of them. Hardened glass had dripped into microscopic stalactite forms at the rim of the opening. Devlin turned around in the cockpit and looked at the eager crew. "Everybody ready?"

"We've got a lot of work to do," Dr. Tyler answered for herself and the unusually silent Freeth.

"Okay, let's move it," Tomiko said.

He eased the impellers forward and guided the *Mote* through the freshly blasted opening and into an enclosed alien sky. . . .

At the Air Force Academy in Colorado Springs, Devlin had spent many clear flying days in a long-winged glider, accumulating cockpit hours above the wooded Front Range. Once the glider's tow cable disengaged from the powered lead aircraft, Devlin had loved to drift along, snug in utter silence within the cockpit, flowing with the wind.

He'd been qualified as a pilot on dozens of different craft, but preferred to study aerodynamics and engine design. He loved to develop useless devices and wacky "better mousetrap" gizmos, built from automobile parts, leftover pieces from model kits, strange components he found on dusty shelves in hardware stores. Even with all of his engineering degrees and military citations, Devlin was proudest of his two trophies from the Rube Goldberg Championship for Delightful and Ridiculous Contraptions.

Back then, that wet-behind-the-ears cadet had never dreamed he'd one day guide a miniaturized craft into the seemingly gigantic body of an extraterrestrial being. . . .

Ready to start exploring, Devlin descended

through the open sky within the lifepod. Unable to keep the grin off his face, he caressed the control panels, whispering compliments to his ship, while glancing at the guardian-angel snapshot of Kelli.

Tomiko worked the external controls and took readings. "Weather report: Ambient air temperature, fifteen degrees Celsius. That's about fifty-nine Fahrenheit, chilly but not unpleasant."

Devlin looked down at the plain of naked gray-green skin. "And our alien friend isn't even wearing a windbreaker."

In the back, Dr. Tyler unbuckled her crash restraint and went to the analytical equipment, switching on the control panels. "I'm going to use the intake valve to draw a sample of capsule atmosphere so I can run a compositional analysis. Give me a hand, Mr. Freeth? Once we learn what this specimen breathes, we can determine more about its physiology." She looked over at the UFO expert for confirmation.

Freeth, though, pressed his face against the opposite window, staring like a tourist. His skin had a chalky look, and his composure seemed ready to crumble. "This is real. After all the time I've waited, all I've believed . . . and now this is real. I can't believe it. This is *real*."

From her analytical station, Cynthia Tyler scratched her kinky blond hair. "Why do you sound so surprised, Mr. Freeth? After your alien dissection video, this must be familiar territory for you . . . though not on this scale."

Freeth avoided answering while Tyler drew an air sample through the intake tubes and squirted the captured gas into a mass spectrometer. At the lab console, she waited for the jagged trace to sketch across the diagnostic screen before she read off the spectrographic results. "Atmospheric analysis shows a composition relatively similar to Earth's, mostly nitrogen, fifteen percent oxygen, and a higher partial pressure of carbon dioxide."

As if anxious to contribute to the mission, Freeth offered his tentative opinion. "It could mean the alien's home planet has a higher concentration of greenhouse gases, perhaps leading to global warming."

"Interesting," Tyler said.

"Or we could simply be testing stale air, contaminated by exhaust from the lifepod."

Freeth looked at the incomprensible readout.

"Specific contaminants or pollutants? Something to indicate that he came from a dying world, an industrial society?"

"None that our instruments can detect. However, the atmosphere within the original spacecraft could have been purified before launch."

"In other words," Freeth said, "we've got data, but we can't draw any conclusions whatsoever."

"That's often the way science works." Tyler gave him a comradely smile. "As I'm sure you know."

Far below them, the motionless extraterrestrial was an astoundingly enormous figure, so huge that Devlin could make out no large-scale features. He recalled the old parable about blind men encountering various parts of an elephant and concluding by touch alone that they had found a snake, a rope, a wall, or a tree.

"It goes on and on, all the way to the horizon," Freeth said.

Without tearing her eyes from the side window, Tyler called, "Are the *Mote*'s cameras imaging all this?"

"Enough pictures to stuff cabinets of government files with plenty left over to fill a scrapbook for our parents." As Devlin brought the *Mote* toward the alien's naked chest, the apparently smooth skin began to appear puckered and rippled.

Tyler turned to the UFO expert beside her, fascinated and eager. "What is your assessment of the epidermis, Mr. Freeth? You haven't told us much about your previous experience. You felt and touched some tissue during your earlier dissection. How does this one compare?"

"I . . . I can't say."

She frowned in disappointment. "Go ahead and share your impressions, Mr. Freeth. If I didn't want your opinion, I wouldn't have insisted that you come along."

He sat back down in his chair, looking defeated. "But I . . . I have no real expertise. I defer to your opinion, Dr. Tyler."

Tyler crossed her arms over her chest, impatient with him now. "Why are you stonewalling? I called in a lot of favors to get you included on this team, and I put my reputation on the line. Don't be coy about contributing to the investigation. That's what you're here for."

She waited. Even Devlin and Tomiko turned around in their seats to see why the UFO expert had fallen silent.

Finally, with his emotions in such a turmoil that he couldn't hold them inside any longer, Freeth spluttered, "But—uh, I've never actually done anything on my own. I've never had a true paranormal experience." He lowered his eyes in shame, and his shoulders slumped.

"What about your video? I'd say that qualifies as an experience."

Freeth rubbed fingertips along his temples as if he had a migraine. "That was . . . well, something of a *simulation*."

Tomiko groaned from the cockpit. "I knew it!"

Tyler looked at him in confusion. "What do you mean?"

"He's saying it was all special effects," Tomiko said.

Tyler's jaw dropped. "A . . . fake?" Freeth seemed to get smaller and smaller in his chair.

Devlin sagged in the cockpit. "Now's a fine time to tell us, Mr. Freeth. At this point, we can't exactly turn around and drop you back off."

"I trusted you. I *recommended* you for this mission, and you never said a word!" Cynthia Tyler's astonishment rapidly evolved into humiliation and outrage. "I'd like to do a little alien dissection on *you*. Director Hunter told me your video was a scam, but I convinced him to take a chance. Now it turns out you're a con artist . . . and I'm a fool." She looked more furious at herself than at him.

"I'm sorry, believe me." Freeth looked in every direction, trying to avoid the glares of his crewmates. He swallowed hard and raised his chin in an attempt to reassemble his dignity. "All my life I've *known* aliens exist, with all my heart—but no one listened. People laughed at me." His freckled face wore a plaintive expression. "So, I concocted a minor deception to help the public see what I knew to be the truth. Is that so wrong?"

Tyler growled, "A lot of people think they *know* things that turn out to be false. They're called crackpots."

"I've been called that plenty of times. Plenty of times." Freeth had been heckled and hounded for years, and now he clearly drew strength from an inner conviction that had always helped him stand against a constant outpouring of ridicule. He dredged up a few scraps of pride and gestured toward the vast alien body below. "But I *was* right, wasn't I? In this instance, the ends justified the means, so I don't have any regrets even with my . . . my white lies exposed. After all the scorn I've taken from the mainstream public and the media, I'm finally vindicated."

"Don't feel vindicated yet. Your 'white lies' got you included on a top-secret mission. You're going to have a lot of explaining to do once we get back outside," Tyler said. "And you are going to clear me of any culpability in this scam."

Freeth looked directly at her. "I thought that if I could just make people more open-minded, alter their attitudes, maybe I could change the world. Your mind was open. And here you are face-to-face with an alien. If humans ever get a chance to meet with a superior extraterrestrial race, think of what that would mean for mankind."

"Slavery? Invasion? Total destruction of the human race?" Tomiko suggested. "Don't you watch the movies, Arnold?"

"You're paranoid." He turned back to Tyler. "I can still be a valuable part of this team."

"Don't expect any authorship credit on a single one of my research papers," she said, as if that were a grave punishment. "Not even an acknowledgment."

Smoothly piloting the *Mote*, Devlin sighed. "Okay, we've all got to get along for the remainder of this mission. Even if he was pulling our legs about the autopsy, Mr. Freeth is still the closest thing to an expert we've got—and we're stuck with him for the duration."

Not mollified in the least, Tyler raked her gaze over the trembling man. "I'd be willing to toss him out the window if I didn't know he'd damage the specimen once our miniaturization field loses its integrity." Then, pointedly ignoring him, she turned back to her atmosphere analysis.

Watching the mission chronometer, Devlin descended toward the alien wilderness of skin.

Chapter 17

Moving at high speed, over a centimeter per second, the *Mote* closed the distance to the gigantic specimen. Cynthia Tyler kept her eyes peeled, trying to understand the amazing sights that bombarded her intense eyes. She still wanted to strangle Arnold Freeth.

"Step on it, Marc. It's been half an hour and we're not even inside the body yet," Tomiko said.

"I'll try to locate some kind of pore or orifice to make our entry," Tyler said, staring out the starboard window. "I'm looking for vestigial hair follicles, blemishes, tiny scars, piles of dead cells."

Pointedly ignoring Freeth, she held a tape recorder near her mouth and documented her observations with a breathless monologue of descriptions, speculations, and simple exclamations. She also added personal asides for herself, suggestions for research journals and possible qualified peer-reviewers.

Because they had been unable to get any interior scans of the body to guide them, Team Proteus had no overall map or structure of the alien's gross anatomy. The specimen was a vast blank canvas upon which she could paint her studies, a mystery to be solved.

For the first time in her life, Tyler would have the opportunity to name the major organs of a new species, to conquer numerous biological formations. Make her mark. Her initial assessments would lay the foundation for decades of further analysis. Even a Nobel Prize wasn't entirely out of the question. . . .

The *Mote* cruised over sweeping gray plains that looked like a bombing range, puckered and uneven. She dictated descriptions of discolorations, fissures, and canyons in the tissue.

"Since the skin is smooth and pale, hair follicles mostly atrophied, the alien obviously does not come from a harsh environment. If we observed large patches of melanin, I might deduce that the alien's sun has a significant output of ultraviolet radiation against which the race requires protection. Given its pale appearance, however, this specimen must come from a world that is far from its sun or has a thick cloud cover."

"Not necessarily true," Arnold Freeth interrupted.

She rounded on him. "Are you *trying* to start a fight, Freeth?"

He shook his head, not backing down from her glare. "I'm used to hostile colleagues, Dr. Tyler."

"I am not your colleague," she said through clenched teeth.

He sighed. "I just wanted to point out that the species could live underground, or in domed cities. Don't limit your possibilities."

With no response beyond a noncommittal grunt, Tyler returned to her dictation.

They soared over glandular openings, pores, craters, any one of which could be a way inside. "The outer layer appears to be keratinized, but without epidermal scales, as in a reptile. On the exterior of the skin—human skin at least—we see only dead cells. The inner cells of our epidermis divide rapidly and force new cells to the surface. The basal layer synthesizes an inert protein called keratin, which is found in hair and nails. This helps outer toughness."

Freeth tried to interrupt, but Tyler cut him off, not wanting to listen. She concentrated on her tape recorder. "I note a pronounced graininess as we grow closer. Perhaps there are outer growths or eruptions from the epidermal cells. The pores appear to be glandular openings, designed to produce mucous or possibly toxic secretions." She turned to the supposed UFO expert as if he were an idiot and needed a translation. "In other words, the skin might feel slimy."

"I knew that," Freeth said. "In fact, there are lots of reports—"

"Hey, Doc," Devlin called back to them, "why don't you choose one of those pores so we can get inside?"

The bumpy epidermal surface resolved itself into a complex forest of growths. Strange nodules swayed on stalks connected to the main skin cells, like balloons on strings, forming a carpet of crowded, shapeless blobs. As the *Mote* skimmed overhead, the weird growths reacted with great agitation, as if a strong wind had rippled across a field of bizarre grass.

"Talk about having your skin crawl," Tomiko muttered.

"They're reacting to us," Tyler observed. The lumps stretched and groped. "Interesting."

"Like wax melting in a lava lamp," Freeth said. "So much for the skin cells being dead, like in humans." He looked over at Tyler, raising an eyebrow. "Right, Doctor?"

Intrigued now, Tyler pressed her face against the window. "We could be observing a post-mortem stimulation response. But the specimen *might* still be alive." She sounded hopeful.

The protrusions swelled to bulbous mushroom-like

heads. Their movement grew more chaotic, like a morass of microscopic eels guarding the skin pores.

"Major Devlin, we've got to get closer to observe them," Tyler said. "I've never seen anything remotely similar."

"Well, it is an *alien*, after all," Freeth pointed out.

"Right. Listen to the *expert*," Tyler said with a sour expression.

His nostrils flared. "Excuse me, Dr. Tyler, but I've spent most of my life studying the stories, the theories, the eye-witness accounts. I have read libraries full of information on any subject connected with life elsewhere in the universe. I am far more familiar with this alien than—"

Before he could finish his sentence, the ends of the stalks split apart like swollen lips to reveal jagged jaws. Tomiko nearly fell out of her co-pilot's seat as the trunks stretched toward their ship. "What the—"

The *Mote* jolted as one of the things clanged against the bottom hull.

Devlin reacted roughly, changing their course as another growth struck with a thump. Arnold Freeth let out a squawk.

The distorted wormlike shapes boiled and changed into a pack of fang-filled monsters, some with bear-trap maws, others with sharp saw blades. The stalks expanded, striking out faster than Team Proteus could get away. Hideous jaws of crystallized teeth careened into the *Mote*'s front window, clacking on the plasglass and leaving a zigzag residue of secretions.

"Whoa! Don't mess with my ship!" Devlin applied a burst to the impeller engines. The surge sent the craft forward and up with a violent lurch.

A swaying skin sentinel whipped toward them like a lamprey, but Devlin twisted the ship out of its path.

Cellular mouths slammed together like hangar doors crashing shut.

Tomiko Braddock, already half off her seat, was thrown to the deck. "Not much of a welcome mat . . . and we aren't even *inside* yet."

Swarms of the bulbous structures rose up like cannibalistic taffy. The *Mote* gained altitude, straining to stay out of reach, but the jaws stretched, showing extraordinary flexibility.

"All right, Freeth—explain *that*!" Tyler looked at him as if she truly expected an answer from him.

Tomiko leapt back into her seat, more flustered at losing her balance than from the attack itself. "Not a good time to be caught without my hands on the weapons controls."

"I didn't have time to be polite." Devlin patted the *Mote*'s control panel. "And not to you, either, baby."

Like witches' claws screeching across a chalkboard, the fang-filled sentinels struck glancing blows off the hull. With a loud thump, one of the "heads" rammed them, rattling the floorplates.

The organic strands grew with impossible speed and elasticity. "What *are* these things?" Devlin asked. The fangs snapped like shark mouths; the fan blades whirred like eviscerating buzz saws.

"I'm thinking, I'm thinking," Freeth cried.

"Enough of this." Tomiko powered up her defensive lasers. When she had insisted Devlin design them into the craft, he'd argued about the need for such weapons on simple exploration missions. Now, though, Devlin promised himself he would buy her a drink.

And a nice dinner.

Make that a lobster dinner. And an expensive bottle of wine.

It might even make Garrett Wilcox jealous. Hmmm . . .

She shot one of the numerous protrusions, and the thing burst with a splat of smoking protoplasm that drifted in gooey droplets. She swept the beam across the writhing tentacular growths, cutting stalks like a harvester slashing a swath through wheat. "Not so tough."

The cauterized stumps melted back into the skin tissue, flowing like organic wax. The severed stalks squirmed and thrashed as if infuriated.

"Only about ten trillion more to mow down," Devlin said.

Like a flat stone that caromed off a smooth lake surface, the *Mote* bounced up and away from the alien's skin. In the main compartment, Freeth finally came to a conclusion. "I remember reading something about starfish, Dr. Tyler. *Pedicels,* a defense mechanism on the skin of an echinoderm, animated scissors to deter parasites."

When the UFO expert mentioned "parasites," Tyler shot a glance over at him. Her brows knitted as she paused to consider. "All right, pedicellariea might be an appropriate analogy. I've seen them under a microscope, and these growths *might* serve a similar protective function." She sounded annoyed that she hadn't thought of the answer herself. "It's not the worst idea I've ever heard."

The once-placid skin surface looked like a boiling cauldron of jaws.

Freeth was too excited to be intimidated by Tyler's scorn any longer. "Maybe they responded because we're made of metal, a completely foreign substance. The alien body's defenses might react against it."

Tyler crossed her arms over her chest, remembering to be skeptical of anything he said. "That's ridiculous. Perhaps you can tell us why a species would evolve to reject tiny bits of metal, Freeth? If I wrote that in a paper, I'd be laughed out of the scientific community. It makes no biological sense."

"On the contrary, think about what this may tell us about the alien's home environment. Why *would* they need defenses against microscopic bits of metal? At our size, what harm could we possibly cause?" He looked down at the snake pit of monstrous protrusions. "Maybe that planet isn't as benign as we first thought."

Tyler thought about that for a moment, then grudgingly spoke into her tape recorder without answering Freeth. "Such a drastic defensive measure would never have developed without the need for survival in hostile conditions. This alien must be programmed—on a genetic level at least—against an invasion or encrustation by foreign objects. *Small* foreign objects. The threat must be sufficient and prevalent enough to warrant such an extreme defense."

"Yeah, interesting, Doctor T." Tomiko's tone said exactly the opposite. "It'll make a fine footnote in an obscure journal, once we're home safe and sound. Right now, we've got to find a way *inside*, or we can blow off our mission right now. Three quarters of an hour wasted already!"

Devlin checked his control panels and engine readings, then glanced at the snapshot of Kelli, as if for support. "Well, we always have the option of charging into one of those pores with all guns blazing."

"You're on, if that's what it takes."

"Pick a pore, any pore," he said, gathering speed. Devlin would bank his life—and the lives of the crew, as well as the survival of his precious *Mote*—upon Tomiko's abilities. "They all look the same. Doc, your insights would be appreciated."

Tyler considered the plethora of possibilities.

"Some of them seem to be follicles, others are glandular passages, while still others could be—"

The vessel reached the top of a parabola, then nosed toward a morass of man-eating mouths, razor-edged sawblades and scissors. Acceleration pressed Devlin back against the seat. Every pore looked like a deathtrap, surrounded by rabid pedicellular guards, but he was in command. The decision was his. "All right. I'll take the large one at eleven o'clock."

As if the pedicels had heard his words, they responded with increased agitation. The fangs seemed to grow sharper, chomping on alien air. The stalks elongated and swayed to cover the deep hole leading into the alien's skin tissue.

Her dark eyes narrowed with grim concentration, Tomiko opened fire like a machine-gunner, slicing down rows of the oozing attackers. Her lasers decapitated the nearest structures and cleared a path to the crater-sized pore, but others flowed over and took their places. Like molten drops of solder, the chopped pedicels extruded new heads and opened fresh mouths.

Gritting his teeth, Devlin rocketed forward, dodging whenever he could. At the edge of the pore, the *Mote* smashed into a pedicel that made a last attempt to stop them. With a clip of their wing, it splattered.

Then the ship plunged into the opening.

Several defeated pedicels drooped over the edge, stretching on absurdly long shafts like Dobermans on bungee cords. One chomped on the casing of the starboard impeller, but Devlin ripped the ship free with a sickening scrape.

The *Mote* shot out of the pedicels' reach, into the depths of the skin.

Devlin switched on the front beams again, shining white cones of light into the unexplored maze of cells. He tried to slow his breathing and cool the prickly thrill-sweat that burst from his skin.

"I hate to raise this possibility," Freeth spoke from the main compartment, gripping his seat with white-knuckled hands, "but what we find *inside* the alien's body might be even worse. . . ."

Chapter 18

Within the containment room, the alien astronaut lay prone—completely enclosed, airtight, protected. Team Proteus was inside now, their strange journey under way, but nothing had moved, nothing had changed.

Sergei Pirov was relieved to be out here, where it was safe. Where he belonged. After so much rushed activity in the past day, he felt weary and on edge. Each breath echoed in his ears, hot against the faceplate. Though his suit's circulation system kept his body cool, he could not make himself comfortable.

Beside him, Rajid Sujatha seemed content to do his work, despite all the constraints imposed upon them. The Bengali doctor went through the procedures, making diligent notes . . . and waiting.

The Russian doctor peered through the lifepod's hazy windows, seeing only tantalizing glimpses of the humanoid body. The alien's egg-shaped head was smooth and infantlike, its large eyelids closed slits with extensive epicanthic folds. Pirov could just see one long arm, a naked shoulder, but not much of the chest or legs. Maybe the alien had tentacles instead of feet?

As a medical researcher, he wanted to feel the alien's skin, its muscles, the hardness of its bones.

He wished he could pry open the eyelids and stare into pupils that had seen the light of distant suns. He wanted to pull back the lips to see teeth that had eaten food from another world, the mouth that spoke an alien language, or recited poetry written under other constellations.

This extraterrestrial specimen could be a biological Rosetta Stone, unlocking amazing secrets. Perhaps if he stared at it long enough, even with his weak and burning eyes, Pirov might solve the mystery of life itself, break the code . . . and understand why this creature had come to Earth.

When he'd been a young boy in Vladivostok, Sergei Pirov had been fascinated with science. Because his family was poor, he'd contented himself with a clunky old microscope discarded by the local university. His father, a hardworking fisherman who barely knew how to read, had obtained it for him because he loved his son. Though he did not understand the mysteries of the universe, the man understood what would make the boy happy.

With voracious curiosity, Sergei had sat with his microscope by the kitchen window, pointing the little mirror to a bright spot in the cloudy skies, while his mother hand-sewed traditional clothes to sell to tourists and rich Party members.

Peering through the eyepiece, he scrutinized a hair-shaft, which looked like a fallen tree under high magnification. He'd pricked a finger and observed his blood, then stained and scrutinized epithelial cells scraped from inside his cheek.

In a drop of murky water taken from a green-scummed meadow pool, Sergei could see a bustling metropolis of strange creatures: coiled green tubes of spirogyra or green algae, amoebas, euglena, protozoans. Blurring, furry feet propelled the ovoid ciliates like aimless bumper cars; when they struck an obstacle, they backed up and puttered off in another direction. He'd kept a little sketchbook, trying to observe and identify as many as possible.

And now, deep inside a mountain installation, he was again an outside observer, still detached and still curious.   ·

Of all the specimens he'd seen in his career, this one required the most objectivity. Just like his old Soviet mentor, Alexei Rokov, had taught him to do. Without imagining the impossible, Rokov never could have developed the miniaturization apparatus back in the 1960s. . . .

If he were allowed to crack open the containment vessel, Pirov might find a thousand answers in only a few minutes. But Hunter had forbidden that. Above, the Director sat alone in the VIP observation deck. Pirov looked forward to seeing Vasili Garamov again, but the Deputy Foreign Minister hadn't arrived yet, which made him even more uneasy.

Had the diplomat been detained on his way into the secure facility? Or had Garamov been held by the Russian government, after they discovered how he'd arranged for the capsule to be brought here in a blatant abridgment of bureaucratic procedures?

Years after Dr. Rokov had defected from the Soviet Union, bringing with him the secret prize of his technology, young Vasili Garamov had been instrumental in cementing a cooperative agreement between the American and Russian miniaturization work, under the aegis of Project Proteus. Garamov had made it possible for Pirov himself to come here.

Guards stood at the armored chamber doors. Technicians moved in the upper levels and outside in the corridor. Taking care of maintenance details while Team Proteus continued their fantastic explorations, Sujatha busied himself disconnecting the now-useless laser-drilling apparatus.

They would have to wait four more hours, trusting the crew would emerge from the alien body with pictures, samples, and more raw information than Pirov could dream of. He wanted to spend the rest of his life in his laboratory office, simply examining the data.

The Russian placed his gloved hands on the impenetrable lifepod, pressing hard to stop his trembling fingers. "They cannot learn everything about the alien in one mission."

Sujatha smiled, content with his assignment. "Nevertheless, that is all the time they have."

Chapter 19

The *Mote* continued into the deep pore surrounded by soft walls slick with secretions. The womblike shaft was curved, lined with what looked like a mosaic of gelatinous tiles. The surrounding light turned reddish orange, then blacker as they followed the serpentine tunnel into the extraterrestrial's dermal layers.

"Now that we're finally inside, we've got four hours to explore and get back out," Devlin said. "Take a lot of notes, Doc."

Cruising at moderate speed, he piloted the ship around curves and organic obstacles. He had always liked to poke his nose where no one had gone before. To him, leaving fresh footprints on an uncharted beach counted for more than all of his degrees and awards. No other place was as unexplored as the microscopic universe, especially here inside an alien body.

Shafts branched out, but he never hesitated, assessing his options in a split second and choosing a direction. Nobody had a map anyway.

Unsettled by the unexpected viciousness of the skin pedicels, Arnold Freeth rebuckled his seat belt and wiped sweat off his forehead. "I hope you're leaving a trail of breadcrumbs behind, Major Devlin, so we can find our way back out."

"That's what the navigation computer is for." Devlin took another sharp turn as the pore twisted. "Even if we get completely lost inside this alien's body, what's the worst that could happen?" Freeth didn't answer.

Intent on the astonishing world around her, Dr. Tyler took meticulous notes about changes in the wall texture. On either side of the *Mote*, small mouths like culverts emptied into the shaft. Viscous liquid seeped out, running up the cellular surface in defiance of gravity. "Those openings must be glandular outlets, releasing pheromones or sebaceous fluids," she said.

Standing at the opposite side window, Freeth added, "Maybe our passage irritates the pore lining and triggers the production of lubricant. Should we go inside one of those glands and have a look around?"

"Any time you want to take a side trip, let me know," Devlin said.

Tyler shook her head. "They're likely to be dead ends, terminating in a pool of fluids waiting to be released."

"Then I definitely don't want to take my nice clean ship in there."

With engines thrumming comfortably now that they had passed the nightmarish skin guardians, Devlin stabilized the ship, then rode through the turbulence as he transmitted a burst to the outside. "Project Proteus, we're proceeding deeper into the alien. You guys should see this. It's like a funhouse at an amusement arcade."

"Yeah, a new theme park—Glandular World," Tomiko said.

With a crackle, Director Hunter's voice came over

the *Mote*'s comm system. "Team Proteus, your transmissions are being distorted by increasing static."

"Not to worry, Felix. We can take care of ourselves. Devlin out."

They descended beyond what, in a human, would have been the gray stratum corneum and into the subcutaneous layers. Tyler pointed out analogies to fatty adipose tissue, sweat ducts, sebaceous glands, recording each one with photographs from hull-mounted cameras, videotapes, and her own verbal commentary.

"Everything you say sounds reasonable, Dr. Tyler," Freeth said, trying to keep the challenging tone out of his voice, "but any conclusions drawn from terrestrial biology could be completely wrong. Human anatomy developed on *this* planet and evolved in *this* environment for millions of years." He tapped on the window. "Believe me, this creature might play by an entirely different set of rules."

"I'm doing my best, Freeth, based on sound scientific principles."

Devlin asked, "What about the theory that mankind was star-seeded, our genetic material dropped onto Earth by extraterrestrials?"

Freeth sounded surprisingly skeptical. "If you swallow *that*, then yes, we would all have a common biological basis."

"Some people will believe anything," Tyler said with a trace of bitterness.

Devlin swerved the vessel around threads of stretchy scarlet fibers that hung down like stalactites. Thick silvery-white liquid traced patterns on the pore wall, glistening like dew-moist spiderwebs in the ship's front lights. Tyler continued to analyze the gridlocked cells that lined the shaft.

Freeth peered from window to window like an anxious puppy. He looked behind them, saw something move, and froze. "Uh, Major Devlin? We've got company!"

A strange shape emerged from an opening in the organic wall—a living blob that bristled with spines and colored masses. The self-contained sack of milky fluid writhed . . . and oozed closer.

"Perhaps it's some kind of glandular secretion." Tyler rolled her eyes. "Nothing to be alarmed about."

As the flexible shape bore down upon them, it grew as large as the *Mote*, a rubbery organic bag filled with gelatinous slime. At its center hung a darker sphere, like the yolk of an egg, surrounded by organelles—rods, spheres, coiled wormlike things.

"That's one mean-looking glandular secretion, Dr. T," Tomiko said.

Tyler reconsidered, her face looking even sharper. "Part of the extraterrestrial's immunodefenses, perhaps analogous to a leukocyte?"

Freeth shook his head. "No, no, I disagree. More likely a single-celled organism, an ameboid creature—either a parasite or a symbiote." He pressed his freckled face closer to the window, watching how the shifting mass changed, then grinned in amazement. "A genuine microorganism from another planet. The very first *xenozoan* ever observed by human beings."

Devlin relaxed at the piloting console. "Mr. Freeth, you saw it first. In my book, that means you have the privilege of naming it for the future of science."

"There'll be plenty of things to name on this voyage," Tyler responded sourly. "We're all going to have a chance to add Latin suffixes to our names."

"Let's write the technical papers later, okay?" Tomiko reached across the control panel to tap the glass coverplate on the mission chronometer. "Got a ticking clock here, three hours and fifty minutes."

The xenozoan drifted closer, a living container of

protoplasm and subcellular matter. At first, the organism moved like an amoeba, pouring nutrient liquid from one pseudopod to the other. Then the protoplasmic mass sprouted a hairy mane of whipping cilia, like the oars on a slave galley, which pushed the single-celled creature toward the *Mote*.

"Think it's a threat, Marc?" Tomiko said.

"*You're* the security officer."

Tyler took furious notes as she watched the ominous xenozoan close the distance. "Let's be reasonable. It can't possibly consider us food of any kind."

As the microorganism came alongside their ship, its cellular membrane extruded fibrous whips like the tentacles of a giant squid. Seven strands reached toward the *Mote*, as if in an effort to grab the ship.

"Uh, let me point out that those skin pedicels shouldn't have reacted to us either," Freeth said. "Let's not take anything for granted."

Tomiko powered up the laser cannons. "Maybe we just need to show it who's boss." She fired a low-power warning shot into the ameboid creature. The thin red laser pierced the rubbery envelope, leaving a foaming trail of vaporized protoplasm. But the blast did no serious damage. The xenozoan kept coming.

"Ms. Braddock, please don't just shoot everything," Tyler chided.

"Damage assessment, Doc. At our size, I can't possibly harm more than one or two cells at a time. Shouldn't cause any problems at all for Big Boy." She gestured out the cockpit window.

Cylindrical organelles in the xenozoan glowed with bluish light, like storage batteries discharging energy. The tentacles crackled like electric whips.

"I've seen enough," Freeth said.

"I hate to say, 'uh-oh,' but I'll say it anyway. Uh-oh." Devlin peered through the cockpit windows into the shadowy distance ahead of the ship. An identical xenozoan emerged from a glandular duct farther down the pore. Extruding electrical cilia, the second extraterrestrial organism climbed toward them.

The *Mote* was blocked from behind and ahead.

"Somebody must have rung the dinner bell," Tomiko said. "Can't figure out why they think we're so appetizing."

"You better aim for the nucleus," Freeth suggested. "That's likely to be the organism's control center, the closest thing to its 'brain.'" Tyler did not contradict him.

Tomiko centered her targeting cross on the spherical nucleus of the first microorganism. "Shooting germs in a barrel. Ready . . . aim—"

Before she could fire, two of the xenozoan's crackling flagellae slapped the *Mote*'s metal hull. A burst of discharged power surged through the frame like a thunderbolt, sending the crew reeling.

Devlin yelled as sparks flew from his control panel. Suddenly, half of the *Mote*'s power systems went dead, and the controls sparked and froze. The deck lurched at a steep angle as their stabilizers shifted. The impeller engines died. A small fire curled up from the cockpit banks. Devlin grabbed for a small fire extinguisher.

The ship's front lights sputtered, then went dark, leaving the crew inside the blackness of the alien's tissue. All systems went off-line.

Devlin searched the diagnostic panel, trying to coax some kind of response from the ship. Anything. But the *Mote* wouldn't move.

The two crackling xenozoans closed in to engulf them.

Chapter 20

Helpless, the *Mote* drifted, dead in microscopic space.

Devlin, who knew every system aboard his ship, scrambled to figure out how he could get the vessel functioning again. Their air would begin to get stuffy in half an hour, but he had far more immediate problems.

With brushing, scrubbing sounds on the outside of the hull, the two xenozoans continued their slow, ominous attack. The creatures pressed against the walls until the *Mote*'s frame groaned.

"Come on, talk to me," he called to the ship. "Snap out of it."

Cynthia Tyler backed away from the side window. The sinuous xenozoan tendrils, made from reinforced protein chains, crackled with blue lighting. The glitter shed an eerie illumination in the dark confines of the pore. The tentacle drew back, like a slave-master's whip. "It's going to hit us again!"

Another surge slammed through the ship, sending a new skitter of sparks from the control panels. Oily smoke oozed from the rear engine compartment.

"Floating out of control, no maneuverability, no defenses." Devlin felt sick at heart. He thought fast. "I'll have to reset all our frozen systems, do a full shutdown and bring us back online from the zero point."

"A restart is good," Freeth said. He stepped back from the microorganisms pushing hard against the window, seeking a way in. "If we can last that long."

"Damn, and I was just about to fire." Tomiko slumped in her seat and frowned at her dark weapons panel. Garrett Wilcox would have chided her for hesitating at the wrong moment. "Maybe I should just swim out there with a baseball bat."

Devlin slammed shut an access panel against the smell of burnt circuits. "You might be better off using one of the sampling rods as a spear."

The second xenozoan approached from above, flagellae extended. The cylindrical organelles inside its body mass pulsed with an energy buildup.

Freeth's brow furrowed as he furiously tried to think of an explanation. "All right, some larger animals on Earth use electric shock as a method to stun their prey, but I've never heard of anything on a microscopic scale. Those cylindrical organelles must be the mitochondria, the powerhouses of the cell, where ATP is generated."

Tyler considered the idea with cautious skepticism. "Why would a microorganism develop such an attack system? What sort of extreme enemies does it normally have to face in its native environment? How can it be aware of mechanical devices on this size scale? It makes no sense."

Devlin brushed past Freeth and Tyler on his way to the engine hatches in the rear. "I've got to get our main control banks restarted, or we're going to be somebody's lunch."

The first xenozoan coiled its flagellae around the *Mote* and drew the ship closer. The cilia were like the moving palps of a spider, scrubbing and chewing, trying to break through the metal armor. They made sounds like bats' wings against the hull.

"An ameboid engulfs its prey within the protoplasm," Tyler said. "Inside the walled-off vacuoles, enzymes slowly dissolve the raw material."

The flowing blob of the microorganism blanketed the rear of the ship, clogging the impeller exhausts. "I'd say these things have similar intentions." Tomiko looked completely frustrated.

With a thud, the second xenozoan struck from the side, limned with bluish light. Devlin looked up from his frantic work in the engine compartment. He thumped the starboard window. "Hey, get out of here."

Unimpressed by the threat, the microorganism kept coming.

Both blobs stretched and oozed around the ship, competing to digest the miniaturized vessel. The microbes wrapped tentacles together, jolting each other with tiny sparks of electricity. The barriers of protoplasm fused into one larger organism, a combined xenozoan twice as powerful as the individual creatures. The flagellae tightened as the microbes worked to destroy the *Mote*.

Cynthia Tyler's expression clouded with seriousness. "I hate to admit this, but Director Hunter was probably correct to insist on absolute containment procedures. If these alien microorganisms got loose in our environment, imagine the havoc they could wreak."

"If their genetics are at all compatible with ours," Freeth added. "That's not very likely."

"Do you have to counter my every statement, Freeth?"

The combined microorganism shimmered, building to a bright pulse, and a third mitochondrial discharge blasted the *Mote*. The ship shuddered, caught within the protoplasmic embrace, and the crew rode through the turbulence.

Devlin stared at his non-functional engines, scorch marks, blown circuits. "Enough already!" Gritting his teeth, he flipped switches, testing power trains and linkages in the circuit housings. He bypassed dead panels, replaced what he could, worked around what he couldn't. "I need a few seconds of peace and quiet to get caught up here."

Tomiko stared at the spherical yolks where braided genetic material hung within the nuclear membrane. "Okay, I'll write them a note and tape it to the window." The structural elements of the *Mote* groaned as the xenozoans clustered tighter, seeking any chink in the ship's armor. Tomiko made a face at them.

Inside the cramped engine closet, Devlin bumped his head on a low impeller cowling. "Sorry, Tomiko. We don't even have a pink bunny to power our systems."

Then, with sudden urgency, she struggled to unfasten her seat restraints. "Wait! We do have the anchor cables, and they don't use electricity. With the switch I can fire a spear right into the nucleus." Tomiko rushed to the side hull, where spring-loaded grappling hooks were mounted to the outside of the ship.

Tyler let a slow smile grow on her hard face. "It'll be like bursting an egg yolk."

Standing against the side hull, Tomiko swiveled the spring-loaded gun in its horseshoe mount, aiming the tube like a torpedo launcher. Then she depressed the release lever to fire the sharp anchor. With a burst of air, the projectile streaked through the protoplasm like a hungry shark cutting the water.

"Come on, come on," she said under her breath.

The hooked tip pierced the first xenozoan's round nucleus, ripping through the membrane and into the packed chromatin-like material. Blue sparks skittered through the odd-shaped organelles, as if she'd unleashed a cellular powerhouse. The *Mote* shuddered as the microorganism reflexively recoiled without releasing its hold.

"Sometimes you've gotta break a few eggs." Using the hand crank, Tomiko withdrew the anchor harpoon like a fisherman hauling in a marlin. She ripped the hook through the nuclear membrane, widening the tear even farther.

Chromatin spilled out in a shapeless mass from the ruptured nucleus, oozing into the surrounding protoplasm. Still clutching the *Mote*, the attacking fused microorganisms convulsed, rocking the vessel back and forth. The second xenozoan linked itself even more tightly with its companion, as if to pick up the slack in the digestion process.

"Shoot the other one!" Freeth said.

Tomiko looked at him with a raised eyebrow. "You don't need to tell me twice." She went to the opposite wall where the second anchor cable waited. She swung the swivel gun and launched the second harpoon.

But missed the nucleus entirely.

Two mitochondria inside the unharmed xenozoan discharged a defensive power burst. Lightning crackled along the anchor cable, scorching the hull again. Tomiko leapt back from the horseshoe mount, afraid of being electrocuted.

When the sparks died down, she angrily reeled in the harpoon, rewinding the cable. Frustrated with herself, she managed to scrape the barbed edges along the nucleus; it was like scalpel blades slicing open a water balloon.

Blue arcs skittered through both of the injured xenozoans, sparkling lights that dispersed and faded into the protoplasm. The *Mote* groaned as the joined microbes writhed in their death throes.

Devlin slammed shut an access panel and pulsed the impeller engines. "Almost got it!" He flipped the switch, shut it off, then clicked over the breaker a second time. Turbines vibrated, sputtered to life . . . and died again. He took a deep breath and caressed the cowlings. Instead of a curse, he whispered encouragement to the ship. "You can do it."

Tomiko finished cranking the second harpoon back into place and locked it down. She wiped sweat off her forehead.

Arnold Freeth gripped a railing at the side of the aft window. "The xenozoans are pulling away, withdrawing pseudopods." The ship lurched as the organisms continued to squirm while they detached themselves.

"All right, Marc. I did my part," Tomiko said. "Here's your peace and quiet."

Devlin clanged his crescent wrench against a shielded transformer.

The UFO expert stared at the first ruptured nucleus, the nucleoplasm streaming out, which formed a blob streaked with colored lines of chromatin and separated into distinct portions. "Believe me, you may have prompted more of a reaction than you intended, Ms. Braddock. That looks to me like the prophase of cellular division, if I remember my biology classes."

"Extremely unlikely," Tyler said with a scowl, not even bothering to take a look for herself. "Given the amount of nuclear damage, I'd expect to see apoptosis, or programmed cell death that's set off when the DNA is damaged. These cells should never be able to recover."

Freeth continued to observe as the broken nucleus took a dipolar shape, stretching into a dumbbell.

"Normally, I wouldn't argue with your medical expertise, Dr. Tyler. But . . . *look*."

The chromosomes elongated like fingers, attaching to spindle lines, like two chunks of wax being pulled apart. Tyler finally shouldered Freeth aside to look at the dividing cells, then at the UFO expert, as if she couldn't decide which was more unbelievable. "Anaphase already. Astonishing—the xenozoan is fissioning. Note the separation of chromosomes along spindle lines."

The single-celled creature pulled itself apart, reabsorbing the cilia and electric-whip flagellae into its main protoplasmic mass. The microorganism drew its pseudopods away from the *Mote*, focusing all its energy on dividing into two equal parts.

"Second organism's doing it, too," Tomiko observed.

"After reproduction, the xenozoans will withdraw and recover," Tyler said. "And then there'll be two more of them."

"Major Devlin, we need to get out of here." Freeth's voice was scratchy with an edge of panic.

The *Mote* lurched as the last clinging pseudopod let go of the hull. The second single-celled creature pulled away, pulsing like translucent clay.

"Now that we're free, we should be able to move." Devlin tried another engine test, got no response, and muttered to himself. He struggled to think of something else to try. "We'll be on our way momentarily."

"Now I can say I'm a mother," Tomiko said, looking out the window. "I made four bouncing baby amoebas."

"Save the cigars for later. We don't have any air to spare." Devlin looked through the small window in the engine closet. The first microorganism had completely divided into two smaller bodies, which were drifting away. His forehead streaked with grease, he eased back out of the engine closet. "How much time do I have until they get hungry again, Doc?"

"I can only answer based on Earth microorganisms, but it won't be long. They'll recover soon and search for food to replenish the energy they just expended."

"Roger that." Devlin picked up his black toolkit and crawled back into the engine compartment. "One hard restart coming up. I'd rather not be here when they snap out of their post-coital bliss."

Chapter 21

When the two VIP visitors finally arrived, nearly two hours behind schedule, Deputy Foreign Minister Garamov was amazed by the hidden high-tech facility, but not in the least impressed with his companion. Congressman Edwin Durston made a show of bluster and indignation, apparently to demonstrate his perceived importance.

Durston had a round, too-expressive face framed by a squarish Lincolnesque beard. He looked ready to go on the offensive at the drop of a hat, and his lips seemed most comfortable in the shape of a scowl.

After intercepting Garamov at the airport, the congressman himself had caused their late arrival, delaying them several times with "just one more minor item," talking on his cell phone, dispatching aides to take care of "urgent matters." Garamov was familiar with such games from politicians in his own country.

After riding in an extravagant limo up the winding roads deep into the Sierra Nevadas, Durston had flouted Proteus checkpoints, demanded more guard escorts than could conceivably have been required, and then complained about lax security.

From far too much painful experience, Garamov knew the Russian bureaucracy was inept and ludi-

crous, but Congressman Durston demonstrated that
American bureaucracy could be downright malicious.

The congressman had emphasized, several times,
that he chaired the committee holding the purse
strings for the U.S. portion of Proteus funding. He
called himself a devil's advocate and remained skeptical about the cost/benefit ratios for the expensive
miniaturization project. As far as Garamov could tell,
Durston didn't know very much about it, however.

Once past the threshold of the underground facility, the Russian dangled a cigarette from his spidery
fingers, trying not to spill ash on the clean concrete
floor, but he could find no ashtray. His features were
sallow and tired, his eyes fiery. After the long flight
from Azerbaijan to Vladivostok, followed by Tokyo,
Honolulu, then San Francisco, he felt haggard and
edgy. He had managed to take a shower in the airport in Hawaii, changed into a drab but less rumpled
suit, and made himself somewhat presentable.

The Deputy Foreign Minister knew he would pay
a dear political price for whisking the alien lifepod
here, but for now he intended to savor every moment
of what the miniaturization technology could do. Perhaps Felix Hunter would salvage this, after all.

Dr. Trish Wylde stepped forward to greet them
just beyond the second guard checkpoint. "I'm sorry,
sir," she said to Garamov without introduction,
"you'll have to extinguish your cigarette before I can
take you into the laboratory levels. We have a great
deal of sensitive equipment."

Garamov knew about Americans and their paranoid anti-smoking policies. "Of course." He took a
long drag before reluctantly grinding it under the
sole of his black wing-tip. Perhaps they didn't *have*
ashtrays in California.

Satisfied, Trish gave them a formal smile. "Welcome to the Proteus Facility, gentlemen. If you'll fol-

low me, I'll expedite your entry into the high-security zone. The team has already been miniaturized and inserted into the lifepod. Director Hunter is waiting for you in the observation deck. He can fill you in on what's happened so far."

"You mean they started without us, even though I sent word that we were on our way?" Durston sounded appalled. Outlined by the anachronistic beard, his cheeks flushed with pique.

"We are tardy, Congressman," Garamov said pointedly. "By a substantial margin, in fact."

Durston seemed to think the world ran according to his own watch. "I apologize for this, Mr. Garamov. Director Hunter has always been arrogant and a bit too self-important with this project. I'll see that my committee deals him a reprimand."

Garamov followed Trish's brisk pace. "On the contrary, sir. I personally gave them a very precise and inflexible timetable. Director Hunter is doing me the courtesy of following it, as I requested. I consider that diligence, not arrogance."

Trish led them to an enclosed elevator, unable to hide her annoyance. "Mr. Garamov is right, Congressman. This is a carefully planned operation, not a diplomatic cocktail party. You weren't supposed to arrive fashionably late."

"Who is this woman?" Durston snapped.

Though he had claimed to be a key player numerous times during the long limousine drive, the congressman had obviously not done his homework. Garamov was glad to fill in details for him. "Doctor Wylde is the Project's chief pathologist, not a hostess, and I am certain we are taking her away from more important duties. Considering your obvious . . . interest in this project, I am surprised you haven't met her before, Congressman."

Impressed that he knew her, Wylde smiled appreciatively at the Russian diplomat. "Director Hunter asked me to lead you to the observation gallery." She pushed the button, and the elevator dropped several stories. "We'll be there shortly."

Felix Hunter already had enough problems to deal with. Armed Marines kept a constant watch on the containment room and its deadly fail-safe sterilization procedures. The two moon-suited doctors stood over the sealed lifepod, ready to assist, impatient to participate. Team Proteus continued to explore the unknown alien landscape, despite increasing static that threatened to cut off all communications.

The last thing Hunter wanted was to entertain two politicians.

Durston pushed past Trish Wylde into the observation deck. "Deputy Foreign Minister Garamov has come a long way for this, Director. You should have waited." Beside him, Trish rolled her eyes; then she left the observation deck, clearly anxious to be back to her duties.

"My apologies, Congressman," he said without meaning it. "We started precisely at the scheduled time." Hunter gave no visible sign of how much he wanted to strangle the man.

For decades, Hunter had grown accustomed to dealing with people like Durston. He had traveled the world, stayed in cultural and industrial cities, met with leaders of industrialized nations. People who *mattered* understood who Felix Hunter was, though few others knew his name . . . which was exactly the way he preferred it. Even his wife, content with her life apart from him in Carmel, didn't know the half of what he did.

He reached out to shake the Deputy Foreign Minister's slender hand. "Vasili, we cannot thank you enough for the opportunity you have offered Project Proteus. I appreciate your faith in us."

The Russian gave him a curt nod and slicked back his dark hair with one hand. "Please remember that, Director Hunter. I may soon be looking for another job."

Hunter motioned the two visitors to a pair of seats. He had requested that the guests' chairs be more plush and raised higher than his own. Tiny touches, harmless concessions.

An avid chess devotee, Felix Hunter enjoyed replaying the games of grand masters. He liked the strategy, but more than that, it forced him to sit still and concentrate, to fine-tune parts of his brain that might not otherwise get exercised. As Project Director and earlier as a corporate captain and manager of a diverse workforce, Hunter had played the game with people, a chess match with infinitely more variations and challenges.

He doubted any other person could have successfully integrated the Cold War miniaturization programs, not even his old college friend Chris Matheson. He'd bridged classification problems and enlisted cooperation from unlikely heroes and public figures, including surprisingly visionary Russians such as Vasili Garamov.

Unfortunately, Congressman Durston had a different agenda every time a funding question arose. However, now that the bearded man saw the sealed lifepod and the actual alien inside, his overblown complaints petered out. True amazement restored some semblance of humility to his round face.

Hunter took his own seat and gave a brief summary of what had already happened. He could see the growing worry on Garamov's face, as well as an eager hunger in the Congressman's eyes.

"You seem to have applied sufficient quarantine

precautions to address all of my concerns, Mr. Director." Garamov leaned forward, paying attention to the spacesuited doctors in the chamber. "Is that my old friend Sergei Pirov? I thought he had been assigned to the actual miniaturization team?"

"Dr. Pirov requested reassignment to this position. Several crew members were changed at the last minute. We had an unfortunate accident during a test mission this morning—"

"What kind of accident?" Durston said. "Why wasn't I informed?"

Somehow, Hunter maintained his patience. "Captain Wilcox was injured, and he's recovering in the infirmary. Consequently, Major Marc Devlin took his place as pilot. Since Major Devlin designed the *Mote* himself and has flown the ship on numerous missions, I have every confidence in him."

He looked over at Garamov. "While miniaturized, Dr. Pirov gave Wilcox emergency medical attention, but he was rather shaken by the incident. Dr. Cynthia Tyler is now part of the exploration team. She is very qualified, and I'm sure she will pursue her research with a high degree of competence."

Durston did not appear satisfied, but the Deputy Foreign Minister nodded. "Sergei has been with the miniaturization program longer than any other person alive. He was Dr. Rokov's protégé before the doctor defected to America." Garamov's expression was mild and gave no sign of holding a grudge about past Cold War struggles. "I am glad you could find an important job for him."

Below, Pirov spotted the two visitors on the observation deck. Recognition was obvious in the old man's expression even behind the transparent faceplate. "Greetings, Mr. Deputy Minister," Pirov said in Russian through the suit microphone.

Scratching his squarish beard, Durston questioned

the wisdom of bringing a "flake" like Arnold Freeth into such an important mission. Hunter indicated the extraterrestrial lying motionless below. "Given the evidence of your own eyes, Congressman, you may have to reassess your definition of a 'flake.' Mr. Freeth believed in UFOs and aliens all along, and he was right."

Chapter 22

Cramped inside the *Mote*'s dim engine closet, dodging shadows from his small flashlight, Devlin caressed the ship, as if he could bring her back to life. "Now let's try it." Around him he could smell the chemical lubricants and the bright odor of soldered metal and burnt fuses.

Outside, the four alien microorganisms recuperated from the fission process. Their organelles glittered and shifted, building up to another deadly charge. The single-celled creatures began to stir.

"Major Devlin, they're moving closer," Arnold Freeth said.

Sweating, Devlin studied the equipment using voltmeters, pulse-scanners, and bypass shunts from his black toolkit. "You're not knocked out for good. I've got faith in you." He worked faster, skinning his knuckles on a metal ridge.

Since his youth, he'd loved to tinker with things, finding that there was *always* an alternative way to accomplish any engineering task. Once, when his sister Lenore went to summer camp, fifteen-year-old Marc Devlin had reconfigured her entire room—the stereo, the vanity light, the blow dryer, the television, even her phone. Thus, when Lenore came home and flipped on the CD player, the telephone rang; when she tried to dry her hair, the TV cycled through its channels.

How could rigging the *Mote*'s engines be any more challenging than that?

The miniaturized ship drifted along, paralyzed and helpless. The first of the four xenozoans extruded cilia and nudged forward. Searching. Hungry.

He slammed a panel shut, and an indicator light winked on, blessedly green. "Ah, thank you!" He kissed the curved metal covering.

When the auxiliary power gauges crept up to sixty percent of total load, Devlin shut off the bypasses and shunted all power into the engines. When he smelled acrid smoke, he scrambled to shut the impeller turbines down again before the short circuits could cause further damage. The green lights flickered off again.

Disheartening, yes. But now, at least, he knew where the problem was located. At least one problem.

Devlin cast a wary glance at the pulsing ameboid cells. The xenozoans had no instinct or memory, and would likely forget about the ship. Probably. But he didn't want to take that chance.

The air inside the ship was growing thick, warm, and stuffy.

He tried to jump-start the engines again, stroking the controls, willing them to cooperate. He felt the ship *trying*. The impeller motors coughed, then hummed. The turbines spun.

He heard Tomiko applauding, and he crawled out of the compartment to take a bow. "The transformer generators will build up our charge again. For now, we can ease ourselves deeper into the pore. We should be reasonably functional in ten minutes." In three strides he was back in the cockpit.

"I'd rather not give the xenozoans ten full minutes," Tyler said, frowning out the window. "They're showing signs of increased activity."

"Let's see what the *Mote* will do if I talk nice to her. We're on our way." Devlin nudged the ship along without headlights, leaving the shapeless microorganisms behind.

"When will I have my laser cannons again?" Tomiko said.

"Working on it. Just don't shoot anything unless you absolutely have to."

Her face brightened. "You think I do this for fun?"

"Actually, yes."

Flying blind in the dark, the *Mote* gathered speed as the engine power cells built up charge. Soon, the overhead cabin lights flickered on inside the craft, then the front cones of illumination shone onto the cellular wilderness ahead.

"If you keep going down the pore shaft, we should find capillaries at its base, feeding subcutaneous cells." Tyler paced the deck in front of her analytical apparatus. "We can cut through a membrane, enter the circulatory system, and begin our overall exploration of the internal territory."

"Beginning our explorations would be good," Freeth said. "The circulatory system will take us away from the xenozoans, like a superhighway."

As the *Mote*'s recovering engines took them down the crimson-hued tunnel, Tomiko gave Devlin a respectful smile. "Not sure Garrett could have pulled us out of that."

"Captain Wilcox would have gotten out and pushed the ship, if he needed to." Devlin shot her a sidelong glance and added, "Not that I'm suggesting it would have been a smart thing to do."

He kept an eye on the energy gauges of the primary power supply and finally reconnected their communications systems. "Steady yourselves. We need to send another message outside." Devlin activated the transmission, gripping his seat as the ship rocked and recoiled. "This is Team Proteus. Hello? Did anybody miss us?"

When Hunter responded, the signal distortion was worse. ". . . lost contact. Severe . . . static." The *Mote*'s windows rattled.

Slowly and clearly, Devlin described the encounter with the xenozoans, but he wasn't sure how many words got through. He heard nothing more than static in response. He looked over at Tomiko. "Don't you feel like Lewis and Clark?"

"Only without a native guide. And don't put *me* in the role of Sacajawea." Once her lasers were fully operational, she breathed a sigh of relief, leaned back, and observed the cellular scenery.

Ahead, bathed in the *Mote*'s bright searchlights, the organic shaft formed a curved barrier. "Bring us close to that tissue wall," Tyler suggested. "I want to study the organelles in a cell that isn't attacking us."

Devlin accelerated toward the pore's terminal end, where Tyler took photographs and recorded her commentary and conjectures on the cellular components and substructure inside the protoplasm. "Notice the equivalents of the endoplasmic reticulum, the lysosomes, vacuoles, tiny specks that might be ribosomes, structural proteins that might correspond to microfilaments."

The UFO expert tried to stay out of her way. "Or all of those things might be something else entirely," he said, doggedly forcing her to keep an open mind. "Form has to follow function, so they may just look similar."

"I prefer to think I know a *few* answers, Freeth. After all, they *do* give out doctorates in *my* field of expertise." Tyler looked down her nose at him. "That darkened line behind the wall must be a capillary delivering nutrients. If we push between the cells, the *Mote* can enter the circulatory system."

"Okay, let's move it. That mission clock keeps ticking down." Tomiko leaned forward. "Should I use the lasers to cut a breach?"

"No need," Tyler said quickly. "Major Devlin, if you nose the *Mote* into the joining of those two cells, we can separate the membrane."

The prow of the microscopic vessel struck the spongy wall, and Devlin added power to the impeller engines. The tiled cellular barrier split open like soft, gelatinous lips and allowed the minuscule vessel to slide through. The membranes folded around them, and the *Mote* passed through into a larger, fluid-filled passage.

Devlin looked at the handwritten card on his control panel. *Think small.*

The ship began to drift in the alien's blood plasma. The widening channel was filled with floating islands, spherical globules, some green, some translucent, others reddish-brown.

As he accelerated through the alien circulatory system, Devlin remembered how much he and Kelli had enjoyed rafting through white water rapids—the Arkansas River in Colorado, the Rio Grande in New Mexico. They both loved the rush against rocks, ducking from the cold splash, guiding their raft around obstacles. It had been too long, and Devlin decided he'd have to do it again . . . even if it meant rafting with somebody else.

Tyler pointed out blood cells as they jostled past. "I'd compare these to human hemoglobin-carrying erythrocytes, larger leukocytes, and smaller platelets."

"Let's just hope the white corpuscles don't try to eat us," Freeth said. "Like everything else around here wants to do."

The arterial tunnels were crowded with sluggish blood cells bumping along. Tyler checked the *Mote*'s velocity gauges to determine the strength of the blood current. "If the alien were dead, there'd be no flow at all. On the other hand, the blood isn't flowing sufficiently to provide the necessary nutrients to sustain life."

"Life, as we understand it," Freeth countered. "Maybe the alien was put into suspended animation, which would slow its systems down to the edge of death. Interstellar journeys take a lot of time, unless the species has warp drive or some kind of faster-than-light travel. Alien astronauts would have to put themselves into cold sleep like this. We just need to find the correct trigger to wake him up."

"If that's what we really want to do," Tomiko said, as cautious as a security officer should be. "I'd want to know a bit more about E.T.'s rap sheet first."

"A moot point," Tyler said, "since we have no idea how to accomplish such a thing. Even if Freeth is correct."

The *Mote* followed the capillary to a junction with a larger blood vessel, then plunged deeper into the fantastic world of the extraterrestrial body.

Chapter 23

The *Mote* soared through curved arteries in the alien's circulatory system. Every cell barrier, every membrane, every tissue matrix was new terrain.

Devlin used his best instincts in following an obvious route into a major blood vessel, while the onboard navigation computer kept track of every move. The ship's spotlights illuminated the plasma and a traffic jam of spherical and donut-shaped cells.

Behind him, Tyler spoke in rapid-fire sentences as she poured data into her electronic notepad and tape recorder. It would take years to distill the information from this mission, but she would have the assistance of squadrons of international scientists.

"Let me know if you see any midi-chlorians, Doc," Devlin said, tongue firmly in cheek. Tomiko jabbed him with her elbow.

"I'm not familiar with the term, Major Devlin," Tyler said.

Arnold Freeth just let out a sigh. "Maybe it's not in your area of research."

A purplish globule drifted past, paused as if inspecting the *Mote*, then drifted onward. Other cells bounced off the hull, like pedestrians jostling each other on a crowded New York street.

Farther into the circulatory system, arterial walls

became thin enough that the vessel's lights shone onto smooth muscle strands laced with bladder-like constructions and pulsing green nodules. Tall sheets of cells hung down like the walls of a maze.

Pipelines of silvery fibers branched and rebranched as they threaded through tissue. At random intervals, photons rocketed down the strands, a chemical/electrical signal passed like an Olympic torch from one cell to another.

"A nerve fiber," Tyler said. "Impulses sent to and from the alien's brain in response to stimuli."

"Nerve impulses are good. If the neurons are still firing, that means the alien is *alive*," Freeth pressed. "His body is still reacting to things."

Tyler looked up from her notes. "To a certain extent. But the low incidence of signals indicates that the alien is much deeper below consciousness than from any anesthetic I know of." She cut Freeth off before he could say anything. "I know, I know. *If* the body works like the ones I'm familiar with."

The *Mote* passed beneath a lacy arched ceiling as beautiful as any cathedral's. Red, violet, and brown nodules hung down like ornaments. Another ganglion flashed a glittering signal that vanished into the thick tissue.

Tyler went to the lab tables and searched her CD-ROM databases, scanning comparative micrographs and tissue structures for ideas. Every similarity she found, though, seemed contradictory.

Ahead, the blood vessel branched into two wide corridors, and the *Mote* followed the main flow of bobbing cells. Devlin easily dodged floating globules and accelerated into a wider artery filled with murky plasma. The fluid churned with turbulence, and glowing sparkles shone through the arterial wall. He kept them steady as the *Mote* jounced through a confluence of blood vessels.

On unsteady feet, Cynthia Tyler came forward into the cockpit. With one look at her face, Devlin could tell that she had cooked up something. "We're deep within the body core now, and we've got to explore further before we start our retreat. If we emerge from these blood vessels into other tissues, I may be able to study major organs."

Devlin watched the mission chronometer tick down. "Roger that. We lost a lot of time because of those xenozoans. Pick a membrane, any membrane."

Tyler stared at the shadowy shapes, strange colors, and weird chlorophyll-based lights activated by biochemical phosphorescence. Ahead, a cluster of shimmering translucent layers blocked one channel like a round stained-glass window. "There. That's where we should go."

Devlin diverted toward the membranous barrier. "Tomiko, if you'd be so kind as to open the door for us?" Her laser sliced a neat incision in the organic wall, splitting the cells apart far enough for the *Mote* to pass through.

Behind them, strange objects—platelet analogs— broke apart and stuck to the breach, sealing the wound. Tyler took dozens of images of the process.

Devlin guided the ship into a heavy forest of massed fibers. Clustered strands formed large caverns filled with a creamy liquid that sparkled with pearlescent light.

Inside the fluid, under the wash of bright illumination, boxy shapes glinted, knotted clusters composed of regular chains of carbon lattice-beads. Startlingly out of place, they were tiny, individual constructions, like a junkyard of automobile parts.

Artificial devices.

"Like little building blocks." Devlin moved the *Mote*'s front lights, playing the spotlight beams over the unusual objects. "Whoa, it's a buckyball grid!"

Tomiko looked sidelong at him. "Being a showoff, Marc? What's a buckyball?"

"Buckminsterfullerene, named after the physicist Buckminster Fuller. A third allotrope of carbon, more exotic than graphite or diamond. A buckyball is a sphere of carbon atoms—at least twenty, but usually sixty or more." Devlin was glad to demonstrate his expertise for a change; at least Tomiko seemed impressed. He pointed out the window. "Those . . . objects look like they've been assembled out of carbon buckyballs and buckytubes, like tinkertoys."

"What purpose could such constructions serve?" Arnold Freeth asked. "They don't look natural."

"Definitely artificial. Buckyballs are far too rare, and I don't believe they occur in nature. On Earth, anyway. I doubt they're an accident."

In front of the *Mote,* the strange devices floated motionless in the murk, all sharp angles and smooth planes, far too geometric. Tiny *machines.* He spun the impeller turbines just enough to maintain their position. "It's like a graveyard of ships. Hundreds of them."

"Even if they are manufactured devices," Dr. Tyler said, sounding uncertain, "how did they get here, inside the organic tissue? I'm sure Freeth can make up an answer."

The floating constructions were immobile, clumped together and shut down. Full of square corners and jointed limbs, nested molecular shapes like leftover pieces grabbed from mismatched model kits, they had a sinister, arachnid appearance.

Devlin noted several different designs. A nagging suspicion in the back of his mind finally led him to guess what the buckyball "bugs" must be.

"It's nanotechnology. Construction techniques on a molecular scale, fabricating devices from the atom up, guided by ultra-compact computer circuits probably made of diamond memory."

Devlin enjoyed talking in engineering terms again, after being surrounded by bio-jargon for so long. "Some university laboratories have already created prototype motors smaller than a pinhead. One rotating three-bladed fan was made of a single molecule, powered by chemical energy. Back in 1989 researchers rearranged thirty-five xenon atoms to form the letters IBM. We've come a long way since then."

Tomiko groaned. "Corporate sponsorship on a microscopic level."

"I've seen theoretical designs for planetary gears and bearings and universal joints made entirely of hydrocarbon molecules. Nobody's been able to build them yet, though. At least, not on Earth." He directed the ship's bright spotlights onto the jumbled constructions. "But maybe our aliens have already achieved functional nanotechnology."

The dormant machines had articulated molecular-lattice armatures, grasping claws, and tools connected to body cores that contained ultra-small integrated circuits, much more compact than the ULSI chip Tomiko, Pirov, and Wilcox had explored that morning.

"Maybe they're switched off," Freeth said. "Or just dormant, like the rest of the alien."

"Could those machines generate the electromagnetic interference that's messing up our communications?" Tomiko asked.

"Affirmative." Devlin's brow creased as his mind worked to understand how the devices functioned. "That nanotech would be as much of a breakthrough in our electronics technology as your observations will be in human medicine, Doc. Command decision: Tomiko and I are going to suit up and go outside to make a closer inspection."

Devlin locked down the *Mote*'s systems and strode to the compartment where the environment suits were stored. Tomiko practically leaped from her chair, ready to go. She shot her anchor harpoons into the nearest membrane wall and tethered the vessel in place.

"Sorry, Doc," Devlin said as he passed Tyler's seat. "Now it's time for *my* expertise."

"But why are you two going?" Freeth's voice was tinged with concern. "Not that I'm volunteering, believe me."

Devlin smiled cryptically at him. "Because, Mr. Freeth, Tomiko and I are the ones who wear the red shirts."

Tyler looked at them strangely. "What do you mean? Neither of you is wearing red."

Freeth rolled his eyes, showing a mixture of alarm and humor. "I'll explain while they suit up."

Chapter 24

Inside the *Mote*'s suit locker hung four slick exploration garments. Director Hunter had required one for each crew member, although in any scenario that forced everyone to suit up and abandon ship, Devlin figured that their best alternative would be to bend over and kiss their butts good-bye.

Tomiko took out the slimmest garment for herself, then handed a larger one to Devlin, teasing. "Just for you, a workman-like coverall designed for engineers and lumberjacks."

"Roger that. You've got me pegged—as long as it has plenty of pockets." Devlin groaned inwardly. Had it been so long since he'd tried to flirt with anybody? He didn't even remember how to do it.

He knew Tomiko must have had her share of boyfriends. Such an intelligent and beautiful woman would certainly have plenty of admirers. He supposed she found Garrett Wilcox fun, sometimes . . . but the cocky pilot had about as much depth as a film of oil on asphalt. She needed a man who was interesting enough to be her match.

As he watched Tomiko slither (he could think of no other word for it) into her silvery suit, Kelli's snapshot seemed to be eyeing him from the cockpit panel. He didn't think she'd disapprove after all this time.

But he was on duty. Time enough to let his imagination run wild later. Maybe. After Team Proteus accomplished the mission objectives.

Devlin climbed into his suit, yanking the tough but flexible fabric over his uniform. The expedition garment was a cross between a scuba-diving outfit and a spacesuit. Intelligent fiber threads sensed his body temperature, his pulse, his blood pressure. The suit could trigger heaters or release coolants to keep him as comfortable as a miniaturized human being could be.

He pulled the snug hood over his unruly dark hair, attached goggles and breathing apparatus. He flexed his arms, tugged on the gloves and wiggled his fingers. He adjusted the life monitors and powerpack at his waist, then strapped on his toolkit, just in case. When he assisted Tomiko in checking her suit, he noticed how well it fit her curves, but didn't dare comment.

Through the suit radio, Tomiko's voice was rich and clear in his ears. "Okay, let's go look at some nanocritters."

"Nanocritters?"

Behind the goggles, her dark eyes crinkled; the curve of her lips was barely visible above the breathing apparatus. "They're smaller than a micron, Marc. I don't want to dignify them with some formal-sounding word." She pushed a button, and the airlock door slid aside.

Pantomiming a gentleman's bow, he gestured for Tomiko to enter the cramped chamber. Egress was via a crude mechanism, like the hatch in an old U-boat. Devlin preferred simple things that were easy to fix, rather than increasingly complicated systems that had few advantages, but broke down more often. He got into the small chamber with her.

"Not much bigger than a telephone booth," Tomiko said as she sealed the door.

He reached down and undogged the hatch. "Ready to get your feet wet?" When the seal breached, external fluid gushed inside, filling the tube.

"That's usually the way to start an important job."

Standing next to Tomiko, Devlin thought longingly of when he and Kelli had taken long, slow showers together. Perhaps his hormones should have miniaturized as well. He forced himself to concentrate on the controls in front of him.

The airlock chamber filled, the fluid level rising past knees, waists, and then over their heads. When the alien liquid reached equilibrium in the cramped chamber, Devlin dropped down and swam out of the *Mote*.

Ahead, the junkpile of nanomachines waited for him.

With languid strokes, Tomiko swam past while he reversed and tugged the hatch back into place. Somewhat awkwardly at first, Devlin paddled through the viscous bath, acclimating himself to the new environment.

Tomiko glided beside him, making him feel clumsy. "Come on, Marc. We need to do this and be back inside. The clock is ticking." She swam ahead, kicking powerfully. "Catch me."

The fluid around them felt thicker than he had expected, with strange, unpredictable currents. When he tried to move, he didn't go precisely in the direction he anticipated. "Takes some getting used to."

Showing off, Tomiko did a graceful somersault. "Must be atomic effects, Van der Waals forces, maybe molecular attraction, and let's not forget the ever-popular Brownian motion."

Devlin looked curiously into her faceplate. He could feel coolants circulating through the snug fabric he wore, the buffet of fluid molecules fizzing against his suit with random atomic motion. "That's a pretty sophisticated analysis for a muscle-minded security specialist."

Her coy laugh came over the line-of-sight radio link. "Don't tell anybody that I'm smarter than I let on. Got to keep up my image." With a slow-motion gesture, she pointed a gloved hand toward the cluster of nanocritters still some distance away. "How far before we separate from *Mote*'s miniaturization field?"

Devlin turned away from the ship and looked toward the motionless devices constructed of fullerene lattices and nanogears, perhaps as many as a hundred of them lined up like cars in a parking lot.

"The subsidiary field generators on our suitpacks keep us linked for quite a distance. When we remain part of the field, we're in our own relative spatial anomaly, confined in this size." He spread his arms, then lost his orientation and had to kick his feet furiously to return himself to an upright position.

A transmission came from the ship. Arnold Freeth sounded very concerned, though perhaps it was only uneasiness at being left alone with Cynthia Tyler. "Are you both all right out there? We've got only two and a half hours left."

Though the two had gone only ten shiplengths from the *Mote*, heavy static crackled through Freeth's transmission. Devlin could hear a dull thrumming in his ear speakers, an undulating pattern just at the edge of the system's pickup ability.

"On our way, Mr. Freeth." The more Devlin thought about it, the more convinced he was that

the interference came from those dormant but still
functional mechanical devices. Perhaps the background signal was a standard carrier wave or a
standby transmission.

Stroking his way forward, Devlin approached the
geometric shapes with caution. Tomiko fanned her
hands and feet to maintain her position, coiled and
wary, prepared to lash out if necessary. If the nanocritters posed any threat, she looked ready to take
them apart using only her gloved hands.

Each machine was half the size of the *Mote*. The
angles were squared off and clumsy looking, functional rather than aesthetic. Devlin recognized the
stacked assembly of spherical baskets, tubes, toruses,
and spindles, interlinked hexagonal graphite grids
that formed a wire-frame skeleton for these
machines.

"Look at the complexity. The design is awesome."
Nested buckytubes contained metal atoms, forming
circuits that were the equivalents of nerve fibers;
other strands looked like muscles. He had heard that,
depending on the direction a carbon sheet was rolled
into a buckytube, the components could exhibit either semiconducting or metallic properties.

Interlocking pistons and nanogears comprised the
mechanical parts, simple clockwork mechanisms that
turned and moved using hydraulic power, articulated joints that bent crablike arms. Each component
was made up of hydrocarbons and metals, impurities
added for specific properties, one atom at a time. The
gear teeth were probably made of benzene, the claw
tips of pyridine.

Devlin scrutinized the range of machines with an
engineer's eye. He saw the same basic body core,
graced with more than one type of manipulative apparatus. Some of the claw arms were large and bulky;
others branched out and got smaller and smaller

until they became feathery grasping digits. "I think each of these devices was designed for a specific purpose."

On such a small scale, the machines would have to operate on straightforward mechanical principles. They reminded him of Victorian contraptions powered not by steam engines but by microscopic atomic batteries, which the nanocritter could convert into usable kinetic energy.

"But for what?" Tomiko asked. "Why are they here, and why are they all shut down?"

"I'm still working on that part." He took a deep breath from his respirator, then swam forward, pulling the toolkit from his hip. "I'm going to tinker a bit."

"See if you can get one of those things to make me a cappuccino."

"It'd have to be a very small cup."

"In that case, make it an espresso."

The closest nanomachine did not react to his presence. Devlin circled, and reached out slowly, carefully, until his fingers touched the side wall composed of carbon lattices. It was like a machine built out of macramé. Through the thin flexible gloves, he ran his fingers along the hull. The giant fullerene molecules seemed strange and insubstantial.

"The carbon grid has a lot of metal inclusions— iron atoms, maybe, or other elements added for conductive properties." He pushed, and the side wall buckled slightly, buckytubes bending and adjusting. The front intake chute was a shovel-like opening through which the nanocritter could "eat" raw materials.

He flexed one of the articulated buckytube arms, which swiveled on a ball joint. Pistons and rolling gears moved like contracting muscles. He shifted the components, prying open side walls to study how the engine was put together. "A thermal power source . . . exhaust-heat radiator fins." He had no idea what to call the strange curved shapes, bulbs and spheres like internal organs, inside the belly of the nanomachine.

The bottom surface of the casing was an embroidery of electronic paths on a thin wafer of hard crystal. "A self-patterned circuit board, much denser than anything we've been able to achieve. I think it's a diamond memory chip, layered with fluorine and hydrogen molecules." Tiny whiskers of carbon tipped with pyridine were raised, as if poised to read data imprinted on the crystal circuit.

Tomiko swam under the nanocritter to see the patterned brain. "Stop drooling, Marc. We're on a tight schedule."

"Roger that. Five more minutes." Devlin contemplated the nanocritter's intake chute, the self-patterned circuit board, the processing machinery. "I bet it has the capability to gather resources and build a copy of itself. Looks like it can imprint a new circuit board and assemble an identical offspring. At this scale, a nanomachine could run around and pick a few molecules at a time, scooping them up with atomic-force apparatus."

Judging from the shape of another component atop the wire-frame chassis, Devlin figured it might be some kind of beacon, a signal emitter and receiver. On such a small scale, though, the generator would be nearly the size of the transmission wavelength itself.

Curious and perplexed, he crawled over the exoskeleton to determine just how much power remained in the dormant device. The signal generator was connected to the power source, large mechanical circuit breakers, and metal lines with closeable gaps, like crude knife switches. He could hear the throbbing standby signal in his ears, much louder now that he was in among the alien devices.

"Careful, Marc. Don't know what these components do."

"Now you're sounding as overprotective as Felix. It's just a simple machine." Moving sluggishly in the fluid, he unsealed his toolkit to withdraw a screwdriver, intending to use it as a prybar or a probe. "Let's see what makes you tick." He used the long end of the screwdriver to prod the ultra-small components, tracing the circuit paths in the complex self-replicating brain systems. He went back to the knife switch next to the signal generator and studied how the component was connected to the power source. "Pretty straightforward."

"Don't get cocky, Marc. I don't want another Wilcox on my hands."

He waved her away. "I know what I'm doing . . . I think."

With just the briefest of contacts, Devlin touched the long end of the screwdriver across the gap in the metal connecting leads, effectively closing the switch. A bright blue spark jumped the gap; on an electron scale, it was an incredibly small fibrillation.

The nanocritter's metal connector clicked into place, holding the circuit closed.

Devlin yanked the tool away, but the connection had been made. The tiny electric arc crackled. Fine whiskers of pyridine and carbon moved, like the fingers of a blind man reading the Braille of fluorine and hydrogen molecules on the diamond memory wafer.

Startled, Devlin kicked backward, careful not to drop the screwdriver.

Another spark connected, and a second switch closed, like a falling line of dominoes. Sensor lights flashed inside the mosaic grid of the nanomachine frame, glowing like eyes. The manipulator arms began to move.

"I don't think you were supposed to do that," Tomiko said.

The chain of awakening circuits continued to build. With a jolt, the nanocritter twitched. Its mechanical pistons and arms jittered as power surged through the linkages.

As the nanosystems surged to full readiness, the dull background tone became a powerful burst of noise, a deep encoded pattern of instructions. The hammering signal undulated in his ears, rising to a skull-shattering peak before warbling down in complicated melodies and octaves. It sounded like a fog-horn through Devlin's helmet radio.

The other nanocritters began to vibrate, glow, stir.

"Whoa, you don't actually want me to go back and turn it off?" Devlin asked. "Do you?"

"Won't do any good. That thing already sent out a wake-up call." Tomiko spun around in the fluid. "The other machines are activated now."

Layer upon layer of transmissions echoed in his head, not just from the one nanomachine, but from others. Many others.

Arnold Freeth sent a message at such high volume that he broke through even the head-crushing signal. "What just happened? What did you do out there? Are you safe?"

"Affirmative. We're both . . . intact," Devlin said. "But I think we'd better get back inside the ship. Right now."

The clustered nanomachines flexed their segmented arms. They oriented their sensors and prepared for whatever mysterious mission lay inside their programming.

"So much for a non-intrusive exploration." He and Tomiko swam forward, racing for the ship's external hatch as if microscopic sharks were chasing them. "I think our mission just got a little more complicated." Devlin cranked open the hatch, and they plunged back into the refuge of the *Mote*.

The nanomachines began to move.

Chapter 25

He couldn't touch the alien directly. His assignment was just to stand and wait and watch, but even so, Rajid Sujatha was proud to be part of the mission.

Team Proteus had only two-and-a-half more hours to map the wilderness of the extraterrestrial body. Holding his breath to hear better inside his anti-contamination suit, he had listened to Major Devlin's intermittent progress reports, though static washed out many of his words.

While Dr. Pirov busied himself rearranging the various medical instruments on their trays, trying to keep busy, Sujatha pressed his gloved fingertips against the curved glassy material of the lifepod window. How he wished he could communicate with the being inside. *Are you a lonesome traveler? An exile? An ambassador? Or were you just lost?*

He never tired of looking at the smooth skin, the large sleeping eyes, the strange features. Through the misted capsule windows, he imagined what lay beyond the tantalizing glimpses. The alien looked so placid, so peaceful. . . .

Suddenly, the lifepod vibrated and hummed. A hiss of vented gas burst through an unseen crack.

Sujatha jerked his hands away. His heart leaped as he staggered backward. "Dr. Pirov! Come and look at this, please." He raised his voice into the suit microphone. "Director Hunter, sir, observe the alien's lifepod."

Pirov whirled, his watery and bloodshot eyes suddenly alert. A sequence of glowing lights and sparkling pathways appeared along the opaque side walls of the container. Another crack opened; more gas vented. Reddish illumination shimmered from deep within the pod.

Outside, everyone reacted quickly. Deputy Foreign Minister Garamov rose to his feet in dismay, fearing that his prize had been damaged. Congressman Durston glanced around as if searching for someone to blame.

Director Hunter scanned the readings on the auxiliary control panels in the VIP observation deck. He flicked on the intercom. "Did either of you trigger any of the systems?"

"Not me, sir," Pirov said. "I was not close. I touched nothing." The Russian pressed down on the lid of the activating lifepod, then ran his gloved fingers over the vibrating surface. His pale blue eyes brightened with alarm, like ice chips sparkling in sudden sunlight. "I do not believe we can turn it off."

Sujatha raised both of his gloved hands. "I also activated no controls, sir. I do not know what caused the change." With all the chamber's fail-safes, backup seals, and anti-contamination lockouts, evacuation was not an option for them. He and Pirov were trapped inside with the extraterrestrial being . . . no matter what happened next.

Pirov leaned closer, searching for visible changes within the pod. "Maybe Team Proteus did something from inside."

A new droning sound came from the capsule's interior, growing louder. Previously unseen slits appeared, along with control markings like illuminated glyphs of an incomprehensible language. Indecipherable phosphors blinked along the sides, shimmering from within the metal.

Pulses strobed quicker, blinking on and off. Steam curled out of broken seals. The gaps cracked wider, as if the pod were a cocoon ready to split open.

Sujatha knew in his heart what was happening. His awed whisper went unheard in the commotion of the control room. "It is waking up."

Hunter nudged a set of controls and barked orders at his communications specialists. "See if you can reestablish contact with Major Devlin inside. Now." The members of Team Proteus had been fully aware of the risks involved, but he couldn't bear the thought of losing the crew. Especially not Marc.

He realized that neither Sujatha nor Pirov had done anything to trigger the change. But how could the *Mote*, no larger than a cell inside the alien's body, have caused such a dramatic change on a macro scale?

Beside him, Garamov and the congressman spoke with excitement to see something happen after staring at the motionless alien for so long. The Russian's long, nicotine-stained fingers fidgeted, as if twitching for a cigarette.

Durston's face hardened and his voice grew deeper, reflecting the no-nonsense gruffness that had gotten him elected. "Director Hunter, remember we're interested in that capsule technology as well as the alien specimen itself. The electronics and computer controls within such a device could offer immeasurable advancement to human technology." Durston's constituents included numerous high-tech Silicon Valley firms. "To be shared with the Russians, of course."

Garamov gave him a look filled with irony. "How generous."

"We're aware of that, Congressman," Hunter said. "Major Devlin is an excellent engineer. Once he returns from this mission, I intend to assign him the task of studying the capsule."

After the miniaturized mission, he hoped Garamov would let them have an additional hour before he dragged the lifepod away and returned it to Russian authorities. The Director would bring in other engineers and specialists, whoever he could find on short notice. Marc probably would complain about having too many people crowded around the capsule, where they could bump elbows and risk damaging the delicate systems.

The humming lifepod reached a crescendo. Both Pirov and Sujatha stepped back, shielding their faceplates as the internal illumination turned an electric green, then dazzling yellow. The capsule's control markings flashed in a frenzy. The throbbing grew louder and louder.

Then all the lights vanished, fading into the alien metal and leaving no mark. The still-closed armored pod became black and silent, as if burnt out.

Durston leaned forward in his chair. "Did it break down?"

Below, Pirov pushed forward like a child inspecting a curious gift. "I believe it is just—"

With a loud hiss and an explosive pop of decompression, the lifepod split wide open. The curved top rose part way up with a smooth motion like the lid of a vampire's coffin at dusk. Gouts of cold white vapor poured down the capsule walls and pooled on the floor.

Automatic security alarms blared inside the underground facility. Rotating amber lights flashed in the corridors. Guards raced into position. Scientists studied their monitors and waited.

Hunter found it all very distracting. "What do you see?"

"Nothing yet, Director, sir." Sujatha wiped condensation off his faceplate and peered into the gaping pod. "Just a moment."

The steam faded. The lifepod lid paused for pressure to equalize as the last wisps of unearthly atmosphere escaped; then the heavy capsule cover slid to one side, revealing the prone form of the gray-skinned extraterrestrial. The alien astronaut remained motionless, still not awake, dead to all appearances. Waiting to be inspected.

"Sleeping Beauty from Mars," Congressman Durston said.

Though protected in their anti-contamination garb, Pirov and Sujatha still hung back. The Bengali doctor heaved an audible sigh over the intercom. "Now you and I must cycle through the full decontamination routines before we can leave. This entire chamber will have to be purged and cleaned."

"I believe it will be at least a day before we are allowed to exit," Pirov said, dismayed at the prospect of the delay, but eager to study the alien.

Sujatha patted the old man's shoulder in commiseration. "I had been scheduled for furlough this evening. I will miss going back to see my daughters, but we must not allow such a magnificent opportunity to pass us by."

From the chair to Hunter's right, Vasili Garamov watched the open lifepod intently, his eyes flashing, wheels turning in his mind. Finally, he reached a decision. "There is now no need to avoid performing a gross body analysis, Director. We should consider having your doctors study what they can."

Now even the congressman looked excited. "Consider it? The capsule's open, and the alien's just lying there. Take a few samples, skin scrapings, draw some blood. Why not? What can it harm?"

Hunter pursed his lips, trying to imagine any negative consequences that might come from intrusive study. "We can't be sure, Congressman."

The Deputy Foreign Minister touched his fingers to the pack of cigarettes in his pocket, as if comforted by their mere presence. "I suggest we let Dr. Pirov study the body, the musculature, the sensory organs. Due to the politics of this situation, it might be more acceptable to have a Russian perform the analysis, even if he is an émigré. It will help my explanations later."

"Maybe we should call in a few more experts," Durston said. "We can assemble an international team, so we don't step on anybody's toes. It might take a few days, though."

"We will not wait a few days, Congressman," Garamov said, his voice sharp. "Please, you must understand the sensitivity—"

Hunter interrupted, "I remind both of you gentlemen that with the lifepod open now, our decontamination problem has increased a hundredfold. Bringing new scientists inside would be impossible at this point. Drs. Pirov and Sujatha are eminent medical specialists. Let's allow them to conduct a preliminary exterior study now, completely noninvasive."

"That would be preferable," Garamov said; he already looked at a loss as to how he could salvage the situation. "If we bring in more people, the chances increase that information will leak to the general public. I do not wish it widely known that Russian fighter jets are in the habit of shooting down possibly peaceful alien spacecraft."

Durston gave a ponderous nod. "All right, why

waste time? So long as we don't begin the complete autopsy until we bring together a full international team."

"Autopsy?" Hunter didn't even try to cover his surprise. "We haven't yet determined if the creature is alive or dead."

Durston waved his hand dismissively.

Hunter reached forward to open a direct channel into the containment room. "Dr. Pirov, you are in charge. Do as thorough an examination as you can with minimal effect to the alien. Don't leave any marks, not even any fingerprints."

From behind his faceplate, Pirov looked at Sujatha with an oddly worried expression, but he understood and acknowledged. The two picked up their instruments and prepared to work on the alien body.

The Bengali doctor grinned at Pirov. "Certainly, this will be remembered as the crowning achievement of our careers."

Chapter 26

Awash in pearlescent nutrient fluid, the once-dormant nanomachines continued to self-activate, swarming like a nest of angry wasps. As signals thundered through the electromagnetic spectrum, additional clusters of machines throughout the alien's body awakened.

The devices moved about, priming their minuscule mechanical systems. Then, following their programming, they began to explore. Something about their search implied hunger and ruthlessness. Devlin put on another burst of speed.

After tugging Tomiko through the hatch, he sealed the lid at his feet. Foregoing the usual double-checks and tests, he pumped the liquid out of the airlock chamber. Within two minutes, the two emerged dripping into the main cabin, grabbing towels to wipe themselves off.

"What did you do out there, Major Devlin?" Dr. Tyler said, rushing forward. "I don't like the looks of this at all."

Arnold Freeth turned from the observation window, blinking rapidly. "Check out that frenzied motion! You really riled those machines."

Outside, the blocky devices behaved like maddened ants, swirling in circles. Machines came together, touched sensor pads to each other, and exchanged information with a crackle of blue energy at contact points; they altered programming on their diamond-memory wafers, shared stored data.

Tomiko narrowed her dark eyes. "Looks like an army regrouping, reconnoitering . . . preparing for an invasion."

In the cockpit, the ship's comm system was a shrieking nightmare of signals, as if the *Mote* were having some kind of a seizure. Underlying it all came a thunderous carrier wave, the standby signal emitted by the tiny machines, which must have been blocking all outside scanning beams. The electromagnetic storm had turned into a hurricane.

Devlin sprinted toward his pilot seat. Wincing, he covered his ears to muffle the undulating feedback until he managed to turn down the speaker volume, muffling the migraine-inducing throbs to a dull whisper.

"Whew, that's a relief."

"Felix is probably having heartburn right now," Tomiko said.

Four nanocritters in the cluster, now fully programmed and functional, spun about like water fleas, then sped off through the pearly fluid. Scouts? Sentries? Couriers? They disappeared into the membrane walls and followed the sparks of a ganglion.

Fascinated and horrified at what he was seeing, Devlin wondered what sort of system could have created such sophisticated microscopic machines—and to what purpose. Through the cockpit window, he watched another one putter toward the tissue walls, tunnel its way through, and disappear into the alien's body cavity.

As she slipped into the copilot's seat, Tomiko tossed back her sweat-streaked black hair, which was somewhat flattened after being tucked into her exploration suit hood. "So what do you think they're going to do? Are they a threat?" She sounded almost hopeful.

"Engineers only know *how* things work, Tomiko. Ask a psychologist for intentions and motivations." He fiddled with the comm system again and received an unpleasant squelch of static. "I'm going to signal Project Proteus, but I'll need to use a lot of power to get through this noise." He bent over the amplifiers and transmission systems.

Devlin dictated a short summary of what they'd encountered, ready to go out in a single burst. No time for rambling conversations. "Everybody hold on for a second. There'll be a power drop, and we may lose a bit of stability." Without waiting for Tyler or Freeth to acknowledge, he diverted energy from the batteries and generators. "This is our message in a bottle. Let's hope it washes up on some friendly shore." His communications burst screamed out like a gammawave comet, an information packet that should have plowed clear of the nano-jamming signals.

He kept his fingers crossed.

The *Mote* lurched as its stabilizers went offline. The deck tilted, and Devlin slid halfway out of his seat toward Tomiko's lap. She raised her eyebrows, as if implying he'd meant to do that.

Outside, the nanocritters reacted to the signal like hornets from a jostled nest.

A dozen of the machines lined up in front of the *Mote*, as if forming a security cordon. Tiny lights blinked in their mechanical bodies, a flurry of hungrily curious sensor eyes gathering data. Grasping claws tipped with benzene molecular teeth flexed and clicked at the end of fullerene-rod arms. Sparks flew from circuit path to circuit path across a densely patterned diamond memory wafer, as if they were considering a question . . . or deciding whether to attack.

"*Somebody* heard your message, Marc," Tomiko said. "Must have sounded like an air-raid siren to them."

The nanocritters hovered like a gang of bullies rolling up their sleeves and ready to do some damage. Aggressively curious, the lead nanomachine crept forward, extending whisker probes with pyridine-molecule sensors. It extended a sharp cutting apparatus at the end of a carbon-matrix arm.

"I'm not sure we should provoke them." Devlin powered up the *Mote*'s impellers and swiftly rotated the vessel away from the line of machines in the pearly fluid. "Let's go explore somewhere else."

"No argument from me." Tomiko touched the weapons controls, reassuring herself that the laser cannons were ready to fire. "No telling what they might do."

The *Mote* streaked away from the agitated machines.

Startled by the ship's sudden retreat, the nanocritters spun about like whirligigs. Two spurted forward to catch the miniaturized vessel, but Devlin accelerated blindly away, banking and curving without waiting to see what they would do next.

Tyler stumbled as she rushed from the laboratory modules to the cockpit. "If we get back into a blood vessel and follow it to a large vein or artery, we'll make much better time away from these machines."

"Getting away is good," Freeth said. "See, Dr. Tyler? We can agree on some things."

"Affirmative." Devlin headed straight for the cell wall ahead of them. Behind, the nanocritters began to close the distance. "Tomiko, if you'd be so kind?"

She sliced a cellular seam with her lasers, and the *Mote* dove through the rubbery organic curtain, split-

ting the tiled chains of cells that held the wall together. The ship jostled into the graceful circulatory
flow among spherical and disk-shaped blood cells.
"Home free."

Freeth joined them in the crowded cockpit, his
mousy-brown hair tousled, his freckled face flushed.
"We're only home free if we don't run into any other
clusters of those nanocritters."

Dr. Tyler looked skeptical again. "How many
could there be?"

With impellers roaring, the *Mote* surged forward
as the capillary widened into a larger blood vessel.
In the arterial stream, they saw no further sign of
tiny machines, though the jamming signals remained omnipresent.

"Two hours left," Devlin said. He didn't think they
had seen the last of the tiny devices. "Let's finish
what we came to do and get out of this alien's body."

Chapter 27

Piloting the ship faster than the flow of blood, Devlin careened into indigo and crimson spherical cells. The flexible globules bounced against the solid hull with wet-sounding thuds, then recoiled into the soft arterial walls.

It felt like cruising with a powerful motorboat through a slow-moving biological Amazon. This stream would carry them toward the alien's primary organs—and away from the mysterious nanomachines. Other than that, Devlin had no idea where they were going.

"That was weird," Freeth said.

"It's an *alien*, remember?" Tyler said sarcastically.

The UFO expert smiled with a moment of self-deprecation. "Thank you for reminding me."

After following the main channel for several minutes, the blood vessel disgorged them into a lumpy forest of tissue, foaming gelatinous bubbles and spheres that extended on branches like rampant fungus growths in a complex cave. Under the glow of the ship's front spotlights, the place looked like an eerie wonderland.

"The lungs! Now we're getting somewhere." Tyler tapped the observation window. "Those nodules must be alveoli, tiny sacks filled with oxygen or carbon dioxide."

"Or whatever the alien breathed on its own world," Freeth said.

Tyler ignored him. "Capillaries touch the alveoli, and gas exchange occurs through the membrane barrier, where blood cells absorb oxygen and deposit the waste product of cellular respiration, which is then exhaled through the mouth or nose."

Frustrated, Freeth chided her again, showing his own impatience. "We don't *know* any of that. Please try to think beyond the human model. For example, fish breathe through gills that take in dissolved oxygen from circulating water. Insects don't even have lungs. Jellyfish and earthworms have no respiratory systems at all—their cells breathe directly through the skin. And every one of those diverse examples evolved right here on Earth. Believe me, this extraterrestrial could be vastly different from what you're hypothesizing."

"Maybe you've got a point, Freeth," Tyler admitted, as if plucking a splinter from her thumb. She pondered the alveolar jungle outside the window. "It's subtle, but there's already something strikingly unusual here. In a human body, blood is pumped through the heart first and then into the lungs, where it receives oxygen before being routed back to the heart for distribution through the arterial system."

Freeth brightened as he understood the implications. "And we've reached the lungs without finding any sort of blood-pumping chamber first. Now there's a major difference in anatomy. On the other hand, who says extraterrestrials have to follow the same blueprint?"

"Thank you for continuing to point that out." Tyler regarded him coldly, annoyed at his constant reassessments of her conclusions. "Tell me, what would your explanation be, Freeth? I'm sure you could publish it in *True UFO Experiences*, or some equally respectable journal."

He didn't rise to the bait. "Well . . . what if the alien doesn't have a single central heart pump, but maybe half a dozen substations, distributed at strategic points throughout the body?" Eyes bright, Freeth was on a roll now. "Redundant backups. Think of it—if a human gets shot in the heart, he's dead. But with distributed pumping stations, the alien could lose one, maybe even a couple of hearts, and still survive."

Tyler looked at the UFO expert as if he'd gone mad.

"Got to admit, it makes engineering sense, Doc," Devlin said from the cockpit, as the ship drifted among the curved alveolar bubbles. "I think you should call them Freeth Pumping Modules."

Finally, in a brusque tone, Cynthia Tyler said, "I suppose it's possible. I'll consider adding the conjecture as a footnote to one of my papers."

As the vessel picked a route through the spongy mass of lung tissue, Tyler returned to her analytical station. "Major Devlin, we've already got a breakdown of the atmospheric composition we encountered when we first entered the lifepod. Would it be possible to fire our sampling snorkel into one of these alveoli? That way I can run a comparative analysis."

They passed a darkened necklace of pinkish spheres, then a group clustered like grapes. As Devlin maneuvered close to the crowded gaseous balloons, Tyler prepped her mass spectrograph. "If we sample *used* air from within the lungs, I can determine how the alien metabolizes what it breathes, which elements it uses, which it discards as exhaust."

Aiming carefully, Tomiko shot the sampling snorkel at the grape cluster. The flexible tube spun out, jiggling with random motion, and punctured a thin wall. She tugged on the hose, making sure it had penetrated firmly.

Pointedly left out of the scientific work, Freeth sank deep into thought, his chin in his hands. His brow furrowed and his fingers moved as he silently ticked off possibilities to himself.

"Mr. Freeth, you look like something profound is on the tip of your tongue," Devlin said.

"I'm trying to decide if the alien could have intentionally implanted those nanomachines within its own body, or if they're an outside infestation." He raised a finger. "Just look at the evidence. Remember those pedicels on the skin and how ferociously they attacked us? The *Mote* isn't much bigger than those nanomachines. What if the pedicels are this species' biological defenses against an outside nano-invasion?"

Tomiko operated pumps to draw a sample of air into a sealed receptacle, deflating one of the alveoli. The sound of whispering wind echoed through the enclosed ship. "Here you go, Dr. T."

"Are you suggesting those devices are *infectious machines*?" Tyler said, looking up from calibrating the mass spectrograph. "Freeth, you're getting carried away with your imagination."

"No, I'm not. Remember how the xenozoans came after us, too? Our ship couldn't *possibly* be a food source for a microorganism, yet they still attacked. Why?" He stood up. "What if those pedicels were developed to prevent foreign nanomachines from infecting the alien's body? And maybe the xenozoans are a second line of defense against anything that manages to get through."

"Whoa, you're painting a pretty grim picture of our alien's home world, Mr. Freeth," Devlin said. "I don't think I'd want to visit there."

"Such natural defenses would take thousands of years to develop," Tyler said. "Impossible."

"Still doesn't explain the nanocritters already inside, and why they were dormant . . . until Major Devlin goosed them." Tomiko worked to detach the sampling snorkel and reeled it back in using the ship's automated systems.

Tyler looked down at the mass spectrograph and began her analysis.

Freeth cleared his throat. "Well, if the alien *intentionally* planted the devices inside its cellular structures, it must have had a reason for doing it." He grew more animated as his ideas became more preposterous. "Given sufficiently sophisticated nanotechnology, a species would be able to do gene splicing on themselves . . . call it micro-remodeling, or interior decorating. After reprogramming their DNA to any new pattern, they could tailor their bodies to whatever standards of beauty or strength they prefer. They could prevent deterioration from aging. They could delete an appendix or facial whiskers or funny-shaped earlobes . . . even alter sexual organs or eliminate gender differences."

"Some of us like the gender differences," Tomiko said.

Tyler shook her head in exasperation. "Freeth, where do you get such strange ideas?"

"You invited him along for his strange ideas, Doc," Devlin pointed out, and she didn't look pleased about the reminder.

Freeth paid no attention to her scorn, letting it run off him just like the words of any heckler on any talk show where he'd appeared. "In my line of work, Dr. Tyler, I'm accustomed to using my imagination instead of being trapped by what I've memorized from biology books. Believe me, if you're going to investigate extraterrestrials, you need to be willing to see not just what you already know, but what is *possible*." He drew himself tall. "Maybe you should try reading science fiction instead of just dry medical journals for a change."

Devlin spun the impellers in reverse and took the *Mote* back into the capillaries. "You'll have to do your atmospheric analysis on the fly, Doc. We're moving on."

Chapter 28

If Dr. Sergei Pirov had been taking written notes, he would have punctuated every sentence with an exclamation point. Despite his personal uncertainty and trembling hands, his concentration never wavered from the task before him once he began touching the alien body.

He owed too much to Director Hunter and to Deputy Foreign Minister Garamov—both of whom were watching now—to do less than his best work.

The extraterrestrial lay uncovered inside its open lifepod, the most amazing specimen Pirov had ever seen. He rattled off observations into the suit microphone that were picked up and captured on audio tape.

Sujatha moved close to him, taking high-resolution photographs of every square centimeter of the unearthly figure. Intent and methodical, the Bengali doctor worked his way lower, down the torso to the exposed pelvic area. "Most unusual. Look, Dr. Pirov, sir—this creature appears to have no genitalia, no reproductive organs whatsoever. At least not where we would expect them to be located."

"That is impossible." Pirov moved to get a closer look at the smooth patch of skin between the alien's spindly legs. "But . . . every higher-order being has sexual development."

"Perhaps the species reproduces by other means." Sujatha raised his bushy eyebrows. "By budding? Or cloning? Or perhaps this is a sterile mule, an engineered organism designed specifically for space travel."

"Yes, perhaps. Perhaps." Pirov could feel an ache in his back and neck, a weary tremor in his fingers. "And where are the excretory outlets? No creature would evolve naturally along these lines." This fact alone would be fodder for numerous scientific debates. "How can we hope to explain it all in only a few hours?" He bit back a groan of disappointment. "Come, let us learn what we can."

Gathering the nerve to poke and prod further, Pirov assessed the muscle tone, the texture of the grayish skin. He touched the wide eyelids, the smooth skin over the cranium, then separated the lips to reveal tiny round teeth like kernels of corn. "No incisors, no canine teeth. Our visitor appears to be a vegetarian."

He felt overwhelmed by how much there remained to do, how much he needed to see. At the same time, he wanted to be back in his laboratory office, studying the results of the analyses. As he grew older, Pirov preferred interpreting data to obtaining it in the first place.

Sujatha applied an electrode thermocouple to the skin. "Body temperature is sixty degrees Fahrenheit."

Pirov looked up from the facial sensory organs. "Not likely its normal range. Now that the pod has opened, the specimen is equalizing with the ambient environment. I do not expect it to remain at the same temperature."

He counted the alien's fingers (four on each hand) and toes (three, in a streamlined hooflike configuration). He examined the tendons in the thin neck, running his fingers along the jawline.

The Bengali doctor continued to take readings at probe points around the slender body. "Most unusual. The body temperature appears to be rising faster than can be explained by simple warmth from the room." He showed Pirov the thermocouple screen. "Something is causing it to heat up. From within."

The Russian ran his thick gloves along the rubbery skin, trying to pick up details. "I wonder what is going on inside there . . ."

With a sense of wonder that overwhelmed even his anxiety about the political fallout from his decisions, the Russian Deputy Foreign Minister watched the succession of images, close-ups, and large-scale anatomy diagrams compiled by Pirov and Sujatha.

Showing considerably less interest, Congressman Durston puckered his lips into a scowl and scratched his squarish beard. "Director Hunter, if that alien should awaken and attack us, what are your defensive options here in the facility?" He looked sidelong at the Marine guards, dismissing them as insufficient. "You've had enough funding to install top-of-the-line systems."

Trying to imagine how the scrawny gray alien could possibly turn into a wild juggernaut, Hunter kept his expression carefully neutral. Years ago, he had formed an opinion of benevolent extraterrestrials from repeatedly watching *Close Encounters of the Third Kind* with his daughter. He simply couldn't picture the delicate, ethereal alien leaping out of its pod, overpowering both doctors, and breaking through the sealed walls.

"As you can see, Congressman, the doctors are inside an armored chamber designed for the most stringent containment situations, proof against the ebola virus or even nerve gas. The foot-thick doors are sealed and locked from outside, the windows are made of reinforced, unbreakable Lexan. No item among the equipment and instruments inside could be used to breach the seal."

"Well, what about that laser drill?" Durston said. "The one they used to burn a hole into the pod?"

"As a fail-safe mechanism, it was designed to require a new focusing rod after one use. The lasing core needs to be replaced before it can be fired again." Hunter managed a smile at the Congressman. "You see, sir, we can be paranoid, too."

Garamov looked at his counterpart. "Congressman Durston, the bigger question will be how to decontaminate and seal the specimen again, so that I can transport it back to Russia."

"Unexpected things still happen," Durston insisted. "What if, in spite of all your plans, an infectious agent gets loose in that chamber? What if someone tries to break free? What if—"

Hunter cut him off with a raised hand. "In such a worst-case event, we have a burst energy annihilation routine, which I can trigger at the last possible moment. A pulse of high-intensity radiation will flash-melt everything inside, disintegrating all possible threats."

"I did not know about this," Garamov said.

"But as a last resort only," Hunter insisted.

"Why, naturally." Durston's close-set eyes gleamed as if he were eager to see the destructive system in action. "So those are the expensive precautions our money has bought."

Thinking about such drastic measures, Hunter could not help worrying about Team Proteus. The terrible static and distortion had prevented any communication for more than half an hour. For all his piloting skill, Marc Devlin didn't know where he was going or what he would encounter. Normally, Hunter could find ways to mitigate dire circumstances, but he felt isolated and helpless outside the Class IV room, out of contact with the *Mote*. Tired of sitting still, he paced the observation deck.

Sujatha looked up at the three men. "Director Hunter, sir, I request permission to make a small incision. Dr. Pirov and I would like to look at the tissue beneath the skin. We can also observe blood coagulation and—"

"Absolutely not," Garamov said without the slightest hesitation. "No physical damage to the alien."

The Bengali doctor looked from Garamov's face to Hunter's. "It would only be a scratch, sir."

"That will be too much." The Deputy Foreign Minister looked over at the Director, prepared to insist, but Hunter deferred to the man.

"It's best to be conservative, Dr. Sujatha."

"I concur," Pirov said, surprising his colleague. "This being's spacecraft has already been destroyed. Perhaps he is an emissary come to open relations with Earth. Or an independent explorer . . . or a criminal, an exile? No one can tell." He looked away, hiding in the shadows of his anti-contamination hood. "We should exercise extreme caution."

Hunter wondered what would happen if the extraterrestrial died. Would comrades come to avenge him, using weapons never before seen on Earth—outside of Marc Devlin's science-fiction movies, that is? He tried to be an optimist, but he had dealt with too many crisis situations in his career. He knew the worst was bound to happen, good intentions notwithstanding.

Nevertheless, no matter how peaceful or harmless this extraterrestrial visitor might seem to be, the interior of its body was probably a ruthless and hostile environment.

And Team Proteus was somewhere inside.

Chapter 29

Cruising through the alien's circulatory system, Devlin focused on covering as much ground as possible before they had to search for an exit. They had seen no further sign of the nanomachines, but the miniaturization field would begin to degrade in another hour and a half.

Not much time, and so much left to discover.

When the *Mote* finally did encounter a distributed blood-pumping substation, Arnold Freeth beamed and blushed so much that even Devlin was embarrassed for him. "I was right." He looked over at Dr. Tyler, as if she would at last forgive him for his false credentials, or at least acknowledge his contribution to their speculations.

But she remained aloof, interested only in studying the heartlike organ. "Let's just figure out what this is. No need to be smug about it."

The major blood vessels converged at an asteroid-sized mass of stringy muscle fibers. The biological pump appeared to be woven from ropes of cells as strong as steel cables. A trifold valve slowly opened and shut ahead of them, regulating the sluggish flow of blood.

Devlin threw the impellers into reverse to hold the ship against the lethargic current that drew them toward the trapdoor opening. As he held the *Mote* steady, the sub-heart clenched and relaxed in a ponderous rhythm so slow that it barely kept blood flowing.

External sonic receptors picked up the heavy vibrations of the beating muscle, like a pounding kettledrum. The bloodstream vortex added turbulence, jostling the ship from side to side.

Spherical blood cells collided with the craft, then recoiled to smash into each other, crowding toward the beating sub-heart. Ahead, the overlapping trifold valves closed again and blocked the way into the first chamber. Each expansion of the tough muscle drew blood into the pumping station, and the subsequent contraction ejected it at higher velocity out the other side.

Pressed against the window, Tyler captured every detail with still images and live video, dictating her own comments and speculations. Hypnotized by the slow beating of the heart subsystem, she even flashed a wonder-filled smile at the UFO expert, then caught herself. She came to the cockpit doorway. "Major Devlin, the contractions are slow and regular, without exerting a great deal of force. I don't think it would pose an excessive danger to us if the *Mote* proceeded into the main chamber itself. It would be a remarkable opportunity to study what's going on here."

Though ostensibly in command of the mission, Devlin was supposed to follow the suggestions of the medical specialist. "Roger that. We're not much bigger than a couple of blood cells anyway, so we can fit through." He looked over at Tomiko for her opinion.

The security specialist shrugged. "No problem. Garrett would have charged right in without even bothering to pause."

He frowned, not wanting to be reminded of the

injured pilot back in the Proteus infirmary. "Captain Wilcox would've wrecked my ship before this mission was over."

Tomiko smiled at him in satisfaction, as if she'd detected the hint of jealousy in his voice. "Well? Let's move it."

"On our way." He slowed the reverse impellers and let the *Mote* drift forward with the increasing flow. "Next stop, Freeth Pumping Module Number One." He wrestled with the controls to steady them through the turbulence as they rushed toward the opening valve.

Drawn in with a gulp of blood, the miniaturized vessel shot through the opening flaps and into a cavern bounded by knotted muscular walls. Caught in a violent eddy, the *Mote* spun around as the carrier fluid pooled within the chambers.

Large, flexible spheroids crashed into each other, bounced apart, and bobbled toward the exit valve, lining up for the next pumping beat that would eject them back into the circulatory system. Devlin struggled to keep the craft in place, shining bright spotlights to illuminate the immense cardiac grotto. "Make your observations, Doc. I don't know how many heartbeats I can hold us here."

Turbulence jostled the *Mote* as crimson muscle walls rushed toward them with the next contraction. The trapped blood swirled, jetting toward the exit valve on the opposite side of the chamber.

Just then the spotlights glinted off geometric shapes, caught a flurry of mechanical movement. More nanomachines.

A pair of purplish blood cells collided with the *Mote*. With a sinking feeling in his chest, Devlin managed to keep the beams on the frenzy of microscopic devices built from carbon-and-metal lattices. The nanocritters bristled with mechanical arms and legs, articulated joints and pincers.

"Whoa, hundreds of them," he said with a whistle. "Maybe thousands."

Bafflingly busy, the frenetic micro-robots swarmed the interior walls of the sub-heart muscle, an army working with cell layers and membranes, adding, stitching, rearranging.

Tomiko stared. "Ever see bees in a honeycomb, crawling around on hive business?"

"Let's hope these don't have stingers," Devlin said. "They're everywhere."

Freeth couldn't tear himself away from the side window. "It might not be anything sinister. Nano-robots could be programmed to carry a person's DNA blueprint and act as scouts, checking cells in the host body to eliminate any mutation, any disease or cancer."

"Objectively speaking those machines do look like they could be repairing the sub-heart wall." Dr. Tyler seemed reluctant to give the UFO expert too much credit. "I guess if Freeth spouts out enough crazy ideas, some of them are bound to be right."

He ignored the back-handed compliment. "Who knows what the alien suffered during its interstellar journey? Not to mention being shot down." Freeth paced from one side window to the other, trying to see through the flurry of blood cells. "My guess is that it used these nanomachines to put itself into stasis before the journey, to keep it alive with the absolute minimum of energy and resources. Then the machines shut themselves down."

"Like putting a car in long-term storage," Devlin said, still working the engines to maintain their position. "You drain the fluids, disconnect the battery, let the air out of the tires, and raise it up on blocks."

Freeth's freckled face was ruddy with enthusiasm.

"Judging by all this activity, the nanomachines are trying to jump-start their host. Maybe they're fixing whatever tissue damage occurred en route, even giving the body a tune-up before it awakens."

Nearby, another group of nanocritters worked industriously. Like cowboys, three of them rounded up an indigo blood cell and stripped off its outer protein sheath. Cooperating like an assembly line of butchers, the tiny devices pulled out the organelles and gulped raw materials into their hungry maws.

Orange heat shimmered from their bottom furnaces, waste thermal energy generated by their furious labors. Mechanical arms and legs moved in a blur as the devices broke down the entire blood cell to separate out desirable resource molecules and protein chains, then discarded the rest of the material. Other nanomachines extruded buckyball chains, fullerene cylinders impregnated with specific elements and molecules at appropriate lattice points. Building blocks.

In fascination, Devlin watched the devices assemble the components based on the blueprint burned onto their reproducible diamond-memory circuit boards. In less than a minute, the construction crew had constructed four nanocritters from scratch, and turned them loose.

Two of the new machines propelled themselves toward the work cluster on the cardiac wall. A third device departed through the widening exit valve and into the bloodstream. The fourth new nanocritter remained within the assembly area and began gathering raw materials from more captured blood cells to build additional nanomachines.

"With a reproduction rate like that, they'll have this alien stripped down to nothing within a day," Tomiko said, "maybe even hours."

"Unless they go outside the body to grab external

raw materials." Devlin felt a cold twist in his stomach as he realized the implications of what he had said. "Whoa! Think of how fast they could spread."

The sub-heart contracted again, ejecting a load of blood through the opposite valve. The nanomachines and the *Mote* anchored themselves in place and weathered the flow.

As the jostling blood cells drained out, Devlin drifted close to the industrious nanomachines that were busily building copies of themselves. A resource-processing device moved toward the vessel, swinging its sensors—not sure what kind of blood cell the *Mote* could be, but obviously hungry.

Suddenly worried about his precious ship, Devlin added more power to the engines, backing cautiously away. "To a nano-construction crew, we must look like a treasure trove of raw materials."

"Keep your distance, Marc," Tomiko said.

With a spurt from its own driving engine, the nanomachine slammed into the *Mote*, spreading a crab-like array of jointed metal legs and claws.

"Hey, don't mess with the ship," Devlin shouted.

Loud tapping sounds echoed through the hull as the device touched the armor plates with pyridine-tipped whiskers, sensor pads, and analysis grids, like a fly sampling a particularly good piece of garbage.

"What is it doing?" Devlin asked. "Leave that alone!"

Freeth backed away from the rear window, where the spidery machine skittered past, clicking and scratching. It banged on the hull with a heavy, grasping claw, searching for weak points.

The sub-heart muscle pumped again, and another gush of blood poured in to fill the chamber, increasing the turbulence around them.

"I'll take care of this, Marc. Don't worry." Before the device could tear off and taste the *Mote*'s armor plates, Tomiko casually blasted the nanocritter with the laser cannon, hurling carbon-lattice debris into the construction area. "No need to take chances."

Suddenly, the swarms of busy nanomachines paused in their work—all of them—as if she had just tripped an alarm. Sending tiny flickers at each other, they pulsed signals through their crude transmitters.

"Or . . . maybe I attracted too much attention."

The swarm of micro-builders dropped their half-assembled machines and moved through the blood fluid, converging toward the debris of Tomiko's target. One half-completed machine struggled to keep pace with the others, a quivering monstrosity trying to follow fragmentary programming.

"That's all the time you're going to get, Doc," Devlin said to Tyler. "I'm getting us out of here before these things get a taste for my ship."

Now nanocritters dropped away from the sub-heart muscle to join the attack squadron. More and more of them, each one intent on the *Mote*.

"Looks like a lynch mob." Tomiko prepared to shoot again, but Devlin stopped her. He increased the impeller motors to a high-pitched whine and shot toward the exit valve. The sub-heart had already begun its next contraction. Blood fluid jetted around the *Mote*'s hull.

As the trifold intake valve opened again on the far side of the sub-heart, Freeth said, "More nanomachines coming in!"

Like police rushing to the scene of a crime, a new flood of tiny devices pushed into the sub-heart chamber, all focused on the same goal. Within moments they could overwhelm the *Mote*. Some of them slashed indiscriminately through crowds of blood cells.

"Looks like the cavalry. And we're the bad guys," Tomiko said.

Before the reinforcements could approach, the sub-heart ejected a load of blood. Devlin drove the *Mote* at full velocity through the widening valve into a large outbound artery. "Time to get out of here."

On the far side of the valve, a new squadron of nanocritters swirled in the plasma fluid, fighting their way upstream. Even outside the sub-heart muscle, the tiny devices crowded toward them from the junctures of veins and arteries.

"I'm afraid that by shooting one machine, you've just activated the alien's defensive systems, Ms. Braddock," Tyler said. "Now, instead of ignoring our ship, the nanomachines see us as a threat."

Flustered, Tomiko looked at Devlin. "What was I supposed to do—let the critter eat us for lunch?"

He muttered out of the corner of his mouth, "Just don't get on my case about my stupid stunt that woke them up in the first place."

"Deal."

Behind them, the pumping station valve opened again, shooting a stream of microscopic devices directly at them. Devlin accelerated blindly into the labyrinth of the alien's body.

Seeing their prey, the coordinated nanomachines closed in for the kill.

Chapter 30

Inside the VIP observation deck, a burst of static came over the comm system, a roaring sound that engulfed distant, distorted words. Felix Hunter could discern a faint voice, lost in the background like a drowning man in a storm. The rest of the message was completely incomprehensible.

Nevertheless, this was their first word from Team Proteus in forty-five minutes. The crew was still alive . . . but maybe in trouble.

He looked intently at the technicians in the adjoining control room.

The skinny communications officer listened on headphones, replayed the burst, and shook his head. "No distinct words, sir."

"Process that and clean it up. Boost the signal to sort out what Major Devlin was trying to say."

"It may take a while, sir."

"Then get started."

Garamov squeezed his long fingers together, massaging his knuckles. "Why has the static increased so dramatically? We need to know what the exploration team is seeing."

"It could be faulty communications equipment," Durston suggested, as if looking for someone to reprimand.

"I highly doubt it, Congressman." Hunter tried to find another reservoir of patience. "We knew beforehand that the alien's body itself exhibits some kind of jamming field."

He stared at the mission chronometer on his control panel, counting down the minutes, and wondered what dire emergencies Team Proteus might be encountering. And he couldn't do a damned thing about it.

Marc can handle it. I'm sure he can.

Five minutes later the comm specialist hurried up to the observation level, sweat glistening on his dark skin. Congressman Durston half rose to his feet, as if expecting that the message must be for him.

The thin black man ignored him and rushed toward the Director. "Sir, with signal-cleanup algorithms we've processed out some of the static from the *Mote*'s transmission." The skinny specialist handed over a small playback pad and pressed the button. "I thought you might want to listen to this up here, rather than over the intercom."

Garbled words came out, distorted through numerous layers of massaging, enhancing, and processing. It was a weird approximation of Marc Devlin's voice. " . . . infestation ### nanomachines ### trying to stay clear ### swarms."

Hunter sat up quickly, ignoring the puzzled looks from Garamov and Durston. "Did I hear that right? Does this mean the alien's body is infested with nanomachines? Is Major Devlin requesting an immediate extraction?"

The technician shook his head. "We couldn't get anything more out of the message, sir. Too much interference. Sorry."

Hunter stifled a groan and sat back in his chair. "Thank you. I'm impressed you could squeeze that much out of the transmission. Dismissed."

Durston nearly choked on a mouthful of questions, but Hunter silenced him with a chop of his hand. His thoughts reeled, and he turned to the Russian Deputy Foreign Minister. Nanomachines might prove even more deadly than the release of extraterrestrial microorganisms from the alien's body.

"This raises the stakes considerably," Garamov said, deeply concerned. He badly needed a cigarette.

With the lifepod wide open, Sergei Pirov leaned over the extraterrestrial body as if he wanted to make love to it. He conducted test after test, while the cameras and Deputy Minister Garamov watched his every move.

Hands steady now, Pirov pried back the wide fleshy eyelid to study a bottomless black eye and shone his bright penlight onto it, as he would have with a comatose patient. "Still no photonic response. I cannot find the pupils, so I am unable to measure any dilation reflex."

On the other side of the pod, Rajid Sujatha played a handheld resonance scanner over the alien's body, scouring every centimeter. They had no idea where the miniaturized Team Proteus had gone or what they were doing. Using sensitive thermocouples to search for a microscopic heat source that could be the traveling *Mote,* he tried at the same time to detect tracer ions the microscopic exploration vessel should have been emitting.

"Most unusual." Sujatha recalibrated the scanner and tested again. "I am detecting multiple energy sources, pinprick heat reservoirs that move. Many, many more than could possibly be the *Mote.*"

Pirov looked at him, startled by the interruption.

Sujatha continued to use his scanner, perplexed at the readings. "I detect widespread thermal spikes in various internal locations, perhaps pinpointing important organs. However, the body's signal distortions continue to confound any detailed analysis."

Pirov ran his gloved fingers along the grayish skin, but he could feel little through the protective fabric. "According to the readings, the alien's body is growing warmer, well above ambient levels. A fever, perhaps? I hope it is not beyond the normal parameters for this species."

Sujatha moved along the alien's chest and legs, without touching the scanner to the skin.

Pirov looked through the corner of his obscuring hood up to the observation deck. Director Hunter sat beside Garamov and the American congressman.

Though he only reluctantly pursued this work, Pirov knew this was their one chance to make genuine progress. He poked and prodded and probed wherever he was allowed.

Somehow, he would understand this alien.

As Pirov's neoprene-sealed anti-contamination gloves brushed the dermal surface, thousands of revived and replicated nanomachines emerged from the alien's pores. They flooded past the safeguards of ferocious skin pedicels, their cooperative allies. Swarms of microscopic machines reached the air, searching for a target.

A specimen.

A host.

Nanocritters climbed like lice over the fabric of Dr. Pirov's gloves and streamed up the coated fibers, searching for a way inside. The devices used sharp molecular-tipped claws and segmented diamond cutting apparatus to hack through the polymer coatings to the threads below.

Chewing, tunneling, burrowing.

One of the scouts sent a signal, and the swarming devices converged toward a target point—the pinprick where the Russian doctor had accidentally stuck himself with the hypodermic needle.

Given time, the tiny machines could have dismantled even the tightest seam of the protective garment. But to them, the pinprick was a gaping doorway as large as a crater. A route inside.

Thousands of alien nanomachines flooded through the hole in the thick layer to the whorled and ridged tip of the doctor's finger. Waves of the relentless devices streamed down the length of his finger to his hand, penetrating the skin.

Once they reached the first capillaries, the nanomachines flowed with the blood and circulated throughout Pirov's entire body.

Within minutes, pumped by the Russian's heartbeat, they had spread out and established primary clusters, transmitting unified commands among the swarms. From cellular base camps, the machines grabbed bits of raw materials from dismantled human blood cells and began to multiply according to their mission programming.

The nanomachines penetrated the nuclei of Pirov's cells. They burrowed into the chromosomes and assessed the human genome.

Then the devices set to work performing the required modifications, slicing out nucleic-acid components that did not fit the prescribed pattern. Using available base pairs, they rebuilt chains of nucleotides in a predetermined order until they crafted another strand of DNA that matched the template carried on the diamond memory wafer of their computer brains.

Based on Earth biochemistry, using only the amino acids, proteins, and base pairs available in human genetics, the design would not be exact. But it was similar enough to the alien's target DNA. The result was within mission parameters.

In a geometric progression, the nanocritters reproduced themselves and diligently worked, modifying and rebuilding. It was an immense task that required millions of microscopic machines to sweep through every biological system inside Dr. Sergei Pirov.

Before long, cell by cell, the thriving mechanical infection would remake this human body into another image, one compatible with the schematics of their creator. . . .

Chapter 31

If the army of nanomachines hadn't been trying to destroy them, Devlin might have enjoyed the mad race through uncharted biological territory. He'd always liked to test his reflexes—often to Kelli's dismay. Despite the earlier need for repairs, he was totally confident in his ship, and the *Mote* performed beautifully, like an extension of him.

As he careened along the alien's bloodstream, dodging corpuscles and choosing branch paths, his reactions were pumped. Devlin couldn't remember having experienced any greater rush of excitement, short of experimental test-flight training for the Air Force.

Nobody else on board considered it fun, though.

"Three more, coming after us!" Freeth called, staring out the window.

Devlin jerked the rudders and lurched the ship to one side, avoiding the new trio of nanocritters that streaked out of a juncture of arteries. The *Mote* collided with a rubbery wall, ricocheted off, and smashed two of the fullerene-constructed devices into scrap.

Making snap decisions, he guided the ship down membrane-lined passageways, between tissue walls. He turned the micro-vessel sideways to slip between the smallest cracks of fibrous muscles. He left the remaining nanohunter far behind, but the microscopic device appeared to be transmitting signals, calling for reinforcements.

"More behind us," Dr. Tyler called.

"And one up ahead. Fasten your seat belt."

The nanocritters swarmed after them like pursuers from an old-fashioned Pac Man game. As a young cadet, he'd spent his share of hours playing videogames (strictly to develop strategy and hand-eye coordination, of course) . . . as well as too much time at home, when he could have been doing things with his wife. Now he hoped all those wasted hours would serve him well.

Without compunction now, Tomiko used her lasers to blast at the aggressive machines. Components of wrecked nanocritters lay strewn in the alien's tissue, a wake of metal parts, as if a squad of robot Humpty Dumptys had fallen there.

But the remaining microscopic hunters refused to break off the chase.

Devlin took the *Mote* on a frantic flight along a striated forest of muscle fibers. The long, smooth cells looked like a packed mat of seaweed hanging down, thick and soft and red. When he couldn't dodge fast enough, Devlin crashed straight through the organic macramé, leaving scattered cells behind. He followed grooves and contours of tissue, away from the converging fleet of artificial devices.

But the nanocritters kept coming.

The ship glided through a filmy layer between the muscle mass and subcutaneous fat. When he passed over a wide rip in the musculature, two nanomachines burst out from below, where they'd been lurking in the crimson shadows. One struck the *Mote*'s bottom hull like a cannonball, but ricocheted off without finding purchase for its articulated arms.

Devlin swerved violently. A few loose instruments clattered to the deck of the main compartment. Tomiko fired her lasers, but missed as he spun through evasive maneuvers. "I can't believe this! They were waiting in ambush. How could they have known we were coming?"

The stunned nano-attacker reoriented itself and joined the second carbon-lattice machine as they streaked into the filmy fluid on an intercept course. The nanocritters used no caution now, did not extend sensors, did not try to probe or understand.

They meant to dismantle the *Mote* without further analysis.

The second machine rammed the starboard engine cone like a kamikaze, knocking the vessel into a spin. From his station at the window, Arnold Freeth tumbled on top of Dr. Tyler, both of them sprawling to the floor of the main cabin. Tyler scrambled away, glaring at Freeth.

Tomiko clenched sweaty hands around her firing controls. "Just get me close enough for a good shot, Marc."

"Affirmative. As soon as I take a break from dodging."

The first nanomachine recovered from its initial abortive impact, spun up, and intentionally collided with the side of the *Mote*. Its benzene-tipped mandibles and articulated carbon hands scratched the wide observation window as it ricocheted off.

"Is that close enough for you?" Devlin asked.

Tomiko fired a shot before she was ready, grazing the mechanical attacker but leaving a black streak of a few dead muscle cells deep beneath them. She swore while Devlin struggled to keep the *Mote* under control.

He applied thrust to pull away, and the impellers roared, but now both nanocritters managed to latch onto irregularities on the hull. With jittery movements they hauled themselves along the external plates, moving with microfiber pulleys and molecular pistons that slid through carbon-walled buckytubes.

Devlin flew in a dizzy corkscrew to throw them off. He could hear the horrendous shrieking of metal edges scraping across the outside of the ship, diamond-tipped apparatus chopping and pounding. Every scraping sound, every gash in the enameled hull surface felt like a wound to his own body.

"I'll get you a new paint job when this is all over. Promise."

Tomiko swiveled the fore and aft laser cannons, targeting the first nanomachine in her crosshairs. "One thing I can't stand, it's rudeness." Intersecting lances chopped the device to pieces, severing fullerene walls and bursting open the hydrogen and fluorine memory layers on the circuit wafer. "And you're not being at all polite."

Melting globules sprayed from the severed nanocomponents like blood. Amputated claw arms flailed about in twitching death throes.

The remaining micro-attacker hurled itself against the *Mote*'s hull. Tomiko's next shot drilled through its body core. As the device shuddered and fell away, it let out an electromagnetic shriek from the transceiver horn, a death cry . . . or an urgent call for assistance.

Arnold Freeth managed to get to his hands and knees. "We have to call for emergency extraction! We never counted on anything like this!" He blinked. "Did we?"

Cynthia Tyler disentangled herself from the UFO expert. "Don't underestimate Team Proteus, Freeth. We can handle this."

Devlin set his jaw in a grim line. "Calling for emergency extraction is problematic right now, since I don't think we can get any signal past this interference—and I no longer have the slightest idea where we are." He flew forward. "But don't worry yet. I am *not* going to be outsmarted by a machine with a brain half the size of a germ."

Cynthia Tyler brushed her jumpsuit off. She offhandedly helped Freeth up, then ignored him again. Looking chagrined, he buckled himself back into his seat. "Sorry about that."

Tyler didn't spare him a glance, focusing instead on Major Devlin. "Go inside that gap in the musculature. If you find a nerve corridor, we can follow the neurons."

"Roger that." Taking a nose dive, Devlin plunged between smooth cells, hoping he wouldn't encounter any nanocritters lying in wait. Bright spotlights slid across reddish-brown organic barricades, yellow streamers, and crimson lace until he found a dark opening where a neural pipeline threaded through the cellular forest.

"Where exactly will this take us, Doc?" Devlin asked. A flicker of lightning shot along the pathway, obscured by a translucent coating that surrounded the nerve strand like insulation on a wire.

Firmly wedged into a seat beside one of the mounted laptop computers, Tyler consulted her reference databases. "I have absolutely no idea."

"Ah, honesty. I appreciate that."

Devlin picked up speed when he found the ganglion path clear. He longed to suit up and go outside to check the damage to the *Mote*, but he could make few cosmetic repairs here on the miniaturized scale.

Tomiko glanced at the mission chronometer on the control panel. "One hour, fifteen minutes. You do have a plan as to how exactly we're going to get out of this mess, right, Marc?"

Now that their flight had become smooth again,

Freeth unbuckled and came forward on unsteady legs. "Do you have some way to send a locator beacon, or an SOS? So they can find us?"

"Good idea, Mr. Freeth." Devlin's fingers danced across the comm controls. Through selective filters he had already damped out most of the caterwauling nanomachine signals in the surrounding tissue, though no outside message had been able to penetrate for the past hour. Now, using the specific frequency and signal-embedding protocol he and Felix had agreed on, he added a signature beacon. "That should produce a recognizable pattern for the Proteus technicians to find us."

A skitter of light flickered along the ganglion like a shooting star. Devlin followed the strand until it linked with an intersection of neurons, where sparkling pulses passed through like bullet trains on intersecting tracks, colliding with enough force that Devlin backed off, shielding his eyes.

"The neural signals are getting stronger," Dr. Tyler said.

"Maybe the alien is waking up," Freeth suggested.

"If he sits up and stretches, we may be in for a rough ride." Devlin veered away from the electrical discharges in the nerve cluster and entered another passage that looked like a glandular opening. Without warning, the *Mote* plunged into a bubbly, foamy mass of tissue. Moss-green forms swirled up in shapeless tangles, like free-form sculptures shot through with coppery chips.

"You take me to the strangest places, Marc. What is *this*?" Tomiko said.

"Another organ of some kind, Doc? I'd love to have some inkling of where we are." Devlin's voice had an edge of frustration. "A spleen or a kidney? The liver? Sweetbreads, gizzard, gallbladder? Maybe even the brain?"

Tyler could only shake her head helplessly. "I can't offer any suggestions, Major Devlin." She scanned her databases for comparable tissue, but found nothing verifiable. She looked over at Arnold Freeth in defeat. "I confess I underestimated just how strange this creature would be."

Without warning, the nanocritters struck again.

A new swarm of machines emerged from the convoluted walls of the strange organ. Wave after mechanical wave, they surged from openings in the spongy tissue, hundreds of devices with pincer arms and groping claws. They surrounded the *Mote* like a wolf pack scenting wounded prey.

"How did they know where to find us? Did they just happen to be in the neighborhood?" The nose of their ship crashed into a blockade of three machines, shattering one and crippling two others. "Don't be shy with your laser here, Tomiko."

She was already blasting right and left. The hot beams sliced the attacking devices into components, lopping off segmented arms, exploding power cells. Devlin spun the *Mote* in a backward loop, throwing off Tomiko's accuracy. She rolled with the motion, adjusting her aim and targeting again. She left a graveyard of metallic and carbon debris behind them.

Devlin's single intention was to get his ship away from this new ambush. "Somehow, they tracked us to this place then set a trap. There's no other explanation for it."

"Awfully goal-oriented critters," Tomiko said.

He flew deeper into the organ's spongy mass. In their wake, dozens of micro-devices lay damaged or destroyed—while tiny reinforcements continued to emerge from the fleshy pockets.

Some nanodevices paused at the microscopic wreckage and began picking over the ruined carbon-lattice hulks, sorting components and raw materials.

The miniature robots set up work crews and went about repairing minimally damaged machines, tearing others apart for scrap. They reassembled new devices from the fullerenes and buckytubes, producing even more hunters.

With a world of resources around them, the nanocritters could copy themselves far faster than Tomiko's quick shots could destroy them. Devlin knew that Team Proteus could never outfight or outrun all of the voracious machines. They had to find another way.

Their best hope was to get out of the extraterrestrial body and escape the trap.

Devlin descended through dark catacombs into a biological wilderness. He had no idea where he was going, and their time grew shorter every second. Now they had only an hour before they grew back to normal size.

The ever-multiplying nanomachines marshaled their forces and continued the hunt.

Chapter 32

Seated a dozen light years away, as far as Team Proteus was concerned, Felix Hunter clasped his large hands around his knees, trying to maintain his composure. After the last fragmented message from Marc, he felt as if he were frozen inside, not knowing what was happening to his crew.

Nanomachines? Swarms? Trying to stay clear? The micro-explorers hadn't been able to get another signal out. The *Mote* could already be destroyed. He should never have sent his son-in-law on the mission.

Hunter loved being at the nexus of every necessary decision, being in charge. Perhaps he should have suited up and gone inside the containment chamber with the two doctors, just to touch the specimen with his own hands. . . .

Vasili Garamov stood up on bony legs and removed a cigarette from his pack. He held it like a talisman in his long fingers, but did not light it. He let out a slow sigh, looking as if he longed for the Cold War days, when no important decision was made outside the confines of a smoke-filled room.

Congressman Durston took great delight in pointing out, "If you want to have a smoke, Mr. Garamov, you'll need to go outside and pass through all the security procedures again. That's probably forty-five minutes, minimum. Think of everything you'll miss."

Garamov's pale face flushed slightly at Durston's taunt. "I can endure."

Sergei Pirov felt something extraordinary happening to his body.

Something terrible.

His skin crawled with electric ants. From the inside. His joints ached and his bones throbbed as he moved. An invisible force seemed to be adjusting his physical form, gradually but inexorably, to a different shape.

After he'd defected to the United States to work for Project Proteus, Pirov had chosen to wear braces on his teeth, even as an adult, to correct years of orthodontic neglect in the Soviet Union. He had endured the constant pressure, the tightened wires and clamps that took years to bring his teeth into the proper position. Brackets, bands, and retainers had aligned his overbite until the teeth looked straight and perfect, an American dream.

Now it felt as if his entire body were undergoing a similar process, completely out of his control.

What is happening to me?

This went beyond his normal body aches, the uncertain tremor in his hands, the queasiness he often felt in his digestive system. This . . . frightened him.

Beside Pirov, the dutiful Rajid Sujatha remained focused on scanning the alien body. The Bengali doctor searched his readings for a blip that would allow him to trace the microscopic ship through the murky interference. "Still no sign, Director Hunter."

Barely able to remain standing upright, Pirov fought to retain his composure. He wanted to leave this chamber, longed to shower and sleep, then spend the rest of his career reading journals and pondering what he already knew.

But a relentless buzzing crackled inside his mind, and his ears rang from spurious signals, sounds he was never meant to hear. Even back at his comfortable desk, he wouldn't have been able to concentrate on reading.

Beads of sweat broke out over his skin, followed by shivers and hot flashes. With disbelieving horror, he realized he must have contracted some kind of fever. An alien virus? Not possible. But still, the heat raged inside his flesh.

He couldn't understand *how* he could have been exposed.

With the alien's lifepod now open, both he and Sujatha might have been contaminated by whatever was on the extraterrestrial's body. But how could that be? He wore full anti-contamination gear and had followed all protocols. He could not possibly have contracted any sort of pathogen from the specimen. Besides, there hadn't been a long enough incubation period.

It was impossible. But still, he felt it happening inside him.

Though it went against strict procedures, Pirov didn't dare mention his symptoms, not with Deputy Foreign Minister Garamov watching him. He could not let them down, and he had already made too many excuses on this vital mission.

He and Dr. Sujatha were sealed within a Class IV containment room. In order to get out, both of them would undergo enormously complex sterilization procedures. Even if he complained about his symptoms, what could anyone do for him now?

Above, Vasili Garamov watched him like a bird of prey, and Pirov didn't dare relax for a moment, though he found it exceedingly difficult to concentrate. No need to bother Director Hunter about his chills, or the Deputy Foreign Minister. Once the mission was over, in an hour, he could arrange for whatever help he needed.

The old Russian doctor remained quieter than usual, doing his work and concentrating on the UFO creature he could see and study. . . .

Deep within his body, ten generations of nanomachines had already reproduced. They rebuilt the aging human on a genetic level, using DNA patterns stored in microscopic computer memories.

Before he could tell what was happening to him, before he realized the fundamental changes within himself, Sergei Pirov became something no longer human.

While Rajid Sujatha scanned for the *Mote*, he detected only static. No discernible blip from the minuscule vessel.

"I cannot locate them." He set the instrument on the surgical table beside him. "No readings. Perhaps they are too deep . . . and they will begin to grow soon. They should be searching for a way out."

Sujatha realized how uncharacteristically silent Dr. Pirov had become. The Russian moved about sluggishly, picking up medical instruments and staring at them as if he'd forgotten what they were for. Then Pirov returned to the naked alien inside the open lifepod and stood motionless, staring. He kept his back turned to Sujatha.

"Are you all right, Dr. Pirov?"

The older man froze, startled, as if he'd been caught doing something illegal. His hesitant voice came over the suit speakers. "I am fine." The timbre sounded thick and hoarse, as if he'd grown oddly congested.

Sujatha waited, but his colleague said nothing more and did not turn around. Frowning behind his faceplate, the Bengali doctor glanced up at the observation deck, but Hunter was busy conferring with the Deputy Foreign Minister.

In a friendly tone, Sujatha attempted to start a conversation with Pirov. "When this mission is over, perhaps you would consider having dinner with me and my girls? We could meet for our next furlough in San Francisco. That would be most enjoyable, I think."

Pirov had never been particularly outgoing, nor was he forthcoming about personal details. The elderly Russian seemed fixated on his work, content to stay in his laboratory or office day after day. But Pirov might have a soft spot inside him. Sujatha thought he could bring the man out of his shell.

Pirov, hunched over the alien specimen, made no response. For the previous three hours, he had dutifully recorded measurements and collected observational data. His gloved hands now clutched the rim of the open lifepod, as if he were about to faint.

Sujatha didn't understand what was wrong. "Dr. Pirov, are you certain you're all right?" He stepped closer, but the Russian did not flinch. "Perhaps I should call Director Hunter? Do you need assistance?"

Pirov's anti-contamination hood and curved faceplate cast his features into shadow. But when he slowly, stiffly raised his head, Sujatha saw past the boundaries of his mask.

The Russian doctor's features had changed.

His head was flatter, and his eyes had enlarged, slanting upward into grossly enhanced orbs. Hanging in threads around his cheeks and neck, bristles of salt-and-pepper hair had fallen out, like shedding fur. Pirov's ears had shrunk against the sides of his head, retreating into his skull. His square chin was now pointed, and his lips had receded. His skin looked grayish.

Astonishingly, Sergei Pirov now resembled the extraterrestrial specimen lying inside the lifepod.

Sujatha reeled backward reflexively and stumbled against the defunct laser drill apparatus. And Pirov was upon him like a wild animal.

The Russian reacted with inhuman speed, crashing a gloved hand across Sujatha's hood. His knuckles caught the Bengali directly on the faceplate with all the power of a sledge hammer. Sujatha's hooded head smacked against the metal elbow of the laser drill, and he felt as if he'd been struck by a high-caliber bullet.

Sujatha fell to the floor. Stunned and terrified, he crab-walked backward to get away from Dr. Pirov. He sounded the alarm.

Above, in the observation deck, Director Hunter and the security guards scrambled to respond. Both Hunter and Garamov shouted into the intercom, demanding an explanation for Pirov's actions.

A hairline crack split Sujatha's transparent polymer face shield. To the thousands upon thousands of reproduced nanomachines that showered off Pirov's glove, the tiny breach was a rift the size of a canyon.

The microscopic devices streamed through the crack and poured onto Sujatha's face, into his eyes and nostrils and mouth. They seeped into every pore, conquering yet another human body.

They had already analyzed the systems from Dr. Pirov and were ready for a second alien conversion. This one would proceed even faster than the first.

Chapter 33

The *Mote* dodged through a maze of blood vessels, stringy fibers, and connective tissue. But nothing gave a clue how to escape from the alien's body. They were much too far from their entry point to follow the original plan.

Since the last skirmish, Devlin hadn't seen any sign of the pursuing nanocritters, but neither had he heard a word from Project Proteus, despite the continued SOS signal.

Now the ship traveled with a flow of loose cells, amber fatty globules, and spindly clusters of crystalline growths. Finally, they reached a large fluid-filled sac that sprawled in front of them. Devlin eyed the roadblock in frustration. "Told you I'd get us here safely, wherever *here* is."

Dr. Tyler studied the liquid-swollen membrane, finally sounding confident again. "That's probably a bursa, or some equivalent cushioning sac between bones and a joint. At least it gives us a sense of perspective."

"Even if this is a joint, though, we can't tell whether we're in a knuckle joint or the hip socket," Freeth countered.

Cynthia Tyler turned to him with a long-suffering

expression. "Unfortunately, you're correct. I guess it doesn't tell us much of anything after all."

The UFO expert looked at her in surprise. "Believe me, I *am* trying to help."

With no point of reference and no reliable monitoring of the distance and speed traveled during their frantic flight, Devlin could only guess where they were. But he was reluctant to admit he was totally lost. "At least Lewis and Clark had the constellations, the horizon, the direction of sunrise and sunset as referents." He made a disgusted sound. "I don't even have a functional compass."

The *Mote* plunged into the murky lubricating sac. The yellowish liquid swallowed them like an ocean of spoiled chicken stock. As the ship hummed forward, visibility in the soupy fluid grew even more difficult. Faint ripples distorted the illumination beams.

"We could put on a blindfold and throw a dart at the map, Marc," Tomiko suggested.

"We don't even have a map to throw a dart at."

By the time the *Mote*'s spotlights glinted off the geometric constructions of carbon lattices, the predatory nanomachines were already whirring toward them.

Devlin slammed a fist down onto the smooth control panel, then immediately brushed the surface, by way of an apology. "If *I* don't know where I'm going, how could they find us?"

"Those things are making quite an effort to go after one tiny ship," Tomiko said.

As Devlin spun the vessel, the attacking nanomachines surrounded them in three dimensions. Tomiko couldn't fire against a whole swarm. "Too many, Marc. We've got to run for it."

He could not hide his exasperation as he dove the

ship downward in a steep arc through the thick fluid, followed by a wake of churning bubbles.

The nanomachines swirled like a cloud of gnats, agitated by the unexpected move. They picked up speed and closed in.

"Maybe it's Arnold they want," Tomiko teased. "We could throw him overboard and see if it works as a diversion."

The UFO expert didn't find the suggestion amusing, but Devlin laughed. "In the movies I've seen, Tomiko, the alien monsters are usually after beautiful Earth women. Want to volunteer?"

"I'm sure there's a compliment buried somewhere in there."

She opened fire and destroyed the two closest microscopic marauders. The hot beams sent froth whirling through the lubricating fluid.

Ignoring the bubbles erupting all around the *Mote,* Devlin plowed ahead with his fingers crossed. Molten fragments of exploded nanomachines caromed off the front viewport and clanged against the hull. Then the *Mote* broke through the cordon with nothing worse than another scratch on the windshield.

The bursa sea stretched to a distant shore of porous openings that pocked a solid plain of bone. The calcified barricade reminded Devlin of massive reefs. "If we hide in there, at least the critters can't come at us from all sides." Without hesitation, he headed toward the honeycombed bone. "Just tell me these caves aren't dead ends, Doc."

Tyler's expression grew more intense than ever. She answered cautiously. "If this were human bone structure, we *might* encounter a spongy marrow tissue where red blood cells are made. That would give us room to maneuver."

Devlin took her answer as a recommendation and shot toward the nearest passageway into the network of bone. The nanomachines followed in their wake, picking up speed.

The ship entered a breathtaking gallery of hard white calcium that sparkled under the spotlights. Devlin flew through one tunnel at a breakneck pace, hooked sideways into another, and followed what appeared to be the clearest path. He executed unexpected turns and random jumps, unwilling to slow even in the confined spaces. "I'm not going to relax a single muscle until I get us all out of this body and back to our own size again, safe and sound."

"Fine by me," Tomiko said, holding on to her seat as he dodged through sharp turns and lacy overhanging loops of hard white mineral.

"We made it into the spongy tissue." Tyler stroked her hands along the window glass as if tracing the bone structure. "Those calcified walls are called lamellae."

"In humans," the UFO expert said, then sat down, as if realizing he was being a pest.

Spherical cells swirled around them, gelatinous masses like bumper cars that drifted toward the outflowing blood vessels. "I presume those are newborn erythrocytes—or the *equivalent* thereof," Tyler added quickly without looking at Freeth. "Red blood cells are a special case, unlike other cells because they have no DNA. They're just bags of hemoglobin. *If* the alien uses a similar process, they arise in the red marrow from pluripotential stem cells, which can also create leukocytes or platelets."

Freeth seemed pleased that she was trying to be open-minded, or at least covering her bases. "Believe me, I don't want to meet any marauding white blood cells. We're having enough trouble with nanocritters at the moment."

Tyler agreed. "A leukocyte wouldn't have the sheer determination those nanomachines are exhibiting." For the moment, at least, none of the attacking machines had managed to follow them.

"And a white blood cell couldn't *track* us, either. It's almost as if—" Devlin stopped in mid-sentence, then groaned. His hands flashed over the comm system controls, shutting down the emergency transmitter. "Our SOS beacon—we've been shouting our location to them everywhere we go." He rested his forehead in his palm. "The critters must have been homing in on the distress call."

Freeth said, "But if Project Proteus was mounting some kind of extraction effort, now they'll have no way of knowing where we are."

"And neither do the nanocritters." Tomiko ran her strong hands up and down the weapons controls, her almond eyes wary. "Personally, I think we're getting the better part of the bargain."

Tyler continued to scan the cavernous passages that blurred past. "Terrestrial bones have a long, hollow shaft that contains the yellow marrow. If this alien continues to have similarities to human structure, we should be able to travel a great distance without any obstruction."

"Roger that," Devlin said. *Full speed to nowhere.*

"Traveling a great distance is good," Freeth said. "Dr. Tyler, human bone isn't this porous, is it?" His voice still sounded a bit tentative, as if he feared she would snap at him for asking a question. "To me, that suggests the species came from a planet with lower gravity than ours, or maybe they evolved from birds, which would give them a strong but lightweight skeletal structure."

Tyler didn't disagree. "Possible, I suppose. But if so, the alien's bones might break if it tried to walk across a room under Earth gravity."

Eager to continue the conversation, Freeth joined her at the window. "Maybe the nanomachines can add metallic atoms to reinforce the bone structure. They could even alter the alien's metabolism and biochemistry to let it breathe different atmospheres and survive under harsh circumstances."

Tyler seemed just about to give him a smile of grudging acceptance when nine nanocritters smashed through the gossamer lamellae around them. The relentless tiny machines streaked into the bone tunnel, cutting off the fleeing vessel both from the front and rear. Freeth let out a startled squawk and scrambled back from the side window.

Tomiko fired at the leading nanomachine just as two more attackers rammed the *Mote* from behind. Devlin put on a burst of speed through a downward-sloping bone passage. A new mechanical attacker crunched into the port hull and slid off, scraping against the bone walls. The spongy calcium catacombs were too cramped for the nanomachines to surround them.

The *Mote* rushed through the marrow fluid, recoiling from impacts with newborn blood cells. Devlin shifted course much faster than he had any right to expect his reactions to handle. "And Kelli said I was wasting my time with all those videogames."

Think small.

Targeting carefully with the rear laser cannons, Tomiko looked for an appropriate cluster of lamellae in the crowded bone walls. "Time for a cave-in."

She hit the nearest nanocritter with a hard blast. The tiny machine broke apart, spreading a fan of fullerene debris, broken diamond memory circuitry, and dangling buckytube arms with metal-atom tips.

Tomiko's rapid pinpoint strikes shot out the overhanging arches of bone, shattering curtain after curtain into hard white rubble. Calcium shards broke away and tumbled to mix with the debris of the de-

stroyed nanomachine, creating a microscopic aster-
oid belt.

The closest two pursuing devices collided with the
wreckage cloud at full speed, like bulls stampeding
into a mine field. In seconds, the passage was
clogged with broken carbon-lattice bodies and bone
fragments.

"Like a pileup in a demolition derby." Tomiko
sounded immensely pleased with herself. She blew
imaginary smoke from her fingertip.

Ahead, the calcium lace expanded into larger grot-
toes and passages. They must be approaching the
open medullary shaft Dr. Tyler had predicted. Devlin
prayed their way would remain clear. The *Mote*
streaked along, leaving a turbulent wake behind it,
and no one knew if they were in the alien's leg, or
a rib, or its little toe.

"Free and clear. I'm going to see just how fast this
ship can go," Devlin said as they burst into an open
area filled with floating cells shaped like fried eggs.
"We've got to make some progress toward getting
out of here."

At the far end of the bone shaft, they would un-
doubtedly encounter another crowded labyrinth of
red marrow, and no doubt a new pack of
nanocritters. . . .

He couldn't understand why the microscopic machines were so obsessive. Certainly, dismantling the
Mote would yield a treasure trove of raw materials
for the assembly of a few more nanocritters. But
judging by the way the devices were already reproducing, they didn't have any dearth of building
blocks. *Why do they hold such a grudge?*

In fact, he could think of no reason why the nanomachines didn't see *each other* as viable meals. Every
one of the finished devices must look like a great big
assembly kit to all the others. If the voracious ma-

chines were programmed to grab any available molecules and build copies of themselves, what stopped them from just attacking each other?

Devlin blinked in surprise and spoke aloud. "Obviously they have some way to tell the difference." He craned his neck around, searching for Cynthia Tyler. "Hey, Doc—how does a white corpuscle understand which cells are benign and which ones have foreign proteins that need to be destroyed?"

"The leukocytes respond to a type of code on the surface of natural cells to distinguish them from foreign objects." She paused and considered his line of reasoning. "Yes. In a similar fashion, these nanomachines must have some way of determining friend or foe."

Devlin sat up straight. After all his years in the Air Force and his training as a fighter pilot, he should have thought of this sooner. "Each one must have a signal generator, like a jet fighter's IFF—the Identify Friend/Foe transmitter. Those devices have got to be sending out ID signals. Otherwise, they'd tear each other apart like hungry sharks."

He grinned with relief. In the red marrow approaching at the other end of the long bone, there must be more nanomachines. Waiting to attack the *Mote.*

There wasn't much time. Less than an hour remained on the mission chronometer, but now he had an idea that might save his crew.

"Simple." Devlin kept his hands on the controls but glanced over at Tomiko. "We just have to fool the nanomachines into thinking that we're one of *them.*"

Chapter 34

When Sergei Pirov turned into a wild man, Garamov couldn't believe what he was seeing.

In a blur, the Russian doctor grabbed Sujatha's protective suit and backhanded him with a resounding crack that sent the Bengali sprawling. Then he went into a frenzy, snarling and screaming as if with some kind of seizure.

Congressman Durston leaped to his feet. "What the hell is he doing down there?"

Hunter pounded on the intercom button. "Dr. Pirov!"

No one could see the old man's altered face inside the hooded suit.

Garamov yelled into the microphone, this time in Russian. Pirov responded by thrashing about, reversing direction, and hurling himself at the far wall like a rabid dog in a cage.

"Get that man up here right now," Durston demanded. "I want to know the meaning of this."

"You are welcome to go inside and get him, Congressman," Garamov said with harsh sarcasm. "He needs medical attention, a sedative at least."

"Impossible. They're sealed in the chamber, and I can't let them out." Hunter spoke rapidly, in control. "This could be a reaction to an extraterrestrial disease. If they're contaminated somehow, we can't risk the contact. No one else goes inside, either. Not until we get some answers about what's going on."

Huddled on the floor, Sujatha scrambled like a beetle to find some sort of shelter. "Director Hunter, help me, please." His faceplate was cracked.

The old Russian doctor ran amok in the containment room. He grabbed trays and flung them at the thick Lexan windows with a clatter. He knocked over an instrument stand and slammed his body against the armored wall, pounding with gloved fists. The sound from his voice pickup warbled up and down, an inhuman wail without comprehensible words.

On the control deck, Hunter used his overrides to activate the facility's full alarm and lockdown procedures. "Standby alert." Magenta lights whirled at corridor intersections in the mountain complex.

Already sealed, the Class IV chamber became armed, systems in place to prevent unauthorized entry or escape—with deadly force, if necessary. An ominous blinking red light indicated the sterilization-burst device powering up.

Hunter wasn't prepared to consider that option. Not yet.

Armed guards rushed to the observation deck, ready to whisk Durston and Garamov to safety. Boots clomping like muffled gunfire, Marines ran along the outside corridors, surrounding the containment chamber at floor level. They held rifles in front of them, their faces stony and grim. A piercing tone signaled that the chamber had reached full emergency status.

Hunter tried the chamber intercom again. "Sergei Pirov, can you hear me?" He maintained a deep, calm voice. "We can't help you unless you explain what's happening."

Unaware of his surroundings, Pirov threw forceps

and diagnostic equipment at the unbreakable windows. The instruments bounced off, leaving only nicks on the glass. With the same tools, he could easily have killed Sujatha, but he ignored the other doctor.

"He is . . . *changed*, Director, sir," the Bengali gasped into his suit microphone. "Dr. Pirov is no longer human."

The transformed Russian turned his hooded head and raised his bulky arms, clenching and unclenching gloved fists.

In the flickering emergency lights and the weird shadows, Hunter could barely make out the old doctor's features, a bizarre distortion, before he turned away and grabbed another tray of instruments. Roaring, Pirov hurled it at the sealed door.

No longer human?

Scalpels, battery-powered laser incision tools, a rotary bone-cutting saw, and medical diagnostic equipment clattered and bounced. Then he turned to the massive laser drill and wrestled with its anchor stand, trying unsuccessfully to uproot the machine from the floor. Sujatha hunched out of the way, trying to avoid the furious, inhuman storm.

Outside the window, Marines extended their rifles. They flinched uneasily, but dared not fire.

Lurching over to the chamber's airlock hatch, Pirov worked with the controls, trying to force the locking wheel, but it would not budge. Then he hammered on the armored autoclave door, to no effect.

Perplexed as well as horrified, Garamov glanced at Hunter in awe. "What is this? Director Hunter, do you have any explanations?"

"I don't think any of us understands, Vasili." Out of nervous habit, Hunter brushed down his mustache. More sweat trickled from his forehead.

Though it had been neutralized by the emergency

lockdown, the keypad exit panel still glowed beside the door. The Russian doctor knew the access code, but he hadn't even bothered to enter it. Why would he try the manual release first? It was as if the man had no memory of who or where he was.

Finally, as if wrestling some sort of control upon himself, Pirov turned to the keypad. Gloved fingers punched buttons with lightning-fast reflexes to enter the code. The panel glowed scarlet, refusing to open the door. Another alarm sounded.

Pirov canceled the entry and stabbed at the buttons again, his fingers an even faster blur than before. When the system denied him a second time, he flew into a rage and punched the panel. His gloved fist smashed it into a sparking eruption of sizzling wires, burned-out indicator lights, and shards of plastic and metal.

"Can't we shoot him with a tranquilizer gun?" Durston said with morbid fascination. "He's like a mad elephant."

"I'm afraid we didn't install automatic tranquilizer guns as part of our standard security systems, Mr. Congressman." Hunter was too concerned for his people to pay much attention to Durston's overblown sense of importance. "Funding constraints, you know."

Garamov glowered at the congressman. "That man is a highly respected researcher and one of the chief medical experts of Project Proteus, Mr. Durston."

"Not anymore," Durston said.

Realizing the futility of his efforts to escape, Pirov paced like a tiger in a cage. His arms swayed back and forth with coiled violence, until he reached an internal crisis. As if his anti-contamination suit had begun to burn his skin, the old man tore at the seals and openings with inhuman strength. He yowled out a primal scream and ripped the tape fastenings, splitting zippers with his fingers. Tiny metal teeth sprayed out like raindrops. The polymer-reinforced fabric dropped into rags.

With an enormous heave, Pirov yanked off his flexible hood, tearing the lapped seams that joined it to his collar. He threw the flopping hood like a projectile up at the observation gallery, where it struck the window with a loud thump.

The hybrid creature that had once been Dr. Sergei Pirov stood fully revealed in the harsh light.

The man's skin was smooth and grayish. Most of his short, salt-and-pepper hair had fallen out like bristly dust. Pirov's eyes bulged, enlarged beyond what Hunter had thought a human skull could accommodate. His nose had melted into the slab of his face, his ears atrophied until they were streamlined nubs against the side of his head.

"On the bright side, now we have *two* specimens." Durston drew in a quick breath, and his eyes narrowed. "And this one's alive and kicking."

Garamov frowned at him in disgust, concerned for both the original alien in the lifepod and the transformed Russian doctor. "Are you certain your security field will hold, Director Hunter?"

"It'll hold." His mind reeled as he tried to formulate explanations, something he could accept. He turned to the Deputy Foreign Minister. "Now I am even more relieved that you didn't let any curious soldiers or local Azerbaijani doctors crack open the lifepod."

"I fear that even this security might not be enough." Garamov couldn't tear his eyes from Dr. Pirov's behavior. "If Sergei gets his way."

The transformed Russian looked up at the men in the observation deck. His narrow shoulders sagged, and he spoke in an unearthly tenor with a newly lipless mouth. "Let . . . me . . . out." He selected each word as if pulling it from an unfamiliar database. "I need . . . to get . . . out."

Hunter didn't answer. The Pirov creature took two long, heaving breaths, and seemed to rediscover his inner emotions. He added a desperate plea, sounding almost human again. "Director Hunter, I have to get out. Please let me. You don't understand what's happening here, what's happening to me." His voice became a mewling cry.

Now that the Pirov-alien could communicate using human words again, Hunter tried to get some answers. "Sergei, you know I can't let you out. Are you able to explain what's happened to you? Do you know what—"

As soon as Hunter denied his request, Pirov became a whirlwind again, smashing equipment, throwing himself against anchored tables. He seemed careful not to harm the lifepod, where the original alien astronaut lay, still motionless. Hunter realized that Dr. Pirov was the alien's counterpart now.

Crouched in a corner under an equipment rack, Rajid Sujatha drew his legs up to his chest. Trying to remain unseen, he touched his cracked faceplate in horror, knowing he must be contaminated, too.

He saw what had become of Dr. Pirov and feared that the same fate lay in store for him.

Chapter 35

The battered *Mote* accelerated toward the opposite end of the long bone shaft. Reproducing blood cells and geometric platelets crowded the fatty globules in the yellow marrow, but Devlin found enough room to maneuver.

With time running out, he kept the ship racing at full speed. He was relieved to have a clear path ahead, yet disconcerted that he had no idea where they were going, or how the team would get out of the alien's body.

In forty-six minutes they would start to grow.

Dr. Tyler looked up from her crude diagrams on the analysis table. "Obviously, bone marrow doesn't offer any egress from the body. We have to work our way outward, through blood vessels and fatty tissue, to the epidermis and another pore."

Devlin noted the dwindling time left on the chronometer. "Roger that, but I'd be more comfortable if we knew we were making progress in the right direction. With all that nanocritter-generated static, it's been a long time since I've gotten a decent reading from the navigation computer."

The vessel rushed along, buffeted by currents in the marrow fluid, the hiss of thick plasma sounding like a waterfall against the windows. After so many

hours, the atmosphere inside the craft had grown
warm and stuffy.

Devlin spared a glance to check the *Mote*'s power
levels: batteries low but within acceptable limits, impellers operating with sufficient fuel. The laser
charges were diminished; Tomiko had used her
weaponry far more than any scenario had anticipated.

At last, given a moment of reflection in the constant tension, Devlin remembered that he had promised himself to buy her a nice dinner after they had
survived the pedicel ordeal. "Are you free Saturday
night?" By now, he probably owed her a month of
fine cuisine. . . .

She looked at him quickly, pleased and surprised
by the offer. "You mean, can I break away from the
wide range of leisure activities available inside the
Proteus Facility? Gee, I'll have to check my social
calendar." She returned her attention to her weapon
control. "But let's get out of here first."

Traveling the length of the bone shaft, they encountered only one nanoscout, which Tomiko blasted
before it could send out an alarm signal. "There'll
be more of those things when we get to the other
end, Marc."

"Affirmative. I'm counting on it." He enjoyed her
startled glance.

Ahead he could see a Swiss-cheese webwork of
bone, calcified curtains that turned the marrow into
a factory maze, where human red blood cells would
have been produced. The bone passages looked like
wormholes in rotted wood. Devlin selected his spot
at a juncture of tunnels with overhanging calcium
fibers. "Here's where we'll go to ground." He rotated
the *Mote*, reversed the impellers, and backed into the
meager shelter. Waiting, like a spider in a hole.

Devlin flicked a switch on the comm system

Keep a lookout, everybody. I just turned our SOS signal back on."

Freeth gaped at him. "But we know that attracts the nanocritters."

"Precisely. But *I* want to choose the time and place for an ambush." Devlin cracked his knuckles, limbering up for action. "I plan to capture a nanomachine. Once we disable it, I'm hoping I can extract its IFF. Then we'll be perfectly camouflaged, a sheep in wolf's clothing."

It would have been so simple to play back recorded alien signals, but the carrier pulse was in a complex, variable code that shifted at random. With so little time remaining, Devlin could not separate out a predictable pattern. He'd have to snatch a transmitter with its programming already built in.

Marrow fluid swirled around them, gently rocking the deck. He shut down their bright spotlights. The SOS beacon fluttered like a matador's red cape for the marauding nanocritters.

"My finger's on the firing button, Marc," Tomiko said.

"Wait for it. Try not to cause too much damage."

The first prowling machines arrived without warning, a hunting pair that streaked out of a side passage toward the miniaturized ship.

Tomiko shifted the targeting cross, then fired a brief burst at the first one, ripping open its chain-link underbelly and shorting out the diamond memory wafer. Then she punched through the fullerene wall of the second device to burn out its power source. The flailing, clacking carbon-lattice claws of the oncoming machines drooped.

Devlin shut down the SOS signal. "Nice shooting. You can hang one as a trophy on your wall."

"I'd need an awfully small taxidermist."

After switching on the spotlights again, he climbed

out of the piloting chair. Tomiko launched the anchor harpoons into the calcified walls. The *thunk* of impact reverberated along the cable.

"Okay, let's suit up. Mr. Freeth, we'll need your help outside. This is going to have to be the fastest jury-rig in history."

The UFO expert was so startled he took a step backward, bumping into one of the detachable chairs and sitting down heavily. "Me? But I don't know how a nanomachine works."

Cynthia Tyler looked at him, her eyes flashing, "Just use your imagination, Freeth. You're good at that."

Devlin clapped him on the shoulder and handed him a slithery suit from the equipment closet. "Here, this one'll fit you."

He and Tomiko pulled on their suits and adjusted the seals while Freeth struggled into his own garb. The UFO expert flexed his arms, fiddled with his gloves, and adjusted the curved faceplate to make sure he could see properly. Tomiko settled Freeth's airtank onto his thin shoulders, cinched the straps tighter, and whispered, "Don't hyperventilate, Arnold. We need your help."

"I'll continue to take readings and measurements," Tyler said. "This will be our last chance. But no heroics out there. Not even you, Freeth."

"Believe me, no heroics," he agreed.

With the three of them crowded inside the airlock tube, Devlin operated the manual valves. Alien plasma fluid streamed around them, squeezing its clammy grip around their legs, waists, and chests.

With their respirators and faceplates in place and line-of-sight radios checked, Tomiko pulled up the hatch. Pushing off from the airlock wall and Devlin's shoulder, she swam out first. The two men followed her into the microscopic bone caverns. Cones of harsh light from the tethered ship cast stark shadows, swaying as the *Mote* was nudged by tricky biological currents.

The dead nanocritters drifted like derelict spaceships.

Freeth thrashed in the syrupy, protein-rich liquid, clearly not remembering his training drill with Dr. Wylde. Tomiko turned backward and pulled him along for a few strokes until he adjusted, and the three of them swam to the pair of burned, pitted nanomachines.

Devlin set his jaw, remembering how simple it had been when the nanocritters were deactivated. Though he still had only a partial understanding of their carbon-lattice structure and buckytube piston mechanics, he had to make some guesses. Right now, with only thirty-five minutes left, he would have to take a few shortcuts.

The two gutted machines hung like junk heaps in the sluggish fluid. One barely attached claw arm dangled like an articulated crowbar. Because the signal generator was on such a small scale, Devlin believed its mechanics would be straightforward and comprehensible even to him. The transmitter's instruction-set memory must be far simpler than the full self-replication and mission programming.

Or so he hoped.

There was no time for finesse. He would remove the transmitter component, connect it to a direct power source from the *Mote*, and coax it into sending the appropriate "leave me alone" signal. It wasn't going to be easy.

He took out his toolkit and set to work with a screwdriver. His gloved hands got past molecular connections, shifting matrices of buckyballs and breaking the bonds between extruded components.

The bell-shaped transceiver seemed intact, but the laser blast had destroyed the controller chip.

As Devlin worked, he gestured to Tomiko and Freeth. "See if you can remove the control chip from the other one. It's a self-contained module below the signal generator."

"It better be a separate component, Marc," Tomiko said over the suit radio. "I sort of fried the main diamond memory wafer on this one."

Amazed at what he was doing, Freeth reluctantly ran his gloved hands over the slippery side of the second nanomachine, touching the burnt crater where Tomiko's laser had blasted apart the fullerene walls. Hardened graphite spears and whiskers of re-arranged carbon broken from the fullerene lattice sprouted like snowflakes around the wound. Tiny bubbles oozed out of the nanomachine's broken side, like leaking blood.

Working together, Freeth and Tomiko removed the intact controller module above the singed diamond memory wafer. They broke the connections holding it to the damaged transmitter and pried it loose. They swam through the murky fluid carrying the delicate black box of impurity-laced carbon webwork back to Devlin.

He lifted the bizarre transmitter construction. Detached buckyballs dropped like marbles, broken out of the structural grid. The clunky, bell-shaped mouth of the device reminded him of a mad scientist's prop from an old movie.

Since their vessel was surrounded by a miniaturization field, he couldn't mount the slapdash transmitter directly onto the hull, but he could tow it behind them. He would use the metal-core anchor cable as a tether and power conduit.

It had sounded like a simple and obvious idea, but when he actually attempted his plan, every step in the process seemed improbable. Devlin had no other choice but to try.

Devlin uprooted molecular-chain wires and bent them with great effort, connecting the components cannibalized from the two machines, a controller and a transmitter. Now he only needed a flow of electrons from the *Mote*'s generators.

Stroking backward in the marrow fluid, Devlin lugged the apparatus to where the nearest anchor cable was embedded in the calcium wall. He let the transmitter float free while he planted his booted feet and uprooted the sharp anchor.

Stringing the cable to the alien IFF device, he tried to make proper connections, conductor against conductor. If he could jolt the transmitter with enough power, the system just might operate according to its self-contained programming. If he'd guessed right, the signal might fool the nanomachines. If not, he had just wasted half of their remaining time for getting out of the alien body.

"Company coming, Marc," Tomiko transmitted.

He thrashed around to see a new machine barreling toward the *Mote*, closing in for the kill. "What have these things got against my ship?"

Overhead, thin bone crumbled away like pieces broken from a glacier. Another nanocritter chewed through the calcium ceiling. This machine had six sharp arms, each one ending in a diamond-edged knife, pyridine-tipped punch, or a sawblade pincer claw.

Sensor lights gleamed like predatory eyes on the wire-mesh body as it scanned the area, then lurched toward the anchored *Mote*, ignoring the miniaturized humans.

Like a bouncer in a biker bar, Tomiko moved to intercept the nanomachines. "I'll handle this little guy. Arnold, you take the other one." She tore the half-severed arm from the wrecked device and shoved it at him. "Here. Show the thing who's boss."

Confused, the UFO expert caught the microscopic spear and held it to do battle against a minuscule Goliath.

"Just get that transmitter functioning, Marc, and you'll save us all."

"Roger that. But no pressure, right?" Devlin worked with fumbling hands, blinking sweat out of his eyes behind the facemask.

With powerful strokes, Tomiko met the multilimbed nanomachine before it could attach itself to the *Mote*. She fought it hand to hand, martial arts in fluid form, using fists and arms to counter the movement of its jointed carbon legs. She grabbed an angular protrusion and twisted it sideways, wrenching the buckytube out of its socket. Sparks glowed in the marrow fluid, and the sheathed-piston limb hung useless.

Now, for the first time, the relentless machine recognized her as a threat.

Tomiko grasped a second pincer, but the nanocritter bore down on her, pushing her backward through the marrow fluid. When she finally found leverage against the curving bone wall, she pressed back, harder this time. The second fullerene limb broke, and she snagged a third as the other arms grabbed for her, sharp tips slashing.

Trying another tactic, Tomiko plunged the attacking machine's spear arm into the porous bone. While the machine strained to disentangle itself, she kicked out, smashing the diamond memory circuit board again and again. Her boot scraped away carefully laid paths of hydrogen and fluorine. Brain damaged, the nanomachine jerked and jittered in a robotic seizure.

The second device swam up from below like a torpedo intercepting a target, and Arnold Freeth jabbed with the jagged end of his spear. He thrust the makeshift crowbar between the clacking components of a pincer claw. He knocked the claw off, then stabbed again. The blunt end of his spear scraped the machine's body core, knocking a few carbon spheres loose, but did no substantial damage.

Freeth struck repeatedly, hindered by the surrounding fluid. Finally, by accident, he smashed an optical sensor. While the disoriented device spun in confusion, he brought the spear down on a second "eye," then a third, blinding it completely. Within moments, he succeeded in incapacitating the device.

Meanwhile, fingers slippery in the thick fluid, breathing hard inside his suit, Devlin finally finished connecting the tetherwire to the controller module of the makeshift transmitter. "Got it! Let's get back inside and see if this thing works."

Leaving their mechanical casualties behind, Tomiko was already stroking for the hatch. The three of them climbed up into the airlock. Freeth, proud of what he had done, sealed the hatch without even being told. As pumps in the floor sucked out the fluid, Devlin yanked down his suit hood and stripped off the environmental suit, gasping. He wiped his face with a towel, anxious to rush for the cockpit.

Cynthia Tyler met him as he emerged from the airlock. "More nanomachines just arrived, Major Devlin. I think they've got us cornered."

Devlin threw himself into the cockpit chair and powered up the impellers, dismayed to see the machines already closing in on their hiding place. "Tomiko, detach that second anchor."

At the controls, she winched the hooked spike out of the bone wall. "Go!" She reeled in the cable as the *Mote* lurched into motion.

Devlin maneuvered the ship out of the protected alcove, trailing the makeshift IFF transmitter in their wake.

The ship streaked away, on the run again, and the nanocritters followed. Three more devices slammed into the *Mote*, clinging hard like leeches. They battered the hull plates, slashing and cutting, using specialized tools.

Still moist and disheveled, smelling of the salty plasma fluid, Tomiko searched for a way to shoot the nanomachines that were already attached to the hull.

The additional weight of the predatory devices made for sluggish handling. The IFF transmitter trailed behind them, still intact and attached. "Time for the moment of truth." Devlin crosswired circuits in the front control board, wishing he had time to double-check the power flux parameters. Gambling, he sent a pulse through the metallic tether.

After a cough of static, the IFF transmitter struggled and glowed. A broadcast came out garbled, distorted—making the attacking machines pause. Devlin worked with the power flow on the cockpit boards, trying to massage the signal. "Come on, come on."

The stolen generator finally sent out a warbling tone that rose and fell unpredictably. The nanohunters stopped in their tracks and then fell back. The *Mote* continued its reckless flight. The three devices clinging to the hull ceased their dismantling activities and waited.

Devlin looked around, eyes wide with hope, holding his breath.

As the makeshift IFF signal continued, the machines detached themselves one by one. Confused, they dropped away into the marrow fluid.

Still sweating, not wanting to push his luck, Devlin accelerated through the bone marrow. From behind, he watched the mechanical marauders hover, as if reassessing their priorities. The stolen identification signal must not be exactly right . . . but it was close.

Finally, the machines disbanded and went about their normal business.

The crew applauded Devlin's efforts. "We're not out of trouble yet." He tried to be modest but couldn't keep the grin off his face.

"Okay," Tomiko said. "About next Saturday night. Are we going to eat in the Proteus cafeteria, or are you a bigger spender than that?"

Devlin laughed. "Tomiko Braddock, I will take you to the best restaurant in Fresno."

"Now *that's* something to look forward to."

The *Mote* proceeded through the network of lamellae until they finally discovered a blood vessel leading out of the dense outer bone, through the alien version of Haversian channels, and through the joint articulation.

Devlin didn't know how long their nano-identifier signal would protect the ship. His main goal was to track down the shortest route to the skin and get away to safety. He'd had enough exploration and excitement for one day, and he had a crew to protect.

According to the mission chronometer, they had only half an hour left.

Chapter 36

Rajid Sujatha's flesh crawled with a life of its own. His muscle fibers were stretching and knotted. His blood sizzled, as if filled with tiny bubbles of charged fluid.

Perspiring heavily inside his anti-contamination suit, Sujatha shuddered. Each breath echoed in his head, like thunder striking his distorted tympanic membranes.

Sujatha forced himself into a sitting position, fighting a wave of dizziness and nausea. Bizarre thoughts hummed inside his head, strange whispering sounds like a swarm of insects that spoke in alien voices.

"No, no, no." The hood microphone picked up his moaning chant and broadcast it over the loudspeakers.

After his initial fury, Dr. Pirov had ignored him. Sujatha had watched the transformed Russian smash laboratory equipment, trying to find some way to break out of this thick-walled prison.

Pirov's wild attack had been a disjointed impulse, a loss of control, and now Sujatha could feel the same thing coming upon himself. A link had broken in the transition between an intelligent human and an extraterrestrial sentience. Both species had violent and terrible evolutionary pasts; atavistic impulses could easily break free.

Groaning deep in his throat, Sujatha focused on the hair-fine crack in his faceplate. It formed a line across his vision, like a barrier separating his human identity from the burgeoning alienness that was attempting to conquer his very being. He struggled for control.

He remembered his experimental rabbit. Gentle and innocent, Fluffy Alice had survived numerous test missions, shrinking and enlarging. The rabbit had lived her life pampered in a cage. Right now, he wanted to stroke her ears, draw calm from the furry animal.

An hour ago, the last garbled broadcast from Team Proteus had been *infestation . . . nanomachines . . . swarms.* By now the *Mote* was probably already destroyed.

"Director Hunter, sir." Sujatha shook his head and blinked. He desperately wanted to describe his symptoms, to perform a last service as a scientist.

"We hear you, Rajid." He could not look up to see the Director in the observation alcove, but he found the rich voice from the intercom reassuring.

Sujatha forced himself not to stop speaking, afraid that if he lost his momentum of humanity, the alienness would crash down around him again. "My vision is blurred and refocused, apparently shifting to different parts of the spectrum. The bright overhead light hurts my eyes." In fact, the glare felt like photonic spikes pounding through his pupils.

Hunter said, "I'm sending Dr. Wylde down to the window outside the chamber. Talk to her if you can. Face to face. It might help."

Sujatha pressed gloved hands against his cracked faceplate, but he could not touch his cheeks. "The orbital cavities around my eyes ache, as if someone is using a rib-spreader to stretch my sockets . . . to accommodate larger eyes . . . like those." He indicated the huge black orbs that Sergei Pirov now blinked at him without compassion or understanding.

After ripping his thick anti-contamination suit to shreds, the unrecognizable Pirov stood with fabric tatters hanging about his shoulders and waist. The transformation complete, his alien body looked smooth and ethereal, a ghost image of a human.

I will look like that soon. It is only a matter of time.

Pirov's bare chest showed only gray skin without fine hair, or nipples, or wrinkles—a body sculpted cell by cell through the work of billions of microscopic machines. It looked like an artificial costume . . . something unreal.

The Pirov-alien looked at him, and Sujatha backed away, afraid of more violence. But by cracking the Bengali doctor's faceplate, he had already done sufficient damage. Sujatha's transformation was now a foregone conclusion.

Pirov cocked his ovoid head, staring with unblinking black eyes, like a bird studying an insect. His lipless mouth moved, and his thin throat rippled. After several tries, the Russian's voice worked again. "Integration is complete. We have incorporated the cultural data reservoir of this life form."

His now-pointed chin jutted toward him. "Rajid . . . Sujatha. We know you. We will soon add your memories to our information pool. Initial adaptation is always hardest upon conquering a new species."

Part of Sujatha, the new alien part, responded to the words with eager anticipation. But his human personality recoiled in horror as he heard the word "conquer."

He could feel implanted thoughts as the massive

infestation stitched programmed memories into his mind. The nanomachines downloaded information from an alien civilization, data that had been stored inside their partitioned supercomputer.

The Pirov-alien pounded again on the thick windows of their prison. The Lexan vibrated but did not break. He looked up to analyze the faces of Director Hunter and Deputy Foreign Minister Garamov, displaying only a glimmer of recognition. Sujatha saw no emotions, no personality on the inhuman face . . . but fragments of Pirov's original memories must have yielded information on how the VIP observers fit in with Project Proteus.

"Our space vessel's flight has been interrupted by military aircraft." Pirov looked over at the still-motionless alien in the lifepod. "Original emissary placed into shock-induced deep stasis. Reanimation delayed." He paused, curious, calculating, and then lost control again. "Let us out!"

Caught in the transition between human and alien, Sujatha was the only one who could explain. He croaked into his hood microphone. "Director Hunter, sir." He could give the necessary clues to help the human race combat this threat. "The aliens do not dispatch a military invasion force." Sujatha shook his head to clear the buzzing from his brain; then a jolt of pain shot down his spine. "Too inefficient."

A crackle of agony came after he had spoken, a punishment from the nanomachines, but he managed to climb to his feet, not afraid of Pirov anymore, resigned to his fate. "They send only a scout ship with one pilot. He contains the seeds of their whole civilization." Within Sujatha's body cavity, the organs felt like loose biological masses spinning about in a rock tumbler.

The Pirov-alien looked at him with a masklike face.

He displayed no expression, no emotion. "We require nothing more than that to subsume a world."

Moving with trepidation, Trish Wylde approached the main windows of the containment room. "Director Hunter asked me to come here, to see if I can talk to them." Perhaps with her pathology expertise, she could learn something, draw important conclusions. But this was so far beyond anything she had ever seen.

The Marine guards stood fully alert and ready, but flustered by not knowing what to do. They couldn't shoot, couldn't run, could only stare at the aliens inside the containment room.

Dr. Wylde tossed her short, reddish hair, screwed up her courage, and pounded on the thick glass to draw Sujatha's attention. When the Bengali doctor turned to her, she noted his waxy, grayish face, his angular features smoothing, his eyes already huge and black, far beyond normal. His bushy eyebrows had fallen out.

Behind him, Pirov no longer resembled a human at all. Hearing her, the Russian doctor launched himself at the window, his slick gray skin striking the glass. His face rippled with loss of control. Trish flinched backward, but held her ground.

Sujatha knocked the Pirov-alien aside, obviously surprised at his own strength. The transformed old man sprawled on the floor, then picked himself up on spindly arms and legs, momentarily disoriented.

Trish tried to be objective, calling upon her knowledge to assess what she could see of the transformation these victims were undergoing. But nothing she'd ever encountered, not even the most extraordinary plague organism, had inflicted such gross bodily changes—not radiation-induced mutations, carcinogens, or birth-defect-causing teratogens.

I could have been in there myself. I wanted to be a part of the mission. But Director Hunter turned me down. Her skin crawled. If she'd won her argument with him, if she'd convinced the Director, then *she* might have turned into one of those creatures.

After being knocked aside, Pirov didn't seem to be alert anymore. The transformed doctor wandered over to the open lifepod and seemed to be waiting for something. For the other alien to wake up?

Trish flicked on the wall intercom. "Dr. Sujatha? Do you understand me?"

The Bengali doctor weaved on his feet, as if trying to remember what he had been doing. Sujatha pressed against the window glass, close to her, and paused, his face falling slack. He said nothing.

"Dr. Sujatha! You're the only one who can—"

He continued to explain the invasion plan, as if he hadn't heard her. "The alien pilot investigates mapped planets until it finds a compatible world, especially an inhabited planet. Then it emerges and releases the nanotechnology infection."

"Like Typhoid Mary."

"The machines replicate and spread, reshaping all native life forms into an alien image. Like this." He held his hands up to his monstrous face. "*Like me.*"

Trish stepped closer to the window, feeling sick. Before anyone knew an invasion was under way, the takeover would be complete. The aliens would have a ready-made colony on Earth without firing a shot.

With a glance up at the observation deck, Trish could tell the diplomats and Hunter were struggling with what they had heard. Congressman Durston wore a sour expression, no doubt already planning to destroy Project Proteus and sterilize the containment chamber.

Trish didn't think Director Hunter would obliterate the threat unless it was genuine, especially not with his son-in-law inside. But such hesitation might prove deadly for the human race. He might have no choice but to take such drastic action.

"How can we stop the invasion?" she asked, hoping the Bengali doctor's thoughts remained clear. "Dr. Sujatha?"

"You cannot." Pirov's alien voice held no doubt at all.

Sujatha squeezed his enlarged eyes shut as bolts of pain rippled through his body, holding his mind hostage. "Only a first step. Pilot establishes a beachhead for continued spread of their civilization. Once native population is subdued and converted to—" He winced with a surge of crippling pain. "Then ships come, commercial vessels, a military fleet, government officials. By the time they arrive, the battle is already over."

Sujatha turned away from Trish and looked plaintively up at Director Hunter. He spoke in a rush, as if fearing he would be stopped at any second. "There is a chance, sir. Unless their pilot transmits a signal that Earth is a prime candidate, that the beachhead is established, the alien civilization will assume he is still traveling from system to system." He fought against a seizure. "You must . . . prevent—" He shouted the final words through his growing agony. "*Signal!* Stop it from being sent."

Like a hunting cat, the Pirov-alien threw himself upon his companion. Sujatha could not back away fast enough. The Russian drove him backward into the wall. Sujatha's head bounced against the thick window, only inches from where Trish stood in the corridor.

The armed Marines scrambled backward, holding up their rifles, but she leaped in front of them, knocking the guns aside. The bulletproof glass should have stopped the weapons fire, but she didn't want to risk the tiniest breach of the chamber.

After fighting off the Pirov-alien, Sujatha could no longer put words together. Within his body, the nanomachines had removed his ability to speak. His limbs watery, he slid to the floor again.

Trish shuddered. Humanity had already received a life-saving stroke of luck when the Russian fighter jets had shot down the UFO, and Garamov's cautious response had been absolutely correct. If the alien pilot had landed on the White House lawn, he would have stepped out and extended a long-fingered hand in a gesture of peace.

A hand crawling with microscopic nano-invaders. Like a Trojan horse.

The struggle was just beginning here inside the Proteus Facility. If a single replicating machine escaped into the open, there could be no stopping the transformation.

The Pirov-alien prowled over to the open lifepod and gestured with spindly fingers. Before long the microscopic devices inside the original pilot's body would bring him out of stasis. And there would be three of them inside the chamber, working together to complete their mission.

Sujatha found it more and more difficult to control his movements. Even his thoughts were being stolen away, one by one, as if a horde of spiders were crawling through his brain, spinning a web of artificial concepts, pricking his cerebrum with poisoned fangs.

He forced himself to think of his family, summoning the image of his beautiful wife, with her light-brown skin, blue-black hair, soft features. He recalled each one of his daughters, how he enjoyed playing games with them—Chinese checkers on rainy days, or badminton in the backyard.

In his heart Sujatha knew he would never again do such things. But the memories remained clear. *His* memories. As long as he kept those, he could retain his humanity.

A bolt of red lightning screamed across his retinas, scrambling his vision and shooting a vertical spike through his brain. But he did not cry out.

Sujatha envisioned his wife again, focused on her dusky features, tried to whisper her name through uncooperative lips. Then, to his horror, the cruel nanomachines shifted the image until he saw her transformed into an oval-faced alien with huge ebony eyes.

He shook his head and vowed not to let that happen. He moaned with despair, the only sound the nanomachines would allow out of his throat.

Sujatha could never replace his wife and his young children, could never erase all the things he had accomplished in his life. Looking at Pirov, knowing that the old man had become a member of a different species bent on the destruction of the human race, the Bengali doctor understood that he must never leave this containment room. And neither could his colleague.

Sujatha knew he would not survive this. He could never go home.

He clenched his hands inside the gloves of his useless anti-contamination suit and wondered how long he could remain *himself.*

Chapter 37

Towed behind the *Mote*, the cannibalized nanotransmitter broadcast its "friendly" signal, sputtering and then starting again. The ever-increasing numbers of nanocritters ignored them and instead concentrated on their own activities, reproducing, spreading, building.

Time was running out for Team Proteus. *Twelve minutes.*

Using his best instincts, Devlin tried to navigate toward the alien's skin surface. He had to find a route that led to a skin pore or a glandular opening. Anything.

As he searched, Devlin pondered the alien's incredible self-defense mechanisms: saber-jawed pedicels covering the skin surface, xenozoan microorganisms, even relentless nanomachine hunters. Though the extraterrestrial astronaut had looked peaceful and benign in its lifepod, the evidence at a microscopic level implied horrific struggles on the alien's home world, warfare unlike anything even the most violent nations on Earth had conceived.

Instead of using competing armies, battles must have been fought through nanotechnology. Clashing genotypes and physical designs must have struggled for supremacy, enemy factions developing defenses down to their very cellular structure. The alien's pedicels, xenozoans, and nanomachines had probably taken the *Mote* for an unrecognized enemy nano-invader that had to be destroyed.

What if such a threat were unleashed on an unsuspecting Earth?

The nanocritters had not yet discovered Devlin's ruse with the IFF signal, but the sea of jamming signals threw off his navigation computer and compass alignment. Amber warning lights flickered on the *Mote*'s control boards, and the power flux jittered.

"She was never designed for this," he muttered. When the IFF signal broke off, Devlin scrambled with his tools and his intuition to coax their stolen signal generator back to life.

Swarms of busy nanomachines worked on the cell structure around them, modifying and rejuvenating the dormant alien body like a vast urban-renewal project. Tomiko tensed at her weapons, but Devlin got the false identifier signal started again, casting just enough ambiguity that the *Mote* was out of range before the nanomachines could rally.

Two lumbering devices blocked the racing ship's passage, by accident rather than by organized ambush. Tomiko destroyed them without a second thought. She frowned at her gauges, saw that she had power for only a few dozen shots more. "Laser cannons running low, Marc."

He flicked a few switches. "I expected the lasers to be used once or twice on a whole mission, for surgical strikes only."

"Been a blast, though, hasn't it?" she said with a smile.

Eavesdropping from the main compartment, Arnold Freeth said, "You're very strange, Ms. Braddock."

Devlin didn't try to cover his smile. "I bet Mr.

Freeth doesn't often get the opportunity to call anybody else strange." He soared past a sheet of fatty tissue impregnated with corkscrewing blood vessels. Tense, he looked at the dwindling time on the chronometer, at the snapshot of Kelli, then flew onward.

"Recognize anything yet, Doc?" He looked back at Cynthia Tyler, who sat tense in the main compartment, strapped into her seat for the final rough ride out of the alien body. "Give me good news."

She continued to stare out at the wilderness of cells and vascular systems. "This looks similar to our initial entry through the epidermis. These walls and the fibrous structure remind me of the hypodermis, and the reticular layer should be the next section."

"Just point me to the nearest hair follicle, or sweat pore, or whatever." He glanced at the mission clock again. *Nine minutes left.*

Impellers whirring, the ship approached a tissue discoloration, a yellowish window like a billboard advertising a particularly fine brand of mucous. "There, Major Devlin." Tyler pointed her slender hand. "Through that barrier. I think it's the bulbous end of a sebaceous gland."

"Exactly what I wanted to hear." Devlin aimed the *Mote*'s prow toward the center of the rubbery wall, then accelerated to ramming speed. "On our way."

On impact, the cell wall split open, and the ship dove into an ocean of pus-yellow fluid. "Now we're making progress," Freeth said.

The overheating impellers carried them through thick turbulence, brilliant spotlights shining out as if through dense fog. The engines groaned louder, fighting through the viscous liquid.

Flying blind, Devlin stumbled unexpectedly into a cluttered construction site of partially assembled nanomachines. "Great, a nanocritter convention." He rolled sideways to avoid ramming several carbon-matrix devices that loomed in front of them.

The nanomachines crowded together, like a large marching band flowing toward the exterior of the alien.

"It's a mass exodus," Tyler said.

"Or a concerted invasion," Freeth said.

Another machine drifted into their path, and the *Mote*'s hull scraped against the multi-armed device. Devlin overcompensated, and on the rebound they crashed into a second machine that was sifting raw materials out of the organic mucous. The wreckage of articulated fullerene arms, imprinted diamond memory flakes, and buckyball gears spun off in separate directions.

Muttering imaginative curses under his breath, Devlin zigzagged through the obstacle course while broken components spanged off the hull.

Long ago, as a test pilot, he'd once flown into a flock of seagulls that had cracked his cockpit windshield, bombarded his plane's sidewalls, and fouled one engine. He'd barely maintained control amidst a spray of feathers and blood.

Now, as he swung around in the thick fluid, the tethered signal generator smashed into the lumbering devices, the loser in a game of crack-the-whip. On Devlin's control screens, the decoy transmitter flickered, and the power flux shut down.

The signal died.

Tomiko reacted instantly. "Step on it, Marc, before they figure out who we are."

Like shadows in the fog, several curious devices moved forward, suddenly noticing the *Mote*. The nanomachines closed around them like a tightening noose.

"I think they already know." Throwing caution to the wind, he soared through the glandular fluid. Currents buffeted them, and the viscous slime flowed across the cockpit windshields like a slow downpour. Devlin could barely see where he was going, but he didn't slow.

Working in eerie concert, a battalion of nanomachines linked claw arms and segmented limbs into a mechanical mesh to block the *Mote*'s passage, like a military roadblock. The impellers spun up with an overworked roar, as if the miniaturized ship were voicing her own indignation. "Everybody hold on!"

Conscious of her dwindling weapons, Tomiko fired only two careful shots. Hot lances burned through the milky pus, opening a breach in the linked barricade of nanomachines, and Devlin rammed through the crumbling blockade. The machines dropped away from each other and streaked after the fleeing ship.

With the jury-rigged IFF transmitter knocked out, the sparking tether cable flailed behind them like a scorpion's tail. As more nanocritters closed in, Devlin dodged left and right, barely able to see ahead of him, but he couldn't let up for a second to wipe away the sweat beaded on his brow. "Hey, Doc, where did you say this gland opens?"

"It should be just up ahead," Tyler said.

The *Mote*'s brilliant beams penetrated the murk, but not far enough.

"I know you'd prefer to deal with one challenge at a time." Tomiko indicated the mission chronometer. "But we've only got seven minutes to get out of here before we start growing."

"Then I hope we're close to the skin surface."

Freeth groaned. "If we don't get out of the lifepod in time, that alien astronaut is going to find an awfully big exploration vessel up his—uh, lap."

"Felix wouldn't appreciate the mess," Devlin said.

Thanks to the dense static, the Director hadn't heard a word from them in an hour and a half. He hoped Felix believed they were still alive. At the very least, he'd be extremely agitated, no doubt regretting his decision to send them on this crazy mission.

In the fluid around them, the nanomachines crowded thicker. The devices had reproduced in wave after wave, far beyond what was required to finish reviving the alien astronaut. Now, in masses, they migrated toward the skin surface, from which they could emerge and sweep across the Earth.

A cold lump formed in Devlin's stomach. If his nanotech warfare scenario was true, then simply escaping from the alien's body would not be good enough for Team Proteus.

Two grappling machines collided with the *Mote* and clung to the hull like lampreys, while others approached from all sides. Devlin put the ship into a violent spin, throwing the nanocritters off.

Desperate, he worked the comm system controls and replayed recordings of the original IFF signal. But no longer fooled, the nanocritters came forward in a redoubled attack. Like torpedoes, the devices rammed the *Mote*.

Tomiko fired eight more times, scoring hits on five devices, but her lasers were growing weaker. According to her gauges, she had only a few shots left.

And the gathered nanomachines were countless.

At last, the glandular fluid spilled out like a slow-motion Niagara, lubricating the walls of a titanic shaft, a bottomless pit in the alien's skin.

"Emergency exit, right this way." Devlin shot out into the pore, spraying mucous behind them. Runnels like protein-thick honey trickled off the windows and hull.

A galaxy of nanocritters lined the opening of the glandular duct. Reacting to the proximity of the *Mote*, they dropped like paratrooper saboteurs. Two machines thudded onto the roof, and Devlin saw no

choice but to fly straight up. "Hang on." He scraped
the upper hull against the flexible gland wall, knocking the clinging devices off. Crushed carbon-lattice
debris tumbled behind them. Devlin didn't glance
back.

"Look at them all!" Freeth said.

A horrendous marching army of nanomachines
lined the pore, thousands upon thousands of them.
Devlin kept the *Mote* in the center of the shaft, out
of their reach. He pulled the control stick toward him
and shot upward, accelerating so hard that his lips
stretched back against his teeth.

A hungry xenozoan moved down the pore wall, a
flowing blob. Suddenly a squadron of nanocritters
engulfed the monstrous microorganism, tearing it
apart like ants on a fat caterpillar. The tiny robots
ripped away protein chains, organelles, and genetic
material, scavenging the necessary resources to swell
their numbers even further. Devlin's stomach twisted
with revulsion.

Six minutes remained on the mission chronometer.

Tomiko stared through the scratched cockpit windshield as they rocketed upward. "Is that what I think
it is? Genuine outside light, way up there?"

"Roger that, and about time, too." Devlin punched
the impellers in a high-G ascent, as if he were testing
a fast jet aircraft. He dodged a few floating nanomachines intent on trapping them, but paid little attention to irrelevant obstacles. He plowed ahead
without pause and left battered devices in his wake.

The *Mote* burst out of the skin pore, and Devlin
let out a whoop of triumph.

"Watch out for the pedicels, Major Devlin," Tyler
said, wiping long strands of permed blond hair out
of her eyes. "It would be embarrassing to be destroyed now, after all our trouble."

Freeth looked at her, wondering whether she had

intended to make a joke. "Believe me, it would be more than embarrassing."

But as the *Mote* rose above the organic dermal plain, they saw that the waving forests of pedicels had been felled, as if by an onslaught of lumberjacks. The alien's gray skin looked like a battlefield strewn with cadavers.

Vicious nanomachines had trimmed all outer defenses and used the pedicels' raw materials to build more and more copies of themselves. The vast epidermis crawled with billions of the tiny devices, all of them ready to swarm outward in an invasion force too small for the human eye to see.

Devlin soared into the blurry white distance of the "sky." Time was running out—five minutes now. Luckily, the tiny locator beacon Dr. Sujatha had installed on the outer glass would help them find the pinprick escape hole in the lifepod's covering.

"Something's not right up there. I can't hear the pinger." He stared through the windowport, searching for the transparent dome far overhead. "And I can't find the ceiling either."

The *Mote* flew and flew, but encountered no barrier. On their minuscule scale, he could see nothing, had no sense of perspective. "We've gone past where we should have encountered the pod glass."

Tomiko strained her eyes, but she saw nothing that would help him. "I'd really like to get through the escape hole before we return to normal size."

Finally, unexpectedly, they reached a metal wall the size of a Grand Canyon cliff. Devlin recognized the outer lip of the lifepod—and understood. "That's why we can't find the ceiling. The pod's been opened."

"Opened?" Tomiko slumped in her chair, looking sick. "Great, and now the containment room has been exposed to all this alien nanotechnology. Just look."

Lines of advanced nanocritter scouts trooped across the edge of the lifepod, spilling onto the floor, onto every surface. *Spreading . . . swarming.*

"Billions and billions," Freeth said. "They must be grabbing raw material from the lifepod itself."

Once the microscopic armies flooded into the room, they would dismantle chairs, tables, equipment, anything to reproduce themselves. An unstoppable, invisible army.

Tyler sounded guilty and tired. "It appears that we're too late."

"Don't jump to conclusions. Now that we're out of the body, we can send a clear signal to Felix. Maybe Project Proteus can come up with some countermeasures." Devlin glanced at the mission chronometer again. "We start growing in four minutes."

"Then at least we'll be too big for the nanocritters to bother us," Freeth said. "That'll be a relief."

"Time to use your imagination again, Freeth." Tyler turned to him, happy to point out something that the UFO expert hadn't realized. "Once we reach our normal size, the nanomachines will infest *us.*"

Chapter 38

As time ran out, the creature that had been Dr. Sergei Pirov became more calculating. And much more dangerous. It would take so little to set in motion the unstoppable invasion.

Even with his brute strength, his muscles and bones reinforced by nanotech modifications, he was not able to break free of the chamber. Armored walls enclosed him, maddened him, prevented him from doing what he *must* do.

Entirely transformed now, his brain buzzed with the need to complete the instructions programmed into him. He had to unleash the replicating nanomachines so the inhabitants of this planet could be subsumed.

It must be done.

Depthless black eyes, designed for the light of a different sun, scrutinized his resources as he tried to determine another way out of the chamber prison. Restless and searching, he prowled among the analytical equipment and medical debris strewn around the chamber.

Slowly, his new mind grasped that breaking free from the containment chamber would be more difficult than it had first seemed.

But not impossible.

*   *   *

Feeling his body change minute by minute, Sujatha
surrendered to the inevitable. He worked at the seals
and zippers of his useless anti-contamination suit.

With a pause to summon his last shreds of bravery
and dignity, he tore the collar seam and removed the
flexible hood. As if he were using a napkin at a tea
party, he gently set the hood on the floor, its cracked
faceplate up. He blinked his grossly enlarged eyes
and drew a deep breath.

Now in the open air, weird smells bombarded him,
chemical traces that he could not understand, scents
processed through altered olfactory sensors. Inhaling
through shallow nostrils and a flattened nose, he
wanted to breathe fresh mountain air again, Ponderosa pine trees and meadow flowers, for one last
time. He wanted to see the spectacular Sierra Nevadas or his beautiful family—not these armored walls
and sterile chrome surfaces. Not the armed Marines
waiting to shoot him if he tried to escape.

He squinted in the too-bright lights, unable to cry,
unable to speak. He wondered if these alien eyes
were even capable of shedding tears. The Pirov creature had stalked away from the window, and Sujatha
felt very alone.

When he cleared his throat, he heard a growling
noise that did not sound like his voice. He thought
he might be able to speak out loud once more,
though the nanomachines might send another puni-
tive jolt to incapacitate him if he openly defied them.
Still, he wanted the chance to strike another small
blow—if he could just think of a way.

With face and head naked, Sujatha looked up to
the observation deck. Felix Hunter, his distinguished
expression now filled with despair, could not tear
himself away from the window. "Director Hunter,
sir," he said, and his voice came out thin and ethe-

real, "please . . . contact my wife and daughters. Tell them I love them."

"Of course," Hunter said. He placed his hands against the high window.

On trembling legs, Sujatha stood. He noticed only a blurred reflection of himself in the shatterproof windows. When he stepped forward to look, the startled Marines backed away and trained their rifles on him. Seeing their terrified faces, he understood all he needed to know.

He turned to Hunter again. "But sir, please do not tell them . . . what really happened to me." He hoped Hunter would find a way to let them know he had ended his life as a hero, or at least a faithful scientist.

If the world itself survived.

Fastidiously, Sujatha pulled off his polymer gloves. His new fingers were long and smooth; somehow, he had acquired an extra joint in each one. When he bent one finger, concentrating on muscle control, the digit curled like a monkey's prehensile tail.

He watched his old fingernails flake off, one by one.

Oddly fascinated, he touched the surface of an equipment table and felt the cool metal, sensing his nerve responses. Heightened neural receptors covered the pads that had once swirled with his personal fingerprints. Now though, his fingertips were completely smooth.

One more step in erasing his identity.

With deep-seated fear, Sujatha touched his face, felt the smooth planes, ran his fingers along the bridge of his nose, which seemed smaller. When he brushed around his eyes, a shower of tiny hairs fell off, his remaining eyebrows and lashes. As he touched the back of his head, dark hair sloughed off to reveal the smooth skin of a bulbous cranium, an ovoid skull.

A deeply human moan of despair came out of his throat.

He remembered how his wife had loved to run her hands through his hair, and how he had kissed her. But now his lips were papery and dry, his face emotionless and alien.

His daughters would run screaming if they saw him now.

"Soon I may . . . not be responsible for my actions, Director, sir," Sujatha said, already feeling the compulsions, so difficult to resist.

His vision lost focus, and the chamber walls shimmered with optical haloes and flares. His modified eyes were not yet fully integrated, making it hard to recognize the open lifepod, the deactivated laser drill, the rotary bone-cutting saws, battery-powered laser scalpels, and medical instruments that were strewn on the floor.

The Pirov-alien picked up tools, inspected them, played with the buttons, trying to understand or remember how the instruments functioned. He cocked his head, ransacking the storehouse of knowledge left inside his brain after Sergei Pirov's original personality had been erased.

Pirov hefted a heavy-duty bone-cutting saw, a powerful device that could have been used to crack open the extraterrestrial's skull, if Hunter had given them permission to conduct a full autopsy. With long, smooth fingers, Pirov flicked it on. The diamond-edged rotary blade whirled, a silver crown of thorns that sparkled in the light.

He stared with huge black eyes and then, with fluid movements that demonstrated that he now had complete control over his transformed body, the Pirov-alien prowled over to the control panel that operated the sealed doors. As the bone saw buzzed, he pressed it against the metal wall. The sawblade whined and sparks flew.

If Pirov cut through the controls, perhaps he could crack open the airlock and emerge into the unprotected atmosphere of Earth. It would only take one breath, one brush of his hand. . . .

Sujatha could never allow him to do that. *I am still responsible for some things. I must do what I can . . . while I can.*

Calling upon his last shred of humanity, Sujatha swayed on his feet, recovering his balance on limbs that no longer functioned the way they'd been born to. He lurched toward the pile of medical devices the Russian doctor had scattered during his rampage. Sujatha still recognized the tools he had used during years of medical practice.

The Pirov-alien had access to all that knowledge in his once-human brain . . . but only if he specifically searched for the information. It would simply be a matter of time before he realized this. The transformed Russian turned his back to Sujatha and continued his work with a grinding shriek against the metal circuitry plate.

The agitated Marines moved back and forth, waiting for emergency orders. In the observation deck, Hunter seemed to be arguing with Congressman Durston, who demanded that he trigger the full-scale annihilation routine at once.

Sujatha stared up at the Director, feeling deep sorrow but doubting anyone could read his non-human expressions. He no longer saw Dr. Trish Wylde outside the window.

He picked up a hand-held surgical laser from the floor. His long, many-jointed fingers wrapped around it like gripping tentacles. He knew how the laser's controls worked. He *remembered*.

Before he could be possessed by an alien imperaive, Sujatha stumbled forward, adjusting the laser calpel to its highest power and deepest cut. He staggered headlong on awkward-jointed legs until he fell into the Pirov-alien. Without saying a word, not daring to hesitate, he rammed the laser against the Russian doctor's back—and powered on the beam.

Smoking flesh crackled as red-hot light cut through Sergei Pirov's spine. Not daring to think about what he was doing, Sujatha ripped the line upward, slicing a deep incision the length of his former comrade's back.

The alien screamed as blackish blood boiled and sprayed through the seared edges of the wound. The laser scalpel burned deep enough to sever arteries and any other organ it encountered. The scalpel beam split the ribs, chopping vertebrae, opening Pirov like an elk gutted by a hunter.

It took all of Sujatha's remaining strength.

Convulsing, the Russian-alien dropped the bone-cutting saw. It spun, bouncing around on the floor with a wild jet of sparks that reminded Sujatha of the fireworks his girls liked to ignite on the Fourth of July.

His limbs jittering, his body already dead, the Pirov-alien collapsed onto Sujatha, twitching and kicking. The cutting laser had severed him nearly in two. An inhuman gurgle came from the Russian's spindly throat. A flow of thick saliva curled out of his lipless mouth as he lay smoking on the floor, huge black eyes dull and unseeing.

Desperate, Sujatha stared at the laser scalpel in his hand. With a few quick slashes he could chop apart the still-dormant alien pilot in the open lifepod, then turn the cutter on himself. That would take care of the other problem.

But even as he considered that option, paralyzing pain screamed through him. His muscles spasmed,

his lips pulled back to expose clenched teeth. He
dropped the laser scalpel and it rolled away into the
clutter of dumped instruments. He couldn't move,
couldn't extend a finger to pick up the scalpel. He
had surprised them when he'd attacked Pirov, but
now the nanomachines froze his muscular controls,
holding him hostage.

Buzzing swarms raced through his body, finishing
the transformation. Sujatha could barely think. His
mind was a constant roar of static now. He couldn't
even see clearly. The lights were so bright. *So bright.*
Gasping, groping for words, he looked up at the VIP
observation deck.

He saw Director Hunter again, watching him in
helpless horror. He thought he saw tears streaming
down the man's face, but he couldn't be certain with
his alien-skewed vision.

Sujatha drew a deep breath full of foul tastes and
strange odors. His mouth worked, his throat constricted, and he tried to make a sound. If only he
could speak one last time, convey his message. A
final plea.

"Director, sir, I beg you. Destroy everything before
it is too late."

Vasili Garamov lurched out of his seat and bent,
retching, over a metal wastebasket. Durston sat with
his eyes wide, his normally florid face pale, but set
with a grim satisfaction.

Hunter hesitated, looked at the chronometer. "I . .
can't. Team Proteus still has a few more minutes. I
have to believe they can pull off a miracle."

Durston swung a fist into his open palm. "Don't
be foolish, Director. Cut your losses."

After the last message from Team Proteus, Hunter
knew deep inside that Marc and his crew could very
well have been the first casualties of the nanoma-

chine threat. He had let his son-in-law down, just as he'd let Kelli down. Too often he'd made promises that he had no ability to keep.

I promised them they'd get out safely.

Garamov came back, looking shaky. He brushed a hand across his lips and nodded, staring at the open lifepod below, at the transformed researchers. "We dare not take additional risks. I give you full authorization. I . . . will deal with my government later. Destroy everything while we still can."

Hunter glanced back and forth between the diplomats, saw the chaos in the chamber below, then stared at the chronometer. If he didn't act fast enough, and a few stray nanomachines escaped, the entire mountain facility would have to be vaporized.

Congressman Durston drew a deep breath. "Be realistic, Hunter, when that other doctor's transformation is complete, the alien in him will try to escape." He squinted down at the smoking corpse on the floor. "But, unlike Dr. Pirov, there won't be anyone in there to stop *him*."

Hunter looked into the sealed chamber, searching for Sujatha's last shreds of humanity. But he saw no glimmer.

He could find no excuse to wait any longer. He *knew* what he had to do.

Garamov sagged in defeat. "Just vaporize the room and be done with it."

With the heavy heart of a caring executioner, Hunter moved to the control panel. Using his private authorization codes, he prepared the sterilization burst, powering up the generators that would release the ionization blast. The final option for Project Proteus. "Sorry, Marc. I don't have any choice."

A new alarm rang through the facility, warning of the impending sterilization routine. "Systems are charging."

When released, a blast of high-intensity gamma rays and extreme high voltage mixed with a wash of plasma fire would melt every single thing inside the containment chamber—the people, the miniaturized Team Proteus, the alien specimen itself, and all of the microscopic nanomachines.

Pulsing alarms echoed off the stone walls; all non-essential personnel evacuated to a reasonable distance from the sterilization burst. Hunter looked at the scarlet light on the control panel, indicating the readiness of the fail-safe routine. He drew a deep breath.

"Mr. Durston and Mr. Garamov, these gentlemen will take you to a place of safety." Hunter placed the two diplomats into the care of the Marine guards, who ushered them out of the observation deck.

Below, at floor level, he himself would stand behind thick lead shields with the last few Marines. And watch the end of it all.

He had a final moment of peace, to think . . . or perhaps it was best *not* to think. Too much time to regret what he knew he had to do. "I'm sorry, Marc. I'm so sorry, Kelli."

"Fifteen seconds," one of the technicians shouted.

The room itself would be cauterized, incinerated, all evidence destroyed. All threats neutralized.

Sujatha dragged himself back to his feet, swaying. He looked over at the corpse of the man/alien he had murdered.

"I . . . I'm sorry, Dr. Sujatha." Hunter's voice sounded hollow over the intercom speakers. His legs felt wooden when he stood, ready to run. He wouldn't have much time to get clear once he set the irrevocable process in motion.

Just then the system light blinked READY. He reached forward to press the "commit" button.

Then the intercom crackled, and he heard a message burst. The communications technician shouted over the intercom. "Director Hunter! We've just received a message from Team Proteus. The *Mote* is on its way out."

Chapter 39

Devlin flew at full speed away from the open lifepod. The impeller motors whirred, straining, growing hot, but still going strong. "Come on, come on!"

An empty gulf of air, no obstacles . . . and an inconceivably vast distance.

They had nowhere to go. "So much for the original plan."

Beyond the lifepod's metal lip, the *Mote* rose into a storm of thermal currents in the open space of the wide room. Devlin wrestled to keep them flying level against hurricane-force stray breezes.

Their carefully chosen pickup point was no longer valid. Simply taking them out through the autoclave again would not work. The nanocritters were everywhere.

"Now that we're out of the alien's body, we should consider Plan B," Arnold Freeth said from the main compartment. "Uh, has anyone *thought* of a Plan B?"

Inside the isolation room, the scale of every object was so great that none of them could interpret what they were seeing. The perspective was too skewed. Devlin had no idea where to fly, except *away* from the swarms of microscopic machines.

Kelli had always complained when he refused to stop and ask for directions.

Devlin fluttered his hands over the controls. "I'm activating our signal beacon so they know where we are—wherever that is."

Only three minutes remained before the miniaturization field began to lose its integrity. If the *Mote* grew to full size in the middle of the chamber, they would all be exposed to the marching nanomachines.

Tomiko shouted into the microphone. "Project Proteus, this is the *Mote*. Hey, Felix—can you read us? We're out of the alien's body in open air, moving away from the lifepod. We are currently open to suggestions." The high-momentum transmission made their flight even more of a violent roller coaster.

Devlin kept flying, muttering to himself as the silence stretched out. "Come on, Felix—answer!"

"Maybe they've given up on us already," Freeth said.

"It's taking too long," Tomiko said. "Let's move it."

Finally, Director Hunter's voice came back full of excitement. "You're alive! Is Marc—is everyone okay?"

"Intact, so far." She looked at the streaming nano-armies below, everywhere she looked. "But a lot of things happened while we were inside. The alien's body was infested with microscopic machines. They've been spreading—"

"We're aware of that, Team Proteus. In fact, you were just moments away from being sterilized." The crew listened in horror as Hunter gave a rapid summary of what had occurred. "The fail-safe incineration device is still primed."

"And I thought things were tough on the inside," Tomiko said.

Devlin piloted them through the lurching turbulence, glanced at the mission chronometer as the number dropped to two minutes. "No time for chit-

chat, Tomiko! Just find out what we're supposed to
do. How do we get out of here? Does Felix have
any ideas?''

The battered vessel soared over an enormous metallic structure that must have been a table or a tray
of equipment. Millions upon millions of creeping nanomachines covered the surface, like endless herds
of buffalo stampeding over the Great Plains.

Freeth looked out the broad window beside his
seat. ''Look how far those things have gotten from
the lifepod!''

''They've probably filled the whole room by now.''
Dr. Tyler's face was white, her mouth drawn. ''They're
on every surface, every object. Pirov and Sujatha must
have spread them around the chamber.''

She unbuckled her seat restraints, lurched forward,
and grabbed onto Devlin's chair. With grave seriousness she spoke into the comm system. ''Director
Hunter, we can't overemphasize the extreme hazard
of this situation. You were right to worry about the
threat. Don't take any chances.''

Arnold Freeth did not argue with the medical specialist. Tomiko and Devlin exchanged a glance. They
all understood what Dr. Tyler was saying.

Hunter, though, sounded equally determined. ''I
don't want to leave any of my people behind. We've
already had enough martyrs on this project.''

Devlin's voice was hoarse. ''Roger that. I'd love to
get out of here, too, Felix, but we can't let you unseal
the room, not even for us.''

Tomiko looked at the mission chronometer on their
control panel, saw the seconds ticking away. ''Our
field integrity fades in a minute and a half. After
that, we start to grow.''

Dr. Tyler lifted her chin. ''Director Hunter, for the
sake of the human race, you've got to proceed with
the sterilization burst.''

"My dad used to tell me that only wimps give up." Devlin had quoted that to Kelli when she was in the hospital, and she'd laughed. Felix Hunter had been there, beside him, and he would remember it, too.

Gritting his teeth, he propelled the *Mote* across the open chamber. The streamlined vessel crashed through air currents like a speedboat on choppy waters. He did not slow for a moment as his engineering mind grappled with the problem. "I regret that I have but one life to give, Felix—well, actually, four lives here inside the *Mote*—but I'd prefer to make the sacrifice some other time. I have an idea."

Hunter's desperate voice came back in a rush, as if he'd been ready to grasp at anything. "I knew you would, Marc, but you'd better talk fast."

"Right now, we're orders of magnitude too small for the nanomachines to infect us. We can *see* them. We're on their scale. We *know* we're clean." Even the crew aboard the *Mote* waited to hear what he had to say.

"And then what, Marc? We have no way to extract you."

"Yes, you do, sir. The same way we got into the alien's capsule. Use the other laser drill to bore a hole most of the way through the window. We can track the beam, and I'll maneuver the *Mote* to the end of the shaft, then blast the remaining glass away. You can trace us by using our beacon. With our own eyes we can make sure there aren't any nanocritters in the vicinity."

Devlin fought with the bucking ship, but his attention focused on convincing his father-in-law. "Apply a positive-pressure air flow to keep the nanocritters from passing through. After we're through the tunnel, Tomiko can toss a thermal grenade to seal the shaft behind us. She's brought plenty along."

Tomiko gave him an I-told-you-so smile.

"Sounds risky, Marc. You know I'd be bending procedures—and putting the planet at risk."

"It's either that or kill us all now, Felix." A low blow, and he knew it—but he was trying to save the lives of his crew. "Give us a chance. I can pull it off. Trust me."

After a brief, frightening pause, the Director agreed. "You know what my choice has to be, Marc. We'll get the laser drill in position."

The distant observation window seemed light years away. On the *Mote*'s control panel, the mission chronometer reached zero. Time had run out.

The miniaturization field would now degrade.

Sick with worry, his head pounding, Felix Hunter issued commands to the trained troops and scientists rushing around in the tunnels. Most employees had already retreated into sheltered rooms. At least Garamov and Durston had been safely placed in protective isolation, where they couldn't countermand his orders, and Hunter's own people here would follow his instructions. He was still the Project Director.

Before the *Mote*'s launch, he'd made a promise. *I'll see that you get out, Marc, safe and sound.* He couldn't give up until he had tried everything.

But if he made a misstep now, he would doom every person on Earth.

It was folly to let his personal feelings endanger the planet. Congressman Durston would insist that it made sense simply to sacrifice the crew members, rather than gamble. Even Vasili Garamov, a much more reasonable man, would agree. The risk was too enormous.

But Hunter had to take it.

He could not simply give up on his hand-picked team. If he abandoned them when he *knew* there was till a possibility to save them, he'd never be able to live with himself. He'd be as soulless as the invading aliens.

But, oh, he was taking a terrible chance.

Grim now, with the authorization codes entered and the fail-safe annihilation systems waiting on standby, Hunter transferred his controls to the sheltered alcove below. The destruction protocol was ready for immediate countdown.

Hunter raced down the access stairs, shouting for the remaining technicians to assist him. Marine guards moved out of the way as Hunter guided the replacement laser drill across the painted concrete into position against the thick Lexan window, where Trish Wylde had stood talking to the infected Sujatha not long before. Now the senior pathologist raced forward, refusing to evacuate with the others, insisting on helping.

Hunter cast a glance over his shoulder and took one last look at the wreckage in the containment chamber, the open pod with the alien body still inside, the burnt corpse of the slain Pirov-alien on the floor. And the monstrous body of Rajid Sujatha, losing its last fragile hold on humanity. . . .

Attracted by the flurry of activity, the Sujatha-alien shambled back toward them and stood on the other side of the window, staring with his enormous black eyes. Hunter flinched, but met the pasty gray creature's gaze, wondering what the altered man saw, what he remembered.

He saw no flicker of Rajid Sujatha in that inhuman visage.

After a long moment, the transformed Bengali doctor turned and took several shuffling steps away. He stood hunched as if ready to fight . . . but the main battle was occurring inside his own body.

Hunter and the technicians worked with the laser

drill. "Calibrate it precisely. We'll have only one shot
and we can't afford any mistakes. Leave a micron of
material, enough that the *Mote*'s own lasers can burn
through. Keep the tracer shining so Major Devlin can
find us."

He turned quickly to Trish Wylde. "And get me a
fan! Just a desk fan from one of the offices. We need
a positive-pressure air flow so that nothing drifts
through the pinhole."

As the final preparations were made, Hunter stood
close to the bulletproof glass, knowing the miniaturized vessel was still far, far too small for his naked
eye to see.

Chapter 40

Loudspeakers inside the containment chamber broadcast all transmissions from Team Proteus as part of the mission, designed to keep the doctors apprised of the *Mote*'s interior explorations.

Now, the alien creature that had been Rajid Sujatha listened to the full plans for the miniaturized crew's escape. The infesting nanomachines tapped into his human memories and knowledge—comprehending what they needed to do.

As the remaining few technicians and Marine guards prepared for the terrible ionization blast, the Sujatha-alien gazed impassively at Felix Hunter. The lean, distinguished-looking Director came closer, a reminder of Sujatha's past and humanity itself. But the barrier between them was much thicker than the shatterproof window. They stared at each other through the impenetrable glass as Sujatha's thoughts and memories flickered like dying embers.

The human being inside him exerted control for just a moment, lurching his traitorous body away. But as the desperately fleeing *Mote* shot toward the window, still too small to be seen, the Sujatha-alien made his way back to where the outside laser drill had burned a new needle-width hole. He stood like a colossus in the torn remnants of his anti-contamination suit, a huge obstruction blocking the way with his sheer bulk.

The nanomachines inside him remained disoriented enough not to comprehend what the body was doing. Sujatha managed to stop short, swaying clumsily in front of the pinhole, but not covering it.

Hunter shouted for the technicians to assist him, working with scanners to detect the *Mote's* position. "Find them! Give me a progress report."

The mission chronometer had reached zero. Team Proteus was already growing larger. Inexorably.

On the far side of the chamber, inside the open lifepod, the original extraterrestrial astronaut twitched.

It began to move.

Hunter felt a deep dread and looked desperately at Trish Wylde as she ran up with the hastily retrieved desk fan. "Hurry!"

The technician checked his scanner again. "Okay, the *Mote* is almost at the glass. Almost there."

Then, in a single, smooth motion, the original alien pilot sat up inside its stasis pod. Its own cautious revival finally complete, after being shocked into deep stasis by the explosion of its ship, the extraterrestrial creature sucked in a huge breath of Earth air.

Hesitated.

Then exhaled.

The enormous black eyes opened, stared at the bright lights, and never blinked. Naked and sexless, the creature flexed its prehensile fingers and its stick-thin reinforced arms.

Satisfied that its body functioned again, the revived alien climbed out of the open lifepod. It took jerky steps, adjusting to Earth gravity, and moved to join its counterpart at the window. They communicated with bursts of compact language, part transmitted signal and part high-speed words.

Next, on the floor of the containment chamber, the burnt corpse of Sergei Pirov also twitched, shuddered, and began to stir. Alive again.

Masses of nanomachines inside the old Russian's body had scrambled to reconnect nerves, joining biological materials into fibers, stitching together the muscles and spinal cord, rebuilding vertebrae with microscopic bricks and mortar.

Before long, the Pirov-alien would also heal sufficiently to join them in their conquest. The three of them would pool their strength and break out of the sealed chamber.

After the mission chronometer hit zero, the *Mote* shot like a bullet across the room, aiming toward the tracer beam. Far below, the exaggerated terrain changed. Broad-stroke details grew more discernible, as if Devlin's eyesight were getting better.

But that wasn't the reason.

"We're growing. I have no way to tell what our relative size is now."

"Okay, let's move it!" Tomiko said. As they crossed the distance, covering inches every second, they could see the glass barrier, the signal indicating the tiny new borehole.

Suddenly, something enormous blocked their way. It seemed to be the size of a planet.

Hunter's voice came over the communications speakers again. "Marc, you're almost there, but Dr. Sujatha and the other alien are trying to prevent you from reaching the window. I think they understand what you're trying to do."

"We're still too small for them to see us," Devlin said. "How can they know where we are?"

Arnold Freeth scratched his mousy-brown hair. "Their bodies are full of nanomachines. They might be able to hear our own beacon. Just like before."

Tyler looked at him and nodded. "Freeth's right, Major Devlin. Remember the SOS signal?" The UFO expert fairly glowed upon hearing her acceptance.

Devlin responded by shutting down the tracking beacon. He sent another message outside. "Mr. Freeth knows what he's talking about, Felix. We'll have to go in on our own now. Watch for the flash from thermal grenades when we're through the window tunnel." Tomiko had already removed the explosives from their storage cabinet.

The monolithic aliens in front of the transparent wall waved huge hands, stirring the air like a cyclone. Devlin fought his way through the whirlpools and vortices toward their only escape route. The *Mote* dodged city-sized hands flailing back and forth.

And all the while Team Proteus kept growing.

"What are those things trying to do? They're too big to capture us." Tomiko looked like she wanted to zap an alien fingertip with her lasers, but she had only a trickle of power left, and no shots to waste.

As they passed under Sujatha's sleeve, a rain of kamikaze nanomachines poured off like lemmings falling from a cliff. Thousands upon thousands of the expendable devices dropped blindly through the air, microscopic paratroopers aiming for the miniaturized vessel.

Most of the nanocritters plummeted toward the far-off floor, but some crashed onto the *Mote*, now only the relative size of wheelbarrows. Using grappling arms to slice apart the metal plates, a full dozen of the carbon-lattice machines began to systematically dismantle the already battered ship.

The screech of tearing metal and the drumbeat of

articulated limbs outraged Devlin. "Come on, come on," he repeated, like a mantra. He hoped the straining impeller engines would carry them to the pinhole, where it *might* be safe.

Seconds ticked away.

Gritting her teeth and growling, Tomiko swiveled the rear laser cannon, aiming at two nanomachines, but Devlin reached over to stay her trigger finger. "Whoa, we've got to save enough power to blast through the glass."

Her tight expression showed her frustration. "Maybe I should just go out and throw a few punches."

A continuous rain of nanomachines fell around the vessel like huge mechanical piranha. Several more attached themselves to the hull.

With the fading miniaturization field, the *Mote* had already grown large enough that the nanocritters looked much smaller, like vultures tearing at a carcass. Therefore, more of the destructive devices could crowd onto the *Mote*'s hull and cause further damage.

"I see the window up ahead," Devlin said, gritting his teeth. "And the beacon."

The giant Lexan cliff rose before them. At their still-microscopic size, the glass looked anything but smooth, with numerous pits and scratches and crystalline notches. The bore-hole tunnel looked like the X on a treasure map.

With a groaning screech, two of the *Mote*'s outer hull plates fell away. Twisted pieces of the plating dropped off like dead leaves.

Arnold Freeth shouted as nanomachines sliced through the roof of the main compartment. A crack of daylight and whistling air burst through.

Buckytube arms reached in, bending the plates back, chewing through the support framework.

Whining pyridine-tipped saws cut into the ship's body.

Devlin closed his ears to the destruction going on behind him, though his hazel eyes stung with tears of frustration. "There's the tunnel right now. On our way." No matter how much he fought with the controls, the *Mote*'s engines could propel them no faster.

In the main compartment, Cynthia Tyler detached one of their chairs and used the shaft to jab at the nanomachines. "Freeth, help me!" She clanged the chair back and forth, trying to beat back the articulated limbs like a lion tamer facing a wild beast.

To her astonishment, the nanocritter grabbed the seat and tore it from her grip. With a blur of metal limbs, the machine hauled the chair through the widening breach in the ship's roof. Outside, a pair of nanomachines ripped the seat to shreds.

Intent on flying, Devlin jockeyed them into position with no time for finesse or delicate moves. He set the groaning impeller motors to hover at the sealed mouth of the tunnel.

Tomiko wasted no time. She fired a blast with her forward laser cannons. The waning power was sufficient to melt away the last micron of glass, opening their escape route. Silica crystals and polymer strands dripped away from the shaft that led outside—their only hope of escape.

With her weapon's last sparks of energy, she scoured away four other nanomachines that made their way along the rugged vertical glass surface, climbing down toward the tunnel and its signal.

"All clear in front, Marc! Let's move it."

The dying laser cannons sputtered, too weak to vaporize the remaining devices on the ship's outer hull, but the energy was sufficient to knock off a few of their mechanical attackers. The dislodged critters tumbled into the open air, their segmented limbs flailing.

Devlin nudged the ship toward the tunnel opening—only to find that the *Mote* had already grown too large to fit into the hole.

They could not get out.

Chapter 41

Wincing at every clash and spark and groan as the brutal nanomachines tore his beautiful vessel apart, Devlin struggled to hold the *Mote* steady—but they had no place to go.

It was a losing battle, and he knew it. His heart wrenched as he made the decision. He had worked for years on designing and building and testing this innovative exploration craft. It was almost a part of him. Now he felt as if he'd let the *Mote* down on her first and only real mission.

"We'll have to abandon ship."

Dr. Tyler said, "And the longer we hesitate, the smaller our chances become."

Freeth steeled himself, obviously not eager to climb outside with the nanocritters around them. "Believe me, that's the *only* thing getting smaller around here."

Moment by moment, the miniaturization field continued to degrade. Their prolonged mission slowed the enlargement process, but still the Team was losing the race against time. While the vessel and crew began to grow imperceptibly at first, they would soon expand much faster, by orders of magnitude. They had to get out of the nanotech-infested room before it was too late.

Even if it meant leaving the *Mote* behind.

"Let's go," Devlin said. "On foot. A fifty-millimeter dash—once we get across the opening." He studied the tunnel through the window, a cave below the wavering ship, seemingly out of reach.

He felt sick at the prospect of casting his lovely vessel to the microscopic wolves. Creating this ship had saved him from wallowing in ever deeper depression after his wife's death. He knew the tiny craft better than he knew his own hand.

But he didn't intend to be one of those captains who went down with his ship in a foolish display of bravery.

Devlin adjusted the shuddering impellers to hold the vessel in position above the drill hole, as close to the window as possible. "That's the best I can do. Tomiko, get everybody to the airlock. We've got to climb across. Every second counts."

She was already out of her seat, clipping the thermal grenades to her belt. Atmospheric currents made the vessel rock and sway.

The clatter of fullerene limbs and pyridine-clawed feet drummed on the outer hull. Another section of the wall plates bent apart from its seams, pried away by powerful nanomachines.

Devlin took one last longing glance around the cockpit. Then he quickly peeled the snapshot of Kelli off the window and tucked it into his jumpsuit pocket before he rushed to join the others at the hatch.

The vulture-sized nanocritters had stripped off the *Mote*'s metal armor as if skinning their prey alive. Like pigs at a trough, the tiny robots crammed against each other, swarming at the roof breach. With diamond-edged jaws, the devices chewed through the hull supports, widening the hole. Trying to get inside. Claws and pincers clacked, scrambled, and poked.

On her way past the laboratory benches, Tomiko snatched a sampling pole from the analysis station. Under normal circumstances, Dr. Tyler might have used it to investigate organic tissue. But Tomiko wielded it like a spear, jabbing at the nanocritters through the ceiling hole.

Just like action hero Nolan Braddock. Her mouth formed a grim smile at the irony. But she had to get it right on the first take.

The machines thrashed with their sharp, jointed limbs. One pincer grabbed the sampling pole and twisted, but Tomiko heaved backward, ripping the machine's buckytube limb out of its socket. She swung again, hard as a ninja warrior this time, driving the others back with a clang of metal against carbon matrix. With a furious thrust, she skewered one device through its optical sensor, then blinded a second one.

She shouted, "Dr. T, bring the other anchoring rope to the airlock and open the bottom hatch. We'll need it to get across."

Her face pinched but determined, Tyler disconnected the metal coils of the anchor cable and hurried with it to the central airlock. Freeth had already opened the hatch, and he helped her drop the barbed end out the open lower hatch.

As even more machines settled on the *Mote*, Tomiko poked the pole repeatedly through widening gaps in the ship's structure. The side hull and windows cracked and split open from the relentless pressure.

Devlin staggered across the main compartment as the ship shuddered in the air, a faithful beast of burden heaving in its death throes. He tried not to think about it. "Tomiko, you're the best athlete around here. You go first. Down the rope, swing across, then anchor it for us on the edge of the drill hole. Now's the time to show off your gymnastics skills."

"Garrett's the show-off," she said with a quick smile. "I'm just a shy girl."

She gave up her battle against the attacking devices. Throwing the spear to the deck, she took the loose end of the anchor cable from Freeth. She jumped into the airlock chamber and squatted at the edge of the floor hatch.

She saw only an infinite sea of empty air at her feet, as if she were about to jump out of a high-flying jet aircraft. Tomiko grabbed the anchored end of the rope, held on, and dropped through the hatch. . . .

Devlin stood with Freeth and Tyler at the airlock door. "Get ready. We've only got a few seconds."

One of the nanomachines ripped out a side window and tried to force its way through the hull opening. Its optical sensors glowed like the eyes of a giant crab. Freeth yanked a laptop computer from its dock on the laboratory desk and tossed it at the tiny robot, knocking the blocky device away into space.

"Mr. Freeth, you next. Then Dr. Tyler." Devlin stood grimly. "I'll go last. She's my ship."

Air currents howled through the peeled-apart wreckage, and the *Mote* pitched about in the wind. The patchwork miniaturization field was failing even faster now. He could see that they were already bigger than when they'd first arrived at the escape hole.

Beneath the ship, Tomiko dangled on the cable. Her muscular legs wrapped around the strand as she swung back and forth. The pinhole in the window glass looked as big as the Eisenhower Tunnel. But the *Mote* filled a space far larger. Had they really been so small only a few moments before?

She twisted her hips to increase the pendular arc. Like Tarzan on a vine, but as light as a dust mote,

she swayed closer to the window. Holding the cable
below her, she thrashed the end like a whip, trying
to strike the opening. The anchor's metal tip brushed
against the crystalline glass like fingernails on slate,
then slipped away.

Far in the distance, she saw shadowy titans, the
looming aliens trying to prevent their escape. Right
now even a centimeter gap was a huge distance for
Team Proteus to traverse.

Nanocritters crawled like mechanical beetles all
over the vessel, dozens of them working frantically,
crawling down, trying to exploit any hull breach.
They had no intention of using the material to assemble more copies of themselves; they wanted only to
destroy. Soon they would reach the undercarriage of
the *Mote*.

If the machines severed the cable from the airlock
hatch, Tomiko was doomed . . . and so was everyone else.

She swung again, practicing her aim, and finally
the anchor hook clanked on the rugged glass, which
looked like an iceberg cliff that extended to infinity.
The hook bounced across the pitted surface, skidded,
clacked against the tunnel opening, but fell again
without finding purchase.

With a gust of air, the *Mote* jolted away, yanking
her and the cable back out of reach. She clung desperately, maintaining her grip with strong fingers.

Panting, she swung back toward the glass wall at
the end of her arc again. This time the hook struck
the melted ridges of the bore hole. The grapple held
just long enough for her to shimmy down the cable.
Rope burn was the least of her worries.

When she finally thumped onto the uneven bottom
of the tunnel, Tomiko kept her grip on the cable and
secured the anchor into a cavity. She wished she had
some kind of rock hammer, anything to gouge the

hole a little deeper. She set the grappling hook as best she could and then pulled on the rope to test it.

Tomiko hunched against a gale-force wind that pushed through the tunnel—the positive-pressure flow Director Hunter had applied to keep the nanomachines from spreading outward. She suspected the ruthless alien devices could still fight their way through the tunnel.

She certainly knew how determined those machines were.

Tomiko dug her feet into the rippled side of the tunnel, held the cable taut, and shouted at the top of her lungs to be heard over the microscopic wind. "Arnold, come on over! Let's move it!"

High above, the UFO expert poked his head out of the hatch. Frightened resignation written on his face, he hesitated, then grasped the cable with sweaty palms. Behind him in the airlock, Dr. Tyler looked ready to give him a push if he didn't move faster.

Tomiko held the rope as steady as she could; luckily, at their size, gravity had little effect. Freeth began to work his way down the rope. . . .

Inside the *Mote*, Devlin swung the sampling spear Tomiko had dropped, using it as a club to batter the nanomachines. The devices looked smaller and smaller, vermin now instead of monsters. His blows dented bead-lattice body cores, bent articulated limbs, smashed optical sensors. But an inexhaustible supply of nanocritters continued to stream down from the full-sized alien bodies. The struggling ship would be completely overwhelmed soon.

Dr. Tyler, looking out an intact window, watched Tomiko grab the UFO expert by the collar and drag him over the rippling glass ledge. She looked strangely relieved to see him safe. "All right. Freeth is secure."

"Go, Doc!" Devlin pummeled two more nanocritters into lumps of carbon mesh.

With a nod, Tyler wrapped her arms and legs around the cable. As if scorning her instinctive fear, she inched downward, clinging to the cable.

The *Mote* dropped with a sickening lurch, and Tyler clutched the anchor rope, nearly jarred loose. Her legs dangled free for a moment, but she caught an ankle around the strand again and pulled her knee over the cable. She hung steady, sickly pale and afraid to move. Devlin yelled at her to hurry.

Inside the besieged engine compartment, the stuttering impellers strained to hold the vessel in place, but gusts of air from the pinhole pushed the hulk farther from the glass wall and down. The cable stretched against the anchor hook until it thrummed with the strain. A random swirl of wind shoved the *Mote* in another direction, closer to the window.

The cable drooped with slack, and Tyler could barely hold on, hanging below the hole now. Slowing her pace with her feet, she tried to scramble up the dangling rope. Standing at the edge of the tunnel, both Tomiko and Freeth reached out for her, calling encouragement.

More nanomachines skittered along the exterior of the doomed *Mote*. The miniaturized vessel had expanded enough in size that the tiny robots could easily squeeze through gaping rips in the hull, crawling between the support framework. Devlin smashed one after another.

Holding on for dear life, Cynthia Tyler made it halfway across the gap.

Several nanomachines dropped onto the connecting cable from the outer hull of the *Mote*. In a rush, the devices worked their way along the rope like big spiders climbing a web, scuttling after the medical specialist.

"Faster, Dr. Tyler!" Freeth shouted. "They're coming!"

The doctor looked behind her to see the mechanical monstrosities closing the distance. With slippery palms, she hauled herself higher, toward the tunnel. The glass wall and the safety of the opening looked very far away.

A draft snatched the *Mote* upward again. One hand slipped, and Tyler dangled, barely holding on until she secured her grip again and pulled herself along.

Tomiko reached out, but her arms could not reach the other woman's. "Just a little farther!"

"Come on, please, come on!" Freeth shouted, his face agonized.

One of the *Mote*'s engines failed at last, its impeller turbine torn out, and the mangled vessel tilted at a horrible angle. Inside the main compartment, Devlin had to grab a side wall just to maintain his footing on the buckled deck. Wind roared through the holes in the hull.

Another five nanocritters broke into the ship.

More attacking devices dropped away and snagged the anchor cable, as if they knew it was their link to the tunnel, their escape route outside. Three nanomachines raced up the rope in the opposite direction, back toward the *Mote*'s airlock.

Back toward Devlin.

Trapped inside, he knew he couldn't wait any longer. But when he looked out through the bottom hatch, he saw another six nanomachines clambering toward him, claw arms clacking.

To his dismay, he watched their claws work at the cable, chewing, cutting. Severing it. "No!" he shouted.

Strands of the anchor rope parted, and the tether broke away from the crippled *Mote*. The long cable fell from the ship, leaving him stranded aboard.

Now he had no way to get across. . . .

As the severed rope dropped away, Tyler swung like a wrecking ball into the vertical wall. Dozens of the dog-sized nanocritters climbed after her from the ragged end of the tether.

Feet slipping, Tyler scrambled unsuccessfully against the pitted glass surface. She seemed to be only a few meters from her destination.

"Pull her up, Arnold. Move it!" Tomiko worked with Freeth to haul on the rope, bringing the doctor closer to the ledge. She looked up with agonized sorrow, knowing Marc Devlin was lost aboard his ship.

Then the nanocritters reached Tyler. One grasped her right foot with a sharp pincer claw. She kicked, trying to break free, and then a second nanomachine skittered onto her back, clawing with sharp metal limbs, hacking at her skin the way they had at the *Mote*'s hull.

Tyler screamed and cursed as blood flowed from slashes in her skin. But she held on.

Lying flat on the glass floor and reaching down for her, Arnold Freeth cried out in earnest determination, "Grab my hand! My hand!"

Tyler tried to climb up, keeping her grip, but even more nanomachines crawled over her body, cutting, chewing, stabbing. Blood soaked her Proteus uniform, and her right leg dangled limp.

Her slippery fingers brushed Freeth's, tried to lock, but she lost her grip. In a reflexive show of bravery that surprised even him, Freeth lunged, managed to grab her wrist, and held tight. "Believe me, I'm not going to let go."

The loose cable dangled below her. Vicious devices continued to climb toward the exit tunnel.

Tyler's face twisted with agony from a hundred shades. The nanomachines, ferocious mechanical pit-bulls, tore at her flesh, vivisecting her. Other devices scrambled to her head, trying to climb higher. 'Can't . . . let them get . . . up there!"

"You can make it!" Freeth pulled on her wrist, determined not to let go.

Tyler's eyes flashed with fear, then decision. "Once again, Freeth . . . we disagree."

As the nanomachines crawled over her shoulders, intent on escaping the containment chamber, Tyler used her last strength to yank her slick hand free from Freeth's grasp.

She closed her eyes and intentionally loosened her grip on the cable, taking with her all the nanomachines that clung to her body.

"No!" He reached for her, but Tomiko held him back.

As she let herself slide downward, Dr. Tyler stripped away most of the remaining devices on the cable like beads popping off a broken necklace. Then she and the nanomachines fell away into the infinite distance, dropping out of sight. . . .

Not letting herself think about what she had just seen, Tomiko kicked the grappling hook away from the glass ledge. The severed cable tumbled down the rugged crystalline wall, carrying with it the last two nanomachines.

Then she looked across to watch the *Mote* falling apart in the sky.

On board, Devlin swung his spear and kicked at the hordes of nanomachines. He had seen Dr. Tyler plummet to her death, and he knew he would be next. Air currents shook the buckling deck; the ship's entire ceiling was gone now. The second impeller engine sputtered. The *Mote* would soon plummet to the far-distant floor.

Far, far above him, the humongous aliens moved about, still trying to block the team's escape. A back-

wash breeze slammed the ship and drove the
wrecked hulk upward against the glass wall, high
above the tunnel.

Devlin tumbled to the deck and reached the crumbling bulkhead just as the last impeller engine died.
The *Mote* began to scrape down the rough glass,
grinding against ledges and scratches.

As the wreckage fell, bouncing on capricious
breezes, he saw the tunnel rushing toward him. He
grabbed the widest hull opening and leaped out,
pushing away with all of his strength. He sailed
across the gap as the magnificent ship tumbled away.

Watching in despair and then surprise, Tomiko reacted in a flash. Devlin nearly missed the edge of the
tunnel, but she fell flat on her stomach and caught
his hands in a stunt that would have made her father proud.

Freeth grabbed for her legs and kept her from slipping as she took Devlin's weight with her arms.

Kicking out, Devlin swung against the uneven surface, trying to get purchase with his feet. With wiry
strength, Tomiko hauled him up into the shaft.

Panting, flushed with adrenaline, Devlin watched
the *Mote* break apart into debris. Its engines fell out;
laboratory equipment tumbled through gaps in the
floor plates. The dead miniaturized ship tumbled
slowly until it vanished far below, where Dr. Tyler
had gone.

Devlin leaned back, his muscles quivering with
shock and exhaustion. He could not afford to mourn
the losses until later. Much later . . .

Tomiko grasped his shoulder, mercifully saying
nothing. He nodded to signal that he was all right.

He looked with dread at the cliff above the tunnel.
The impact of the dying vessel against the glass wall
had jarred loose a new flood of clinging nanomachines. They had leaped from the wreckage like arti-

ial fleas and now skittered down the pitted surface
the window.

Freeth's muddy eyes were wide, his freckled face
ilky and pale. He stared out into the open air, as
hoping to catch another glimpse of Cynthia Tyler.

In an instant, Devlin pulled himself together. He
as in charge here, and he damned sure wasn't
ping to let anyone else die. He hauled the UFO ex-
rt to his feet. "Hurry! We're already growing."

Tomiko took the lead as the three of them lurched
to a run along the pinhole tunnel through the ob-
rvation window.

An army of nanomachines rushed after them.

Chapter 42

Finally healed and resurrected, the creature that ha
been Sergei Pirov sucked in a deep breath, stretchir
his diaphragm, spreading ribs, filling lungs. Ali
again. He lay on the cold floor of the containme
chamber, legs jittering with random muscle twitche
Nanomachines surged through all the body's dar
aged systems, completing emergency reconstructio

The huge, bottomless eyes blinked once, then r
mained open and staring, seeming to grow eve
blacker.

Sufficiently repaired to return to the all-consumir
task, his alien body rolled over, leaving a dryir
bloodstain on the floor. The pool of blood itse
seemed alive, writhing . . . *shrinking* as the tiny de
vices used organic material for their own purpose:

Pirov made no sound of pain or exultation as th
burn scar faded along his spine, the skin cells fizzir
and foaming in an organic froth. The flow of disc
ored fluids leaking from his wounds slowed, the
stopped.

He was ready to continue the fight.

Slowly, Pirov rose to his feet, refamiliarizing hir
self with his own muscles. Though eerily silent, th
three identical aliens communicated with each oth
through signals and complex codes, formulating

ombined plan. Together, they would break out of
he chamber.

With long, steady strides the Pirov-alien went to
in his companions—to join the struggle, to do
ore damage.

In front of where the laser drill had punched
hrough the glass, the original alien pilot lurked as a
ntry. The extraterrestrial creature stood so close to
he unbreakable Lexan window that Felix Hunter
ould see the contours of bones and musculature, the
mooth skin that was infested with furiously replicat-
ng microscopic invaders.

Hunter's mind raced. *We will all look like that, if a
ingle nanomachine escapes.*

At the beginning of their journey, Team Proteus
had entered through pores in that placid-looking
kin, eager to explore in the name of science. Now
unter wished he'd never attempted the scheme,
ever listened to Vasili Garamov's idea to use the
iniaturization project. There had been too little time
o plan, too many uncertainties.

But if he *hadn't* brought the lifepod here, if Gara-
ov had simply delivered the crashed lifepod into
he hands of curious Russian scientists without
roper precautions, a local medical examiner in Azer-
aijan would have cracked open the lifepod and
ade a routine inspection of the body, probably
earing nothing more than latex gloves and a cotton
reathing mask. The examiner, far out of his depth,
ould have released the nanomachines . . . and the
festation/invasion scenario would already be play-
ng itself out.

The battle for Earth would have been lost.

Still, Hunter had had no business sending Marc
evlin and his team on such a risky, unpredictable
ission. They'd had no idea what dangers they

might encounter inside an alien body, where the
would go, how they would respond to unpredictabl
hazards, and survive. . . .

Now, the Sujatha-alien and the resurrected Piro
moved to the door-control panel. The two of ther
went back to work where the Russian doctor ha
been trying to cut an opening with the battery
powered rotary bone saw.

Sujatha bent to the floor and picked up the dis
carded laser scalpel with which he had—temporar
ily—slain Sergei Pirov. He flicked on the burning re
knife, trying to use the cutting tool for another pur
pose entirely.

Out in the corridor, Trish Wylde waited besid
Hunter, desperate for some signal from Team Pro
teus. "How much longer can we wait?"

Magenta alarm beacons continued to flash. The las
of the technicians and scientists had ducked into the
designated shelters. The control lights for the annih
lation sequence glowed ready, waiting for the fina
code that would unleash a sterilizing blaze. Besid
Hunter and Wylde, a few remaining Marine guard
stood stony-faced, as if they knew they might be o
a suicide assignment.

He stared at the digital chronometer on the wal
his eyes burning. "Come on, Marc!"

The Sujatha-alien paused with the laser scalpel i
his hand, as if he had momentarily forgotten how th
instrument worked. Then he applied the hot beam t
the armored wall. Though designed to burn incision
through flesh and bone, not metal, the laser scalpe
heated the armor plate, finally burning through th
first layer. Smoke and sparks spurted upward. Wit
infinite patience, he moved a centimeter at a time.

Beside him, the Pirov-alien picked up his bon
cutting saw again and powered on the motor. Th
whir sounded like a dentist drilling teeth. He applie

ιe spinning diamond blade to the control panel, slic-
ιg circuits, apparently hoping he could hot-wire the
ead systems.

One of them would soon cut through. The impris-
ned aliens needed only to create the tiniest breach—
nough for the microscopic nanomachines to escape.

One of the Marines said, "We need to get behind
ιe lead shields, sir."

"Not until I hear from Major Devlin." Even to his
wn ears, he sounded stubborn and foolish.

The *Mote*'s beacon had cut off, so the Proteus tech-
icians could no longer locate the miniaturized ship.
Iunter had no way of knowing where the vessel
ʌas, or if the crew had survived. It seemed like such
long shot.

Pirov pushed the bone-cutter harder against the
ʌall, chopping deep scars into the tough alloy plates.
"Sir, if we don't trigger the sterilization blast in
me—"

"*Not* until I hear from Major Devlin."

With sweat running down the sides of his tanned
ιce, Hunter hunched in front of the tiny pinprick. A
esk fan roared next to the borehole, blowing air to
tall the oncoming nanomachines. On one finger he
eld a lump of epoxy, ready to cover the hole as
ɔon as he saw the signal flash.

"Marc, please hurry," he whispered through
Ienched teeth.

Team Proteus *must* be almost through. They had
ɔ be on their way. How could he give up now, when
is crew was on the verge of being safe?

With an angry shout, Congressman Durston strode
ed-faced into the corridor outside the chamber, fol-
ɔwed by the Russian Deputy Foreign Minister and
ʌo flustered guards. "Why haven't you pushed the
·utton, Director? This delay is unconscionable!"

"Congressman, you must get behind the barri-

cades!" One guard actually tugged on Durston's arm
but the man yanked his elbow away.

Pale-faced and jittering, Garamov looked franti
for a cigarette. The crisis had actually forced him int
an alliance with the congressman. "You know w
cannot hesitate, Director Hunter. You are playin
with the lives of every person on Earth. This hesita
tion is madness."

Hunter had no legitimate arguments, no defens
against their demands. "You should have stayed ir
your protected room, gentlemen. Get behind thos
lead barricades and prepare." He swallowed hard
"I have transferred the detonation sequence to m
command console here."

Inside the chamber, Sujatha had succeeded in cut
ting the first layer off the wall plating. He dropped
it to the floor with a clatter and methodically begar
to work on the next section.

The Pirov-alien extracted a handful of wires and
began to cross-connect them, ignoring the spark
around his fingers.

"So order the blast!" Durston yelled as Garamov
and a Marine guard pulled him toward the lead
shielding.

With a sick feeling, Hunter knew the diplomat
were right. Everything was about to fail. He hac
given Devlin and his crew their best chance.

Sujatha peeled away yet another thin section of the
armored plating, then used the laser to cut deeper.

"Sorry, Marc." Hunter reached forward to sea
the hole.

Chapter 43

Helping each other in a mad rush, the three survivors of Team Proteus raced along the tunnel. Their panting breath echoed in the narrow space, accompanied by the rush of wind from outside.

Devlin could see he was already ten times his former miniaturized size, and growing fast. The walls were closing in.

At first the pinhole through the glass wall had been big enough to accommodate the *Mote* three times over—a substantial shaft the relative size of a subway tunnel. But now the long shaft constricted around them.

"Keep running!" Devlin shouted.

Tomiko sprinted ahead, leading the way. Freeth staggered along as if barely able to keep his body moving. Devlin pushed him onward. "Dr. Tyler bought us some time. We can't waste her sacrifice." The UFO expert found a reserve of strength within himself.

Behind them Devlin heard a terrible clicking sound, hundreds of sharp carbon-lattice legs scraping on the fused glass floor. Seeking a way out.

Previously, only two of the nanomachines had been large enough to threaten the entire vessel; now the tiny marauders looked like robotic tarantulas as large as toy poodles. "Don't let them nip at you heels, Mr. Freeth."

Freeth yelled as one of the nanomachines leaped onto his back, reminding him of his awful last sigh of Cynthia Tyler. Devlin smacked the device off before it could do more than scratch the UFO expert.

Another nanocritter fastened onto his own thigh but Devlin battered it away. Freeth stomped a third under his heel, crushing its outer carbon-weave casing. Both men began smashing and stomping as the nanomachines continued to surge forward. Devlin felt like Gulliver against an army of robotic Lilliputians.

"Don't waste your time fighting them," Tomiko shouted over her shoulder. "Just run! We're growing too fast."

Devlin and Freeth left the wreckage behind and raced through the howling wind, ignoring the attackers except for an occasional kick to boot one backward. The relentless nanomachines, focused on escape now, did not even stop to cannibalize components from their damaged comrades.

Ahead, Tomiko could see light, the other side of the window opening. Air pressure from the outside fan whipped them like a storm, seeming to shove them backward like an invisible hand. The gale became stronger as they approached the other end. As they grew, the uneven spots on the glass floor became smaller, smoother . . . and very slippery.

With the rough ceiling closing down around them they had to crouch as they ran. Devlin wiped dripping sweat out of his eyes as he duck-walked on bent knees. It was already hard to breathe. "If we're caught inside this pinhole when we return to normal size, it'll squeeze us like toothpaste in a tube."

Freeth needed no further encouragement.

*   *   *

The detonation button glowed scarlet, the ionization blast ready. The timer remained frozen. Congressman Durston looked as if he would explode first, though. "Now! You must end it now!"

"One more minute, that's all I ask." Hunter had no idea how close Team Proteus was. Had they entered the tunnel yet? Had some disaster befallen them? He looked over his shoulder.

Trish Wylde grabbed one of the congressman's arms, while Vasili Garamov took the other, after a long and meaningful glance toward Hunter. "Come, Congressman," said the Russian. "You and I must get behind the barricade. The Director cannot set off the sterilization protocol until we are safe."

With seconds ticking inexorably away, Hunter hunched close to the needle hole. His heart pounded. He placed a flat microscope slide directly under the opening. If something had happened to the *Mote*, he hoped the team members could jump onto the glass. Marc would lead them through the tunnel.

"Your minute is up, Director Hunter." From the edge of the lead-shielded alcove, Edwin Durston did not look like a man who was accustomed to being ignored. "I order you to sterilize the room *now*."

Hunter looked up to see all three aliens working together to rip off the wall plates. They had already stripped several layers from one section. Bent plates lay strewn on the floor among the scattered medical equipment.

The Sujatha-alien continued cutting with his laser scalpel. Pirov pushed harder with the bone-cutting saw. The creatures would break through at any moment.

Garamov's plea joined Durston's. "Your crew is dead already. Enter the code!"

As if they had heard and understood, the three aliens stopped their activities. In unison, they turned to stare through the thick glass, daring Hunter to challenge them. He shuddered, but refused to back away.

The extraterrestrials turned back to their destruction.

"You're right." Hunter's words were like nails hammered into a coffin lid. "We can't wait any longer."

If the *Mote* itself had been able to pass through the vessel should have reached the tunnel exit long before now. Even if their communications were down, as the ship grew, he should have been able to see it like a gnat in the air.

Hunter looked one last time at the microscopic slide and the pinprick, and murmured a quiet farewell to his friends, the team members he himself had chosen, to Marc Devlin. Along with Pirov and Sujatha, they would join Chris Matheson as martyrs to the miniaturization project.

"Everyone brace yourselves."

Tomiko finally reached the drop-off at the end of the passage and lurched to a stop, staring at what looked like a bottomless pit. Ahead of her yawned an immense glass cliff . . . with the platform of a microscope slide waiting for them. Far too far below.

"Great, we're trapped."

Hunter must have been trying to hold the glass slide close to the pinhole, but on their size scale, even his fraction of a centimeter looked like an immense drop. She had no way to contact the Director; the nanocritters had destroyed their communication system along with the *Mote*.

Devlin and Freeth hurried to catch up, scuttling ahead with bent knees and hunched backs. They dropped to all fours and began to crawl in single file

ιs they grew to fill the tunnel. The voracious ma-
hines skittered closer like a stampede of scorpions.

Tomiko held out her thermal grenade, ready to
hrow it into the tunnel. The flame front would blast
»ack the approaching devices and fuse the glass. And
he shockwave would hurl all three of *them* out into
»pen space.

"Move it!" She squatted at the mouth of the hole,
»arely fitting through, and peered over the edge. "Of
:ourse, there's no place to go once you get there."

Then Tomiko brightened, remembering her physics
ιtudies of mass, and air resistance, and gravity. She
ιet down the thermal grenade at the edge of the
ιhaft. "Use this, Marc. You'll have to jump . . . and
ιope."

"Go, Tomiko!" Devlin scrambled ahead with
ʼreeth close behind him. The tunnel had no room
ʼor them.

With whipcord muscles, she leaped over the edge,
»ut into open space. Garrett Wilcox would have
ʼelled like a wild man at the top of his lungs, spin-
ιing in a cannonball tuck through the air. She pre-
ʼerred to fall with a little more dignity.

As she tumbled downward, Tomiko drifted like a
ιust mote, jounced along by the fan's air current.
·ler miniaturized body was blown against the outer
ϟlass wall and skidded the remaining distance down
ο the microscopic slide.

Tomiko landed with a thump, her hands slipping
»ut from her, and she crashed on her face on the slick
ϟlass surface. Not exactly graceful, but thankfully no
»ne was watching.

The microscope slide trembled as if from an earth-
ιuake, vibrations caused by Hunter's unsteady
ιands. She got to her feet and stared up at the tunnel
mouth, calling after Devlin.

Inside the claustrophobic shaft, he and Freeth

pulled themselves forward, belly-crawling. The wall
and ceiling squeezed around them like a fist. The
now-smooth glass brushed their shoulders.

The swarms of nanomachines were right behind
them.

"This is the end of the line. We'll be crushed in
here," Freeth panted, his voice filled more with despair than terror. "At least our bodies will plug the
hole."

"Come on, Mr. Freeth. You can make it."

When Devlin reached the end of the passage, he
grabbed the thermal grenade Tomiko had left for
them. Around the UFO expert's body, he could see
the nanomachines scuttling like silvery crabs, racing
ahead now that the two of them blocked the strong
wind.

Four of the devices had clambered up Freeth's legs,
but he kicked them off in disgust, smashing them
like cockroaches against the glass tunnel wall. He
and Devlin slapped at each other's clothes, crushing
the nanomachines that clung to him.

"Go, Mr. Freeth. You've got to jump first."

The UFO expert could barely wriggle out of the
mouth of the pinhole. "I'm stuck."

Devlin shoved him through the bottleneck and sent
him tumbling into open air. He hoped Tomiko would
catch Freeth—or at least break his fall.

Next, he clasped the thermal grenade in one hand
and lowered himself over the edge of the tunnel with
the other. He gripped the uneven ledge with his fingers, supporting his minuscule weight.

Above, thousands upon thousands of the tiny nanomachines streamed along the tunnel floor and up the
walls, robotic lice anxious to get out.

Devlin thumbed the activator on the grenade and
lobbed it up into the opening. The weapon rolled

toward the masses of nanocritters. Devlin released his hold on the edge and let himself fall backward.

With a flash, the grenade incinerated all the nano-machines nearby and melted the end of the glass, sealing the tunnel.

Hunter saw the pinpoint of light just as he started to withdraw the slide. "There they are! It's the signal." Down on the glass, he could now discern tiny specks, flickering dots that moved about. "I've got Team Proteus!" Before his eyes, they began to grow into visible human beings, three of them.

Only three of them.

Hunter pulled the slide away and with his finger slathered a glob of fast-drying epoxy over the pinhole, adding an additional seal to the melted glass. He tried to keep the slide steady as he hurried gingerly away.

Inside the containment chamber, the three aliens threw themselves into their dismantling work with renewed fury, as if they realized the miniaturized team had escaped.

The tiny figures crowded together on the slide had become miniature people about a centimeter tall. If Hunter moved too quickly, he'd knock them off—but he had to get behind the protective barricade.

The aliens would breach the containment any second now.

He handed the slide to Trish Wylde, who had returned to grab him. She cradled the slide to her chest and ducked into the lead-shielded alcove, where the Marines, Garamov, and Durston already huddled. With the crew ready to tumble off, Wylde set the slide on the ground and backed away, careful not to step on them.

As Hunter ran for the protective wall, he caught one final glimpse of the trapped alien invaders. Two of them had been Sergei Pirov and Rajid Sujatha. All three stopped their work and turned to look soulfully at him, as if he'd betrayed them. Finally accessing lost memories, they knew what he was about to do.

Hunter tried not to think of the two good doctors who had already vanished. He ducked back and entered the commit code. "Sterilization sequence *now!*"

He squeezed his eyes shut as a searing white blast filled the containment room, accompanied by a muffled boom and a high-pitched blast of static.

The ionization flash incinerated everything inside the chamber, boiling away outer surfaces of glass and metal, cremating the three aliens in a fraction of a second and vaporizing every nanomachine.

The pulse made the lead shield vibrate. Several banks of corridor lights sizzled, then went dark before emergency illumination kicked in.

Beside Hunter, the surviving members of Team Proteus finished growing to full size again. Devlin, Tomiko, and Freeth stood holding each other, trembling from their ordeal.

Chapter 44

When the radiation alarms finally signaled that the vicinity was safe, the stunned Proteus staff, Marine guards, and shaken politicians emerged from their shelters.

"Not exactly the showcase mission you wanted, Felix," Devlin said. "But I'm still glad you let me go along."

"Nobody else could have pulled it off," Tomiko added, touching his arm.

Hunter started and stopped, his mouth dry and empty of words, but full of emotion. Finally, he could only choke, "Whenever you feel you're ready, we'll need a full debriefing from you and the . . . surviving crew."

Devlin nodded, not looking forward to the task.

Hunter placed a strong, paternal arm on his son-in-law's shoulder, and they stepped around the lead barricade together.

The interior of the sealed containment chamber looked as white as snow, every surface dusted with a fine layer of ash, as if a cleansing blizzard had covered all evidence of the aliens and their nanotechnology. . . .

Devlin stared at the aftermath. "Felix, you did

more than you should have. Anything else . . . would have cost us the planet.''

Hours later, when his terror had faded and self-protective arrogance returned, Congressman Edwin Durston prepared to leave the Project Proteus facility, calling for his limousine and escorts. He seemed anxious to take Deputy Foreign Minister Garamov back to the San Francisco airport and see him off American soil.

Garamov had already made several urgent phone calls to Moscow, though the first three had been misrouted. Finally reaching the correct department and an administrator who seemed ready to listen, Garamov started to explain what had happened to the alien lifepod—but the administrator didn't know what he was talking about. Apparently, the paperwork regarding the extraterrestrial artifact had been lost or misfiled. He asked for Garamov's name and contact number, but the Russian diplomat hung up on him.

Garamov walked with jerky, exaggerated motions as he followed the congressman to the cave opening and the fresh, thin mountain air. A damp mist had settled over the Sierra Nevadas, which began to glow pearlescent with the approach of dawn.

As soon as he stepped into the fresh morning air, the Deputy Foreign Minister yanked a cigarette out of his suit-jacket pocket and lit it in a rapid, smooth movement. He took a long breath of the acrid tobacco and exhaled with a sigh. Director Hunter noticed that he had bought a pack of an American brand, probably at the airport just after he'd arrived.

"All evidence is gone," Garamov said to Hunter. His tone was difficult to interpret.

Hunter stood beside the two diplomats, looking into the sky, where the stars were vanishing with oncoming daylight. "We both know that any other research protocol would have released the nanotechnology infestation, Vasili." Even realizing that, though, Hunter's heart felt heavy.

"But perhaps that solves my most pressing problem," the Russian said. "I no longer need concern myself that my next assignment may be as an environmental monitor in Novosibirsk. It is one of the most polluted cities in the world, you know." He took another drag, consuming a third of his cigarette in one deep breath. "Considering the alternatives, perhaps this debacle turned out for the best."

Durston grumbled, his mind already made up. "Well, I'm not convinced this couldn't have been handled better. I intend to file my personal report to the committees in charge of your Proteus funding, Director Hunter. You can expect to answer a lot of questions in closed-door hearings."

Weary of the politics, Hunter turned to the florid-faced man. "And I will defend them. I stand by my decisions throughout the mission."

He would have to cope with the disaster, hoping that the miniaturization project would remain intact despite the losses of Sergei Pirov, Rajid Sujatha, and Cynthia Tyler. The Class IV containment room was destroyed and was still hot with residual radioactivity. The sophisticated exploration vessel had been torn apart by the nanomachines.

The official limousine eased out of the fenced parking area and crunched across the gravel toward them. Durston tugged on his tie and jacket, flushing red and sweating profusely. "No excuses, Director Hunter. We are very displeased with how you responded to this emergency situation. Mr. Garamov and I barely got out alive."

Garamov tossed his cigarette butt on the ground and crushed it into the gravel. "Regardless of Russia's official response when I return home, Congressman, perhaps my word will carry weight in your government's investigations. I will not support any censure against Director Hunter. Bear in mind that *I* was the one who insisted on using the miniaturization technology to attempt a non-invasive investigation. *I* demanded that absolutely secure precautions be instituted. The Director followed the most prudent course of action."

Hunter's patience finally snapped. "If it wasn't for Project Proteus, Congressman Durston, all of Earth would be infected by now." He narrowed his eyes and stared at Durston until the congressman backed down, looking impatiently at the approaching limousine.

Politics be damned. "Think of that while you write your report, sir."

Under the supervision of Chief Pathologist Trish Wylde, medical technicians collected data on the effects of miniaturization. Inside the Proteus recovery room, medical techs ran a battery of tests and checkups on Devlin, Tomiko, and Freeth, as well as treating cuts and scrapes from their battles with the nanomachines.

The UFO expert sat in quiet shock for some time, staring down at his hands, as if wondering how he could have lost his grip on Dr. Tyler. Minor wounds marked his skin where the nanocritters had attacked him, but he considered himself lucky. Freeth lifted his arms while Trish Wylde poked and prodded him, remembering when she had taken him through his rushed training. He still couldn't believe everything he had been through.

Finally, like a dam breaking, he began to talk nonstop, asking questions and recounting parts of their mission. Trish listened, nodding at appropriate moments; then she jabbed a needle in his arm to take a blood sample and wrapped a cuff around his elbow to take his blood pressure.

Recovering in the infirmary bed on the other side of the room, but wide awake, Garrett Wilcox watched the process, looking from Devlin to Tomiko. "Man, I wish I could have been there." He shifted his burn-damaged leg and winced. "But considering what happened, maybe I was the lucky one after all."

"Take any consolation you can get, Garrett," Tomiko said, watching as crimson blood from her arm slowly bubbled into a syringe. "Major Devlin did a perfectly fine job of filling your shoes." She coyly raised her eyebrows.

"Roger that, and I still destroyed my own ship." Devlin tried to relax, knowing his blood-pressure readings would be off the scale. "Garrett, if *you* had wrecked the *Mote*, I'd have given you a couple of black eyes." He heaved a deep sigh and let his shoulders slump. "At least I've got no one to blame but myself."

Felix Hunter strode into the recovery room, looking pleased with himself. When he saw Marc Devlin, he stopped short of giving his son-in-law a hug and stood at a professional distance.

Devlin got up off his medical bench, dangling a lead to the blood-pressure cuff behind him, to the consternation of the medical technician. "I knew you wouldn't leave us behind, Felix."

Trish Wylde turned toward the Director, her short reddish hair in disarray, her pretty face drawn with concern. "I'm very sorry about Dr. Tyler," she said, looking guiltily at him. "When I came into your office, I never meant to cast doubt on her qualifications. I'm sorry I questioned her place on the team. That was selfish of me, and such jealousy has no place in the Project. I was out of line."

Trish walked around the padded table so she could face the Director. "Cynthia was an excellent researcher, an invaluable part of the team. What she did probably saved the rest of the crew. Maybe even all of humanity."

Freeth nodded, his eyes moist. "Believe me, there's no doubt about it."

"Next time, Dr. Wylde." Hunter looked at her with his intent, expressive brown eyes. "I made you a promise."

After his extensive debriefing, Arnold Freeth stood near the portal guard's glass cage. He held out his hand while Director Hunter paid him. In cash.

The bills blurred out, one at a time, like playing cards from a hustler. Freeth could barely follow the counting. "There you are, Mr. Freeth. One thousand dollars, which constitutes your consulting fee of five hundred per day for two days. As agreed."

The UFO expert was ecstatic to receive such a large payment, more than he usually got as a bonus or a salary, though he wasn't about to confess as much now. Besides, he was proud to have had some small part in saving Earth.

"Uh, can I have some paperwork for this? A receipt or a written record?" He seemed embarrassed. "Because of my profession, I . . . tend to get audited often. Only serves to enhance my belief in government conspiracies."

Hunter stood firm, his mustache a dark line across his upper lip. "Sorry, Mr. Freeth. Nothing you can trace back to this mountain facility."

"You did sign the agreement and confidentiality forms, Mr. Freeth," Devlin said. "We tend to take those things seriously."

"Then how do I record this on my taxes?" Freeth looked from one man to the other.

"You don't."

"Paying way too much for a man with admittedly bogus credentials, aren't we?" Tomiko Braddock said, lounging against the rock wall next to Devlin. She gave Freeth a teasing look. "But I suppose Arnold did turn out to be a good addition to the team."

Squirming, he seemed overwhelmed. "Thank you for letting me see that I was right all along . . . even if I did doctor my video a little."

Devlin placed a brotherly arm on Freeth's shoulder. "You proved to be just as useful as Dr. Tyler had first expected, Mr. Freeth, fake autopsy or not."

He gestured out into the sunlight, where the government sedan had already been pulled inside the staging area within the chain-link fence. "Let's take you home."

Later, alone deep within the underground facility, Felix Hunter stood just inside the silent miniaturization room. The lights had been dimmed. He cradled the white experimental rabbit. Absently, he scratched Fluffy Alice's ears, pondering what he would write in his letter to Rajid Sujatha's family.

The Proteus guards, scientists, and technical support staff were stunned and subdued, the near-miss casting a pall too heavy to be lifted by their survival and triumph. No one else had come into the dim chamber.

He stared at the translucent prismatic grid that lined the floor and ceiling inside the focal point of the miniaturization beams. The technical stations were empty. Repairs and further testing would start within a day or so; he wondered if Project Proteus would ever be allowed to conduct experimental missions again.

The rabbit hung in his arms like a furry pillow, plump and content. She sniffed his finger.

It would be such a tragedy to lose everything now What a boon it would be to worldwide industry if he could establish cooperative research agreements and technology transfers for the innovative shrinking process. Medical uses, data storage, military applications, materials studies, scientific analysis, cargo transportation.

He supposed even micro-tourism was an option.

Feeling stronger than he had since before his daughter Kelli died, Hunter vowed not to let this disaster shut down the project, as the debacle with Chris Matheson had done all those years ago. He would fight, as always, using every weapon at his disposal.

And, in the great chess game of international politics, Felix Hunter knew he could win.

Chapter 45

"Believe me, when you government types interact with paranormal investigators, it's rare that anything positive comes out of it," Arnold Freeth said on the drive out of the Sierra Nevadas.

His conversation with Devlin was entirely different from their initial meeting just the day before, though his enthusiasm was tempered by delayed stress at what they had been through. "We've all heard stories of Men in Black who show no identification, drive unmarked cars, and represent ultrasecret organizations."

"Whoa, what secret organizations? You mean like . . . Project Proteus?" Devlin asked with a sidelong grin. He picked up speed, not particularly impatient but just hating to drive too slow.

"Okay, is that so far-fetched?" Freeth seemed comfortable to be wearing his professional white shirt, tie, and sport jacket again. "I was very suspicious of you at first, Major Devlin. I thought you might drug or hypnotize me at the end of the mission. I've heard that the CIA has some sophisticated brain-wiping technology."

Devlin steered with one hand as the downhill grade became steeper and the curves sharper in the high foothills. "Why would we want to do that, Mr. Freeth?"

The UFO expert gave him a concerned frown. "You're not going to make me . . . disappear, are you? After all we've been through together? I may have been gone for two days, but sooner or later someone will notice. I have plenty of connections, speaking engagements, colleagues in the business."

"Relax, Mr. Freeth. Think about it. If a prominent and outspoken flying saucer expert simply vanished off the face of the Earth, don't you think that would raise more eyebrows than if we simply left you alone?"

Devlin flicked his turn signal, then stomped down on the accelerator to roar past a slow-moving pickup on a tight mountain curve. Earlier, Freeth would have been spooked by the maneuver, but now that he'd seen Devlin's piloting skills through the hazards of an extraterrestrial's body, he had no concerns about mere roads and hills.

They drove for a long time, finally emerging from the foothills into the grassy bowl of the Central Valley, heading west toward San Francisco. The broad, brown expanse spread out before them like an agricultural ocean.

Freeth fidgeted in the front seat of the sedan. "Aren't you afraid I'm going to talk? What if I tell the whole world?"

"You signed the papers and contracts, sir. We could prosecute you to the fullest extent of the law." Devlin showed no concern. "Besides, I think you have more integrity than that."

"But the public needs to know about these things. Believe me, there have been too many cover-ups already."

"And if you do, we'll deny everything." Devlin gave him a wry smile. "Just think it through."

Freeth pursed his lips in exasperation. "I've talked about other people's UFO encounters for years, and now I have my own incredible *real* adventure to talk about. I want to tell the world that we had an extraterrestrial sealed in a lifepod. I want to reveal that our government has developed cutting-edge miniaturization technology as part of a covert international project. I can truthfully say that we explored inside an actual alien's body."

"Don't forget that we saved the Earth from a deadly nanomachine infestation as part of the bargain," Devlin added as he raced across the flat farmlands.

With a disappointed groan, Freeth leaned back in the seat. His voice slowed as the implications hit him. "Of course, all the evidence was destroyed. The aliens and the nanomachines were vaporized."

"Mr. Freeth, people will believe or disbelieve you, according to your past. You've been saying crazy things for years, and you've been heckled for it—but you do have your followers. Dr. Tyler even believed you, and Director Hunter gave you the benefit of the doubt. You claimed to have done an alien dissection for home video. Do you think you're going to win any new adherents by adding the miniaturization part to your story? Or the nanotechnology invasion?"

Freeth's freckled face trembled on the verge of a pout. "The whole fantastic voyage sounds so improbable that even *my* core audience might have second thoughts."

Devlin shook his head. "Mr. Freeth, I've grown to respect you. You have a fiery dedication and a persistence in the face of impossible odds. Most people lack that. You have accomplished something truly remarkable, whether or not anyone else believes you."

The UFO expert sagged in the seat and looked out

to see the familiar territory racing by. Traffic picked
up as they headed toward the sprawling Bay Area
cities. He pounded his fist on the seat beside him
"But it *is* true, damn it!"

"Roger that. And you know the truth. Does any
thing else really matter?"

By himself on the long drive back to the Proteu
Facility, Devlin had plenty of opportunity to reflec
and plan. The sun set behind him, changing the chap
arral colors with dusk.

When he got back, his first priority would be to
find a good restaurant in Fresno, as he had promised
Tomiko, for Saturday night. He doubted the daugh
ter of Nolan Braddock and Kira Satsuya would be
satisfied with a cheap burger joint.

As he drove into the Sierra foothills burning with
sunset light, Devlin let his mind wander, digging
himself free of the gloom that surrounded his
thoughts of the three lost medical researchers. He
thought of an old command adage: Any mission in
which personnel are lost is a failed mission.

Despite the ordeal, though, he wouldn't have given
up the opportunity for the world. And Devlin would
have words for Felix Hunter if the Director tried to
choose a different pilot for any upcoming mission.

A different, more personal pain came when he
thought of the *Mote,* his beautiful ship. At least he
had managed to rescue his picture of Kelli.

He promised himself that he would redesign the
vessel, call up the *Mote*'s old blueprints and modify
them to include new ideas and improvements based
on his actual mission experience. He touched the
snapshot, still in his pocket—he and his wife
drenched from a water-balloon fight—and smiled, already rushing ahead with his dreams.

The *Mote 2* could be even better than the first. If

Project Proteus continued—and he had no reason to believe otherwise, given Felix's talent for negotiations and fixing problems—he would construct a new vessel. Before long, Team Proteus would have an even more sophisticated ship to use in their miniaturized explorations.

The universe was vast, even on a microcosmic scale.

ACKNOWLEDGMENTS

I couldn't have done all the research and technology aspects of this book alone. For sanity checks, ideas, and advice, I relied on the medical expertise of Dr. Ann Weller, the biological expertise of Patricia MacEwan, and the military and physics expertise of Doug Beason. I'm sure mistakes still slipped through, but they are far fewer in number because of the assistance these people generously offered.

At Signet Books, Doug Grad and Laura Anne Gilman helped me work through manuscript after manuscript and were even willing to look at the roughest of drafts to help shape the book into its final form.

My agents, Robert Gottlieb and Matt Bialer, saw the potential in this project and had faith in me from the beginning. Marty Greenberg provided essential ideas and input.

At WordFire, Inc., Catherine Sidor (as usual) did an enormous amount of work transcribing my microcassette tapes, offering suggestions, and helping with the editing chores. Diane Jones and Diane Davis Herdt were my guinea-pig first readers, whose comments led to major plot overhauls. And, of course, my wife, Rebecca Moesta Anderson, was involved in every step of this project, from the brainstorming to the final edit.

I'd also like to thank Eric Ellenbogen and Ben Melnicker for making it possible to revive *Fantastic Voyage* and for giving me complete creative freedom to tell the best story I possibly could.

KEVIN J. ANDERSON has played in many different universes, from *Star Wars* to *X-Files* to those of his own creation. Most recently, his original prequels to Frank Herbert's *Dune*, *House Atreides* and *House Harkonnen* (cowritten with Brian Herbert), became international bestsellers.

His work has been translated into 27 languages and has sold nearly 13 million copies worldwide. During a promotional tour in 1998, Anderson established the Guinness World Record for "Largest Single-Author Book Signing." He is currently at work on three volumes of a new science fiction epic, *The Saga Of Seven Suns*.

ANDERSON'S research has taken him to the deserts and ancient cities of Morocco, inside the Cheyenne Mountain NORAD complex, into the Andes Mountains and the Amazon River, inside a Minuteman III missile silo and its underground control bunker, onto the deck of the aircraft carrier *Nimitz*, to Maya, Aztec, and Inca temple ruins in South and Central America, inside NASA's Vehicle Assembly Building at Cape Canaveral, onto the floor of the Pacific Stock Exchange, inside a plutonium plant at Los Alamos, and behind the scenes at FBI Headquarters in Washington, D.C. Anderson lives in the Colorado Rockies, where he is an avid mountain climber.

He also, occasionally, stays home and writes.

www.wordfire.com and www.dunenovels.com